LIVY'S WOMEN

Livy's Women explores the profound questions arising from the presence of women of influence and power in the socio-political canvas of one of the most important histories of Rome and the Roman people, *Ab Urbe Condita* (From the Foundation of the City).

This theoretically informed study of Livy's monumental narrative charts the fascinating links between episodes containing references to women in prominent roles and the historian's treatment of Rome's evolutionary foundation story. Explicitly gendered in relation to the socio-cultural contexts informing the narrative, the author's background, the literary landscape of Livy's Rome, and the subsequent historiographical commentary, this volume offers a comprehensive, coherent, and contextualised overview of all episodes in *Ab Urbe Condita* relating to women as agents of historical change.

As well as proving invaluable insights into socio-cultural history for Classicists, *Livy's Women* will also be of interest to instructors, researchers, and students of female representation in history in general.

Peter Keegan is a Professor in Roman History at Macquarie University, Australia. His research ranges from sexuality and body history to the spatial dynamics of social relations in urban and periurban contexts and the epigraphy of ephemeral graffiti and death. His recent publications include *Inscriptions in the Private Sphere in the Greco-Roman World, Graffiti in Antiquity, Roles for Women and Men in Roman Epigraphic Culture,* and *Written Space in the Latin West 200 BC-AD 300.* He has also contributed a range of book chapters, journal articles, and conference papers on the subject of gendered discourse in historical and sub-literary texts.

LIVY'S WOMEN

Crisis, Resolution, and the Female in Rome's Foundation History

Peter Keegan

Routledge
Taylor & Francis Group

LONDON AND NEW YORK

First published 2021
by Routledge
2 Park Square, Milton Park, Abingdon, Oxon OX14 4RN

and by Routledge
52 Vanderbilt Avenue, New York, NY 10017

*Routledge is an imprint of the Taylor & Francis Group, an informa
business*

British Library Cataloguing-in-Publication Data
A catalogue record for this book is available
from the British Library

Library of Congress Cataloging-in-Publication Data
Names: Keegan, Peter (Lecturer in Roman history), author.
Title: Livy's women: crisis, resolution, and the female in Rome's
    foundation history/Peter Keegan.
Description: Abingdon, Oxon; New York, NY: Routledge, 2021. |
    Includes bibliographical references and index.
Identifiers: LCCN 2020042527 (print) | LCCN 2020042528 (ebook) |
    ISBN 9781138553255 (hardback) | ISBN 9780367706906
    (paperback) | ISBN 9781315148489 (ebook)
Subjects: LCSH: Livy. Ab urbe condita. | Women—Rome—
    Historiography. | Rome—History—Empire, 30 B.C.–476 A.D.—
    Historiography.
Classification: LCC PA6459.K44 2021 (print) | LCC PA6459 (ebook) |
    DDC 937.007202—dc23
LC record available at https://lccn.loc.gov/2020042527
LC ebook record available at https://lccn.loc.gov/2020042528

ISBN: 978-1-138-55325-5 (hbk)
ISBN: 978-1-315-14848-9 (ebk)

Typeset in Sabon
by KnowledgeWorks Global Ltd.

CONTENTS

LIST OF TABLES

FOREWORD

Setting the scene

Between republic and empire – the late 30s/early 20s BCE and the early decades of the 1st century CE – the years of the Augustan dispensation saw T. Livius (known more familiarly to a modern readership as Livy) write a history of Rome from the foundation of the city.[1] With one quarter only of the scope and bulk of its production extant, Livy's annalistic record takes us from the wanderings of Trojan Aeneas to 167 BCE and the dying throes of a conflict that would mark the birth of a new power in the Mediterranean. Scholars of the recent age have commented at varying length on his literary technique, narrative artistry, and rhetorical aptitude.[2] A few knowledgeable students of Graeco-Roman historiography have evinced a belief in an overall design to the Livian corpus and speak of organisation and critical intent.[3] Nonetheless, whether AUC history is approached from the hypercritical perspective of *Quellenforschung* (source criticism),[4] quarried for its philological reserves of Latinity and style,[5] or interrogated as unintentional witness to the Augustan milieu,[6] a question intrudes.

Livy himself tenders the problem in his opening preface.[7] The genre of the composition is *res populi Romani*, history of the Roman people. Its subject matter comprises *vita*. Livy exhorts his ancient audience to embrace the stuff of life itself, in its ethical and political manifestations (*mores, artes*). The domain of content is apposite: at home and in the army (*domi militiaeque*). Livy's publication is, in part, a social document, intended to instruct and edify in matters of human interest. The historian "speaks" to his audience about the issues which warrant representation – and it is one of these issues, the role and function of women at key turning points in Rome's history, which this volume addresses.

Representations of women appear frequently in the surviving books of Livy's monumental history of Rome, a city which in the historian's time was the capital of a growing Mediterranean-wide empire.[8] Even a casual reader of Livy's record of the achievements of the Roman people *a primordio urbis* (Liv. 1 pr 1) – namely "from the foundation of the city," a phrase which is traditionally rendered in more generic terms as *Ab Urbe Condita* (AUC) history – will register the presence of women, frequently at pivotal moments in the story of Rome's archaic and classical past. Whenever this occurs, the women Livy represents may appear as named subjects of particular episodes in the city's developing narrative; or as unnamed categories or collectives of person, socially, culturally, or biologically defined as female, and depicted in various urban or rural spaces across a range of mythological, semi-legendary, or historical events in the traditional chronology of ancient Rome.[9]

At first glance, to the modern consumer of personalities or events drawn from recent, remote, or fictional historical narratives, this may not seem especially out of the ordinary. After all we live in an age when historical subject matter is crafted more and more into works of creative literary, theatrical, and cinematic art – and, even more perfidiously to many, contemporary news is rendered problematic in the face of disinformation, data manipulation, and negotiated falsehood. Nonetheless, in relation to the composition of history in general, and the representation of women in particular, there are three important aspects of Livian historiography which require critical attention.

The first issue bearing on the composition of AUC history and the inclusion of women in Rome's legendary (mythological), semi-legendary (archaic and early republican), and non-contemporary (middle-late republican) narrative concerns the relationship between Livy's personal story and his historical precedents and sources. While little is known about Livy's formative years, and especially that time forever changed by the battle of Actium,[10] it is logical to infer that the historian's individual experience mirrored that of most persons living in such a seismic period of political upheaval.[11] What is often underestimated, however, in regard to what men and women living in Rome saw, felt, and knew about the changing political landscape following a century of civic violence – and, contingently, those histories which incorporated representations of men and women participating in transformative social and political events – is the concurrent and profound impact of these events on republican society, on social relations, and on individuals living through such times. In particular, it will almost certainly have been the case that Roman women were prone to the imperatives of time, accident, and changes as they manifested themselves in the evolution of other, apparently unrelated, social institutions. As a consequence of the interrelated political *and* social upheavals affecting Rome during the 1st century BCE, then, Livy will have seen gradual, or in some instances radical, changes to the roles of certain Roman women, changes reflected in the actions of powerful non-Roman women. Examining the ways in which women are depicted in Livy's narrative of Rome from its foundation in the 8th century BCE to the end of the war with Perseus in 167 BCE should always bear in mind what personal experience the historian possessed and to what information he had access in relation to elite and subaltern Roman and non-Roman women, his knowledge and awareness of the social categories of women (freeborn, libertine, enslaved) and their daily lives, and his understanding and reaction to those changed female roles which developed over the course of his lifetime.

Livy's historical context, his perception of contemporary Roman and non-Roman women, and his responses to experienced and anecdotal changes in female roles, will also have been informed in small or large measure by his reception of the corpus of literary, documentary, and epigraphic sources which survived to the late 1st century BCE and the ways in which these texts transmitted female imagery, behaviour, speech, and thought. In this light, earlier historiographical sources that refer incidentally to women or include representations of women in brief vignettes or longer episodes range from the records of the notable events of each year known as the *Annales Maximi*, which were displayed in black ink on a whitewashed wooden board and otherwise preserved on wax tablets bound in *codices*, to known writers dating from the first Roman historian, Q. Fabius Pictor, who wrote the history of his city in Greek at some point during the late 3rd or early 2nd century BCE, to the annalistic narrative of a certain Fenestella, writing in the later years of the Augustan principate and under Tiberius. While only fragments of many of these texts survive into the present age, the range of extant references to named and anonymous girls and women, and to occasional larger female groupings, display something of the variety in the categories of fictive, ambiguous, and authentic historical context where they are situated within the broader annalistic frame, and to the breadth of information in the original, complete texts Livy will have been exposed.[12]

While the extent to which he will have had access to published sources pertaining to the history of Rome remains uncertain, Livy will have had the opportunity to peruse the archives of the Atrium Libertatis on the Capitoline, the *bibliotheca* in the Temple of Apollo on the Palatine, and the library in the Porticus Octaviae next to the Theatre of Marcellus.[13] In addition to the many lost, forgotten, and only partially extant catalogue of literature dealing with historical subject matter, these public collections will also have held in reserve many of the sources which modern scholars of Graeco-Roman antiquity identify as canonical texts: the Sicilian histories of Antiochus, Philistus, and Timaeus of Tauromenium; the universal history of Diodorus Siculus and the *Antiquitates Romanae* of Dionysius of Halicarnassus; and the contemporary historical narratives of Herodotus, Thucydides, Polybius, and Sallust. It should be remembered that these purpose-built architectural spaces will have featured marble, mosaics, stucco, and, importantly, paintings and sculpture, all of which combined to provide decorative programs that enhanced and embellished the collections of book rolls, as well as intentional contexts for the reception of manuscripts about a diversity of cultural production (war, politics, and the law; poetry, philosophy, grammar, and rhetoric; architecture, science, and technology; chronological and topical historical manuscripts, family records, and biographical profiles).[14] Finally, from the streets of the dead lined with the funerary monuments of deceased elite, freed, and slave men and women to the dedicatory, legislative, and political record of the city, the urban and peri-urban spaces of Rome displayed hundreds of thousands of epigraphic texts that preserved individual memorialisations of ideal and authentic lived experience as well as official formulations of civic patronage, obligation, and service.[15]

All in all, Rome's multifarious historical record occupied the papyrus rolls or bound *codices* preserving literary, scientific, and reference literature, to which Livy could refer in the course of composing his voluminous work. These texts were stored in the libraries that belonged to the Roman people and in the town house and country villa collections of wealthy, educated private individuals belonging to the senatorial and equestrian *ordines*, and which were dominated by those texts considered to be the most important and influential of the time (e.g., Homer, Euripides, Pindar; Horace, Propertius, Vergil; and the like).[16] Otherwise, the shadow of the city's historical tradition could be traced on the arches, tombs, temples, reliefs, and statues of the classical city. Regardless of the genre of text, its location, and its subject matter, even casual perusal of the Roman manuscript, documentary, and epigraphic tradition, the writer of AUC history could read about the political, military, economic, social, and cultural evolution of Rome from humble origins to Augustan restoration – and, whatever the medium or mode whereby the city's past was transmitted, the presence of women could not be ignored.

The second historiographical element bearing on Livy's representation of women in AUC history relates to a question of style. Unlike modern professional historians, who in the main would adhere to a methodology based on the careful presentation of relevant evidence and coherent argument, Livy's approach to writing history skews more toward a predilection for stylistic expression, not necessarily at the expense of historical substance, but certainly with a view to memorialisation of the authorial voice to the same extent as explication of the past. According to this view, Livy – indeed, most ancient historians – "wrote to be read or heard for pleasure,"[17] a motivation that would – and, as noted previously, in the modern era of broadcasting or publishing "alternative" information, does – entail adding details to a narrative which may not always align scrupulously to the definition of facts but which make the story more interesting.

In this regard, the modern scholarship of ancient historiography has devoted considerable time and effort to addressing the manner in which Livy fashions his narrative structure, to the political and philosophical frames of reference he applies to his historical episodes, and to the form and function of his characterisation of particular individuals, whether as identifiable persons or classifiable groups of women or men.[18] A great deal can be learned from these careful, critical studies about how best to describe Livy in terms of his literary style, compositional strategy, and historical perspective. Moreover, it is possible to acquire crucial insights from these studies into the psychological and sociological nature, as well as the historiographical purpose, underlying Livy's inclusion of specific persons featured in his AUC history.

Finally, while the scholarship of many generations affords the modern reader of Livy a broad understanding of his approach to the construction of narrative and character, and a window into his historical aims and method, specific questions still remain unresolved in regard to the ways in which, and the reasons why, Livy incorporates women into what has been described as his broader historiographical project.[19] In general, to what extent does Livy's representation of women draw on, conform with, or challenge the social protocols and cultural precedents of female depiction in the prevailing literary tradition? More particularly, did Livy represent women differently from the Roman historians on whose work he relied and with whose narratives Livy's readership will have been familiar? Should we regard Livy's representation of women as incidental or instrumental to his historical purpose? Finally, to what extent was Livy's approach to the representation of female subjects in his historical narrative – namely, the rhetoric of gendered historiography – adapted, appropriated, or avoided by contemporary and later Roman historians?

It is undoubtedly coincidental to exploring these particular questions of historical method and gendered representation, but I would argue it is no accident that a woman, and no ordinary woman at that, is mentioned in the very first sentence of Book 1 of the AUC. Her name is Helen, *the* Helen, famously known as Helen of Troy. After leaving Sparta with the young Trojan prince Paris, Helen, wife of the Spartan king Menelaus, would be understood in the minds of many, from antiquity to the modern age, as a major – if not *the* – cause of the legendary conflict known as the Trojan War. Immortalised in Homer's epic poem *Iliad*, Helen, or, more particularly, her elopement, is commonly portrayed as the spark igniting a decade-long struggle between the armies of Achaean Greece, united under Menelaus' leadership, and those forces allied with the city of Troy.

How Livy deploys the name of Helen, with all the weight of the literary and iconographic tradition associated with her story, and within what historical context he inserts her designation, is of particular interest. "First of all, then," Livy begins,

> it is generally agreed that when Troy was taken vengeance was wreaked upon the other Trojans, but that two, Aeneas and Antenor, were spared all the penalties of war by the Achivi, owing to long-standing claims of hospitality, and because they had always advocated peace and the giving back of Helen.[20]

What is fascinating about Livy's introduction to his first book of Roman history – the history of a quintessentially patriarchal society where men held and exerted power in roles of political leadership, moral authority, social privilege, and control of property – is that he took the conscious decision not only to include reference to a woman but to implicate her in the survival of male protagonists, one of whom (Aeneas) would prove integral to the foundation of Rome, and, in turn, to the origins of one of the most powerful male-dominated cities in antiquity.

Even more significant to Livy's positioning of a woman in relation to the historical genealogy of neonate Rome – where, according to AUC history, Aeneas founded Lavinium, his son Ascanius founded Alba Longa, his son Silvius founded a number of Latin colonies, and so on until Romulus founded Rome – is the historian's choice of a very particular *kind* of woman. Known to all in classical antiquity with even a passing acquaintance with the literary tradition of the Greek epic cycle,[21] the Homeric poems, *Iliad* and *Odyssey*, and a range of rhetorical, comic, and historiographical works,[22] Helen was deeply embedded in the story of the Trojan War. Perhaps as, or even more, familiar to a readership contemporary to the period during which Livy was composing the first of 142 volumes of history were the representations of Helen in the Latin poets.[23] It may even be the case that Livy was privy to the first inklings of the Helen who would feature in the second book of Virgil's *Aeneid* – a representation only to appear fully-fledged in published form after the death of Augustus in 14 CE.[24]

Prior to the composition of Livy's AUC history, Helen played important roles in a range of cultural media.[25] Familiar, we must assume, with the varied genres of literary and iconographic production where representations of Helen appeared, and the breadth and depth of cultural reception in those contexts where her images were consumed,[26] Livy deliberately included a reference to her name as part of the wider establishing frame for Book 1 of his history of Rome. Livy introduces his readers to the legends of Aeneas and Antenor, thereby linking the Trojan War, with all the cultural capital the epic cycle entailed, to the founding of settlements in Italy. To the extent that the victorious Greek forces exempted Aeneas and Antenor from summary execution in the aftermath of Troy's defeat, the historian casts each of the Trojan men as deserving due consideration. In explaining why the Argive forces withheld the punishment otherwise meted out to their (Aeneas and Antenor's) fellow Trojans, Livy identifies three reasons: one, the exercise of hospitality (*hospitium*), widely understood in the ancient Mediterranean as a personal relationship that could lead to (and, in the succeeding chapters of Book 1, will entail) the foundation of alliances between communities; two, recognition of the desire in both men not to prolong the conflict and to negotiate a peaceful settlement; and three, related to the second motivating factor, Aeneas and Antenor being favourably disposed to surrendering Helen. In naming Helen, Livy may characterise her as an object under male control, in one sense, as a good or chattel able to be traded in kind; at the same time, acknowledging her will have confirmed, implicitly yet inescapably, Helen's agency in deciding to leave Sparta and her husband-king. In the same way, by virtue of her role in the narrative of the Greek epic cycle, Livy affords his readers the opportunity to reflect on Helen's nature as the focus of male desire *and* the model of female desire. At one and the same time, mention of her name will have sounded the ultimate warning against the consequences of marital instability – in this instance, adulterous action resulting in prolonged international conflict, the fragmentation of Achaean and Trojan personal relationships, and the destruction of social communities alike. Likewise, Livy will have reminded his readers that Helen must always be understood as the archetypal *exemplum* of the desirability of maintaining, or at the very least restoring, marital stability, something achieved in this case at inestimable personal and social loss. Finally, by identifying (implicitly) her elopement as one of the primary causes of the Trojan War *and* characterising (explicitly) her return as a key factor in resolving the conflict – certainly the Argives believed that Aeneas and Antenor held both views – Livy embeds Helen in the historiographical architecture of Rome's foundation.

This interpretation of Livy's use of a notable woman's name (a notorious, Greek female, no less) at such a key moment in Rome's historical narrative – when the tradition of the city's foundation was first conceived, both as it had been transmitted to the historian and in terms of his particular version of AUC history (*iam primum omnium satis constat*) – opens up broader consideration of the questions relating to female representation in Graeco-Roman antiquity. However, before looking more closely at Livy's insertion of a woman – whether a woman like Helen, embedded in a tradition where myth and history combine; or a woman like Lucretia, part of a legendary story about an early period in Rome's history already grafted to folklore before it was memorialised in written form; or even women like the *matronae* agitating for repeal of a sumptuary law (the *lex Oppia*), a female collective acting at a time (the first decade of the 2nd century BCE) when events and personalities were preserved in the historical record – as a locus for understanding how naming or otherwise portraying a woman may be situated within the historian's broader rhetorical strategies, moral principles, and thematic frames, something should be said in relation to our current state of knowledge about women in antiquity in general, and Roman women in particular.[27]

Information about Roman women is almost exclusively derived from male sources. This is not to say that Roman women could not read or write; some certainly could.[28] Nor, given the wealth of pertinent material culture – in particular, funerary inscriptions and statues – should we limit our search for understanding to the literary record.[29] Archaeological traces can reveal aspects of Roman women's daily life. Paintings, ceramic wares, relief panels and friezes, commemorative statues, monumental sculptures, funerary altars and stelae, domestic, ritual and decorative artifacts[30] – all speak in fragmentary and context-specific voices about Roman family and household, work and leisure, worship, and social obligations.

What anyone interested in knowing about and understanding Roman women must acknowledge is the problematic nature of our sources – namely, that women are either excluded from or embedded within culturally prescribed representational media – and the variety of nuanced theoretical approaches to them.[31] Integral to our engagement with the surviving sources is awareness of the historical discontinuities between seemingly familiar social and legal categories and their expression in Roman antiquity.[32]

Roman women were bound by the inextricable connection in the Roman *familia* – at least, as it has been portrayed to us in the extant literary and material evidence – between biological and social reproduction.[33] Of course, biology in the Roman world, as elsewhere, was not the only determinant of women's lives; society influenced reproduction as much as natural capacities. Each of the societies that eventually made up the Roman Empire shaped reproductive life in its own way. And in the ancient Mediterranean world, there was no room for choice: a woman did not choose celibacy, she did not choose marriage, and she did not choose remarriage after widowhood – at least in the privileged circles spoken of in the majority of written sources. Social factors, then, must be taken into account, since to a large extent society regulates the biological destiny and therefore the mortality of women. Once human beings begin to act socially to regulate reproduction, women naturally become the focus of such efforts.[34]

A paradigm for this reproductive discourse in the representation of Roman women is prevalent in the epigraphic record. From the memorial of Claudia[35] to that of Allia Potestas[36] and well into the Late Imperial period of Christianised antiquity, funeral epitaphs, and commemorative inscriptions deploy a catalogue of social characteristics consistent with a typology of the ideal Roman woman: faithful bearer of legitimate children; prudent manager of the household; obedient daughter, faithful wife, diligent mother.[37] Literary and documentary texts reiterate this conflation of biology and virtue.

The promotion of citizen marriage and procreation is a constant in iconographic, inscriptional, legal, and literary sources concerning Roman women.[38] Due to the lack of sanitation and hygienic practices, in combination with ignorance of microbiology and effective pharmacology, maternal and neonatal mortality was high in ancient Rome. While well attested in the sources, the evidence for maternal mortality is anecdotal only. Statistical *comparanda* drawn from similar but later societies (e.g., 18th-century rural England) suggest an average rate of 25 maternal deaths per 1000 births. Studies of the rate of death in early childhood estimate that around 30 percent of new-born infants born alive died before the age of one.[39] As part of Roman birthing ritual, new-born children (if not abandoned) were picked up by their father to signal his acceptance of their legitimacy – confirmation of the free Roman woman's role as *matrona*, producer and nurturer of legitimate offspring.

Female infants were named on the 8th day after birth. Whatever their origins, freeborn Roman women in the republican period had essentially only one name, their father's *nomen* in feminine form (which was not lost by marriage or exchanged for the husband's name); imperial women added praenomina corresponding to that of their fathers. In similar fashion, if individuals were related, we may distinguish elder and younger sisters by the prefixes *maior* and *minor*, while the eldest is often designated *maxuma*. However, this is how modern scholars often differentiate one girl from another in a family (Octavia *maior*, half-sister of Augustus, and *minor*, his sister-german, Mark Antony's fourth wife). So, Octavia minor is simply called *Octavia C.f. soror Augusti Caesaris*: Octavia, daughter of Gaius Octavius, sister of Augustus Caesar. Note that the *nomen* is followed by some form of filiation, in this case the father's praenomen – C (*aius*), in the genitive or possessive case, plus *f* (*ilia*), daughter. Significantly, while the abbreviation *f* (*ilia*) is nearly always given when the father's name appears, the word *uxor* (wife) seems as often omitted as present when the husband's name appears.

Of course, status and family stamped the individual as a participant in the social order, providing the sureties of physical integrity and legal recognition. Therefore, if not freeborn (an *ingenua*) or freed (a *liberta*), then the enslaved woman (*serva*) theoretically, and often practically, lacked any rights or claims. Existing without ethnic or national heritage, and lacking any socially acknowledged kin, the *serva* was given a single name by her master or mistress.[40]

Originally, at marriage, a Roman woman was usually transferred into the authority (*potestas*), in this instance, *manus*, of the father (*pater*) of her husband's *familia*, of which she became a member, leaving her own *familia*.[41] However, from an early period, this transfer began to be avoided, at least in wealthy families; thus, the woman, along with rights to her dowry and inheritance, was retained in her *familia* of origin. *Manus* was very rare by the end of the republic and virtually extinct by the mid- to late-2nd century CE. By then, most wives were either in the *potestas* of their own pater, or legally independent, and entitled to own their own property.

The constraints upon Roman women with regard to political activity are well known. They did not vote, could not hold (secular) office, and their presence, it seems, was forbidden in voting assemblies, although by the early 3rd century CE this rule was no longer being adhered to. Aulus Gellius tells us that "women have no part in the *comitia*."[42] This may be true, but clearly women could be present in public assemblies. We hear of Sempronia, widow of Scipio Aemilianus, brought out into a public meeting by a tribune.[43]

Some constraints seem to have been imposed by the moral authority of tradition. Valerius Maximus writes of women's "natural condition and the modesty befitting the *stola*," which should ensure their silence "in the forum and law-courts."[44] Ulpian offers the opinion that "women should not undertake the functions of men," nor act "contrary to the modesty befitting their sex."[45] These traditional expectations of propriety were eventually encased in law.[46]

Exceptions, in the form of public demonstrations by women, are rare. One famous occasion was public interest in 195 BCE in the repeal of the *lex Oppia*, a law which had restricted the ornament of women. Another notable occasion was a demonstration against a tax, which was to be imposed on

Rome's wealthiest women in 42 BCE, with the demonstrators "pushing their way into the forum."[47]

Otherwise, certain priesthoods might bring eminence. The *flaminicae* had station as wives of the *flamines* – at least of the *flamen Dialis* and the *flamen Martialis*, and probably of the *Quirinalis*. But the Vestals held office in their own right, the college of the six Vestal virgins being one of Rome's most remarkable institutions.[48] Unique among women in the Roman Republic, the Vestals might hold title to property in their own right. Augustan legislation would later allow the mothers of three children (or of four children if freedwomen) the privilege of not requiring a guardian: the *ius trium (quattuor) liberorum*.[49] Even a woman of such eminence as Agrippina the Younger, as the mother of only one child, would never have automatically enjoyed this freedom.

There seems to have been an at least partial gender differentiation in religious observance. Oaths are an interesting case. Aulus Gellius reports that Roman women did not swear by Hercules.[50] Occasionally, a specific ritual took women away from the world of men and into a secretive cult.[51] At other times, they were conspicuous – both in traditional and new religious observance. With reference to the year 212 BCE, we learn that "crowds of women were to be seen praying and offering sacrifice in accordance with unaccustomed rites";[52] and leading matrons might take striking initiatives – for instance, Caecilia Metella's single-handed purification of Juno the Deliverer's desecrated temple.[53]

All this might seem rather limiting. All the same, Roman women were not closeted: unlike Greek women of the Classical period, they moved freely in public spaces, attending social gatherings, and civic events.[54] Indeed, the women of the Roman aristocracy were part of their families' conspicuous place in the Roman community.[55]

In earlier studies, by which we might refer both to 19th-century scholarship and to the "first wave" of recent feminist writings, it became commonplace to stress the division of public and private. Classically, with reference to Greece, this will be the *oikos* (house) and *polis* (state). Does it hold good for *domus* and *res publica*? Certainly, the distinction will need to be blurred in the Roman case. Much business, for instance, was conducted in the *domus*, and much of women's business, as we can see, was conducted out of doors. Important political arrangements might occur over dinner. And, as we have seen, women were present – there and at family councils. The evidence is thin, and what survives relates to extraordinary times. But when Brutus and Cassius conferenced after the murder of Caesar, the women of the household were present and one, at least, made her views known.[56] Women served as agents of their families. In January, 62 BCE, faced with a worsening political crisis, Cicero consulted his friend Q. Metellus Celer's wife Claudia and sister Mucia.[57]

Roman women who crossed the line between public and private did so at risk. Those women who took an improper interest in political or civic affairs might be targeted (by satirists, moralists, and historians alike) for polemical abuse, their roles being recast (and their very status being redefined) as those of prostitute, procuress, or actress (the last considered a sordid, disreputably-professional occupation). Nonetheless, there can be no doubt that the social transformation of Rome in the second century BCE (and subsequently) had affected the opportunities offered to women of the Roman political elite, especially in the last century of the republic. Valerius Maximus identifies women – Amasia Sentia (Maesia of Sentinum), Gaia Afrania, and Hortensia – advocating in public.[58]

As members of a family that was busily engaged in changing the nature of Roman government forever and drawing on their traditional status within a leading family, the women of the Julio-Claudian household had access to power on an unprecedented scale.[59] Much could now be done within the household without the suggestion of improper female intervention, or much could be suspected of having been done behind closed doors.[60] The role of women in the leading Roman families became ever more prominent as political power (in the conventional sense) centred in fewer hands.[61] In the time of Claudius' principate, there was a distinct lack of male Julio-Claudians surviving, which meant that women naturally gravitated toward the centre of imperial activity in politics and consequently generated more references in the historical sources. For instance, Tacitus reports the articulateness of women speaking as defendants in trials before the Senate.[62] Pliny describes the galleries of the Basilica Iulia as lined with men and women, hanging over in their eagerness to hear and see events transpire in the centumviral court.[63] And the subject of the so-called laudatio "Turiae" pressed for investigation of her parents' murder and threatened civil litigation to defend her rights under her father's will.[64]

Formal and social limitations may be adduced in support of a general principle of restricted female legal activity[65] but the evidence of over 600 written decisions and rulings (responsa) dating from 117 to 304 CE – issued in reply to letters submitted by female Roman citizens who were sui iuris, resident in the provinces, and belonged to all of the social orders – situates women working within the legal system.

Opportunities were also offered to women outside the elite, though almost exclusively confined to the contexts of domestic labour (cloth and food production, storeroom and provision management; hairdressing, personal care; midwifery, wet-nursing, child-minding) and commercial activities (spinning fibre, weaving cloth, working wool; bar and retail service, market trade, workshop production), entertainment (actors, dancers, musicians), and social relations (wives, mistresses, sex workers).

The epigraphic record of Rome's capital (CIL VI) reveals the potential for significant female participation; for instance, in purveying or procuring indispensable and discretionary items. The tituli officialium et artificium for familiae privatae list women as suburban agents comprising individuals as self-sufficient as the local popa for perishable foodstuffs and as commercial as the *negotiatrix frumentaria et legumenaria* for supplementary and staple nutritional requisites. Such participation may also be found in those persons catering or ministering to personal and domestic well-being, from the *pedisequa* to the *vestiplica*.

Recent scholarship on Roman women – elite and non-elite; freeborn, freed, and enslaved; married, divorced, widowed, and independent; Italian and non-Italian; and so on – concerns issues of social condition and gender, variations among cultural ideals and accepted practices, and critical readings of female representation in the extant record. Despite limitations of survival and male-centred production of source material, interest continues in situating Roman women within their socio-cultural contexts and teasing out how they may have understood themselves, each other, and the ancient world in which they lived.

The range of information that archaeological, documentary, epigraphic, historical, and literary studies – and, far less frequently, the preserved fragments of authentic female voices – has revealed about women in antiquity is impressive. However, it is equally clear that the present study of female representation in a work of annalist history conceived and composed by a man can only proceed after recognising the limitations to acquiring knowledge of ancient women. Imposed by virtue both of the predominantly male-authored, commissioned, or produced categories of evidence that survive into the modern age and of the comprehensively male-exclusive control over the lives of women, their means of personal or communal expression, and how they might have desired themselves to be known, remembered, and represented, acknowledging the extent to which our access to women of the classical past remains restricted is essential.

With this in mind, that Livy chose to include a woman's name in the opening lines of his AUC history – a name which, as we have seen, will have carried significant cultural freight for every reader of literature who possessed even passing acquaintance with the Greek epic cycle and Helen's role within that tradition – should demonstrate that any caveats regarding the degree to which the women of classical antiquity can be known are negotiable. As modern historians of the ancient world currently apply the tools of textual analysis, understanding the conventions governing a literary, documentary, or epigraphic genre is not simply fundamental to reading a crafted textual artefact: sympathetic comprehension of the principles governing the production of a category of literature illuminates how the information provided by a work that incorporates those principles is shaped. In line with this proposition, whether poetry or prose, fiction, philosophy or history, epistolary or legal papyrus, formal inscription, votive epigraph, or ephemeral graffito, careful reading of any ancient text, produced according to conventions and under conditions known to limit or exclude access to information about women, can provide additional insight into the basic material of ancient history.

The present volume aims to read AUC history in this way, studying the perturbations arising from Livy's insertions of women in the socio-political canvas of foundation history in order to foreground female experience and representation. In doing so, *Livy's Women* will probe the link between the episodes containing references to women in prominent roles and the historiographical treatment of evolutionary facets of the nascent Roman *res publica*. This association will entail a discussion of Livy's notion of exemplary storytelling, of correspondences between legendary/attributable and domestic/public history, and of resonances between the textual treatment of Rome's origin and expansion and the late republican/early imperial cultural and intellectual milieu in which AUC history was written.

To contextualise Livy's interposition of women in the dense, composite superstructure of his annalistic narrative, Chapter 1 will elucidate the connection which exists between the stated aim of his historiographical project and the practical application of that argument. Introducing to the reader the consistency and vigour of Livy's gendered exposition of Roman history (*res Romana*) will require a focused overview of the subtle propositions that the annalist outlines in his introductions to Books 1 and 6.

Of course, Livy may conform to the structural conventions of traditional Roman historiography, but his authorial choices suggest a conscious manipulation of the accepted narrative frame. Chapter 2 will explore how Livy uses the *topos* of a public debate, set against the background of a collective demonstration of women, to address matters of gender and social history.

In the same way that Livy deploys a very particular discourse of gender relations in service to his historiographical project, so the author's orientation and distribution of participants provides his readers with clear points of historical and socio-cultural reference. Chapter 3 will examine Livy's treatment of non-Roman female characters across the surviving narrative to illustrate the critical purposes underpinning his use of gendered categories of person.

Two final, interdependent elements of AUC history will be considered: the extent to which the roles assigned by Livy reflect a traditional or revisionist interpretation of gender; and the degree to which Livy's narrative framework represents a complex amalgam of authentic historical data and secondary oral-literary superstructure. By examining a variety of rhetorical instruments used with episodes involving significant women in the foundation history, Chapter 4 will explore the link between the *topoi* used by Livy in his depiction of female engagement in the process of history and key terms which signal those moments of change. With respect to the historicity of the AUC, it will be argued that throwing a spotlight on the gendered lens Livy overlays on particular crucial events in Rome's foundation narrative affords opportunities to test the degrees of correspondence between points of historical tension in his overarching annalistic reconstruction.

Rather than rehearse the weight of argument presented during the course of the volume, a brief Afterword will address in general terms what seems most urgent in relation to Livy's representation of women: his conception of gender as compared with traditional Graeco-Roman constructions of female and male; to what extent he draws distinctions between public and private in episodes where incidents involving women play out in civic, military, and other male-exclusive contexts; and how he negotiates conjunctions of literary and historical narrative when he includes named, anonymous, and collective female protagonists in the canonical and lesser known events comprising Rome's foundational story.

Notes

1 A recent review of conjectured dates for Livy's composition of the first pentad in Vasaly (2018: 3) leans towards the late 30s or early 20s, which coincides with C. Octavius' defeat of the joint naval forces of M. Antonius and Cleopatra VII off the coast of north-western Greece on the second day of September in 31 BCE. According to this revised chronology, the formulation of AUC history will have run parallel to the seismic events that followed Actium: surrender of Antonius' nineteen legions, capture of Alexandria and suicide of Antonius and Cleopatra, senatorial award to the victor of honours, titles, and privileges, and the beginning of a political regime that would evolve into a system of government known to later generations as the Augustan principate. See also Bayet (1940: xvii–xviii); Luce (1965: 238); Burton (2000: 446): contra the traditional date of publication between 27 and 25.

2 Exemplary studies include McDonald (1957); Walsh (1970); Stadter (1972); Luce (1977); Lipovsky (1984); Moles (1993); Miles (1995); Feldherr (1997); Jaeger (1997); Forsythe (1999); Chaplin (2000); and Vasaly (2018).

3 Since only Books 1–10 and 21–45 of an original corpus comprising one hundred and forty-two volumes survive in manuscript – along with a collection of brief ancient summaries (*Periochae*) covering every book in consecutive order (with the exception of those for the years 137 and 136 BCE) – it is only speculative to propose a structural frame for the historian's overarching scheme. Nonetheless, tentative conclusions relating to the organisation of the surviving work can be found in Syme (1959: 28–42); Walsh (1961: 5–8), (1974: 8–10); Stadter (1972); Luce (1977: 3–32); Briscoe (1981: 397, bibliography); and Kraus (1994: 9–16).

4 On the effort of *Quellenforschung* to identify the literary sources Livy used and to describe how he used them, see, e.g., Luce (1977: xv–xxvii) and Richardson (2015).

5 For detailed discussion of Livy's use of Latin and narrative style, see, e.g., Walsh (1961: 245–270), Leeman (1963: 190–197), and Burck (1934), (1992).

6 Discussion of Livy's incidental and intentional references to events and personalities dating to the period of Augustan rule is considerable. See, e.g., Syme (1959), Mette (1961), and Miles (1995: 110–136).

7 For analysis of the Preface to Book 1 of Livy's history, see Moles (1993: 141–168) and Woodman (1988: 128–134). How Livy's elaboration of his historiographical aims and focus in the first of his major prefatory essays (the other significant introductory passage is found at 6.1.1-3) provides an entry-point into understanding the role of female representation in his wider historical narrative. It should be noted that Livy includes other subsidiary passages that similarly mark important turning points in Roman history (2.1.1-6; 7.29.1-2; 21.1.1-3; 31.1.1-5).

8 References to the representation of women in Livy's history of Rome can be found in a number of journal articles and book chapters. Representative studies

include Smethurst (1959); Balsdon (1962: 21–43); Watson (1979); Donaldson (1982: 103–112); Bryson (1986); Hemelrijk (1987); Scafuro (1989); Joplin (1990); Evans (1991); Joshel (1992b); Baumann (1993); Moses (1993); Brown (1995); Claasen (1998); Beard (1999); Mustakillio (1999); Vandiver (1999); Matthes (2000: 23–50); Koptev (2003); Milnor (2005: 154–184); Mastrorosa (2006); Freund (2008); Welch (2012); Chiu (2016: 19–62). Most of the scholarship dealing with the function of women on the pages of Livy focus on mythological, legendary, and historical episodes from the first pentad (Books 1-5: 8th century-389 BCE), the repeal of the *lex Oppia* (34.1-8: ca. 195 BCE), and the account of the Bacchanalian conspiracy (39.8-19: 186 BCE) To date there is no critical survey of the full catalogue of named women or categories of female (e.g. mothers, wives, daughters; elite, freed, and slave women) introduced in the extant pages of AUC history.

9   Livy's compositional method of dividing AUC historical narrative into "episodes" – what is conventionally termed *Einzelerzahlung* or "unit narration" – is discussed by Witte (1910: 270–305, 359–419); cf. Walsh (1970: 24–26).

10 For information about Livy pertaining to his relationship with Augustus and the *princeps'* regard for the historian, his style, his views about historiography and literary expression, and his celebrity, see Liv. 4.20.5-11; Quint. *Inst.* 2.5.20, 10.1.32, 39, 8.2.18; Tac. *Ann.* 4.34.3; Suet. *Claud.* 41.1, *De Historicis et philosophis* 21.39; Plin. *HN* 2, 5-7; Sen. *Ep.* 100.9; *Controv.* 9.1.14, 9.2.26.

11 All who lived in the city of Rome and the Italian peninsula will have felt the impact of events associated with the conflict following Caesar's death and the decade of unrest following the formation of the Second Triumvirate in October 43 BCE. For a comprehensive scholarly overview of the historical, sociopolitical and cultural narratives of this period, see Bowman, Champlin and Lintott (1996: 1–69, 414–433, 782–978); for a brief profile of the years 44–33 BCE from the perspective of the Roman people, see Parenti (2004: 187–221).

12 For the fragments of the Roman historians in the surviving literary record, see Cornell (2013). 1. **Annales Maximi:** (a) F10 = Dion. Hal. *Ant. Rom,* 8.56.1-4 (foundation of the temple of Fortuna Muliebris in memory of the women who convinced Coriolanus to end his threatened assault on Rome; cf. Liv. 2.40.9-10, 10.23; Dion. Hal. *Ant. Rom.* 8.26; Fest. 282; Tert. *De monog.* 17.3; Val. Max. 2.1.2; Serv. *Aen.* 4.19; *vir. ill.* 19.5). (b) F12 = Liv. 8.18.11-12 (appointment of a dictator in 331 BCE to carry out the expiatory ritual of fixing a nail following the conviction of matrons for poisoning; cf. *Inscr. Ital.* 13.1, 33-5). 2. **Q. Fabius Pictor:** (a) F4a = Dion. Hal. *Ant. Rom.*1.76.3-79.4 (account of the ancestry, birth, exposure, rescue and upbringing of the twins Romulus and Remus; cf. Plut. *Rom.* 3.3, 4.3-5.5; Zon. 7.1-2). (b) F6 = Plut. *Rom.* 14.1 (reference to the four-month interval between the foundation of the city and the rape of the Sabine women; cf. Liv. 1.9.1-13.6; Ov. *Fast.* 3.167-244; Plut. *Rom.* 21). (c) F7 = Dion. Hal. *Ant. Rom.* 2.38.2-40.2 = L. Cincius Alimentus F3 = L. Calpurnius Piso Frugi F9 (account of the Tarpeia story; cf. Ov. *Fast.* 1.261; Prop. 4.4). (d) F11 = Dion. Hal. *Ant. Rom.* 4.30.2-3 (reference to the murder of Arruns Tarquinius by his wife Tullia; cf. Liv. 1.46.3-48.7; Ovid. *Fast.* 6.587-624, Zonaras 7.9; *vir. ill.* 7.15-19; Varr. *Ling.* 5.159; *ap.* Gell.18.12.9). 3. **L. Cincius Alimentus:** F3 (Tarpeia; cf. Q. Fabius Pictor F7, above). 4. **A. Postumius Albinus:** F3 = Serv. *Aen* 9.7.10 (record of the derivation of the name of Baiae, referring to a certain Boia, nursemaid of Euxinus, companion of Aeneas; cf. *OGR* 10.1; contra Lyc. *Alex.* 694; Polyb *ap.* Strabo 1.26, 5.245; Sil. *Pun.* 8.539, 12.114-15; Serv. *Aen.* 3.441, 6.107, 9.707; Eust. *Od.* 24.465 p.1697, 24). 5. **M. Porcius Cato:** (a) F8 = Serv. *Aen.* 6.760 (Lavinia, wife of Aeneas, mother of Silvius; cf. Liv. 1.1.7, 1.1.9-11, 1.2.1-2, 1.3.1-4; Dion. Hal. *Ant. Rom.* 1.59.3-60.1, 64.1, 70.2; Virg. *Aen.* 7.70-75, 96-101, 363-370).

(b) F10 = *OGR* 12.5-13.5 (Amata, wife of Latinus; cf. Dion. Hal. *Ant. Rom.* 1.64; Virg. *Aen.* 12.593-613). (c) F14 = Dion. Hal. *Ant. Rom.* 1.75.4-84.1 (see Q. Fabius Pictor F4a, above). (d) F16 = Macr. 1.10.11-17 (Acca Larentia, wealthy prostitute and benefactor to the Roman people, recipient of tomb and annual funerary cult; cf. Liv. 1.7; Plut. *Rom.* 4.5, *Quaest. Rom.* 35; Gell. *NA* 6.7). (e) F109 = Festus 320 (a list of women's dress that Cato is otherwise known to have regarded as extravagant and deserving of censure; cf. Liv. 34.1-3, 3.9. 7.3, 7.6, 39.44.2; Val. Max. 9.1.3; Plut. *Cat. Mai.* 18; Plin. *HN* 34.31). (f) F119 = Charis. 128; Serv. *Aen.* 4.698-9 (description of women's hairstyles in the past, part of a diatribe against women's luxury in the Rome of Cato's time; cf. Plin. *NH* 28.191). (g) F145 = Serv. *Aen.* 3.63.-4 (description of the dress of Roman women in mourning; cf. M. Porcius Cato F119, above). 6. **L. Cassius Hemina:** F28 = Non. 90M = 129L (reference to female participants in the cult of Magna Mater; cf. Liv. 29.14.5-14). 7. **C. Acilius:** F8 = *OGR* 10.1-2 (etymological report of the deaths of Baia, mother of Euxinus, and of Prochtya, buried on a nearby island; cf. Naevius fr. 12 Strzelecki; Virg. *Aen.* 9.712; Dion. Hal. *Ant. Rom.* 1.53.3; Plin. *HN* 3.82). 8. **L. Calpurnius Piso Frugi:** (a) F3 = *OGR* 10.1-2 (Prochyta; cf. Acilius F8 above). (b) F7 = Dion. Hal. *Ant. Rom.* 2.38.2-40.3 (Tarpeia; cf. Q. Fabius Pictor F7, above). (c) F16 = Dion. Hal. *Ant. Rom.* 4.15.5 (designation of Juno Lucina, Libitina, and Juventas, goddesses concerned respectively with childbirth, burials, and men of military age). 9. **C. Fannius:** F2 = Charis. 158 (reference to Metallis or Megallis, wife of Damophilos of Enna, whose ill-treatment of her slaves on her country estate was said to have caused the initial outbreak of the slave war; cf. Diod. Sic. 34/5.2.10). 10. **Vennonius:** F1 = *OGR* 20 (the divine origin of Romulus and Remus; cf. Liv. 1.4.2; Dion. Hal. *Ant. Rom.* 1.77.2; Conon *FGrHist* 26 F1 (xlviii); Ov. *Fast.* 3.21; Tib. 2.5.51-4; Serv. *Aen.* 1.273; Plut. *Rom.* 4.2-3; Aug. *Civ.* 18.21). 11. **Cn. Gellius:** (a) F1-5 = Dion. Hal. *Ant. Rom.* 2.31.1, Charis. 67-8, Gell. *NA* 13.23.13 (account of the rape of the Sabines, incl. a reference to Hersilia; cf. Liv. 1.13; Ov. *Fast.* 3.167-244; Plut. *Rom.* 21). (b) F7 = Charis. 68 (a possible reference to a trial of Vestal Virgins on a charge of having had sexual intercourse; cf. Liv. 8.15.7-8 [Minucia], *Per.* 14.7 [Sextilia], 20.4 [Tuccia]). 12. **L. Coelius Antipater:** F42 = Serv. *Georg.* 2.345 (relating to the story of the ill-fated marriage of Masinissa and Sophoni(s)ba, daughter of Hasdrubal; cf. Liv. 30.12.11-15.8; Diod. Sic. 27.7; App. *Pun.* 27.111-28.120; Zon. 9.13.2-6). 13. **Valerius Antias:** (a) F1 = *OGR* 19.1-4 (reference to Amulius ordering Rhea Silvia to become a Vestal Virgin; cf. Liv. 1.3.9-11; Dion. Hal. *Ant. Rom.* 1.71.4, 76; Plut. *Rom.* 3.3). (b) F2 = *OGR* 21.1-22.1 (a version of the story of Rhea Silvia's twin children being raised by Faustulus' girlfriend Acca Larentia; cf. Dion. Hal. *Ant. Rom.* 1.84; contra Liv. 1.4; see also Q. Fabius Pictor F4, L. Cincius Alimentus F1, M. Porcius Cato F14, above). (c) F3 = Gell.*NA* 7.7.5-8 = C. Licinius Macer F27 (record of Acca Larentia bequeathing her property not to the Roman people but to Romulus). (d) F5 = Plut. *Rom.* 14.7 (record of the number of Sabine girls seized by the Romans in other sources: 30, 527 [Antias], 683 [Juba = *FGrHist* 275 F23]; cf. Cic. *Rep.* 2.14; Liv. 1.13.6-7; *vir. ill.* 2.12; Dion. Hal. *Ant. Rom.* 2.47.4). (e) F8 = Arnob. *Adv. nat.* 5.1 (reference to Egeria's advice regarding the trapping and questioning of Faunus and Picus Martius; cf. Liv. 1.19.5; Ov. *Fast.* 3.285-348; Plut. *Num.* 15.3-10). (f) F20 = Plut. *Mor.* 323 C-D (account of the miracle of Servius' head bursting into flames as his wife Gegania lay dying, and with his mother and other women in attendance; cf. Liv. 1.39.1-3; Dion. Hal. *Ant. Rom.* 4.2.4; Ov. *Fast.* 6.635-6; Val. Max. 1.6.1; Plin. *HN* 2.241, 36.204; Flor. 1.1; Zonar. 7.9.2; Serv. *Aen.* 2.683; *vir. ill.* 7.1; Lydus, *Ost.* 5). (g) F29 = Gell. *NA* 7.8.3-6 (the unedifying tale of P. Scipio Africanus keeping a beautiful female prisoner to use for his sexual pleasure; cf. Polyb. 10.19.3-7; Liv. 26.50; Sil. *Pun.* 15.268-85; Dio Cass. fr. 57.43; Val. Max. 4.3.1; Frontin. *Str.* 2.11.5; Polyaenus, *Strat.* 8.16.6; *vir. ill.* 49.8; Amm. Marc. 24.4.27; Zonar. 9.8.5). (h) F54 = Liv. 39.41.5-6 (report of Q. Naevius Matho's conduct of crimes alleged to have been associated with the Bacchanalia and renewed poisoning investigations, both in Rome and rural communities; cf. Liv. 39.8.8, 40.37.4-7, 43.2-3, 44.6). 14. **L. Cornelius Sisenna:** (a) F32 = Non. 348M = 551L (possibly reference to a woman responsible for the betrayal of Venafrum or Nola, ignoring her duty to her *patria* and perhaps her husband to protect her lover; cf. App. *B Civ.* 1.41.183, 1.42.185; contra Liv. *Per.* 72 [Ser. Sulpicius Galba]). (b) F90 = Non. 255M = 387L (reference to the siege of Aec(u)lanum, describing either the massing of men and women on the walls in order to attempt to repel the besiegers or to surrender; cf, Liv. 31.44.4; Varro *ap.* Gell. *NA* 3.10.7). 15. **C. Licinius Macer:** (a) F1 = OGR 19.5-7 = M. Octavius F2 (account of Amulius' violation of Rhea Silvia; cf. Liv. 1.3.11-4.3; see also C. Valerius Antias F1, above). (b) F2 = Macrob. *Sat.* 1.10.17 (the secondary version of the legend of Acca Larentia; cf. M. Porcius Cato F16, above). F12 = Malalas 7.178-80 Dindorf (a rationalising version of the story of Romulus and Remus, with references to Lycaena, a local countrywoman, and Ilia the twins' mother, a priestess of Ares; cf. Q. Fabius Pictor F4a, above). 16. **Lutatius:** (a) F2 = Serv. *Aen.* 9.710 (reference to the nursemaid Boia; cf. A. Postumius Albinus F3, above). (b) F12 = OGR 10.1-2 (etymological references to Baia and Prochyta, Aeneas' relative; cf. L. Calpurnius Piso Frugi F3, above). 17. **Munatius Rufus:** (a) F2 = Plut. *Cat. Min.* 36.5-37.9 (reference to the reconciliation of Munatius and M. Porcius Cato Uticensis, effected by his second wife Marcia). (b) F3 = Plut. *Cat. Min.* 25.1-12 (the story of how Cato "loaned" his wife Marcia to Hortensius so she could bear him children; cf. Plut. *Cat. Min.* 52; Strabo 11.515; Luc. 2.326-91; Quint. *Inst.* 3.5.11, 10.5.13; Tert. *Apol.* 39.12; Hieron. *Adv. Iovinian.* 1.46; August. *De bono coniug.* 21). 18. **M. Tullius Cicero:** (a) F2 = Plut. *Cic.* 20.3 (account of Cicero's wife Terentia relieving him of domestic worries and sharing his political anxieties; cf. Cic. *Fam.* 14.5.1; *Att.* 9.6.4, 11.9.2; Diod. Sic. 40.5; [Sall.] *Inv. in Cic.* 2.3; Plut. *Cic.* 29.2-4, 30.4; *Ant.* 2.2). (b) F6 = August. contra *Iul. Pelag.* 5.23 = Jul. Aeclan. *Ad Turbantium* F180 De Coninck (account of the calming of the demonstration against Roscius Otho, incl. a reference to a virtuous woman; cf. Plut. *Cic.* 13.2-4; Cic. *Leg.* 2.38-9). 19. **C. Oppius:** F1 = Gell. *NA* 6.1.1-5 (story of the impregnation of Pomponia, wife of P. Cornelius Scipio Africanus, by Jupiter in the guise of a snake; cf. Liv. 26.19.5-9; Sil. *Pun.* 13.637-44, 615). 20. **M. Actorius Naso:** F2 = Suet. *Iul.* 52.1 (reference to C. Iulius Caesar's affair with Eunoe, wife of Bogudes, ruler of Mauretania alongside Bocchus, during the African campaign of 47–46 BCE). 21. **M. Tullius Tiro:** F2 = Plut. *Cic.* 41.2-5 (apologetic account of the reasons for Cicero divorcing his wife Terentia and remarrying a younger girl; cf. Dio. 46.18.3; Cic. *Att.* 12.11, 12.12.1). 22. **Calpurnius Bibulus:** F1 = Plut. *Brut.* 23 (reference to Cato's daughter [and Bibulus' mother] Porcia's profound emotional reading of the depiction of Andromache's farewell to Hector, doomed hero fighting in vain for his city's preservation; cf. App. *B Civ.* 3.13.47). 23. **Q. Dellius:** F2 = Plut. *Ant.* 59.6-8 (description of Cleopatra VII's poor relations with many of Antonius' friends). 24. **Imp. Caesar Augustus:** F8, 10, 15, 19 = App. *B Civ.* 5.42.182; Serv. *Aen.* 8.696; Suet. *Aug.* 62.2; Dio Cass. 48.44.4 (references in passing to Fulvia, Atia, Scribonia, and Livia Drusilla respectively). 25. **C. Julius Hyginus:** F3 = Gell. *NA* 6.1.1-5 (story of Pomponia and the snake; cf. C. Oppius F1, above). 26: **Fenestella:** (a) F13 = Macr. 1.10.5-6 (record of the trials of the Vestals in 114–113 BCE, specifically Aemilia and Licinia; cf. Liv. *Per.* 63; Ascon. *Mil.* 39-40Sr = 45-6C; Cic. *Brut.* 160, 161; Dio

Cass. 26 fr. 87.4; Plut. *Mor.* 284A-C; Obseq. 37; Oros. 5.15.22). (b) F16 = Plut. *Crass.* 4-5 (story of two slave-girls attending to M. Licinius Crassus' needs during his time of refuge in Further Spain from the purge of Cinna and Marius.

13 Atrium Libertatis: Ov. *Trist.* 3.1.71; Plin. *NH* 7.115, 35.10, 36.23, 24. 25. 33. 34; Isid. *Orig.* 6.5.2. Palatine Apollo: Suet. *De gramm.* 20; Ov. *Trist.* 3.1.63; Hor. *Ep.* 1.3.17; Suet. *Aug.* 29; Plin. *NH* 7.210, 34.43; Tac. *Ann.* 2.37, 83; Fronto, *Ep.* 4.5; Dio Cass. 53.1; Serv. *Ecl.* 4.10; Plin. *Ep.* 1.13; Gal. 13.362. Porticus Octaviae: Plut. *Marc.* 30; Ov. *Trist.* 3.1.69; Suet. *De gramm.* 21; CIL 6.2347-9, 4431-5, 5192. On the libraries in the Atrium Libertatis, the Temple of Apollo, and the Porticus Octaviae, see Dix and Houston (2006: 671–688, with references and bibliography).

14 For a catalogue of book lists on papyrus, their characteristics, and exemplary collections in Roman libraries, see Houston (2014: 39–86).

15 On the roles of men and women in Roman epigraphic culture, see Keegan (2014).

16 Strocka (1981) and Dix and Houston (2006) outline the evidence for Roman libraries in the 1st century BCE and the creation of large private collections in Italy.

17 Oakley (1997: 3) includes the surviving works of Herodotus, Thucydides, Sallust, and Tacitus in this assessment of the literary approach of ancient historians.

18 Exemplary studies include McDonald (1957); Walsh (1970); Stadter (1972); Luce (1977); Lipovsky (1984); Moles (1993); Miles (1995); Feldherr (1997); Jaeger (1997); Forsythe (1999); Chaplin (2000); and Vasaly (2018).

19 Kraus (1994: 13).

20 Liv. 1.1.1: *iam primum omnium satis constat Troai capta in ceteros saevitium esse Troianus: duobus, Aeneae Antenorique, et vetusti iure hospitii et quia pacis reddendaneque Helenae semper auctores fuerunt, omne ius belli Achivos abstinuisse.*

21 Burgess (2001: 89, 149) argues that the lost poems of the epic cycle (including works such as *Cypria, Aethiopis,* the so-called *Little Iliad, Iliupersis, Nostoi,* and *Telegony*) are not only younger than the poems of Homer but also, as traditionally supposed, composed with the sole purpose of completing the story of the war as told in the Homeric poems. It follows that, if the Cycle poems as we know them are later than the poems of Homer, then the tradition that they represent is not only old but also independent of the Homeric tradition. Known representations of Helen in the lost poems – as well as in archaic and classical images relating to these representations – will have supplemented, and no doubt complicated, Livy's knowledge and understanding of her character, personality, behaviour, and actions as represented in Homer.

22 References to Helen in Greek literature other than those already cited can be found in works of the following writers: Hesiod (didactic poetry and mythography); Alcaeus, Ibycus, Sappho, Stesichorus, Alcaeus, and Alcman (lyric and martial poetry); Aeschylus and Euripides (tragic poetry); Aristophanes; Plato and Aristotle (comic poetry); Gorgias, Isocrates, and Theocritus (encomiastic poetry); Herodotus and Thucydides (historiography).

23 Enn. *Iphigenia* 101 Jocelyn; Catull. 68.87-93; Lucr. 1.464-465, 473-474; Hor. *Carm.* 1.15, 4.9.13-16; *Serm.* 1.3.107-110; *Ep.* 17.42-44); and Prop. 2.1.49-50, 3.28-29, 32.19-32, 34.87-88; 3.8.29-32, 14.19-20.

24 Verg. *Aen.* 2.567-588, 601-602; 6.494-519.

25 Blondell (2013).

26 The extent to which representations of Helen were both familiar and subject to revision and adaptation is well exemplified by a post-pharaonic graffito

opposite a sculpted figure of a beautiful Egyptian female ruler in Luxor Temple. Incised at the base of a papyrus-capital column, the graffito juxtaposes an apparent depiction by a Graeco-Roman tourist of a statue of Helen's infamous lover, Paris, with a statue of queen Nefertari. One of a number of inscriptions of late pharaonic through Graeco-Roman date clustered in the east side of the south end of the first open court of Luxor Temple, this graffito is a single example of a far wider phenomenon and sheds light on the degree to which Helen's story had permeated Mediterranean cultural perception. For detailed discussion of the depiction of Paris in Luxor Temple and the implied substitution of the statue of Nefertari as an *eidolon* of Helen, see Manassa (2009).

27 What follows is very much drawn from the long-standing study of women in antiquity – and Roman women in particular – undertaken by Drr. J. Lea Beness and T.W. Hillard, both affiliated with the Department of Ancient History at Macquarie University. To both my colleagues I owe a significant debt.

28 For a useful survey of the quantitative problems associated with the phenomenon of literacy, see Harris (1989), Humphrey (1991), and Thomas (1992). The introductory chapters and bibliographies in these studies provide an excellent overview of the issues and a comprehensive entry-point into the continuing debate. For specific instances of women writers, see Plant (2004).

29 On what conclusions can be drawn from the corpus of private Latin inscriptions from Roman Italy in the republican and imperial periods about the identity, social condition, and cultural activity of men and women participating in the process of epigraphic commemorations and dedication, see Keegan (2014). For an overview of the issues relating to the representation of Greek and Roman women in sculpture from the fifth century BCE to the second century CE, see Barrow (2018).

30 Studies of clothing, cosmetics, hair and hairstyling, and textiles in Greece and Rome include Grillet (1975); Harrison (1998); Wyke (1994); Croom (2002); Wild (2003a); Wild (2003b); Cleland et al (2007); and Olson (2009).

31 For useful introductions to the source material for information about gender, sex and sexuality in Graeco-Roman antiquity, see Dover (1978); Blok and Mason (1987); Foxhall (1998); Dixon (2001); Doherty (2001); Deacy and Pierce (2002); Skinner (2005); and Williams (2010).

32 Important overviews of Graeco-Roman social and legal categories such as adoption, adultery, marriage, pornography, and rape can be found in the works of Treggiari (1991); McGinn (1998); Lindsay (2009).

33 On the family in Greek history, see Patterson (1998); on the family in ancient Rome, see Dixon (1992).

34 In relation to the reproductive economy of classical antiquity, an understanding of Aristotle's philosophy of biology is especially formative. For a close study of the philosophical and historical issues arising in Aristotle's biological works, see Lennox (2001).

35 *CIL* I² 1211 = *ILLRP* 973 = *ILS* 8403.

36 *CIL* VI 37965 = *CLE* 1988.

37 An overview of the breadth of scholarship can be found in Bérard et al³ (2000), including seven online supplements (http://www.antiquite.ens.fr/txt/dsa-publications-guidepigraphiste-en.htm). Bodel (2001: 1–56) provides a splendid introduction to the kinds of historical evidence provided by Greek and Latin inscriptions. For a useful bibliographical survey of material written about Greek and Latin epitaphs, see Pfohl and Pietri (1983).

38 Cic. *Top*. 14; Gell. *NA* 18.6.8–9; see also Crawford (1996.2: 801–809) for the *lex Iulia de maritandis ordinibus* (18 BCE) and *lex Papia Poppaea* (9 CE); and Treggiari (1991: 60–80) for discussion of the Augustan legislation governing

marriage, which created a system of rewards for married persons and parents and penalties for the unwed and childless.

39 Demand (1994), Gourevitch (1996), and Bonet (1998) provide informative outlines of childbirth, infant diseases, and mortality in ancient Greece and Rome.

40 On Latin cognomina, personal names in the Roman world, and Roman ono-mastic practice, see Kajanto (1965); Salway (1994); and Cheesman (2011). For an overview of slavery's place in the fabric of Graeco-Roman society, see Wiedemann (1981) and Bradley (1994).

41 On the categories of mistress of the household (*materfamilas*) and respectable married woman (*matrona*), see Hallett (1984) and Dixon (1988).

42 Gell. *NA* 5.19.10.

43 Val. Max. 3.8.6; (Auct.) *de viris illustribus* 73.

44 Val. Max. 8.3.

45 *Dig.* 3.1.1.5.

46 Ulp. 11.2.

47 Liv. 34.1–8; App. *B Civ.* 4.32.4. On both episodes, see Ch. 2.

48 For a useful general estimation of the priestesses who tended the temple of the Roman goddess Vesta, see Wildfang (2006). On Roman priests and priestesses in general, see Rüpke (2007).

49 For references to episodes featuring Vestal Virgins, see Ch. 1.3 and 4.2; Fig. 1.1 (Bk. 5, 63); Fig. 1.2 (no. 4, 18, 24, 31, 32, 35, 39, 41); Fig. 1.3 (Bk. 1, 4, 5, 8, 14, 20).

50 Gell. *NA* 11.6.

51 Ov. *Ars am.* 3.635–6; see Brouwer (1989) for a detailed study of Bona Dea, the "Good Goddess."

52 Liv. 25.1.

53 Julius Obsequens 55.

54 Nep. *Praef.* 3.6–7.

55 E.g., Aemilia, sister of L. Aemilius Paullus: Polyb. 21.36.

56 Cic. *Att.* 15.11.

57 Cic. *Fam.* 5.2.

58 Val. Max. 8.3.1–3; cf. Quint. *Inst.* 1.1.6; App. *B Civ.* 4.5.32-34; Dio Cass. 47.14.2-5.

59 For a portrait of one such woman, Antonia Minor, see Kokkinos (1992).

60 Cf. Cass. Dio 53.19.1-3.

61 On the evolution of female-prominent influence in the early imperial period, it is difficult to avoid considering the life and career of Livia Drusilla, wife of the first *princeps* Augustus. See, e.g., Purcell (1986); Wood (2001: 75–141); Barrett (2002); Harvey (2020).

62 Tac. *Ann.* 6.49.3 – the mother of Sextus Papinius: 37 CE; 16.30.4 – Servilia, daughter of Barea Soranus: 66 CE.

63 Plin. *Ep.* 6.33.

64 *CIL* VI 1527, 37053.

65 *Dig.* 48.2.8, 50.17.2; Gai. *Inst.* 4.13.11; cf. *CJ* 2.12.8, 22.6.9 pr., 2.8.8.2, 2.12.1.5, 48.16.4, 16.1.32.

ACKNOWLEDGEMENTS

The people I have to thank are many. Firstly, I would like to thank my wife Cathy. She has always been my most ardent and valued supporter. I owe her a great debt of love and gratitude.

I must also thank my boys (Tom, Jack, and Dominic) for tolerating my absences (in thought and location) and for their invariable support and encouragement.

In helping me to write this book or for help with its development over the years or for references, conversations, emails, off-prints, advice and inspiration I would like to thank (in alphabetical order) David Christian, Suzanne Dixon, Elaine Fantham, Michele George, Sandra Joshel, Alison Keith, Maxine Lewis, Judith and Sam Lieu, Kristina Milnor, Nicholas Purcell, Brent Shaw, Christopher Smith, Mary Spongberg, Andrew Wallace-Hadrill, and Greg Woolf.

Four scholars need to be singled out for special thanks. During my time at the British School at Rome in 2019, I was fortunate enough to share a resident's reading table with Professor Ron Ridley, whose deep and profound expertise in Livian scholarship is well known. I am grateful to him for offering his enviable insights and expertise in support of the final phase of my writing project. Alanna Nobbs acted as the energetic supporter of an Honours project that began with an historiographical dissection of Livy's first pentad and ended with a review of a select proportion of those episodes including individual women or female collectives in the surviving books of AUC history. It is embarrassing to think what I might have produced without her help and advice. Her criticism and encouragement, along with a constant stream of ideas and references, made the writing far more enjoyable, and far more rewarding, than it would otherwise have been. Lea Beness has played an important role in my work since I had the pleasure of convening the unit *Women and Gender in the Ancient World* as I commenced my doctoral program. Her knowledge of ancient concepts of gender and sexuality and of the many ways that women have been represented in classical literature and art has been a constant source of inspiration and assistance. It is true to say that without Lea I would not have understood the significance of the historical material I was exploring. Finally, Tom Hillard has my gratitude for two (though undoubtedly on reflection many more) reasons. First, for bringing me to the study of the ancient Roman world at Macquarie University, where my years here engaged in research and education have taught me more about classical antiquity than I thought possible. I am also grateful to Tom for the time I have spent as his colleague. His eagerness to share and debate ideas, his rigour and inquisitiveness in the field and on the page, and his acute understanding of how fluid is our knowledge of gender and sexuality in classical antiquity – all these have provided the best of examples.

I would also like to thank the library staff of the British School at Rome, the Department of Classics, Columbia University, New York, and the Institute of Classical Studies, London. I am grateful for their thoughtful curation of resources, readiness to provide a reference at short notice, and consistent *bon homie*.

Thanks, finally, to Elizabeth Risch, Ella Halstead, and Amy Davis-Poynter at Routledge for their guidance, encouragement, and enduring patience throughout the editorial process.

1

AUC HISTORY

Women and the art of exemplary storytelling

1.1 *Res novae* and *mores maiorum*: *exempli documenta, haec tempora,* and the resonances of change

The prominence of individual or collective female activity in certain episodes of Livy's *Ab Urbe Condita* (AUC) presents the critical reader of Graeco-Roman historiography with a difficulty and a duty. The problem is a matter of emphasis; the obligation, one of explanation.

The latter first. Any treatment of Livy's interposition of women in the dense, composite superstructure of his annalistic narrative must elucidate the connection which exists between the stated aim of the ancient writer's historiographical project and the practical application of that argument. In other words, to appreciate the consistency and vigour of Livy's gendered textual exposition of Roman history (*res Romana*), the modem interpreter requires some familiarity with the subtle propositions which the annalist outlines in his introduction to Book 1.

This task requires a sympathetic imagination. In this respect, it is hard to accept R.M. Ogilvie's assessment that Livy's *praefatio* is "the preface of a small man ... who writes ... to enshrine in literature persons and events that have given him a thrill of excitement as he studied them"; nor is P.G. Walsh's assertion that, "if the Preface is any guide ... moral and patriotic considerations are united for didactic purposes" completely satisfying.[1] Rather, in line with the increasing respect accorded to Livy's literary and historiographical intelligence, I would argue that Livy sought to redefine the writing and interpretation of AUC history – that is, the representation of Rome's historical past – albeit within the formal structural limitations of conventional annalistic practice.

Without avoiding the complexity of discussion which naturally attends such a reading of Livy's famous Preface,[2] the following observations are cited for consideration. First, the opening words of the historian's long, intensively personalised introductory period establish the desired relationship between writer and reader.

Whether the task I have undertaken of writing a complete history of the Roman people from the very commencement of its existence will reward me for the labour spent on it, I neither know for certain, nor if I did know would I venture to say. For I see that this is an old-established and a common practice, each fresh writer being invariably persuaded that he will either attain greater certainty in the materials of his narrative or surpass the rudeness of antiquity in the excellence of his style.[3]

By virtue of the fact that the opening words of his Preface possess a very particular metrical pattern, Livy draws attention to the relationship between poetry and history.[4] Recognition of this association immediately compels the historian's readership to engage thoughtfully with the writing of a history intended to teach moral and ethical lessons. The unsettling effect created by Livy's inclusion of a poetic metre is at first glance solely a stylistic issue. Notably in this regard, Quintilian, who recognised the quality of Sallust as a historian, contrasts his austere and epigrammatic *brevitas* with Livy's *lactea ubertas* ("milky richness"), a style that, while lush and vivid, avoiding all harshness and in which the periods run along smoothly, still provides a richly fertile historical narrative suitable for nourishing the reader.[5] Associated with the question of style, however, is the existence and continuity of an ancient argument best exemplified by the diverging historiographical approaches of the 5th century BCE Greek writers, Thucydides and Herodotus, a difference regarding respectively the distinctiveness and assimilation of poetry and history.[6] In the simplest terms, while the histories of Herodotus and Thucydides both drew inspiration from oral history, the poetry of the Greek epic cycle and the *Iliad* and *Odyssey* in particular, Thucydides broke from Homer's grip and took a different approach to observing the landscape of historical memory and conveying the world's reality. Of course, when the Homeric epics were composed, usually dated to the 8th century BCE, poets were the only historians. Although it does not follow that poets would always scrupulously adhere to truth, veracity in historical narration relied significantly on a poet's reputation in public opinion. Naturally, the common use of written records and the rise of prose histories drew into contention unquestioning acceptance of truth-telling in relation to the genre of poetry, regardless of the merit in which the composer was held. When this tension between the writing of poetry and history is admitted, the rhetorical ploy underpinning Livy's provocative beginning guarantees the participation of his readers.

Second, this reciprocal involvement in the writing of AUC history is explicitly articulated in Section 10 of the Preface:

There is this exceptionally beneficial and fruitful advantage to be derived from the study of the past that you see, set in the clear light of historical truth, examples of every possible type. From these you may select for yourself and your country what to imitate, and also what, as being mischievous in its inception and disastrous in its issues, you are to avoid.[7]

In the light of Ogilvie's interpretation of these words, the force adhering to Livy's claim – that history offers examples ("set in the clear record of a nation") of every sort of conduct (*exempli documenta*) – is novel and original.[8] As C.S. Kraus notes, there is "a direct, personal relationship between the ego of the text and this *tu*: history is understood – even made – in the space between them."[9] This kind of view resonates in certain ways with recent reassessments of how we read the past. More and more, modern historiography has moved beyond the preoccupation with factually accurate data drawn from approved historical sources, passive reception of canonical prose history, and valorisation of static written records and literary accounts.[10] In line with Livy's explicit acknowledgement of the permeable nature of history and the agency of the consumer of the historical tradition, there is merit in studying the past wherever it may be illuminated. For scholarly historical inquiry in the 21st century, this approach draws on a constantly evolving corpus of non-prosaic, archaeological, and epigraphic evidence: literary, documentary, and material sources of knowledge outside the medium of historical writing that preserve the memory of the past as cultural knowledge.[11] In much the same way, a majority of the men and women living in late republican Rome accessed their culture in a wide variety of forms: for those who were wealthy persons educated in the elite curriculum (mythology, Greek and Latin language, literature, and rhetoric), traditional historiography afforded a very particular opportunity to engage with narratives of the past; for those with functional, little, or no literacy, the formal memorials of the past, displayed in the architectural, aesthetic, and inscribed topography of city and *suburbium*, and the performative historiographical traditions of theatre, recitation, and procession.[12] With this in mind, the ancient reader of Livy's Preface could not help but register the implied interdependence of narrative and artefact – that is, the discursive monument of annalistic history and the narrative episodes of historiographical storytelling – and the mediating role ascribed to the complicity between creator and observer.[13]

Third, setting this in the milieu of the *saeculum Augustum* – the period of socio-historical change marking Rome's conceptual transition from oligarchic to dynastic rule, linked intrinsically to the lifetime of Augustus – Livy's historical *monumentum* can be viewed as an attempt to reconstruct Rome in a representational and referential sense.[14] As the historian observes mid-way through his prefatory manifesto,

The subjects to which I would ask each of my readers to devote his earnest attention are these: the life (*vita*) and morals (*mores*) of the community; the men and the qualities by which through domestic policy and foreign war dominion was won and extended. Then as the standard of morality gradually lowers, let him follow the decay of the national character, observing how at first it slowly sinks, then slips downward more and more rapidly, and finally begins to plunge into headlong ruin, until he reaches these times (*haec tempora*), in which we can bear neither our diseases nor their remedies.[15]

While it cannot be verified – either by historical research or the sequential comparison of symbolic discourses (that is, literary texts and visual images) – if Livy or his late republican contemporaries were aware of the qualitative leap embodied in the transition from Republic to Empire, the possibility of an ancient historian coming to grips with intellectual, moral, and emotional conceptions similar to those of Augustus should be entertained.[16] Despite this uncertainty, it is reasonable to propose that Livy meant his version of the existing tradition to extend and outstrip the pessimistic and moralistic imperatives of his Roman historiographical predecessors, and to interrogate the tensions between topical and timeless meanings across the continuous process of *res Romana*. In one sense, the very novelty of his historiographical project necessitated Livy's adoption of a ritualistic structure which emphasised customary references and recollected previously assimilated material.[17] The effectiveness of his intention to use the past as a conduit, through which he might facilitate contemporary change, depended very much on the degree of familiarity in the conveyed content of the message.[18]

This brings us face-to-face with the inclusion of women among the conventional themes and figures of Livian historiographical narrative, a project which must be contextualised within the world of the Augustan revolution and the emergence of the socio-political phenomenon of the Julio-Claudian dynastic *familia*. No one would underestimate the major transformations in Roman society and government during the period from the death of Julius Caesar to the death of Augustus (44 BCE–14 CE). Central to our interest here is social reform. At the very least, effects on women of the period during which Livy prepared, composed, and published his AUC history would have been paradoxical. On the one hand, the Augustan programme embraced a moral rejuvenation of Rome: a very public assault on social trends which were regarded as detrimental to the spiritual well-being of the Roman people.

In this regard, consider the following observation:

> Augustus claimed both to revive the past and to set standards for the future. ... The aim of the new code was no less than this, to bring the family under the protection of the state – a measure quite superfluous so long as Rome remained her ancient self. In the aristocracy of the last age of the Republic marriage had not always been blessed with either offspring or permanence. Matches contracted for the open and avowed ends of money, politics or pleasure

were lightly dissolved according to the interest or the whim of either party. Few indeed of the great ladies would have been able – or eager – to claim, like Cornelia, the epitaph "A wife once only, this stone declares."[19] Though some might show a certain restraint in changing husbands or lovers, they were seldom exemplars of the domestic virtues of the Roman matron – the Claudia who "administered the household, worked the wool."[20] Their names were more often heard in public than was expedient for honest women: they became politicians and patrons of the arts. They were formidable and independent, retaining control of their own property in marriage. The emancipation of women had its reaction upon the men, who, instead of a partner from their own class, preferred alliance with a freedwoman, or none at all. With marriage and without it, the tone and habits of high society were gay and abandoned. The New State supervened, crushing and inexorable.[21]

This assessment of the Augustan national programme can be found in *The Roman Revolution*, Ronald Syme's idiosyncratic and controversial study of the transformation of state and society, the violent transference of power and property, and the establishment of dynastic rule between 60 BCE and 14 CE. A product of its time – the third decade of the 20th century – it is essential for a modern reader to note the irony with which he artfully blurs the distinction between clever and precise allusion to the evidence, the historian's observation, his own opinion, and mimicry of the tone of his conservative sources and the Roman moral tradition. Nevertheless, as Syme noted, the proposed revival demanded a return to traditional *mores*. One focus was the sanctity of the family. A graphic illustration of this can be found on the reliefs which flanked the long exterior walls of the *Ara Pacis Augustae* (the Altar of Augustan Peace), a monument commissioned by the Roman Senate in 13 BCE to honour the return of Augustus after 3 years in Hispania and Gaul and consecrated in 9 BCE. Kleiner points out that integrated family groups of men, women, and children appear here for the first time in surviving Roman state art.[22] At the same time featured in this revival were the traditional roles of women – roles constrained, but not without authority. The virtues, the power of womanhood, were to the fore in this moral revival, nowhere perhaps more manifest than in the grand figure of nurture on the left-hand panel of the east face of the *Ara Pacis*: "the ever-controversial personification of peace and plenty, Tellus/Italia."[23]

Of course, as with any form of discourse – and the construction of Roman historical accounts, and Livian historiography in particular, should be preeminent in relation to what follows – this kind of iconographic image can be viewed from a variety of standpoints. Late republican and early imperial freedmen and women as well as their freeborn offspring, for example, commissioned funerary portraits which appear to have been based on current and earlier aristocratic models.[24] But the degree to which these representations of Roman men, women, and children spoke of Augustan ideological concerns is a moot point. If, as noted above, it is acceptable to posit that an artistic monument was just as often a "document" to be "read" with a particular meaning in mind, how should we interpret the marked differentiation between the portraits of idealised young men and women, and the sombre, static, and oftentimes unflatteringly realistic depictions of older men and women? Is it enough to suggest that these funerary reliefs sought only to highlight the legitimation of the Augustan ideal of *familia*, and the roles which this socio-cultural conception assigned to individual members of the *domus*? It has been argued that slaves and freedmen were among the most enthusiastic consumers of Augustan assertions about respectability and that they attempted to use the tools he offered in order to claim a higher status for themselves.[25] However, there may well be other meanings to these images, over and beyond those portrayed in the accepted terms of the included or dominant population, and it is as well that the extant remainders of marginal groups be viewed accordingly. So, it might be that the *libertini* and their freeborn descendants wished to speak to others of their class and gender about matters more of concern to them than to their former owners, the current elite. For instance, it is possible to see that the representations of a freedman's or woman's identity at death distinguish a specific type of work from the property relationship that defined his or her submission to an ex-master; and that these portraits (with their accompanying inscriptions) assert a claim to physical movement in the material and social world otherwise limited by the freed status.[26]

As a single example of the variety of alternative modes of historical expression and reception practised under Augustan rule – and an instance not only familiar to the late republican and early imperial readership of AUC history but undoubtedly known to the historian himself – the case of Marcus Vergilius Eurysaces and Atistia is pertinent.[27] Constructed around the end of the Republic, the tomb of Eurysaces was one of the largest and best-preserved funerary monuments in Rome, and its sculpted frieze commemorated the activities associated with the named owner's profession. Drawing on information provided in the monument's façade inscriptions, we learn of his Roman citizenship and foreign descent, the first signalled by his *tria nomina* and the latter encoded in the derivation of his cognomen. In addition, Eurysaces listed his titles – a *pistor*, or master baker; and *redemptor*, contractor of bread – occupational categories which Cicero found somewhat problematic, given the Roman elite's disdain for commerce and labour.[28] Other evidence pertaining to the attested relationship between husband and wife can be gleaned from a full-length marble relief portrait of a man and women dressed in Roman attire, their heads turning towards each other, and a marble epitaph. In regard to the second datum of evidence, Atistia is represented as the "best of wives," a "wonderful woman" whose remains are preserved "in this breadbasket" – an extraordinary metonymy between the memorial of the dead and the cooperative activity of the living.[29] In addition, the tomb's topographical placement, just outside the Porta Maggiore and off the intersection of two major metropolitan roads and its monumental size reflect the wealth of the baker and the prosperity of his business enterprise. Even though the commemorated individuals belong to a higher status affiliation than many *libertini*, there is more than meets the eye (namely, whose eye) when viewing ancient evidence of this kind.

Commemorative, memorialising discourse like the funerary monument of M. Vergilius Eurysaces – a civic memorial transmitting socio-economic and familial information through traditional commemorative strategies – provides the modern reader of AUC history with a qualitative framework for understanding the late republican and early imperial milieu within which Livy composed his narrative. In this light, it is reasonable to imagine the historian referring to a plethora of visual cues, curated, inscribed, and otherwise constituted in the built fabric of urban space throughout and around the Augustan city so as to fashion his account of Rome's past. As such, Livy selected his corpus of exemplary narrative episodes and his catalogue of illustrative socio-cultural and psychological representations of men and women not only from a range of extant literary historical sources but also from a number of architectural structures, commemorative, dedicatory and funerary monuments, and topographical features.[30]

In relation to the epistemological significance of the Roman historical enterprise, the literature of the Augustan period is similarly revealing on a number of levels.[31] Not only does its interest in a revered past record for us otherwise lost lore; it rewrites it, according to contemporary needs. Virgil's Dido and Creusa are very suitable cases in point. Virgil represents Dido against a background of specifically Roman cultural norms in her political, religious, legislative, and architectural practice. But a narrative concerning the origins of the political, religious, and military institutions of a state that places a woman at its head[32] poses a serious threat to Roman cultural conventions, since these institutions were reserved almost exclusively for upper-class citizen males at Rome. As a woman operating in the public sphere, Dido necessarily constitutes and is constituted as a disruptive force in the *Aeneid*. In accordance with Roman discursive codes about the female, therefore, the focus of the narrative narrows to Dido's sexuality; so that her political and military ambitions come to be subsumed by her inappropriate erotic desires.[33] Viewed through this androcentric elite Roman perspective, Dido's nationality (a Carthaginian) and gender ideologically render her socially disruptive and, therefore, sexually deviant.

The sexual ideology implicit in the Dido episode of the *Aeneid* recalls Livy's inclusion of Helen of Sparta/Troy as he commenced his history of Rome. Virgil, too, incorporates a similar figure of passion and volatility, albeit a portrait at length rather than in passing: the representation of a woman whose qualities contrast with Aeneas' order and control, traits that Virgil associated (or, rather, wished to identify) with the Rome of his own time. In this sense, the Dido episode shows significant points of contact with the social and moral concerns addressed in the *leges Iuliae* of 18 BCE, the year after Virgil's death.[34] Introduced by Augustus, the effects on women of the *lex Iulia de adulteriis coercendis*, or the Julian law on restraining adulteries, were explicit. The *lex Iulia* established an assortment of sexual misdemeanours punishable by the state. In general, these offences related to something called *stuprum*, which encompassed adultery and *incestum*. *Stuprum* referred to associations with single or widowed women, and with boys. A class of women was specified on which *stuprum* was not committed, principally slaves and prostitutes. Incest in the Roman world included both sexual relations between primary kin and marrying within the proscribed degrees of relationship, whether natural or by adoption. Adultery, then, came to be used specifically of relations with a married woman; and, importantly, for the first time became a criminal offence, although men did not encounter equivalent treatment to women when the law was applied.[35]

In addition to the many and varied provisions of the *lex Iulia* intended to suppress those forms of non-marital sexual relations considered unacceptable by Roman society, particularly adultery, a father was specifically allowed to impose summary justice on a daughter caught in the act of adultery in his or his son-in-law's house. Gardner notes that, as this justice had to be imposed immediately, and as the father was obliged to kill the adulterer as well (and must not kill either without the other), "[this provision of the law] in effect constituted a restriction on the *ius vitae necisque* [*paterfamilias*'s right of life and death], and it is possible that the intention was in practice to discourage such killing."[36]

These instances should make it fairly clear that the law was intended primarily to preserve the chastity of women within marriage. Sexual relations with marriageable women were not to be encouraged, since they undermined that marriage and production of legitimate children on which the continuance of the *familia* depended. The chastity of men did not matter, so long as they kept away from other men's wives, and there were plenty of legal alternatives available.

In association with the *lex Julia*, the stipulations of another piece of social legislation, the *lex Papia Poppaea* of 9 CE, ended any legal liability for women to be assigned a tutor if they had three children (four, for a freedwoman).[37] The more wealthy and influential women could, on formal exemption conferred by the *princeps*, claim the right without having given birth to the requisite number of children. It should be noted here that additional benefits granted by this "privilege of children" (the so-called *ius liberorum*) included fast-tracking of the *cursus honorum* for husbands and male kin (what should be understood as the anticipated career path in the public domain for elite male citizens) and exclusion from the penalties Augustus had imposed on the childless in regard to the receipt of bequests. Of course, given the elementary nature of medical diagnosis and treatment, not to mention the kinds of care afforded after birth, it is a matter of conjecture if women considered the relief provided under the legislation particularly beneficial; specially freedwomen, whose children born before their manumission were not included in the calculation. Where the person giving financial and other support to the manumitted female was also married to the woman, the tutelage might not be a burden, only, naturally, while marital relations remained satisfactory. Daughters whose father remained alive were compelled to wait until such time as they became orphans or were freed before they could receive any advantage from producing the requisite four children. In sum, the *lex Papia* considerably increased the freedwoman's powers of testamentary disposal, as against her patron, so long as she bore children.[38]

Therefore, the laws of 18 BCE and 9 CE did not so much recognise marital relations as punish reproductive abstinence. While marriage could remove some, but not all, of the disability, the production of legitimate children completed the process, and fertility could also bring rewards. Those chiefly affected by the penalties imposed on the unmarried were the well-to-do. Clearly, one at least of the aims of the original legislation (though not the only one) was "to stabilise the transmission of property and consequently of status" among the Roman upper classes. Just as clearly, due to exemptions bestowed by imperial favour upon the influential and their friends, and the clearly defined elements of disclosure incumbent upon the parties involved, the legislation proved (at the very least) ineffective.[39]

When viewing Virgil's representation of Dido in relation to the social reforms of the principate, while it would be naive to suppose that the *Aeneid* was no more than an Augustan policy statement circulated as literature, there is compelling evidence that the poem was in broad accord with the politics of the new regime.[40] The close temporal conjunction between the promulgation of the moral legislation of 18 BCE in Augustus's name and the publication of the Aeneid on Augustus's authority the next year suggests that Dido's sexual transgressions may be related to Augustan efforts at appearing to regulate female sexuality. In the same light, however, establishing the partiality of Livy with regard to the reforming objectives of the Augustan principate remains elusive, to some extent due to the fragmentary and historically distant nature of the surviving corpus, but in large part because the historian's narrative remains separate from the broader political project underway in the city of Rome and across the fabric of the Roman state.[41]

Situating Livy within this brief and highly selective survey of historiographical practice during the transformative period of the Augustan principate foregrounds the fact that composing a history of Rome would always, but especially in times of social and political transition, result in a dynamic work of historical literature – articulated from the many varied narratives of past generations; sensitive to the traditional structure of the annual magisterial cycle, receptive to the transmission of national rules of conduct and codes of behaviour, and alert to the representative catalogue of exemplary characters.[42] From the time when he first contemplated his monumental task to the moment his AUC was first written down, more than 500 years after it began happening, Livy would have stitched together his narrative from *all* the sources of information and inspiration available to historical writers of his time. In a sense, for the modern reader, just as much as Livy's contemporary audience, the history which some will have for so long read as Rome's history pure and simple becomes a palimpsest, rich in layers. There is much to be learnt from reading between the lines and attempting to discern the other readings – not least about the aims of the dominant text. Whether the Augustan version overlays all is another matter entirely, and a consideration which, in the end, need not distract from the present investigation.

In this context, Livy's representation of women looms larger than one might expect in a canonical history of Rome comprising, in the simplest terms, a combination of foundation legends and formative episodes that describe the primordial origins of city and state (Books 1–10) with a cyclical, sequential catalogue of political and military events and personalities (Books 21–45). According to this formulation, while a significant amount of ink has been committed to Latinist literary critiques, topical studies, and thematic examinations of episodes including depictions of female behaviour, speech, and active participation in the course of making Roman history, in the main these studies have focussed on episodes and women located within the temporal and spatial limits of Livy's first pentad (Books 1–5) and only rarely on events in the period of the Middle Republic (Books 21–40). In regard to this selective scholarly interest, marked by a preoccupation with the earlier, legendary stories of Rome's foundation, prime examples from the first pentad are Livy's account of the abduction and rape of the Sabine women (in Book 1) and his coverage of the legendary heroines Lucretia and Verginia (in Books 1 and 3, respectively); and, for the later pentads, his treatment of the debate on the repeal of the *lex Oppia* in 195 BCE (at the beginning of Book 34), and his account of the Bacchanalian crisis (in Book 39).[43]

On a purely statistical basis, episodes recorded in AUC history including references to women – identified by name, designated by kinship or marriage, or otherwise cited in collective terms; and involving significant, peripheral, or incidental female activity – may be found throughout the extant record of Livy's *res romana*.

Using Table 1.1 as a guide, the initial calculation of narrative locations where Livy includes representations of women is instructive. In the surviving volumes of AUC history (Books 1–10, 21–45), Livy identifies by name 46 legendary or historical women and 5 female deities or divine beings; additionally, he refers to 8 unnamed female characters and 17 categories or collectives of women. A review of the outline summaries of otherwise lost books of AUC history (the *Periochae*) reveals a further 17 named individuals, a lone goddess, 3 anonymous women, and 2 female collectives. All in all, across a chronological period of 800 years, extending from the mid-8th to the late 1st century BCE, the Livian tradition includes 94 representations of women in a total of 82 narrative episodes: 59 episodes in the extant

Table 1.1 Structure, female representation, and chronology of AUC history (extant and summary)

Book	Women	Events
1	Helen, Lavinia, Creusa, Rhea Silvia, Larentia, *Carmenta*, the Sabine women, Hersilia, Tarpeia, *Egeria*, Horatia, Tanaquil, Tullia, Lucretia	Pentad I (Book 1): from the founding of Rome to the expulsion of the Etruscan kings
2	Vitellia, Cloelia, Veturia, Roman women, *Fortuna Muliebris*, Oppia	Pentad I (Books 2–5): from the beginning of the
3	Roman *matronae*, Racilia, Verginia	Republic to the sack of
4	"Woman" cited in C. Canuleius' proposal for the right of *connubium*, the Ardean *virgo*, Postumia	Rome by the Gauls
5	Roman *matronae*, Women of Veii, *Juno Regina*, Roman *matres*, Ar(r)uns' wife, soldiers' wives, Vestal Virgins and L. Albinius' wife, Vestal Virgins and the sacred hearth	
6	Roman *matronae*, the Fabiae Ambusti	Pentad II (Books 6–10):
8	A woman from Pandosia, Cleopatra and Olympias; Minucia, the *ancilla,* and 20 *matronae* accused of poisoning	from the refounding of the city and the political evolution of the
10	Roman *matronae*, Verginia, *Pudicitia Patricia*, and *Pudicitia Plebeia*	constitution to the expansion of Roman power in Italy
14	Sextilia	Pentads III and IV (Books
19	Claudia	11–20, lost): from 292 to
20	Tuccia	218 BCE, including the First Punic War [Lost]
22	Busa	Pentads V and VI (Books
24	Wife of Hannibal; Damarata, Heraclea, and Harmonia; Roman widows	21–30): the Second Punic War (218–202 BCE)
26	Mistress of Campanian deserter; Vestia Oppia and Pacula Cluvia; wife of Mandonius, daughters of Indibilis, and other young unmarried women; the fiancé of Alluccius	
27	Young woman from Tarentum; Polycratia	
29	Claudia Quinta, daughter of Hasdrubal's sister, Sophoni(s)ba	
31	Apega	Pentads VII-IX (Books
34	Roman and Latin women agitating for the repeal of the *lex Oppia* (*frequentia mulierum, agmen matronae, coniuratio muliebri, secessio mulierum, seditio muliebrium; coetum muliebris, honestae feminae; filiae, uxores,* and *sorores; intercursus matronae; sociorum Latini uxoribus*)	31–45): the Macedonian and Eastern Wars (201–167 BCE)
35	Apamae (mother and daughter)	
38	Chiomara; Cornelia Maior and Cornelia Minor	
39	Hispala Faecenia; *scortum* from *Placentia*	
40	Theoxena	
41	Orthobula	
45	Roman *feminae*	

(*Continued*)

Table 1.1 Structure, female representation, and chronology of AUC history (extant and summary (*Continued*)

Book	Women	Events
48	Publilia and Licinia, *nobiles feminae*	Pentads X-XXIV/V (Books
50	Laodice	46–142: 166–9 BCE):
51	Wife of Hasdrubal	from the Middle Republic
52	Cleopatra Thea, wife of Demetrius III	to the Early Principate
57	Women of Vaccaea	[*Periochae* only][44]
59	Widows excluded from *lustrum*; Cleopatra III; Sempronia, wife of P. Cornelius Scipio Africanus	
60	Cleopatra Thea, wife of Demetrius II	
63	Aemilia, Licinia, and Marcia, Vestals	
68	Mother of Publicius Malleolus	
72	Woman, rescuer of Ser. Sulpicius Galba from captivity	
89	Bastia, wife of Mutilus	
103	Pompeia, wife of Caesar	
106	Julia, daughter of Caesar	
111	Cleopatra III	
112	Cornelia, wife of Pompey; Cleopatra III	
116	*Venus Genetrix*	
125	Fulvia, wife of M. Antonius	
127	Fulvia; Octavia, sister of C. Octavius/ Caesar Augustus	
130	Cleopatra VII	
131	Cleopatra VII	
132	Cleopatra VII; Octavia	
133	Cleopatra	
140	Octavia	

historical record and 23 references in the epitomies of the remaining lost books.[45] To this tally can be added 100 items that should be understood in relation to the primary episodes featuring women in the extant books of AUC history and 53 references that provide incidental representations of named and unnamed women and categories of women (*feminae, mulieres; filiae, matres, sorores, uxores*).[46]

As outlined previously, the quantitative residue of female representation in AUC history reflects traditional Roman historiographical practice. In relation to historical writing composed and transmitted prior to the end of the Augustan principate, it must always be remembered that Roman society excluded female participation from all formal political offices, effectively limiting a woman's political role to the provision of advice and the deployment of matronal influence (*materna auctoritas*) within predominantly domestic contexts in the daily lives of elite senatorial families. In light of the social and cultural prescriptions on women in Roman antiquity, traditional annalistic narrative dealt almost exclusively with important political and military events in the city of Rome, the Italian peninsula, and the wider Mediterranean (either in contact with the Roman state or under Roman rule). As such, and in line with dominant ideological attitudes to women and gender relations in the ancient world, Roman historical writers will only infrequently have identified historical traces of female activity important enough to record.

To be clear, in comparable Greek literature dealing with expansive narrative treatments of significant historical subject matter the frequency of female representation is similarly slight. Herodotus refers to women 373 times; Thucydides, less than 50, and – unlike Herodotus – never in any detail.[47] By contrast, there are more than 130 references to women in the extant text of Polybius'.[48] In this regard, knowing that Livy's AUC history, in particular the third decade dealing with the Second Punic War, has an extremely close relationship to the surviving portions of the Polybian account[49] – and regardless of whether Livy used Polybius directly, or whether the similarities are the consequence of either Livy employing a source who had himself used Polybius, or else of Livy's source and Polybius depending on a common source – it is notable that both historians refer to women; and, at first glance, that Livy appears to do so as frequently as his Greek counterpart. That the work of both historians is profoundly fragmentary limits any comparison to the extant literary material:[50] as to whether either historian incorporated representations of women into their lost narrative accounts less or more frequently, or to a degree equivalent to the number of times tallied from the surviving literature, must remain speculative. In regard to Livy's history, the *Periochae* shed some light on this question, but using these summaries to interpret the historian's project will, in the final analysis, reflect the interests and emphases of the author(s) as least as much as those of Livy; and the fact that the *Periochae* of the surviving books sometimes fail to correspond to Livy's narrative gives further pause for thought.[51]

To the modern reader, this representative quantum is disappointingly slight. Nevertheless, despite the skewed preponderance in Livy's history of source material featuring the historical representation of women, a contextual analysis of these placements aggravates an initial suspicion. Regardless of the category of female included in the historian's depictions, the statistical corpus of instances where Livy provides annalistic (discursive) or narrative (story) representations of women are situated invariably in contexts of cultural, economic, military, political, religious, or social change or crisis.

Table 1.2 provides a condensed template of those distinctive historical elements which frame Livy's gendered *exempli documenta*. Reviewing the tabulated scaffold provides a snapshot of information immediately prior to the beginning, or following on from the end, of an episode in AUC history featuring female representation of one or more kinds. What becomes clear as one moves methodically from one narrative element to another is the importance assigned by the historian to each of the women represented in each episode. Although identified by name only, we have already

Table 1.2 Structural relationship of narrative elements before and after major episodes of AUC history featuring representations of women

	Pre-episode	Episode	Post-episode
1	Capture of Troy and massacre of Trojan citizens.	HELEN (wife of Menelaus and Paris; indirect saviour of Aeneas and Antenor). 1.1.1	Aeneas and Antenor survive the aftermath of Troy's defeat. Both will be known as conditores (founders).
2	Confrontation between Latin and Trojan forces under Latinus and Aeneas.	LAVINIA (wife of Aeneas; regent after his death and preserver of the Latin State). 1.1.7, 9-11; 1.2.1-2; 1.3.1-4	Aeneas founds Lavinium and his son Ascanius (Iulus) founds Alba Longa. (Latins/Trojans)
3		CREUSA (mother of Ascanius). 1.3.2-4	
4	Amulius expels Numitor, seizes the crown, murders Numitor's sons, and compels R(h)ea Silvia to become a Vestal Virgin.	R(H)EA SILVIA (mother of Romulus and Remus). 1.3.11; 4.1-4	Romulus and Remus survive exposure.
5	Romulus and Remus are suckled by a she-wolf until discovered by Faustulus, the king's flockmaster.	LARENTIA (wife of Faustulus; primary caregiver to Romulus and Remus). 1.4.6-8	Romulus and Remus thrive into adolescence under Larentia's care.
6	Romulus kills Remus.	CARMENTA (mother of Evander; revered as divine and an interpreter of fate) prophesies that Hercules will join the company of the gods. Evander (king of Pallantium), standing in judgement over Hercules for the murder of the shepherd Cacus, who stole the cattle Hercules had pastured nearby, finds in the hero's favour. 1.7.8-10	Romulus introduces magisterial emblems, institutes the right of asylum, and creates the senate.

(Continued)

14

Table 1.2 Structural relationship of narrative elements before and after major episodes of AUC history featuring representations of women (Continued)

	Pre-episode	Episode	Post-episode
7	Romulus, Rome's first king, fails to secure alliance and the right of intermarriage with neighbouring nations.	The SABINE WOMEN (abducted and raped by Roman men; married to their abductors and rapists; guarantors of Rome's survival). 1.9.1–13.6	Rome and the Sabines arrange the terms of a treaty, declare an end to their war, and unite to become a single state.
8	Romulus routes the Antemnates, a people of the Sabine nation, and captures Antemnae, their city.	HERSILIA (wife of Romulus; mediator between Sabine women and parents). 1.11.2	Romulus pardons the Sabine women's parents and grants them Roman citizenship.
9	The last of the wars between Rome and the Sabines begins.	TARPEIA (daughter of Sp. Tarpeius, commander of the Roman citadel; betrayer of the city's security). 1.11.5-9	The Sabines occupy Rome's citadel. Romulus and Hostius Hostilius defend Rome against the enemy incursion.
10	After the formation of alliances and closure of the Temple of Janus, Rome faces the threat of idleness (otium).	EGERIA (nymph; divine adviser of Numa). 1.19.5	Numa, Rome's second king, establishes Rome's ritual calendar.
11	Rome and the Albans conclude the earliest formal treaty. The Horatii and Curiatii, triple brothers, represent their nations in battle to satisfy the conditions for peace.	HORATIA (sister of the Horatii; betrothed to one of the Curiatii). 1.26.1-14	The Roman people (Quirites) acquit Horatius, victor over the Curiatii but his sister's murderer, of treason.
12	Tyranny threatens Rome in the aftermath of the murder of L. Tarquinius Priscus, Rome's fifth king.	TANAQUIL (wife of Lucumo, that is, L. Tarquinius Priscus; ambitious advocate on behalf of her husband's and Servius Tullius's careers) TARQUINIA (daughter of Tanaquil; wife of Servius Tullius), and Tanaquil's granddaughters. 1.34; 39; 41	Servius Tullius, Rome's sixth king, accedes to the throne, unelected by the people but without opposition from the Senate. The sons of Rome's fourth king Ancus Marcius, instigators of L. Tarquinius Priscus' assassination, go into exile.

(Continued)

Table 1.2 Structural relationship of narrative elements before and after major episodes of AUC history featuring representations of women (Continued)

	Pre-episode	Episode	Post-episode
13	Servius Tullius' reign faces a deadly threat from within the royal household.	TULLIA MINOR (younger daughter of L. Tarquinius Priscus and Tanaquil; wife of L. Tarquinius Superbus; high-spirited, greedy, ambitious, and violent) and TULLIA MAIOR (elder daughter of Priscus and Tanaquil; wife of Arruns Tarquinius; unlike her sister in every way). 1.46.3–48.9; 59.13	Lucius Tarquinius ("Superbus") denies his father-in-law burial, ordered the death of the leading nobles, and commenced his reign as Rome's seventh king unelected by the people and without confirmation of the Senate.
14	Lucius Tarquinius Superbus rules Rome as a tyrant. Sextus Tarquinius, his son, emulates his father's example.	LUCRETIA (daughter of Sp. Lucretius Triciptinus, wife of L. Tarquinius Collatinus). 1.57-58	Brutus incites the army against Superbus. The Tarquins are expelled from Rome and the Senate and Roman people establish the *res publica.*
15	Young men of high birth, incl. the brothers Vitellii and Aquilii, instigate a conspiracy to restore the Tarquins.	VITELLIA (sister of the Vitellii; wife of Brutus; mother of Titus and Tiberius) exposes her sons to the conspiracy by virtue of her kinship. 2.4	The conspiracy is uncovered and appropriate measures taken. Envoys of the Tarquins are treated according to international law. The consul Brutus orders the execution of all conspirators, including his sons, Titus and Tiberius. The informer Vindicius receives a financial reward and his freedom.

(Continued)

16

Table 1.2 Structural relationship of narrative elements before and after major episodes of AUC history featuring representations of women (Continued)

	Pre-episode	Episode	Post-episode
16	Conditions to establish a treaty marking the end of war between Rome and Clusium are confirmed. These include withdrawal from Veientine territory and surrender of Roman hostages.	CLOELIA (a young unmarried woman) liberates her fellow female hostages and leads them home. 2.13.6-11	The Etruscan king Lars Porsena recognises Cloelia's courage and conduct; cf. Horatius Cocles (Liv. 2.10) and C. Mucius Scaevola (Liv. 2.12). Given the choice of which half of the remaining hostages might be returned, CLOELIA nominates the *impubes* (underage boys). She is honoured with an equestrian statue on the highest part of the Summa Via. Peace between Rome and the Etruscans is restored.
17	Cn. Marcius Coriolanus leads a Volscian army against Rome.	VETURIA and VOLUMNIA (mother and wife of Coriolanus) advocate for peace in the enemy camp (called to act by a deputation of *matronae*). 2.40	Coriolanus withdraws his forces from Roman territory. Rome defeats the Volscians and the Aequi. Sp. Cassius Viscellinus is accused of aiming at regal power and executed.
18	Domestic conflict between patricians and plebeians distracts from the greater threat of war with Veii and the Volscians.	OPPIA (Vestal Virgin) is accused and convicted of unchastity (in response to soothsayers' pronouncement that sacred functions had been profaned). 2.42.11	Civic dissension escalates and the Veientine and Aequo-Volscian wars begin.
19	The city is stricken by an epidemic.	Roman *matronae* (*stratae matres*) respond to the Senate's call for all citizens to pray for an end to the pestilence. 3.7.8	People throw off the effects of the epidemic and public health is restored.

(Continued)

Table 1.2 Structural relationship of narrative elements before and after major episodes of AUC history featuring representations of women (*Continued*)

	Pre-episode	Episode	Post-episode
20	The Sabines invade Roman territory and threaten to breach the security of the city's walls.	RACILIA (wife of L. Quinctius Cincinnatus) prepares her husband to meet a deputation of the Senate, charged to deliver the call for her husband to accept the office of *dictator*). 3.26.9	Victory against the Aequi is quickly secured. Cincinnatus relinquishes dictatorial command and returns to his farm and RACILIA.
21	After the formulation of the Twelve Tables under the direction of the First Decemvirate, the Second Decemvirate rule unfairly and administer justice poorly.	VERGINIA (daughter of L. Verginius, centurion; fiancé of L. Icilius, trib. pleb.) is killed by her father to prevent the decemvir Appius Claudius claiming her as his slave. 3.44, 49	Divided and perplexed, subject to a confusion of contradictory advice, the laws promulgated by L. Valerius Potitus and M. Horatius Barbatus (the Valerio-Horatian legislation dealing with *plebiscita, provocatio,* and *sacrosanctitas*) are ratified. Appius Claudius may have been tried and may have committed suicide.
22	The period of the Decemvirate ends.	The tribune C. Canuleius refers to the category of "woman" (*femina*) in the context of a proposal to recognise the right of *connubium* between patricians and plebeians. 4.4.10	The consular tribunate is instituted.
23	Ardea is captured by the Volsci.	The Ardean *virgo* (daughter of a plebeian family) is desired by young men of both plebeian and patrician stock and is ultimately abducted by young nobles. 4.9.4-6	Rome lays siege to Ardea, relieving then colonising the city.

Table 1.2 Structural relationship of narrative elements before and after major episodes of AUC history featuring representations of women (*Continued*)

	Pre-episode	Episode	Post-episode
24	Domestic strife ensues (plebeian tribunes against *interreges*; patricians against plebeians), leading to the prosecution and conviction of C. Sempronius on grounds of disgrace during the Volscian war.	POSTUMIA (Vestal Virgin; sister of the wife of T. Quinctius) is accused wrongly of unchastity and acquitted. 4.44.11-12	A slave plot to set fire to the city is foiled. Renewal of hostilities with the Aequi is mooted.
25	Report of a national Etruscan uprising reaches Rome.	Roman *matronae* offer up solemn petitions to the gods (to ward off destruction from the houses and temples of the city and from the walls of Rome, and to divert the fears and alarms to Veii if the sacred rites are duly restored and the portents expiated). 5.18.11	Rome captures Veii.
26	M. Furius Camillus marshals the resources of war and religion against Veii, conducting the ritual of *evocatio* to persuade the tutelary deity of the enemy city to leave Veii and accept a new home in Rome.	Women of Veii (and slaves) hurl stones and tiles from the roofs of houses as the Roman assault on the city intensifies. 5.21.10	The enemy forces of Veii are massacred, the city stripped of its enormous wealth, and all freedmen sold into slavery.
27	Camillus directs Roman forces to attack Veii on all sides, distracting defenders from the tunnel under the citadel.	*JUNO REGINA's* cult statue is removed to a new permanent home on the Aventine in Rome. 5.22.5-9	Like the fall of Troy, Veii is defeated after a siege lasting 10 years by strategy and subterfuge.

(*Continued*)

Table 1.2 Structural relationship of narrative elements before and after major episodes of AUC history featuring representations of women (Continued)

	Pre-episode	Episode	Post-episode
28	The capture of Veii is announced in Rome after many years of undecided warfare and numerous defeats.	Roman *matres* offer thanksgiving to the gods, filling the temples in anticipation of the Senate's order. 5.23.3	The Volscians and Aequi sue successfully for peace.
29	M. Furius Camillus is impeached by the plebeian tribune L. Apuleius and banished from Rome. Ambassadors from Clusium appeal to Rome for support against the Gauls.	The wife of A(r)runs (a wine importer from Clusium) is seduced by a certain Lucumo (a young man of considerable influence, also from Clusium). 5.33.3	Arruns leads the Gauls across the Alps and urges them to attack Clusium. The Gauls migrate into Italy.
30	The Roman army led by Q. Sulpicius makes its stand (on 18 July 390 BCE) against the forces of the Gauls under their chieftain Bennus. On the left bank of the Tiber where the Allia joins the main river, Rome is overwhelmingly defeated.	In a reference to the battle of the Allia make their way to Veii, the wives and children of defeated commanders and soldiers are mentioned. 5.38.5 (cf. references to "women and children" at moments of national crisis and military disaster: e.g., 5.21.11; 5.42.4; 6.3.4; 9.17.6; 29.17.6; 29.28.3).	The city of Rome is occupied by the Gauls in the aftermath of the battle of the Allia.
31	The Gauls enter the city of Rome. Men of military age, able-bodied senators, and their wives and children, occupy the citadel and Capitol.	The Vestal Virgins and the Flamen Quirinalis take the sacred objects (*sacra*) from Rome. Leaving the city, Lucius Albinius orders his wife and children to vacate their places in his wagon for Rome's *sacerdotes publicae* and the *sacra*. 5.40.10	The Flamen Quirinalis and the Vestal Virgins safeguard the *sacra*. The Gauls massacre the elder senators who remain in the city (outside their houses, arrayed in their magisterial dress). The occupation of Rome is completed.

(Continued)

Table 1.2 Structural relationship of narrative elements before and after major episodes of AUC history featuring representations of women (Continued)

	Pre-episode	Episode	Post-episode
32	The Gauls are defeated and withdraw from the city. M. Furius Camillus addresses the proposal of the tribunes to transplant the entire population to Veii and abandon the city as the capital of the Roman world. The dictator speaks instead about rebuilding Rome and restoring the city's religious traditions and monumental grandeur.	JUNO REGINA, Roman matronae, and the Vestal Virgins are identified as central to the religious identity and customary tradition of the city. 5.52.10, 13-14	The city of Rome is rebuilt.
33	Rome fights against the Etruscans, culminating in the surrender and looting of the town of Sutrium.	Camillus refers to the Roman matronae who contributed towards the necessities of the commonwealth (the first time, to assist the government to discharge its responsibility under the vow of Camillus which he had made before the capture of Veii; the second occasion, when the ransom was being raised to buy off the Gauls). 6.4.2; cf. 5.50.7	Camillus celebrates Rome's triumph over the Etruscans. New citizens are enrolled and further rebuilding of the city is undertaken.
34	In retaliation against the Antiates (who surrendered their city and territory to the Romans) and Tusculum (allied to Rome), the Latins set fire to Satricum and attack Tusculum. A Roman army marches to defend Tusculum.	The temple of MATER MATUTA (goddess of the early morning light) at Satricum is spared from the fire set by the Latins which consumes the remainder of the city. The humiliation of one of the daughters (the FABIAE AMBUSTI) of M. Fabius K. f. M. n. Ambustus (cos. tr, 369 BCE) leads Ambustus to decide that something must be done. 6.33.4-5; 6.34.5-11	The consuls L. Sextius and L. Aemilius Mamercinus enact the Licinio-Sextian rogations and the reforms of 367–366 BCE.

(Continued)

21

Table 1.2 Structural relationship of narrative elements before and after major episodes of AUC history featuring representations of women (*Continued*)

	Pre-episode	Episode	Post-episode
35	The settlement after the Latin War (340–339 BCE) provides Rome with a secure system of incorporated states and subject allies.	MINUCIA (Vestal Virgin) is accused of unchastity on the evidence of a slave, tried and found guilty by the college of *pontifices*, and buried alive near the Colline Gate in the Campus Sceleratus ("the accursed field"). 8.15.7-8	Rome fights against the Ausones of Cales (the first Latin colony established by Rome after the settlement of 338 BCE).
36	The Aurunci, at war with the Sidicini, appeal to Rome, desert their *oppidum* (then destroyed by the Aurunci), and fortify their most important settlement, Suessa Aurunca. Rome does not send an army to support the Aurunci, instead dispatching a military force to engage the Ausones of Cales, now allied with the Sidicini. Cales is besieged, captured, and colonised, but the Sidicini remain unsubjugated. Finally, while a census is conducted and Acerrae is incorporated as a *civitas sine suffragio*, rumours of Samnite unrest and a Gallic War lead to the appointment of a Dictator and Master of Horse.	A young woman (*ancilla*) informs the aedile Fabius Maximus Rullianus that twenty *matronae* (incl. CORNELIA and SERGIA, who suicide when confronted) brewed poison responsible for a spate of deaths among leading citizens in Rome. Accomplices of the *matronae* inform on a large number of other women, leading to the conviction of 170 in total. 8.18.4-9	Rome goes to war against the Volscian town of Privernum. Rome is victorious, Privernum capitulates, and the town is granted Roman citizenship.

(*Continued*)

Table 1.2 Structural relationship of narrative elements before and after major episodes of AUC history featuring representations of women (*Continued*)

	Pre-episode	Episode	Post-episode
37	The gravity of the Neapolitan War and the threat of war with the Samnites result in the creation of the dictatorship of the plebeian M. Claudius Marcellus. Patrician and augural objections lead to his resignation. Fourteen *interregna* lasting 70 days follow, and a plebeian Poetelius is elected to the consulate before the patrician Papirius Cursor. A crisis in the Struggle of the Orders eventuates.	A solitary woman from Pandosia stands between the mutilated body of Alexander, king of Epirus, and a crowd pelting it with javelins and stones. She cremates what remains of the body and returns the bones to Metapontum, thence to Epirus and the king's wife CLEOPATRA and his sister OLYMPIAS. 8.23.16-17	Rome declares war on Samnium.
38	The Samnites raid Campania but are routed and killed. To the north, Etruscans, Samnites, Umbrians, and Gauls form an alliance in Etruria.	Excluded by the patrician *matronae* from the cult of PUDICITIA PATRICIA on the ground that she was married to a plebeian, VERGINIA founds a rival cult of PUDICITIA PLEBEIA. 10.23.1-10	Q. Fabius Rullianus commands Rome's victory against Sentinum, opening the way for Roman hegemony in peninsular Italy.
	NB Books 11–20 are no longer extant; brief summaries only exist.		
39	The consul Curius Dentatus defeats Pyrrhus (275 BCE), expelling him from Italy. The state is declared ritually cleansed after a *lustrum* (274 BCE). A treaty of friendship is concluded with Ptolemy II Philadelphus of Egypt (273 BCE).	SEXTILIA (Vestal Virgin) is condemned for adultery and buried alive. Per. 14.7	Rome subdues Tarentum. The Tarentines are given peace and freedom.

(*Continued*)

Table 1.2 Structural relationship of narrative elements before and after major episodes of AUC history featuring representations of women (Continued)

	Pre-episode	Episode	Post-episode
40	Caecilius Metellus defeats a Carthaginian army commanded by Hasdrubal and organises a spectacular triumph (featuring 13 enemy leaders and 120 elephants). The consul of 249 BCE, P. Claudius Pulcher, loses the Battle of Drepana against the Carthaginians after ignoring a bad omen and famously throwing the sacred chickens into the sea, saying, "Since they do not wish to eat, let them drink" (*bibant, quoniam esse nolunt*).	CLAUDIA (sister of P. Claudius Pulcher, cos. 249 BCE) berated a crowd hindering her return home, saying, "Oh, that my brother were still alive and commanded a navy" (*utinam frater meus viveret: iterum classem duceret*). Because of this, she was fined. *Per.* 19.8-9	Caecilius Metellus (*pontifex maximus*) ensures that Aulus Postumius (*flamen Martialis*) remains in the city even though he wants to wage war. The war against the Carthaginians is conducted successfully by several commanders. C. Lutatius defeats the Carthaginian navy in the final battle of the First Punic War near the Aegetan Islands.
41	L. Caecilius Metellus (*pontifex maximus*) saves the *sacra* from a fire in the Temple of Vesta. Faliscan, Sardine, and Corsican revolts are suppressed.	TUCCIA (Vestal Virgin) is condemned for adultery. *Per.* 20.5	War is declared against the Illyrians, who are defeated and surrender. Gauls from across the Alps invade Italy; the Roman people and Latin allies cross the Po for the first time and are victorious over the invading army.
42	The Carthaginian army, under the leadership of Hannibal, surrounds and comprehensively defeats a larger Roman force commanded by L. Aemilius Paullus (cos. 219, 216 BCE) and C. Terentius Varro (cos. 216 BCE). Loss of manpower is enormous: 45,500 infantry, 2700 cavalry, and an equivalent number of citizens and allies; 3000 infantry and	BUSA (a woman from Apulia) aids Roman soldiers escaping from Cannae to Canusium, providing them with corn, clothing, and money for the journey. 22.52.7; 22.54.4	Despite significant losses – two consuls and two consular armies; the allegiance of Hellenistic southern provinces (Arpi, Salapia, Herdonia, and Uzentum), the towns of Capua and Tarentum (two of Italy's largest city-states), the Greek cities in Sicily, and the Macedonian king, Philip V – Rome refused to negotiate surrender. Instead, the Senate redoubled the nation's

(Continued)

Table 1.2 Structural relationship of narrative elements before and after major episodes of AUC history featuring representations of women (*Continued*)

	Pre-episode	Episode	Post-episode
	1500 cavalry taken prisoner; 2000 fugitives from the unfortified village of Cannae; 7000 from the smaller Roman camp and 5800 from the larger.		efforts, declaring full mobilisation of the male Roman population, raising new legions, enlisting landless peasants and slaves, and revising battlefield doctrine to accommodate Hannibalic tactics.
43	Fearing that his grandson Hieronymus is not competent to inherit, much less wield, sovereign power, Hiero (tyrant of Syracuse) resolves to exclude the transfer of regal power on his death, leaving Syracuse a free state.	The daughters of Hiero (DAMARATA and HERACLEA) oppose their father's testamentary plan, anticipating that the administration of all affairs would be conducted by themselves and their husbands, Adranodorus and Zoippus. 24.4.3	Syracuse dissolves its alliance with Rome, expelling all Roman citizens from Sicily and siding instead with Hannibal. Hieronymus expresses the opinion that all of Sicily should be conceded to him, and that dominion of Italy should be the possession of Carthage.
44	After Hieronymus is assassinated, accord is eventually reached between the various factions in Syracuse. Hippocrates and Epicydes (two Carthaginian citizens of Syracusan origin who Hannibal had sent to conclude the initial alliance with Hieronymus) claim that the council plans to deliver the city into Roman control.	DAMARATA (wife of Adranodorus) urges her tyrant husband to retain sovereign power at whatever cost and by whatever means. 24.4.3; 24.22.8-11; 24.25.11	Adranadorus, who had been the power behind Hieronymus until his murder, is killed on suspicion of plotting a coup. Damarata (wife of Adranadorus), Heraclea (wife of Gelon) and her daughters, and Harmonia (wife of Themistus), are put to death.
45	To address domestic issues arising from the Hannibalic War, Rome's censors concentrate their attention on the regulation of men's morals (*mores hominum*), the chastisement of vices (*castigandaque vitia*), and the poverty of the treasury (*inopia aerarii*).	The property of Roman widows is acquired to sustain the state's impoverished treasury. 24.18.13-14	Stern authoritarian measures counteract some of the evils that the disaster of Cannae and the ensuing climate of war spawned. Rome recaptures Casilinum, thereafter serving as a base of operations against rebellious Capua. Hannibal is unsuccessful in his attempts to seize the town of Nola.

(*Continued*)

Table 1.2 Structural relationship of narrative elements before and after major episodes of AUC history featuring representations of women (*Continued*)

	Pre-episode	Episode	Post-episode
46	Rome besieges Capua.	The mistress (*scortum*) of a Campanian deserter informs the proconsul Fulvius Flaccus about the machinations of leading Capuan citizens who sought Hannibal's aid in raising the Roman siege of the city as well as information that Numidians are in the Roman camp playing the part of deserters. 26.12.17	Fulvius Flaccus captures the messengers sent to enjoin Hannibal's support, scourges them with rods, cuts off their hands, and sends them back to Capua. This action breaks the city's spirit, which eventually turns on its leaders and betrays their cause. Before the gates of the city are opened, a number of Capuan senators take poison to spare themselves the anticipated punishment.
47	Rome defeats Capua by laying siege to the city. Against a decree of the Senate, the proconsul Fulvius Flaccus executes the leading citizens of Capua, Capuan citizens in Cales, and the rebellious leaders of Atella and Calatia.	While Rome fights in Campania, VESTIA OPPIA (of Atella) sacrifices every day for the safety and victory of the Roman people; and PACULA CLUVIA (formerly a prostitute) supplies food to needy captives. 26.33.8	Capuans appeal to Rome regarding their plight, but the Senate finds the proconsul's behaviour in keeping with the office of a magistrate.
48	P. Cornelius Scipio Africanus successfully assaults New Carthage. After the city falls, the Romans gain control of the Carthaginian hostages, prominent members of local communities.	Accompanied by the daughters of Indibilis (ruler of the Ilergetes) and other young unmarried women, the wife of Mandonius (brother of Indibilis and fellow ruler of the Ilergetes) pleads before P. Cornelius Scipio Africanus on behalf of all of the female hostages of the Carthaginians for good treatment. 26.49.11-16	Scipio entrusts the female hostages to a man of proven character with instructions to protect their modesty as he would do with the wives and mothers of guests.

(*Continued*)

Table 1.2 Structural relationship of narrative elements before and after major episodes of AUC history featuring representations of women (Continued)

	Pre-episode	Episode	Post-episode
		Soldiers bring before P. Cornelius Scipio Africanus, the fiancé of Allucius (an elite young Celtiberian), with whose betrothed and parents the general meets, offering her safe return in exchange for Allucius' friendship (*amicitia*) and a good opinion of the Romans. 26.50.1-14	Tarentum is captured, the population put to the sword, 30,000 slaves captured, and silver and gold, statues, and paintings were taken as spoils of war.
49	The consul Q. Fabius lays siege to Tarentum.	The commander of a guard of Bruttians (provided to Tarentum by Hannibal) desired a young Tarentine woman (*muliercula*), sister of a soldier in the army of the consul Fabius. On her brother's direction, the young woman persuades her lover to betray the defence of a place in the citadel over which he had command. 27.15.9-11	
50	Philip V of Macedon drives off Roman forces under P. Sulpicius, after raids on the Peloponnesian coastline between Sicyon and Corinth.	POLYCRATIA (wife of Aratus, one of the leading men of the Achaeans) is abducted and taken to Macedonia with the prospect of a royal marriage. 27.31.8	The Romans install a garrison at Cyllene in Elis and fend off a Macedonian attack (during which Philip is thrown from his horse but recovers to fight on foot). The king escapes laden with massive spoils (including 4000 captives and 20,000 cattle) and in possession of the Elean fort of Phyrcus.

(Continued)

Table 1.2 Structural relationship of narrative elements before and after major episodes of AUC history featuring representations of women (*Continued*)

	Pre-episode	Episode	Post-episode
51	A sense of crisis settles on Rome, fueling nervous superstition and wild reports of prodigies. In response, the state order religious measures, culminating with the importation of the Magna Mater.	The city's most prominent married women (*matronae primores civitatis*) receive the cult statue of the Magna Mater, passing her from one to another in orderly succession. Singled out due to her chastity, CLAUDIA QUINTA assists in conveying the goddess into the Temple of Victory on the Palatine. 29.14.12-14	The Senate administers the resourcing of state revenues, the renewal of local, regional, and international alliances, and the rebuilding of military strength.
52	P. Cornelius Scipio Africanus commences military operations in North Africa. Various tribes ally with Carthage against Masinissa.	The daughter of Hannibal's sister is married to Mezetulus, the ruler of the Massylians, in an attempt to shore up Numidian resistance against Masinissa. 29.29.12	Masinissa defeats Numidian forces allied with Carthage, promises Mezetulus impunity and restitution of his property, and so brings him over to his side.
53	P. Cornelius Scipio Africanus blockades Utica and defeats Carthaginian and Numidian forces. Syphax abandons Hasdrubal. Masinissa claims the Numidian throne and launches a campaign against Syphax, who is defeated and taken prisoner.	Hasdrubal arranges a marriage between Syphax and his daughter SOPHONI(S)BA (daughter of Hasdrubal; wife of Syphax and Masinissa), who prevailed on her husband to renew Numidia's alliance with Carthage and pursue the war with Rome. Masinissa allies with Rome, defeats Syphax, takes possession of the Numidian capital Cirta, and marries Sophoni(s)ba. Scipio demands that she should be surrendered. To avoid this fate, Sophoni(s)ba takes her own life with poison given to her by Masinissa. 29.23.3-6; 30.3.4; 30.7.8-9; 30.11.3; 30.12-15	The Carthaginian assembly accepts terms for the secession of conflict with Rome, ordering Hannibal and Hanno to end the Italian campaign and return to Africa. Hannibal presses for peace, but Rome finds the terms he proposes unacceptable. Negotiations break off, resulting in the decisive battle of Zama Regia and Carthaginian defeat.

(*Continued*)

28

Table 1.2 Structural relationship of narrative elements before and after major episodes of AUC history featuring representations of women (*Continued*)

	Pre-episode	Episode	Post-episode
54	Nabis (sole king of Sparta, 207–192 BCE) rules as a tyrant.	APEGA (wife of Nabis) subjects Argive women (*singulae illustres*, and *plures genere inter se*) to suffering and violence and steals nearly all their gold jewellery and valuable clothing. 32.40.10-11	Nabis executes 80 of the principal young men (34.27.8: *principes iuuentutis*), exiles the wealthiest and most prominent Spartiates who were his enemies and gave their property as well as their wives and daughters (34.35.7: *liberos coniuges*) in marriage to newly freed helots.
55	Rome quells a slave uprising in the cities of northern Etruria, defeats the Boii in Cisalpine Gaul, and attends an ultimately inconclusive conference with Antiochus III at Lysimachia. War with Spain is averted temporarily and a decision regarding a declaration of war in Greece (against Nabis of Sparta and others) left to T. Quinctius Flamininus. Hannibal flees to Antioch.	The *frequentia mulierum* or *agmen of matronae* agitate for the repeal of the *lex Oppia*. 34.1.5-7; 34.8.1-2 *Representations of Roman and Latin women in narrative and reported speech:* 1 The *coniuratio muliebri*. 34.2.3 2 Roman women, characterised in the speech of M. Porcius Cato as *secessio mulierum, agmen mulierum* and *seditio muliebrum*. 34.2-5 3 Roman women, characterised in the speech of L. Valerius as *matronae, coetum muliebris, honestae feminae* and *filiae, uxores*, and *sorores*. 34.6-7 4 The *intercursus matronae*. 34.5.8-9 5 Latin women (*sociorum Latini uxoribus*). 34.7.5-6	Rome goes to war in Spain and against Antiochus III.

(*Continued*)

Table 1.2 Structural relationship of narrative elements before and after major episodes of AUC history featuring representations of women (Continued)

Pre-episode	Episode	Post-episode
56 Rome fights against the Gallogrecians (Tolostobogii, Tectosagi, Trocmi).	Held captive with other Tectosagi prisoners, the unnamed wife of the Tectosagi chieftain Orgiago [cf. Plut. Mor. 258 D-F; Polyb. 21.38; Val. Max. 6.1.ext.2; Flor.1.27.6: CHIOMARA] is raped by the commander of the guard. The centurion promises her freedom in exchange for gold. At the exchange, Chiomara orders her kinsmen to kill the centurion, whose head she carries with her and presents to her husband on her return. 38.24	Rome is victorious against the Tectosagi.
57 P. Cornelius Scipio Africanus is impeached, intervenes to prevent the imprisonment of his son L. Cornelius Scipio Asiaticus (also under prosecution) and retires to Liternum where he dies.	The Senate beg P. Cornelius Scipio Africanus (cos. 205 BCE) to arrange the marriage of his younger daughter CORNELIA MINOR to Tiberius Sempronius Gracchus (cos. 177, 163 BCE). CORNELIA MAIOR is married to P. Cornelius Scipio Nasica Corculum. 38.57	The prosecution of Lucius resumes. He is imprisoned for misappropriation of funds collected from Antiochus and eventually pardoned by the tribune Tiberius Gracchus (elder son of Tib. Sempronius Gracchus and CORNELIA).
58 In contrast to Cn. Manlius, C. Flaminius and M. Aemilius maintain military discipline and defeat the Ligurians. M. Furius Crassipes seeks an excuse for war with the Cenomani who are guiltless of any provocation. M. Fulvius Nobilior	The events in the account of the suppression of the Bacchanalia include the following female protagonists: HISPALA FAECENIA (a freedwoman prostitute), DURONIA (mother of P. Aebutius; wife of T. Sempronius Rutilus),	Q. Marcius Philippus (pr. 188 BCE, cos. 186 BCE), who assisted his colleague Sp. Postumius Albinus in the suppression of the Bacchanalia, suffers a serious defeat in Liguria. M. Fulvius Nobilior hosts the *ludi Tauri* vowed during the Aetolian War;

(Continued)

Table 1.2 Structural relationship of narrative elements before and after major episodes of AUC history featuring representations of women (Continued)

	Pre-episode	Episode	Post-episode
	celebrates a triumph over the Aetolians; and Cn. Manlius Vulso celebrates a triumph over the Gauls in Asia, despite unfavourable reports of diminished military discipline under his command. It is recorded that Manlius' triumph introduced *luxuria* into Rome.	AEBUTIA (paternal aunt of P. Aebutius), SULPICIA (mother-in-law of Sp. Postumius Albinus, cos. 186 BCE), PACULLA ANNIA (a Campanian woman reputed to have admitted men to the previously all-female initiation rites of the Bacchanalian cult), and numerous women initiates (priestesses, wives).	L. Scipio celebrates *ludi* vowed during the war with Antiochus III. Gaul invades north-west Italy and Greek embassies lay various complaints against Philip V who sends his own representatives to reply.
59	A spate of poisonings in the municipalities and rural communities is investigated, leading to the condemnation of about 2000 persons. Large conspiracies of shepherds are broken-up and the remainder of the Bacchanalian investigation is prosecuted, resulting in arrests and imprisonments on a large scale.	39.8-19 Invited to dinner by L. Quinctius Flamininus, a prostitute (*scortum*) from Placentia with whom the Roman commander is profoundly smitten tells him that she has never seen anyone carry out an execution with an axe and would very much like to see it. While the girl is reclining in Lucius' lap, a man already condemned to death is beheaded.	The censor M. Porcius Cato, scion of an ancient patrician clan and notorious for his strictness, expels several prominent senators from the Senate, including L. Quinctius Flamininus, whom Cato charges with the murder of the Gallic chief who had come before him seeking the protection (*fides*) of Rome.
60	A list of prodigies precedes a long account of the major crisis in the Macedonian royal house. Philip V's actions are decried by the Macedonians and his desire to recommence war with Rome reported to the Senate.	39.43.2-4 After her sister ARCHO (daughter of Herodicus; wife of Poris, first among the Aenianes) dies, THEOXENA marries Poris and cares for Archo's sons. Hearing about Philip V's edict to arrest the children of those he had ordered executed (including Herodicus), she vowed to kill the children rather than let	Events in Macedonia reflect the consequences of *indisciplina* and *discordia*. Macedonian hatred against Philip V's actions intensifies and the king's bitterness against the Romans becomes more pronounced. The seeds of the Macedonian War are sown.

(Continued)

31

Table 1.2 Structural relationship of narrative elements before and after major episodes of AUC history featuring representations of women (Continued)

Pre-episode	Episode	Post-episode
	them fall into Philip's hands. Poris arranges for a ship to carry himself, his wife, and his children away from Aenia, but the king's troops pursue them in an armed boat. Theoxena urges the sons of Archo and Poris to end their lives by the sword or poison, then flinging her arms round her husband she plunges into the sea. 40.4	
61 Rome and Italy experience a devastating plague.	QUARTA HOSTILIA (wife of C. Calpurnius Piso, pr. 186 BCE; mother of Q. Fulvius Flaccus, pr. 187 BCE) is accused of murdering her husband, consul for 180 BCE, a charge given added weight when her step-son Flaccus (who had failed three times previously) is declared consul in place of his step-father. Flaccus' death coincides with those of the praetor Tiberius Minucius and many distinguished men of all ranks, investigated on order of the Senate in relation to cases of alleged poisoning. 40.37.5-7	Rome fights against the Ligurians in northern Italy and the Celtiberi in Spain. Genthius (king of the Labeates) is accused of mistreating Roman citizens and Latin allies under his dominion. Three priests (the pontifex maximus, a triumvir epulo, the rex sacrificulus) die from the plague. Three thousand cases of poisoning outside the ten-mile radius of the city are brought to trial. Q. Fulvius Flaccus celebrates a triumph for his successful campaign against the Celtiberi.

(Continued)

Table 1.2 Structural relationship of narrative elements before and after major episodes of AUC history featuring representations of women (Continued)

	Pre-episode	Episode	Post-episode
62	Civil strife in Aetolia intensifies when the chief magistrate Eupolemus puts to death 80 illustrious citizens (belonging to the faction of Proxenus) to whom he had assured restoration of their native country Hypata	After her husband speaks well before the panel ordered by the Senate to negotiate the factional rivalry undermining Aetolian political stability, ORTHOBULA is convicted of poisoning Proxenus and sent into exile. 41.25.6	Ambassadors return from Aetolia and Macedon, saying that they had not secured a meeting with Perseus and that war was being prepared and would not be further delayed. Further embassies similarly encounter varying degrees of success.
63	Perseus flees in the aftermath of the battle of Pydna and Rome's defeat of Macedonian forces.	Crowds of Roman men and women (*feminae*) fill the temples to give thanks to the gods at the arrival of news of the defeat of Perseus. 45.2.7	Rome receives news of the defeat of Genthius.

noted the historiographical and ideological significance adhering to Helen by virtue of the Greek epic narrative which notionally precedes Livy's reference and to the specifically Roman foundation stories which follow. In this regard, of equivalent interest is the frequency with which each specific instance of female participation in the ebb and flow of monumental Roman history appears to coincide with a particular and fundamental moment in narrative time.

Of course, any view relating to this intriguing interpolation of Roman and non-Roman women in AUC history should not subsist solely on recourse to the plausible accumulation of data. To assume the impact of argument on the influence of coincidence is a hazardous transaction. However, with all cautions and reservations, and in light of the evidence provided in Table 1.2, it seems permissible to suggest that some purpose resides in Livy's choice to accommodate representations of women within the overarching AUC frame of annalistic structure and historical continuity. Here it is sufficient to note in passing the proximity to gendered participation of such pivotal events in Roman history as the assimilation of regional Italy, the expulsion of the Tarquinian dynasty, the codification of Decemviral legislation, the migration of Gauls across the Alps, the Licinian-Sextian rogations, the expansion of Roman hegemony into peninsular Italy, Roman resilience in the aftermath of catastrophic military defeat at Cannae, and the prosecution of the Bacchic cult. Thus, certain extended passages in AUC history can be adduced that concord nicely with the presumed emphasis on gender. And, as should be clear on even a casual reading of the preceding catalogue, Livy's gendered historiographical strategy aligns instructively with historical events of transformative significance – episodes featuring innovative or revolutionary solutions to historical questions relating to cultural practices, economic conditions, military conflicts, political rivalries, and social reforms. The strategic incidence of female representation, then, may be associated with those moments of crisis or rebellion in Rome's historical record where the stability and traditions of the *urbs* and *res publica* (*mores maiorum*) face a critical challenge. In strictly historiographical terms, Livy introduces representations of women at those moments in AUC history when Rome encounters the shock of new things (*res novae*) and follows a course of action leading either to broad societal change in one form or another or reverts to the *status quo* until such time that the historical trajectory for change reasserts itself.

Again, though, perhaps these attestations reflect adventitious alignment. To confront the claims of statistical imbalance and incidental composition, and to avoid the error of identifying cogency of argument with potency of theory, this inquiry will begin with an examination of the rape of Lucretia. This initial close reading should introduce the salient elements of the thesis linking women to episodes involving crisis and revolution (*res novae*) and begin to address the possibility that Livy consciously deploys women in situations which challenge, threaten, or change what was old, traditional, and ancestral about Roman society (*mores maiorum*).

1.2 The rape of Lucretia: gender, crisis, and the *res publica*

As is the case with regard to many of the episodes in AUC history where women are represented – and particularly so in relation to traditional narratives from the period before written accounts were first recorded – no contemporary source exists for the story of Lucretia. Information about Lucretia, her rape and suicide, and the historical consequences of these events have only been transmitted in the later works of Livy and Dionysius of Halicarnassus, both narratives drawing on the treatments of earlier writers who composed their versions during the 3rd and 2nd centuries BCE.[52]

Despite the essentially domestic details of Lucretia's personal history, the actions described in the traditional record cause a revolution that leads to a radical transition of Roman government from a regnal to a republican state. In the aftermath of Lucretia's death, the Roman state transforms from the absolute rule of kings to a political system comprising an advisory council formulating consultative decrees and directing foreign policy (the Senate), holders of official authority over particular geographic areas, responsibilities, or tasks (magistrates), and legislative assemblies tasked with the election of magistrates, declaration of wars, ratification of census results, approval of legislation, and making determinations in cases of appeal. As a result of such a momentous socio-political development, the bare bones of Lucretia's story will have been inextricably woven into the fabric of Rome's foundation history. In brief, a fundamentally private episode in the lives of elite Roman citizens transcends the boundaries of familial household drama, inscribing a tale of physical and psychological duress onto the discursive surface of memorialising historiographical storytelling.

The gist of the tale is easily rendered and eminently memorable. Well-to-do young fighting men, home on a leave of absence from the siege of an enemy town, in the process of comparing notes about their wives, devise a method of determining which one of their spouses behaved in the most exemplary manner. Visiting their homes unannounced, the men quickly come to agree that Lucretia stood out as excellent in every way. The king's son, Sextus Tarquinius, overwhelmed with lust to possess Lucretia, rapes her at the point of his sword. Although Tarquinius expresses regret afterwards, Lucretia is unmoved; even when he cycles in rapid succession from love to pleading to threats of disgrace, Lucretia does not relent, instead calling together a family council to judge Tarquinius' actions rather than determine her response. Explaining that it is their duty to determine what penalty is due to her violator, Lucretia pronounces herself as equally deserving of punishment, plunging a knife which she had concealed beneath her dress deep into her heart. Passing the bloody blade between them, Sp. Lucretius Triciptinus (her father), L. Tarquinius Collatinus (husband), P. Valerius Publicola, and C. Iulius Brutus (fellow *primores*) swear an oath not to suffer the depredations of Lucretia's rapist or any other who would act as king in Rome.

They bear Lucretia's body to the forum, the sight of which ignites popular discontent. Brutus recounts the shameful history of regal Rome, inflaming all those present to take up arms against Etruscan rule.

Any contextual treatment of the narrative of Lucretia's violation confronts reader and investigator alike with the extent to which Livy has historicised the major preoccupations of his opening foray in the annalistic tradition. Consider the deployment of significant male protagonists prior to the unfolding of Lucretia's story. First in line is L. Tarquinius Superbus (Tarquin the Proud), Rome's seventh king. Earlier in Book 1, Livy recounts the manner in which Tarquinius acquires power. Surrounded by a group of armed men and seated on Servius Tullius' throne, he addresses Rome's elders in the senate house, denigrating his father-in-law's status (as a slave born of a slave), his unorthodox accession to the throne (bypassing election by the Senate and the people), and political actions (favouring the lower classes of Rome over the wealthy). Confronting the king with the same accusations, Tarquinius carries Servius Tullius outside and throws him down the steps of the Curia.[53] Dazed and unattended by his retainers, the king is assaulted and murdered as he returns to the royal palace. Regicide by proxy and usurper of dynastic rule, then, Tarquin the Proud is characterised by action and disposition as the archetypal objectification of arbitrary or despotic rule (*tyrannis*). Once he occupies the throne, Superbus is responsible for preventing the burial of his predecessor, eliminating his political rivals, and requesting a bodyguard. Moreover, he abrogates patrician authority and the popular vote, and resorts to the politics of terror – namely, the execution or relegation of, and confiscation of property from, a prescriptive and arbitrary cross-section of the aristocratic population. We may add to these actions his failure to consult the Senate on issues of war, peace, and treaties, his establishment of external alliance through marriage to consolidate internal security, his exercise of deception to reinforce his authority over the Latium region of Aricia by fraudulent liquidation of a forthright neighbouring rival, and his imposition of artificial (as opposed to constitutional) unity on the body politic of a regionally expanded *urbs condita* by reform of military organisation.[54]

Next, we meet Sextus Tarquinius – youngest son of the tyrant Superbus and the pivotal agent of violation and retributive dynastic expulsion in the coming narrative – who is shown to have inherited and internalised the qualitatively un-Roman disposition and rational temperament of his father. This portrayal is explicitly formulated as a reflection of Superbus' policy of deceit and trickery:[55] his simulated desertion from Rome; his energetic activity within Gabii; his appointment as army commander; his intuitive interpretation of Superbus' instructions (obtained by intrigue); and his subsequent wholesale betrayal of the town to the Roman king, including his use of an extensive variety of methods by which he rid himself of potential rivals, and his appeasement of surviving sentiments by the liberal dispensation of money and spoils of war (the equivalent of bribery and corruption).[56]

In a like vein, the king's younger sons, Titus and Arruns Tarquinius – sent to consult the oracle of Delphi regarding the determination of a dreadful portent causing their father a painfully disquieting anxiety – reveal a significant imperfection of character, the desire to reign (*cupido regnum*), and a concomitant disposition towards the kind of self-seeking and secretive behaviour associated with excessive ambition and a conspiratorial nature.[57]

Finally, Lucius Iunius Brutus – nephew of the tyrant king and the spirit destined to deliver the Roman people – is depicted as deliberately assuming an artificial disguise that differs markedly from his innate intellectual capacity and temperament.[58] Importantly for all that follows, this representation is grounded in the premise that pretence may be excused if faced with the extremities of unrestricted power and tyrannical rule (*dominatio*). Brutus' psychological and behavioural façade – the figurative depth of physical and mental excellence enclosed within the superficial hollowness of his outward appearance – echoes strikingly Romulus' assumption of the emblems of authority and active concealment of his true feelings when he deceptively lures visitors to Rome in order that the sheer masses might be turned into a people in the proper sense.[59] Without attaching undue significance to the literary and conceptual relationship, it is interesting to note that, in episodes when Rome's constitution might be ratified and sustained, Livy's rhetorical composition of AUC history emphasises the relationship between appearance and reality.

In addition to this extensive exposition of male *dramatis personae*, when Livy introduces Lucretia to the reader, her presence in the narrative is triply predicated by the considerations of military men belonging to the first rank.[60] Youthful and princely, they form part of a siege mounted by the Roman king against Ardea. Beleaguering the wealthy Rutilian town is a long-drawn-out affair, and the young men enliven the vacant periods of protracted inactivity by engaging in the rituals of eating and drinking together characteristic of small aristocratic groups, the elite Roman fraternal associations (*sodilitates*).[61] This alignment of contributing factors – desire for wealth and authority (*cupido*), leading to external conflict (*causa belli*), and interspersed by long hours of enforced leisure (*otium*) – precipitates a gathering of like-minded individuals related by circumstance, status and, in some cases, blood: Sextus Tarquinius, Tarquinius Collatinus, and an indeterminate brotherhood of military companions.

Of immediate significance is the fact that women form the subject of a wholly male rivalry. Livy describes a struggle between minds which emulates the exertions of military battle temporarily sublimated due to the contingencies of the entrenched siege. In this light, the apparently casual observation that "by chance ... the talk turned to the subject of their wives"[62] foregrounds the exercise of the mental faculty as the foundation of the coming competition. It is at this point – where the mimetic contest becomes figuratively inflamed – that Collatinus interposes a denial of reliance on discourse alone.[63] He proposes instead the efficacy of pursuing a proactive policy of rational engagement in achieving a resolution of conflicting views.

It is important to note that Collatinus amplifies the notional objectification of the absent wives as surrogate spoils of young men's striving to equal or excel each other (*aemulatio*) by categorising Lucretia in terms of the quality in which her superiority consists. This express definition of female worth is to be found in the character (*ingenia*) most prized by men: the domestic conduct of their spouses.[64]

With the rules of the contest established and accepted, the winner is easily determined. On the one hand, the royal daughters-in-law are observed as active participants in a banquet characterised by an extravagance of eating and drinking; that is, as sharing in a similar kind of entertainment favoured by, and conventionally regarded as the prerogative of, their husbands. On the other, Lucretia is depicted as devoted to that most traditional of all female activities, working in wool; so too, she is seen to be assiduous in the running of household affairs, and shown to display the hallmarks of patient fidelity usually ascribed to the ideal wife of Homeric epic, Penelope.[65] Given the possibility that Collatinus' earnest and urgent exhortation might represent an authorial intervention – designed to emphasise the importance of the faculty of critical engagement in understanding the experience of personal history – the reader would certainly focus on Livy's recognition of Lucretia as possessing the esteem of the female contest. As such, Lucretia can only be identified as the embodiment of conventional womanhood (*muliebritas*), conferring by reflection the highest acknowledgement of manliness (*virtus*) on Collatinus.[66]

At this point in Lucretia's story, the reader (whether a contemporary of the Augustan age or a modern interpreter of AUC history) will recognise the allusive links to the archetypal contest of wives treated in the judgement of Paris.[67] In affording this opportunity, Livy consolidates the literary and artistic resonances by introducing the motif of guest-friendship abused. On one level, this reminds his audience that the Roman pedigree of Trojan and Greek influences and the assimilation of regional Latium may be connected to similar betrayals of ancient hospitality (*hospitium*) in the annals of AUC history. Additionally, by inserting another character flaw at this point to complicate Sextus' thirst for power – namely, unbridled lust (*mala libido*) – Livy may be seen to tie together his historiographical perception of the experiential threads of *res Romana*. Just as the traditional female virtue of chastity (*pudicitia*) is typified by the working of wool (*lanificium*), and the archetypal male character flaw of personal desire for regal dominion (*regni cupido*) by the transgression of acceptable social practice or ancestral custom (*mores maiorum*),[68] so the depraved and inordinate desire which seizes the fledgling tyrant Sextus Tarquinius is represented by the hostile and forceful violation of the female body.[69] Underpinning this willful inclination to violent physical pollution is the two-fold embodiment of male perception: the beauty of the female form and the esteemed (and verifiable) purity of the female body.

What is unavoidable here is Livy's thematic emulation of the narrative thrust. The spark which inflames Sextus' libidinous impulse is seen to be an intrinsically neutral combination of innate factors which can equally intensely generate individual and collective estimations of approval and respect. Inordinate or wilful desire (*libido*) born of inherited attributes of character – hunger for power (*ambitio*), longing to possess (*cupido*), inclination to deceive (*fraus*), and propensity for violence (*vis*) – taints Lucretia's qualitative attributes. These female qualities are otherwise viewed as male signifiers of domestic rectitude and conventional female virtue (*ingenium*) – what can be described as masculinist appropriation typical of patriarchal societies like ancient Rome or Greece which view *all* aspects of personal and cultural identity through a very particular interpretative filter. In other words, Lucretia has become the reflexive eye of Livy's reconstruction of the annalistic "Roman" ("man" and "woman") and "society." In her predicament, the reader must confront the consequences of choosing a particular moral or ethical course for individual well-being, domestic concord, community satisfaction and social stability, and the role which these selective mechanisms have played in determining the *res gestae* of Roman history.

In his portrayal of the meeting between Lucretia and Sextus, Livy continues to compound the exposition of individual qualities of character exemplary of those historical factors seen as disruptive to social stability. The historian is at pains here to alert his audience to the ease with which an individual of Sextus' calibre might subvert the fidelity expected of friendship (borne of age, status, endeavour, and blood) or the trust conferred by hospitality. One might also note the degree to which the rational assessment of opportunity and circumstance coexists with a correspondingly intense affective engagement of subjective desire.

Similarly, Livy parenthesises Sextus' articulation of identity to Lucretia with the young man's invasive and oppressive usurpation of his desired object's physical being and rational heart. Male and female are consequently identified as existential composites of intellect and affection. Like all previous perceptions, it should be clear that this association is exclusively male. Just as the fulfilment of domestic obligation and the display of patient fidelity establish Lucretia's qualifications as the best of wives (in the eyes of her husband and his companions) or her qualities of beauty and tried purity as the most desirable of women (in Sextus' estimation), so the young tyrant distinguishes his own individuality by imperative word and minatory act. These are interwoven into a portrait of a person who favours obedience to authority as opposed to individual liberty.

As such, the object of male rivalry and desire is rendered voiceless in Livy's narrative economy. This discursive strategy is epitomised in Sextus' tense prelude to seduction. How, then, is the reader to delineate the tenor of Lucretia's resistance, except as an artifact of the male imagination? If we accept the logic of this outlook, the evocation of the female mind and will (albeit *in extremis*) must be viewed as an externalisation of male cultural values, and Lucretia becomes, in consequence, the genderless idealisation of male expectation filtered through Livy's narrative lens. As a result, the historian isolates Lucretia's disgrace – suffered by an aristocratic female if even thought to have committed adultery with an individual of inferior status – as an object of fear or dread far outweighing apprehension of death. Such a concept should be regarded as a narrative insertion, which speaks more to a symbolic order of patriarchal customary practice than of an irruptive linguistic core of authentic female socio-cultural concepts. In other words, what Livy's narrative categorises as a quasi-compulsion capable of subduing the otherwise inflexibly resolute chastity of *muliebritas* personified is not unbridled lust or even the threat of violent death but the indignity and humiliation adhering to the perceived sexual transgression of established hierarchical social boundaries. At this point in the retelling, female propriety (*decor muliebris*) is considered superordinate to unprovoked violation or murderous intent.

Taking into account the preceding mimetic/semantic assimilation of the female by the "superior" agents of a patriarchal linguistic code, the hypothetical fate projected onto Lucretia by an increasingly desperate and unexpectedly thwarted Sextus effectively impinges on the male ethos which holds such factors as reputation and legitimacy (that is, status and inheritance) as prevailing signifiers of individual, gentilician, and broader social identity. In other words, just as the standing of each elite political *vir*, his *dignitas*, was dependent upon the honour he had acquired through the holding of magistracies, so the perception of appropriate female conduct may be categorised as a yardstick by which the attitudes and expectations of male peers measured and evaluated social worth. Thus, any formulation of the degree to which Lucretia's violation impinges on the status of her husband, father, and other male relatives – and on any bonds of filial feeling determined by claims of *amicitia* or *patrocinium* – must be conceived within a masculine forum.

It is not surprising, then, that neither Lucretia summons those most affected by the social ramifications arising from her calamitous dishonour; nor should we fail to expect the explicitly affective characterisation of her response to such profound misfortune. What I find instructive is the extent to which Livy invests in his depiction of Lucretia's narrative role qualities determinative of *virilis* rather than *muliebris ingenium*.[70] She is resolute in the face of Sextus' erratic and increasingly frenzied seductive strategies, and she is similarly stoic in the shadow of violent death. Moreover, she succumbs to her rapist's persuasions only when presented with the irresistible logic of an intellectually conceived scenario that effectively embodies the lesser of two evils. It should be noted that she possesses the presence of mind (and the implicit concern for the reputation of her male kin) to gather a crucial quorum of the implicated male community – a "domestic court" (*iudicium domesticum*), as it were, to ascertain the circumstances, examine the witness, and pass judgement on this shocking occurrence.[71]

What can be well with a woman when her honour is lost? The marks of a stranger, Collatinus, are in your bed. But it is only the body that has been violated; the soul is pure.[72]

Importantly for Livy, despite her tears, the words he assigns to Lucretia underline a decidedly masculine preoccupation with the impact of a slighted reputation, the reciprocity of retributive justice, the primacy of the male in determining the outcome of domestic affairs, and the significance invested in the continuity of tradition and the priority of ancestral *virtus*.

But pledge me your solemn word that the adulterer shall not go unpunished. It is Sextus Tarquin who, coming as an enemy instead of a guest, forced from me last night by brutal violence a pleasure fatal to me; and, if you are men, fatal to him.[73]

Finally, she commits suicide, choosing to fall by her own hand rather than exist as a witness to (and reminder of) Tarquinian *dominatio*.[74]

Within the representation of Lucretia as historicised subject and sexual identity, this compressed juxtaposition of idealised male and female signifiers allows us to place in perspective and evaluate Livy's focus on ethics, practice, and sexuality. In keeping with all that has gone before, it would seem unlikely that Livy can do more than render his own subjectivity problematic. While he might call into question (by drawing attention to) the ambivalent basis of his society's most fundamental inter-relational (and hence cultural) concepts, the historian is never able to discard the particular masculine and aristocratic ideological worldview from which he reconstructs his discourse on *res gestae* and *annales*, and through which we can interpret the historiographical metanarrative of AUC history.

In this light, the voice given to Lucretia in the textually fixed moment between rape and suicide does not so much identify Livy as allowing to his subject her own subjectivity as leaves the reader with an uneasiness in relation to the historian's representation of gender.

"It is for you," she said, "to see that he gets his deserts. Although I acquit myself of the sin, I do not free myself from the penalty. No unchaste woman shall henceforth live and plead Lucretia's example."[75]

This discursive tension fails to denaturalise the traditional concepts associated with gender construction. Instead, Livy's representational strategy highlights the locus of contradictions in problematic areas of AUC history. This is achieved by challenging or distorting certain facets of the fixed identities usually assigned to female (but not just female) characters. Invariably informed by the cultural, historical, and conceptual limitations inherited from the hegemonic discourse of his male Roman imagination and patriarchal social milieu, Livy nevertheless occasionally explicates the disparity between female referent and male signifier. In the process, he marginalises the familiar appropriated or displaced figures of women and the lionised or eulogised generations of men so as to question traditional explanations of *res Romana*.

To this end, Lucretia's clipped, emphatic declaration manifests the introspective severity and overriding discipline of the stoic.[76] In a sense, "her" words amount to a condensed declamation on the subject of *pudicitia*: the measure of its worth in relation to the guardian of its condition; how its loss through violent imposition impinges on the guilt or innocence of the violated party; its extortion viewed in the context of (and as justification for) communal retaliation; its equation with the hostile abuse of guest-friendship, and by redaction with the violence committed by use of arms; and, integral to Livy's rhetorical complexity, the recognition of its possession by the female as the guiding principle of her existence and sole rationale of decisive action.

Contrasted to this elaboration of single-minded and clear-sighted resolution of intention, the reader finds a structurally enclosed and thematically dense expression of an explicitly representative aristocratic male ethos. Not only is a distinction drawn between an offence springing from compulsion and a fault of omission, but a qualitative division between the mind and the body is elucidated on the basis of a polarity between the antithetical extremes of transgression and prudent deliberation. More than the retrojection of contemporary legal opinion, Livy's interpolation of an attitude towards personal culpability subtly parallels the various ambiguities already outlined in his textual exposition. Bracketed by Lucretia's "virile" resolve, the collective (if hierarchical) male response might promise to fulfil her call to retaliatory action against Sextus, but also evokes a sense that her purity of purpose has been figuratively diluted (if not polluted). Certainly, it is difficult not to regard Lucretia's separation of responsibility for familial retaliation and individual reconciliation as a veiled rebuke to men whose determination falls short of the ideal that she expects of herself. As such, while Lucretia acquits herself from any charge of wilful transgression (as do her companions), she cannot excuse herself from punishment (a course of action which the elite male gathering hopes to forestall or subvert). In sum, there is agreement that the seed of incrimination lies in voluntary intellectual engagement; but consensus falters over the exculpation of guiltless yet irreducible violation.

How is the reader to explain Livy's explicit narrative contention over an undeniably transgressive act in a specifically gendered context? Perhaps the clue lies in Lucretia's last words: "no unchaste woman shall from this time live to plead Lucretia's example."[77] The faculty of invention which Livy generally brings to bear on his reconstruction of speeches or dialogue is especially transparent in this evocation of future time (the historian's own?) and of idealised ratiocination. Surely the modern reader cannot expect

Lucretia to accept the burden of disgrace so flagrantly imposed, so judiciously deplored, and so deeply felt. Indeed not! Yet to do so conforms attitudinally to the process of mimetic transfer previously encountered, albeit in a viscerally extreme form. In the same way that Lucretia and her aristocratic female peers (the king's daughters-in-law[78] functioned as the alternative space within which Collatinus and his companions might sublimate and expend potentially disruptive agonistic energies, so the social and personal impact of Lucretia's attitudinal transfer may (but, in this instance, cannot) be reversed. If the effects of Lucretia's disgrace were to rebound on her familial and gentilician relations, the consequences for those males associated with Collatinus by ties of consanguinity or friendship would be far-reaching and possibly harmful to the broader social stability. Therefore, the ancient logic pervading Livy's gendered narrative of res privata/publica demands Lucretia's annihilation. Her father, her husband, and their amici cannot pronounce or administer the only judgement permissible under the tenets of this symbolic order. To do so would itself represent a deliberate and unconscionable transgression of intrinsic and prescriptive boundaries. These cultural limes preclude any admission that female space (muliebris ingenium) overlaps the sphere (and can be determinative of the standards) of male action (virtus or virilis ingenium). To exercise ultimate control over Lucretia's fate would be to openly avow implication in the course of events which led to her disgrace. In paraphrase, "I kill (or demand the death of) Lucretia, because Sextus raped her, and her condition brings me dishonour. But Sextus raped Lucretia because I pandered her (mind and body) in a contest between wives, and her victory brought me honour." The interpenetration of male and female identity exerts a problematic tension on the dynamic warp and weft of Rome's social fabric.

And so Lucretia takes charge of her highly particularised sphere of personal influence. Recognising that her death will restore the fragile equilibrium that exists between the conventional (if clearly ambiguous) binarisms which comprise the ideological species of the Roman community, Lucretia completes the tricolon of thought, word, and deed by silencing the seat of her passions and wisdom. Prefigured and premeditated, her act of self-extinction symbolises the ideal subordination of self-interest to the requirements of community welfare (bonum publicum). Equally, it illuminates in its finality the problematic interventions of Sextus, Collatinus, and the associated representatives of male gender and aristocratic class. Finally, it presages the appropriation and embodiment of this highly desired and exemplary behaviour in that most unlikely liberator, L. Iunius Brutus.

I say "unlikely," and yet the hidden depths of Brutus' character are already known to the reader. In fact, while the other protagonists remain perversely ignorant of his true nature, Livy's audience is well-prepared for the transformation (or, more appropriately, the shedding) of persona to reveal his authentic ingenium. All the more puzzling, then, that the historian implicates the traditional liberator of Rome as party to Lucretia's ideologically inept, if superficially supportive *iudicium domesticum*. So, Livy does not mention Brutus' inclusion in the magisterial system as tribune of the Celeres,[79] whose attendant status undermines the degree of astonishment which the assembled male population (even if not the various members of his extended family) should have expressed. These non-linear insertions can be viewed as contingent on the intended frame of Livy's narrative structure. Just as easily, the reader could associate such identifiable textual anomalies as further indication of the annalist's subtly crafted historiographical theme. On the one hand, Lucretia – as the ideally constituted representation of *muliebris ingenium* – exposes the transgressive potential inherent in the mimesis of aristocratic competition within a social context of gendered relations; on the other, Brutus – typologically "perfect" *imago* of liberation from tyranny (*conditor reipublicae*) – lacks the will to intervene in the unjust tenure of ambitious and dominating men until forced by circumstance and the ineffable requisites of familial piety. To these ends, Livy coopts the crucial narrative impetus to revolution (Lucretia's rape) as the means by which the traditional utopian articulations of *pudicitia* and *libertas* might be critically represented.

Distilling this discussion to its essential ingredients, I offer the following points for consideration. Although it is beyond the capacity of literary-critical, philological, or "scientific" historians to confirm or deny the sources or means of transmission of AUC history – nor is it possible to proffer more than a tentative reconstruction of the transition from monarchy to republic – I suggest that the account contained in Livy can provide us with valuable evidence about the historiographical crisis fabricated and explored in episodic fashion throughout his version of the annalistic tradition. Further than this, instead of viewing the so-called historical romance centring on the rape of Lucretia with hypercritical skepticism, it may be seen that Livy's climactic period of prose narrative gathers, focuses, and illuminates a variety of disparate elements of character. In turn, such a treatment could only be regarded as a conscious attempt to provide a structural and semantic conclusion to whatever rhetorical and critical discourse the historian has interwoven through his preceding exposition of archaic Roman history.

1.3 Egeria, Carmenta, and the Vestal priestesses: *exempla* and the male imagination

To round off discussion of the argument regarding Livy's representation of women within the frame of his broader historiographical project, two case studies conclude this chapter. Each inquiry is self-contained and focusses on compositional strategies and thematic issues. The first explores the historian's use of female categories – the nymph, the prophetess, and the priestess – to tease out notions of literary authorship, civic authority, human society's relationship with the divine, and the concepts of religious faith and historical belief. The second examines Livy's approach to the representation of women in a non-Roman context (the Greek city-state of Syracuse in the late 3rd century BCE) and how the intersection of elite domestic and political concerns places pressure on the fragile, porous boundaries between the household and the state.

Intentionally brief, both studies demonstrate in capsule form the overarching contention which the preceding lengthy discussion of Lucretia's story introduced: namely, the historical precondition or agent for society's re-evaluation of the *status quo* – whether the tradition under pressure relates to a particular cultural, economic, political, religious, or social practice – is the catalyst for action incorporating individual women, a female collective, or a combination of both, leading to a resolution or complication of the original motivating factor, either in the form of a partial or complete change to existing practice. In the case of the episode involving Lucretia, the tyrannical rule of the Etruscan Tarquin dynasty (what precedes the episode) may be seen to impact on a range of traditional Roman socio-political relations and cultural values, resulting in Lucretia's rape and suicide (the episode), which in turn precipitate the end of monarchical rule in Rome and the establishment of a republican form of government (what follows the episode).[80] The following case studies illustrate the manner in which Livy introduces into traditional AUC discourse memorable narrative episodes incorporating representations of women so as to identify, explain, and create a permanent record of moments in legendary or historical time (*res Romana*) when the usual or expected order of Roman society (*mores maiorum*) changed in radical, incremental, or transient ways (*res novae*).

With all that in mind, Livy's citations of the goddess Egeria and the prophetess Carmenta – early on in Book 1, well before the transformative events subsequent to Lucretia's rape and suicide – can be viewed as illustrative of his historiographical method: discursive annalistic presentation (historical information) and immersive narrative representation (literary recreation).[81]

Egeria – described by Livy as a divine being or *dea* (goddess); represented in other literary sources as a mythological spirit of nature taking the form of a beautiful maiden who inhabited rivers or woodlands[82] – is a figment of Numa's imagination. The creation of a fictive mythological counsellor aligns neatly with the evolutionary agenda of Rome's second king. Following on from his predecessor Romulus' foundation of the city by force of arms, the reader learns that "Numa prepared to found the city anew by laws and customs."[83] In this context, Egeria's active engagement in establishing traditional sacral practice and institutionalising specialised sacerdotal offices is an invention of male intellect. As Livy notes, Numa's concern that peaceful conditions in Rome would lead to indiscipline and idleness prompted the introduction of a counterbalancing influence: in this case, fear of the gods.

> But, as this would fail to make a deep impression without some claim to supernatural wisdom, [Numa] pretended that he had nocturnal interviews with the nymph Egeria; and that it was on her

advice that he was instituting the ritual most acceptable to the gods and appointing for each deity his own special priests.[84]

According to this formulation, Egeria is the objectification of male rationality. In the same way, Carmenta serves to reify the sufficiency of masculine power. Livy refers to Carmenta immediately after his account of Rome's foundation, when an enraged Romulus kills his brother Remus, takes on the mantle of sole rule, and the city is named after its founder. As the original episode in AUC history – arising from a moment of extraordinary crisis contingent on the consequences attending contempt for the sanctity of Rome's newly raised walls – one should expect Romulus' first actions as king to be significant. In this light, he addresses particular military and religious exigencies: fortification of the Palatine hill and proper conduct of divine worship according to traditional Latin and Greek rites. In regard to the latter, Livy provides a basis for the cult of Hercules at the Ara Maxima by including a version of the legend of Hercules and Cacus. This story features Evander, king of Pallantium, as his city's benefactor, in no small part due to the status and knowledge of Carmenta, his mother.

> [Evander], worthy of respect because of his knowledge of letters –
> a new and marvelous thing for uncivilized men – was still more
> revered because of his mother Carmenta, who was believed to be a
> divine being and, in the days before the arrival of the Sibyl in Italy,
> regarded with wonder by all as an interpreter of fate.[85]

The status of her son is conferred by association.[86] Her productive ability (prophetic utterance) is bequeathed to Evander as an inherited attribute enhancing his personal identification.[87]

Each characterisation performs a double aetiological function: the origin of a customary socio-religious institution;[88] and the source of a valued facet of the hermeneutic (male) self. In this rhetorical formulation, Egeria is the figurative signifier of Numa's reasoning mind, and Carmenta is the intuitive construct of Evander's intellectual invention. Even more resonant is the observation that Livy pursues his historiographical project in the same manner. Numa (like Evander) is a fictive reproduction, designed to exemplify an originary impulse. This principle gives rise to certain religious *mores* which transform early Roman *vita*. He is a most experienced and knowing *vir*, whose *artes* reinforce the disciplined superstructure of the growing *urbs*. He is a creation, and Egeria is the by-product of his thought. If this is a valid interpretation, then "woman" (divine or human) must be seen as a device employed by Livy to clarify the limits of the male body: heart and mind, individual and social.

This is not to say that Livy invents from a vacuum. Rather, I mean to suggest that he distorts and manipulates the received tradition familiar for the most part to his Augustan audience. In this connection, the reader encounters the designation of virgins for Vesta, embedded in the chapters detailing Numa's religious innovations.[89] Here, Livy is explicit in nominating a secure genealogical link between the heritage of the Vestal priesthood and the birth right of Romulus. For one reason, it would seem: so that a *sacerdotium* of *virgines* should not attract the appellation of *alienus*. Although Numa allegedly acted on the advice of a goddess, the appointment of girls of marriageable age to a significant participatory position within the overwhelmingly male religious hierarchy is clearly regarded as contrary to normative practice and demands subtle, almost forensic argument to support its inclusion in such a publicly sanctioned textual history. Even given the incontrovertible existence and valorisation of the office, Livy is required to sacralise its image. Not with the external trappings of magisterial duty granted in perpetuity, but with a physical objectification of sanctified flesh. While male authority is rendered visible by the representational identification of material dress and emblems of office, female alterity or otherness is made visceral by the referential application of material control.

Just as Numa's invention of Egeria and Evander's appropriation of Carmenta reflect Livy's gendered formulation of the male body, the historian's inclusion of an authentic female referent (the *Vestalis*) is structured so as to map out the designated contours of male sanction by comparison with the delimitations of female space. And so Livy reiterates Numa's duplicitous congress with Egeria (now his wife), emphasising its physical singularity and its specificity of purpose.

> There was a grove through the midst of which a perennial stream flowed, issuing from a dark cave. Here Numa frequently retired unattended as if to meet the goddess, and he consecrated the grove to the Camenae, because it was there that the meetings with his wife Egeria took place.[90]

In essence, there is a place for "woman" in the scheme of AUC history, dedicated by (and to) "man." Of necessity, it must be remembered that the rationale underpinning any encounter with this Other (*virgo, Vestalis, dea*) is the product of male rhetoric. For the syntactic evidence of this semantic reading, we need look no further than the relative clause of alleged reason which encodes Numa's authorship of Egeria's space and his explanation of her existence. Male and female are indeed *unius corpus*; in a sense, the rhetorical conjunction of imperial reason.

The historiographical frame for these episodes is consistent with the proposition already confirmed in relation to Lucretia's story. Prior to introducing the myth of Hercules and Cacus, featuring Evander and reference to his mother Carmenta, Livy recounts the events leading to the foundation of the city of Rome.[91] Here, the direction that Rome's historical trajectory will follow is very much contingent on how Romulus proceeds in the wake of killing his brother Remus. In this regard, the mythological interlude confirms the wisdom of Romulus' first act – attending to the city's ritual obligations – and provides legal precedent for the constitutional measures the newly installed king introduces afterwards.[92] In similar fashion, Livy situates Numa's invention of Egeria in the shadow of mooted change to Rome's ideological direction. After forming treaties of alliance with neighbouring states and closing the temple of Janus, the city exchanges the threat of military conflict for the twin perils of peacetime, *indisciplina* and *otium*. To combat these hazards to maintaining social order and stability, Numa creates a fictive divine counsellor, effectively justifying the cessation of Romulus' previous emphasis on military action in favour of widespread religious reforms.[93]

1.4 Damarata, Harmonia, and Heraclia: Livy's assignation of moral weight

In this light, focussing on the identification of specific norms, ideologies, and obligations allows the reader to chart any coherent patterns which interpenetrate Livy's gendered transactions of *res Romana*. To this end, I am especially drawn to the account of tyranny, betrayal, conspiracy, rebellion, and murder which follow the death of the Syracusan ruler Hiero in 215 BCE.[94] In particular, one should note the following intellectual and affective concerns which appear to shape and control Livy's reconstruction of a pivotal historical episode in the *res externa* of Roman-Carthaginian relations during the first years of the Second Punic War.

First, a disruptive intersection of *res privata* and *publica* is mediated through the expression of female *ambitio*. The explicit interdependence of Damarata's and Heraclia's opposition to their father's wish to bequeath political freedom to Syracuse, and Hiero's inability to separate the interests of household and state in his dying instructions is crystallised in the association between gender, affiliation, and genealogy, and a specific moral and mental constitution.

> This plan of [Hiero's] his daughters strenuously opposed. They anticipated that the boy would enjoy the name of royalty, but that the administration of all affairs would be conducted by themselves and their husbands, Adranodorus and Zoippus, for these were left the principal of his guardians.[95]

As resistance to her deceased father's wishes plays out, Damarata – female, wife, and daughter – is characterised as "puffed out" with haughty feelings (which arise from her belonging to a family of kings) and as having an imperious or overbearing disposition (typical of or "natural" to a woman, in a definitively bad sense). According to Livy's profile, she is "swelling with the pride of royalty and female presumption."[96]

Second, it is possible to apprehend a familiar tricolon of thought-word-deed, by which the affective overwhelms the rational. This process causes a supervention of constructive policy and a concomitant upheaval of normative relations. Hiero's clear-sighted discernment of the potential for injurious disorder of the body politic and for the despotism of arbitrary rule following his death – and his desire that Syracuse is left in a condition of political freedom – is opposed by his daughters. They are compelled to take a stand against his policy, as a result of their firmly held opinions.[97] This belief leads to ingratiating speech, enticement and provocation, rebuke, and recommendation, all of which is specifically gendered.[98] Warning Adranodorus – who, in succumbing to his wife's entreaties, will be responsible for the radical turning of Syracusan politics to the Carthaginians – Damarata recommends that:

> Now was the favourable time for seizing the government, while everything was in confusion in consequence of liberty being recent and not yet regularly established; while a soldiery supported by the royal pay was to be met with, and while generals sent by Hannibal and accustomed to the soldiery might forward the attempt.[99]

Such communication instigates a transformation of political influence, a temporary vacillation of masculine will, and an eventual capitulation in the hope of revolution and seizure of power.

Third, Livy may be seen to deploy certain formulaic motifs which facilitate critical interpretation through the recitation of lessons already learned. In this case, he incorporates the death of exemplary restraint as the catalyst for an objectification of alterity in the socio-political order. This translates into a manifest and (by now) familiar sequence of commonplaces (*topoi*): the display and condition of tyranny; the death of innocence through partisan rivalry and conspiracy; and the outbreak of violence and disorder (necessitating the arming of citizens and other emergency measures), which arises from despotic crime and lust, and which is signalled by an advocate of freedom and moderation.

Last, the reader cannot help but discern the problematic permutations which demark Livy's reconstruction of the existing density of AUC tradition as most ambiguous in a gendered context. These are most notable in the chain of violent events which spring from the *oratio obliqua* of Sopater,[100] asked by the senate and his colleagues to address the people after the murder of Adranodorus and Themistus within the curial walls. Free from any suggestion of complicity in the *coniuratio* against the royal house, and stained with the blood of liberty's enemies, this individual is thus sanctioned as the mouthpiece of socio-political reconstitution – yet another Brutus holding aloft the dagger of popular vengeance. But the literal and figurative gap between appearance and reality is considerably wider in this episode. Predicated by a crucial misinterpretation of (or, rather, overreaction to) Sopater's accusations against the violence and impiety perpetrated through a youth by his unscrupulous and embittered guardians, the autocratic disposition of Adranodorus and Themistus is mimetically transferred to the machinations of Damarata and Harmonia (daughter of Gela, Hiero's eldest son and deceased ally to Carthage).

> But those wives of royal blood had infected them with this thirst for royalty, one having married the daughter of Hiero, the other the daughter of Gelon.[101]

Nowhere more explicitly does Livy deploy the issue of gender as a signifier of transgressive interaction between private temperament and civil discord. For not only does a praetorial edict condemn the wives of the conspirators to death, but Heraclia (daughter of Hiero, wife of Zoippus) and her daughters – in the most melodramatic and rhetorically decorous of circumstances. The authorial intention is unequivocal and confirmed in parenthesis by explicit preface and postscript. The shedding of female blood (*virgines*, *innoxia*) – in a context materially associated with the destiny of the household, and replete with the lexicography of violation and inverted normative behaviour (*invidia*, *matris cruor*) – is deemed the response of a mob suborned by intemperateness, angry passion, and immoderate desire.

> Such is the nature of the populace: they are either cringing slaves or haughty tyrants. They do not know how, with moderation, to spurn or to enjoy that liberty which holds the middle place; nor are they generally wanting ministers, who pander to their resentment, who incite their eager and intemperate minds to blood and carnage.[102]

The common masses are transformed into the bloodthirsty and irrational embodiment of *tyrannis*, exterminating innocent and guilty alike. And all due to the irremediable failure of the many to apprehend the intermediary action of true independence from restraint.

As previously observed, Livy's gendered historiography in relation to Syracuse during the period of the Second Punic War is located at the nexus between key points of historical contestation and resolution. During his long rule, Hiero had kept order in Syracuse but, in the prelude to the narrative passages featuring Damarata and her sister, his influence had waned in old age. At the same time, in the aftermath of Hannibal's victories, Hiero's son, heir, and co-regent Gelo declared his allegiance to the Carthaginians, setting off a period of dynastic strife and rebellion. Then Gelo died suddenly in mysterious circumstances, "so timely a death as to taint even the father with suspicion," and not long afterwards Hiero too passed away after a 54-year reign.[103] The deaths left Syracuse with a power vacuum; and, with Hannibal using spies, agents, and envoys to keep abreast of developments, the stage was set for Carthaginian and Roman allied factions within the city to struggle over the succession. "Hiero's death changed the whole situation," claimed Livy, and rule passed to Hiero's 15-year-old grandson Hieronymous. When he assumed the throne at Syracuse real power lay in the hands of Hieronymous' uncles, Adranodorus and Zoippus (husbands of Hiero's daughters), who had been appointed as guardians to the young king, along with 13 Syracusan noblemen.[104] The struggle for power at Syracuse initiated a period of violence, intrigue, and assassination at the court of the old king. There was turmoil and conspiracy as agents of both Rome and Hannibal vied for influence with various factions. In the aftermath of Hiero's death, a plot on the life of the young heir was exposed, implicating one of his guardians, the pro-Roman Thraso (falsely accused, according to Livy).[105]

As expected, when inescapable challenges threaten a community's established political order and customary social practice in this way, Livy incorporates very particular representations of women into the historical narrative. What should be clear is that the women in this episode of AUC history – Damarata, her sister Heraclea and her daughters, Harmonia, and the wives of the conspirators – are non-Roman (Hellenistic Greek) elite females. They are not the first non-Roman women to be represented in situations of conflict, crisis, or rebellion in AUC, but, at least as far as Damarata is concerned, Livy characterises her exhortations to her husband, the nonagenarian regent Adranodorus, in similarly negative terms to other non-Roman women appearing prior to or after Book 24.[106]

> Damarata, [Adranodorus'] wife, the daughter of Hiero, still swelling with the pride of royalty and female presumption, called him out from the presence of the ambassadors, and reminded him of the expression so often repeated by the tyrant Dionysius, that a man ought only to relinquish sovereign power when dragged by the feet, and not while sitting on horseback.[107]

While Adranodorus' susceptibility to Damarata's advice (*muliebria consilia*) is not wholesale, the fact that he can be swayed at all by her blandishments to seize the tyranny and resist the Romans at all costs sets the scene for the frenetic period that follows. The historiographical frame within which Livy's representation of the royal women and female children is located may thus be summarised as follows: Hiero's testamentary desire to end monarchical rule and reconstitute Syracuse as a free state is resisted by the king's surviving heirs, especially so by his daughters, and in particular, Damarata. Here, the threat of new things (*res novae*) – namely, the creation of a radically transformed political constitution – gives rise to a savage familial rebellion with the sole objective of retaining inherited power and influence, culminating in the assassination of Hieronymus, Adranodorus' attempt to seize power and subsequent death, the brutal slaughter of every man, woman, and child related to the royal family (including Damarata and Harmonia), and Rome's eventual sack of Syracuse in 212 BCE.[108]

1.5 Conclusion

The work of over 40 years, Livy's AUC history may draw largely on (now almost completely lost) older historical narratives as well as Polybius. However, while he may have relied on sources like Coelius Antipater, Licinius Macer, Q. Aelius Tubero, and especially Valerius Antias and Claudius Quadrigarius for the content of his AUC, if nothing else, the overview in this chapter of his historiographical method sheds light on Livy's relationship to the ideological objectives of the Augustan principate and, in equal measure, the value he clearly placed in dressing historical transmission in contemporary literary dress using a rich formal tradition. In this process the connection to the annalists – with their formula of a report continuing from one year to the next, lists of elections, officials, and prodigies at the year's transitions – would have been rather a hindrance both to a freer conceptual perspective on the form and function of history and to the production of a literary structure within which that historiographical project might best be situated. This tension is especially evident in Livy's attention to the arrangement of narrative episodes within an overarching structural frame. That said, whether dramatic individual actions like a military battle or a speech in a political assembly, or the characterisation of his male and female characters, Livy succeeds in his attempt to give a modern literary form to historical tradition.[109]

Moreover, what will have become clear over the course of discussion is Livy's application of a particular historiographical strategy involving episodes that feature representations of women. We saw in the last chapters of Book 1 how the historian prefaces the story of Lucretia with precisely the mixture of socio-political circumstances (arbitrary, unrestrained exercise of power, and despotic abuse of authority) most susceptible to inflammatory action (radical uprising, armed struggle, and structural reformation of the state) – needing only a provocative act (the rape and subsequent suicide of a chaste married woman) to provide the appropriate spark. So too, the episodes featuring Carmenta and Egeria early in Book 1 and Damarata, Harmonia, and Heraclea in Book 24 display a similar historiographical template. In brief, this template comprises an episode in which mythological, legendary, or historical women, Roman or non-Roman – lean on detail, classically strict in word use and syntax, and compressed for impact (annalist); or extensive, eloquent, and very much a literary artefact (narrative) – is embedded between two historical conditions. The condition that precedes the episode may be termed the precipitate event, comprising, in relation to the examples discussed in this chapter, circumstances such as conflict with neighbour states, death of a family member, tyrannical rule, and military siege). The condition which follows the episode depicts the consequent action, consisting of such events as the reform of religious practices, foundation of constitutional processes, formation of a new political system, and sack of a city and annihilation of dynastic line. Regardless of the category of female deployed in these internal narrative episodes (nymph, prophetess, aristocratic wife, and foreign royalty), it is the fact that the story includes women which alerts the reader to a turning-point in AUC history on the one hand and helps the author to shape the trajectory of the surrounding historical events on the other.

In order to elaborate on this conceptualisation of Livian historiography, the next chapter will explore the structural, descriptive and thematic *variatio* which Livy brings to bear through his gendered narrative as expressed in situations depicting collective female action. If successful, the reader should understand more clearly to what extent Livy intended his distinctive annalistic treatment of episodes incorporating significant female activity to explain and clarify a personal and critical standpoint regarding the tensions and ambiguities of Rome's social fabric. To this end, attention will be paid to how Livy uses the *topos* of a public debate, set against the background of a collective demonstration of women, to address matters important to his historiographical project.

Notes

1 Ogilvie (1963: 25–26); Walsh (1970: 66). These scholars epitomize the legacy of the *Quellenforschung* and *Einserzählerungen* models first articulated in Nissen's 1863 *Kritische Untersuchungen über die Quellen der vierten und fünften Dekade des Livius* ("Critical Inquiries into the Sources for the Fourth and Fifth Decades of Livy") and Witte's 1910 "Über die Form der Darstellung in Livius' Geschictswerk" ("Concering the Shape of the Narrative in Livy's History"). On Livian scholarship over the past 150 years, see the introduction to a recent anthology of readings on Livy in Chaplin and Kraus (2009: 1–14).

2 Scholarship on Livy's Preface is immense. For a useful bibliography, see Moles (1993: 162 n.2).

3 Liv. 1 pr. 1–2: *facturusne operae pretium sim, si a primordio urbis res populi Romani perscripserim, nec satis scio, nec, si sciam, dicere ausim, quippe qui cum veterem tum volgatani esse rein videam, dum novi semper scriptores aut in rebus certius aliquid allaturos se aut scribendi arte rudem vetustatem superaturos credunt.*

4 *facturusne operae pretium sim* (1 pr 1) possesses a dactylic rhythm (where a stressed syllable is followed by two unstressed syllables). Quint. *Inst.* 9.4.74 confirms the word order. On the challenge posed by Livy's inclusion of poetical metre in a work of history, see Ogilvie (1965: 25) and Moles (1993: 141).

5 Quint. *Inst.* 10.1.32; cf. 4.2.45. For interpretations of the phrase *lactea ubertas*, see Hays (1987).

6 On historiography's debt to epic in relation to Herodotus and Thucydides, see Rutherford (2012). On the relationship between historical poetry and the formation of historical writing in the practice of Herodotus, Thucydides, and their predecessors, see Porciani (2017).

7 Liv. 1 pr. 10: *Hoc illud est praecipue in cognitione rerum salubre ac frugiferum omnis te exempli documenta in inlustri posita monumento intueri; inde tibi tuaeque rei publicae quod imitere capias inde foedum inceptu foedum exitu quod vites.*

8 Ogilvie (1963: 28).

9 Kraus (1994: 14).

10 Cf. Chaplin and Kraus (2009: 3): "The gap between history and literature, which formerly coincided with modern academic categories (themselves equally the products of nineteenth-century German scholarship), is a wholly regrettable distortion of the ancient understanding of history as a form of literature."

11 For a succinct outline of recent approaches to Roman historiography, see Dench (2009).

12 On the variety of ways in which ancient persons experienced the past in late republican Rome, see Sandberg (2018).

13 On ancient audiences and expectations, see Marincola (2009).

14 On the idea of the *monumentum* as a useful tool for studying space and memory in Livy's construction of history, see Jaeger (1997: 15–29). For a dispassionate examination of the far-reaching revision of Roman historiography under Augustan rule, see Toher (1990).

15 Liv. 1 pr. 9: *ad illa mihi pro se quisque acriter intendat animum, quae vita, qui mores fuerint, per quos viros quibusque artibus domi militiaeque et partum et auctum imperium sit; labente deinde paulatim disciplina velut desidentes primo mores sequitur animo, deinde ut magis magisque lapsi sint, tum ire coeperint praecipites, donec ad haec tempora quibus nec vitia nostra nec remedia pati possumus perventum est.*

16 For a discussion of the forms of memory making that supported reconsideration of the past in Roman antiquity, see Flower (2011: 3–17).

17 On Livy's use of spectacle within the historiographical tradition both as a means to engage the gaze of his audience and as a visual image of the cumulative power of the Roman past, see Feldherr (1998: 4–50).

18 Kraus (1994: 6) has observed that, as far as the composition of his AUC history is concerned, Livy's position in relation to the Augustan programme of wide-ranging political and social reforms "has attracted more attention than any other single issue" in the scholarship dealing with Roman historiography during the Augustan principate. Treatments of any parallels between the consolidating principles of the principate and the overarching unifying aims of Livy's monumental project include those of Phillips (1982) and Deninger (1985). Assignation of the degree to which the historian aligned with, adverted to, or actively critiqued Augustus can be found, respectively, in Syme (1959: 76) and Woodman (1988: 128–140) (Livy as propagandist and encomiast); Burck (1991) (Livy as admirer); and Mette (1961), Petersen (1961), Badian (1993), and Miles (1995) (Livy as critic).

19 Prop. 4.11.36: *in lapide hoc uni nupta fuisse legar.*

20 *CIL* 1^2.1211 = *ILS* 8403: *domum servavit, lanam fecit.*

21 Syme (1939: 444–445).

22 Kleiner (1978: 772).

23 Kellum (1994: 26). While there have been many attempts to identify this figure – was she Venus, for instance? Or possibly Ceres? – in the end it scarcely matters. For all intents and purposes, the image most likely presented an intentionally multiple iconography. For the ancient viewer, the significance of the image resided in the representational strength and indelibility of the female figure.

24 Kleiner (1977).

25 Zanker (1988: 291–295).

26 On imperial ideology and perceptions of women's roles in the freed and slave populations of Augustan Rome, see Joshel (1992a).

27 Petersen (2006: 95–120).

28 Cic. *Off.* 1.151, 3.57. CIL 1.1203 (N. façade): [Est hoc monimentu]*m Marcei Vergili Eurysacis pistoris redemptoris apparet.* CIL 1.1204 (W. façade): *Est*

hoc monimentum Margei [sic] *Vergilei Eurysacis pistoris redemptoris apparet.*
CIL 1.1205 (S. façade): *Est hoc monimentum Marci Vergili Eurysac*[is]. To
make complete sense of this repeated message, *apparet* ("it seems," "it is apparent") might be reimagined as *apparitor* (public servant). On the interpretation
of the façade inscriptions, see Petersen (2006: 253 n.13).

29 CIL 1.1206: *Fuit Atistia uxor mihei/femina opituma veixsit/quoius corporis
reliquae/quod* [sic] *superant sunt in/hoc panario* ("Atistia was my wife. She
lived as a wonderful woman, the remains of whose body which survive are in
this breadbasket").

30 For a list of non-literary (in large part, man-made, but also natural) structures,
monuments, and features created or crafted to transmit historical capital of
one kind or another, see Steinby (2000).

31 On contrasting views of the Roman historiographical project – ranging from
the construction of history as a sequence of myth-making embedded in and
illustrative of contemporary political debates to the creation of a range of
monuments and memorials that participate in and contribute to the making of
history – see the essays in Sandberg and Smith (2018).

32 Verg. *Aen.* 1.364: *dux femina facti.*

33 Keith (1997).

34 For an overview of legal and historical features of the *lex Iulia de adulteriis
coercendis*, see Corbett (1930: 133–146); Csillag (1976); Raditsa (1980);
Richlin (1981); and Fayer (1994: 212–269).

35 Gardner (1986: 124–125).

36 Gardner (1986: 7).

37 On the terms of the *lex Papia Poppaea*, see McGinn (1998: 70–104).

38 Gardner (1986: 194–196); McGinn (1998: 72–84).

39 Wallace-Hadrill (2009: quote, 253).

40 On Vergil's concept of history, see, e.g., (2009: 125): "There is little doubt that,
for Vergil, Augustus is the *telos*, that is, the *aim* of history."

41 Kraus (1994: 8); cf. Kraus and Woodman (1997: 70–74). On approaches to
aesthetic, historical and political issues arising within the context of "Augus-
tanism" (that is, the view that contemporaries of Augustus, especially writers,
shared sensibilities, ideas and attitudes), see Kennedy (1992) and Galinsky
(1996).

42 Pittenger (2008: 9 n.23, with bibliography): "The formation and growth of the
Roman historical tradition – often loosely, if somewhat inaccurately, termed
annalistic – is an extremely complex and controversial subject ... The once
widely accepted view of a monolithic development simply will not hold."

43 The Sabine women: Bryson (1986); Stehle (1989); Miles (1993); Brown (1995);
Beard (1999); Vandiver (1999). Lucretia and Verginia: Galinsky (1932);
Bryson (1986); Joplin (1990); Schubert (1991); Joshel (1992b); Bauman (1993);
Moses (1993); Calhoun (1997); Vandiver (1999); Matthes (2000); Donaldson
(2002); Koptev (2003); Freund (2008). The repeal of the *lex Oppia*: Balsdon
(1962: 32–37); Hemelrijk (1987); Hillard (1989), (1992); Mustakillio (1999);
Milnor (2005: 154–184); Mastrorosa (2006). The Bacchanalian conspiracy:
Fraenkel (1932); Gelzer (1936); Meautis (1940); Balsdon (1962: 37–42);
Pailler (1988); Rousselle (1989); Scafuro (1989); Takács (2000).

44 References to mythological, legendary, and historical women in the *Periochae*
of Livy's lost AUC history (Books 11–20 and 46–142): 14.7 (Sextilia, Vestal condemned for *adulterium* and buried alive); 19.8-9 (Claudia, sister of
P. Claudius Pulcher, consul, fined for loyalty to the brother defeated against
Carthaginian navy after ordering sacred chickens drowned); 20.5 (Tuccia, Vestal condemned for *adulterium*); 48.13 (Publilia and Licinia, *nobiles feminae,*

executed for murdering their husbands, former consuls); 50.4 (Queen Laodice, daughter of Seleucus IV, wife of Perseus, Macedonian ruler); 51.5 (wife of Hasdrubal the Boetharch, Carthaginian commander in the third Punic War, kills herself and her two children); 52.11 (Cleopatra Thea, wife of Demetrius III Nicator, daughter of Ptolemy VI Philometor); 57.7 (Vaccaean women and children, killed by men of the city under siege); 59.7, 14 (widows not included in *lustrum* of 126 BCE; Cleopatra III, marries uncle Ptolemy VIII Euergetes II [Physcon] ca. 142–140 BCE; Sempronia, wife of P. Cornelius Scipio Africanus, sister of the Gracchi, suspected of poisoning Africanus); 60.11 (Cleopatra Thea, wife of Demetrius II Nicator, killed husband and Seleucus, her son); 63.4 (Aemilia, Licinia, and Marcia, Vestals condemned for *incastitas*); 68.9 (mother of Publicius Malleolus, killed by her son); 72.4 (woman who released Ser. Sulpicius Galba from captivity in Lucania); 89.9 (Bastia, wife of Mutilus); 103.2 ("wife of the *pontifex* Metellus" = Pompeia, wife of Caesar); 106.1 (Julia, daughter of Caesar, wife of Pompey); 111.3 (Cleopatra); 112.3, 6 (Cornelia, wife of Pompey; Cleopatra); 116.2 (*Venus Genetrix*); 125.2 (Fulvia, wife of M. Antonius); 127.2 (Fulvia; Octavia, sister of C. Octavius/ Caesar Augustus); 130.1, 3 (Cleopatra VII); 131.3 (Cleopatra); 132.2 (Cleopatra, Octavia); 133.1, 2 (Cleopatra); 140.2 (Octavia).

45 The chronology of AUC history: Books 1–5: from the foundation of the city to 390 BCE; Books 6–10: 389–293 BCE; Books 11–20: 292–218 BCE; Books 21-45: 218–167 BCE; Books 46–142: 167–10/9 BCE. For a detailed outline of gendered incidents in the extant Livian *corpus*, the reader should refer to Table A.1, located in the Afterword of this volume, as identified in Fig. 1.1 above, additional fragmentary references to women in AUC history are located in the summaries of the lost books of Livy's history known as the *Periochae*; for specific references, see the preceding note (n.42).

46 *femina(e)/mulier(es)*: In addition to those references subsumed within broader annalistic or narrative episodes treated explicitly in Fig. 1.1-3 (66 items) – 1.1.11 (Lavinia); 1.4.7 (Larentia); 1.9.16 (characterisation of women's affective nature in Romulus' justification of the abduction and rape of the Sabine women); 1.13.7 (the names of the Sabine women, or of their husbands, are given to the *curiae*, selected on grounds of age or personal distinction); 1.34.8 (Tanaquil); 1.46.2, 7 (Tullia); 1.57.6, 58.4, 6, 7 (Lucretia); 2.13.6, 11 (Cloelia); 2.40.1 (Volumnia); 2.40.9 (Veturia); 3.26.9 (Racilia); 3.50 (Verginia); 4.4.10 ("woman" cited in proposal for right of *conubium*); 5.4.11 (Ap. Claudius Crassus refers indirectly to Helen, for the sake of whom "a city was once besieged by the whole of Greece for ten years"; cf. 1.1.1); 5.21.11 (women from Veii); 5.33.3 (wife of Ar(r)uns); 5.40.10 (wife of L. Albinius); 8.24.17 (Cleopatra and Olympias); 10.23.3, 10 (women attending religious rites of Patricia Pudicitia); 22.52.7, 54.3 (Busa); 24.22.8, 24.2 (Damarata); 24.26.1, 9 (Heraclea); 26.12.17 (wife of Campanian deserter); 26.33.8 (Vestia Oppia and Pacula Cluvia); 26.49.11-16 (the wife of Mandonius, the daughters of Indibilis, and other young unmarried women); 26.50.1-14 (the fiancé of Alluccius); 29.29.12 (marriage of alliance between the Massylian ruler Mezetulus and the daughter of Hannibal's sister); 30.3.4, 7.8, 11.3, 12.11, 15, 15.5, 7 (Sophini(s) ba); 32.40.11 (women robbed by Nabis of money, clothing, and jewellery); 34.1.3 (reference to "woman" in the *lex Oppia*); 34.2.2, 3, 6, 7, 8 11, 14, 3.1, 8, 4.1, 6, 7, 10, 15, 18, 5.5, 12, 13 (women in M. Porcius Cato's speech against repeal of the *lex Oppia*); 34.6.1, 8, 10, 7.3, 4, 5, 9, 11, 12 (women in L. Valerius's speech against repeal of the *lex Oppia*); 34.25.5 (Apega, wife of Nabis); 38.24.2, 4, 8, 10 (wife of the chieftain Orgiago); 38.57 (Cornelia Maior and Cornelia Minor, mother of the Gracchi); 39.11.4, 7, 12.4 (Sulpicia); 39.11.5

(Aebutia); 39.10.2, 12.2, 13.1, 3, 19.6 (Hispala Faecenia); 39.14.7 (Bacchanalian priestesses); 39.8.5, 7, 13.8, 10, 14, 15.9, 12, 17.5, 18.6 (Bacchanalian
adherents); 39.43.2-4 (*scortum* from Placentia); 40.4.13 (Theoxena); 40.37.6
(Quarta Hostilia); 41.25.6 (Orthobula) – and in relation to sacrificial notices
and prodigy lists that comment *inter alia* on the biological sex of infants or
animals pertinent to particular items (8 instances) – 22.1.14 (hen); 25.12.14,
27.37.11, 43.13.3 (heifers); 27.11.5, 27.37.6, 31.12.6 (children of uncertain
sex); 28.11.3 (lamb) –, Livy includes 37 references to the terms *femina(e)* and
mulier(es) at these points in AUC history: 1.29.5 (Latin women cry plain-
tively as Alba Longa falls); 1.34.2, 3 (wife of Arruns, brother of Lucumo [L.
Tarquinius Priscus], son of Demaratus of Corinth); 5.42.4 (Roman women
and boys shriek as the Gauls occupy Rome); 7.13.6 (comparison of cowardice in battle to the cowering of women behind a rampart); 3.5.14 (crowd of
men and women fill all Rome's temples, imploring the protection of the gods
from the invasion of the Aequians); 3.68.8 (T. Quinctius Capitolinus refers to
the proverbial quarrelsomeness of women when framing his argument that
individual desires must be subordinated in order to achieve *concordia*); 6.3.4
(women and children weep as they process in exile from Sutrium, a city allied
with Rome under Etruscan siege); 6.25.9 (crowds of Roman men, women and
children go about their daily lives unencumbered by fear after the Tusculans
sue for peace); 7.6.5 (crowds of Roman men and women throw offerings and
fruit after M. Curtius' *devotio*); 9.17.16 (to exemplify the hallmarks of a fee-
ble military opponent, Livy refers to Darius III "trailling women and eunuchs
after him, and weighed down with gold and purple trappings"); 9.19.7 (alleged
saying of Alexander of Epirus, the Molossian, referring to the quality of his
Asian opponents: "and he would have said that he had fought wars against
women"); 10.28.4 (comparison of the courage in battle against Roman soldiers of Samnite men to women); 22.7.11 (Roman *matronae* wandering about
the streets after Trasimene); 22.55.3 (Roman women lament in the aftermath
of Cannae as a state of panic takes hold); 22.60.2 (Roman women mingling
in the Forum with men after Cannae); 24.8.11 (wife of Otacilius, daughter of
Q. Fabius' sister); 24.41.7 (wife of Hannibal, from Castulo in Spain); 25.1.7
(crowds of Roman women sacrifice in the forum and Capitol, offering prayers
to the gods); 26.9..7 (Roman women wail in private houses and *matronae*
pour into the street after Hannibal crosses the Volturnus); 26.36.5 (senatorial women supporting the Roman treasury); 27.31.8 (Polycratia, wife of Aratus, a leading Achaean); 27.45.7 (Roman men and women line the route of
C. Claudius Nero's forced march north to Picenum, uttering vows and prayers
and words of praise); 27.51.9 (Roman men and women observe thanksgiv-
ing for the victory at the battle of the Metaurus); 28.19.13 (Spanish women
supplying arms to men defending Castulo); 28.20.6 (Spanish men, women,
and children massacred by Roman soldiers at Illitirgi); 28.22.6, 23.2 (Spanish
women and children massacred by their own people in Astapa); 29.17.15-16
(A Locrian ambassador exploits the rape and abuse of *matronae*, *virgines*, and
mulieres in order to highlight the wartime experiences of his people); 29.28.3
(Carthaginian men, women, and children fill up all roads in every direction after
Rome lands in northern Africa); 31.44.4 (removal by Athenians of representations of Philip and his male and female ancestors); 33.21.4 (wife of Attalus of
Pergamon); 35.26.5 (wife of the Antigonid Craterus); 35.47.5, 6 (Apama, wife
of Amynander, daughter of Alexander of Megalopolis; Apama, wife of Seleucus
I, daughter of Apama I and Amynander); 32.21.24 (reference to daughters and
wives in the speech of Aristaenus, a praetor of the Achaean League; in relation to Philip V of Macedon's abduction of the wife of Aratus); 32.36.10 (wife

of T. Quinctius Flamininus); 36.24.10 (Aetolian women, children, and non-combatants gather in the citadel as Roman forces sack Heraclea); 37.5.1 (Aetolian women bringing weapons and stones to defend the walls of Lamia); 38.21.14 (Gallic women unfit to bear arms at the battle of Mt. Olympus); 38.22.8 (Gallic men, women, and children are wounded in Rome's assault on Mt. Olympus); 38.36.5 (Campanians granted right to take Roman citizens as wives in plebiscite of 188 BCE); 39.14.7 (Pergamene women viewing Diophanes from the city walls); 39.44.2 (M. Porcius Cato's censorship directs women's jewels, dresses, and vehicles worth more than 15.000 asses to be listed at ten times their value); 39.49.8 (Messenean men, women, and children pour out to see the hostage Greek general Philopoemen); 40.38.6 (deportation to Samnium of Ligurian freemen, women, and children); 41.11.5 (Histrian women and children massacred on the walls of Nesactium); 42.5.3 (wife of Perseus); 42.16.8, 9 (wife of Attalus I Soter's brother, Attalus II Philadelphus); 42.29.3 (wife of Prusias, king of Bithynia); 43.10.5 (Illyrian/Macedonian women raise a din as Perseus approaches the city walls); 44.32.3 (wife and mother of Gentius, ruler of the Ardiaei); 44.32.11 (Macedonian women bringing provisions to the soldiers' camp near Pydna); 45.24.11 (Reference in speech of Astymedes to Rhodian men and women surrendering themselves and their wealth to Rome).

47 For discussion, see Wiedermann (1983: 162–169) and Harvey (1985).
48 See Mauersberger (1968: cols. 406–408).
49 Levene (2010: 126–163).
50 The extant writing of each historian constitutes only about a quarter of the original work.
51 On the *Periochae*, see Begbie (1967); Stadter (1972); and Brunt (1980).
52 Liv. 1.58-59; Dion. Hal. *Ant. Rom.* 4.64-84. Lost sources: e.g., the history of Fabius Pictor (Dion. Hal. *Ant. Rom.* 4.64); a *praetexta* of L. Accius, possibly the *Brutus* (Cic. *Sest.* 123); cf. Varro, *Ling.* 6.7, 7.72.
53 Liv. 1.47. On the historian's representation of Tullia Minor and her role in the death of her father and the usurpation of his throne by her husband, see Chapter 4.
54 Liv. 1.49.
55 Liv. 1.53.4: *minime arte Romana fraude ac dolo adgressus est* ("[L. Tarquinius] resorted to the policy, so unlike a Roman, of deceit and trickery").
56 Liv. 1.53.1-10.
57 Liv. 1.56.4-6, 9–12.
58 Liv. 1.56.7-8.
59 Liv. 1.9.6: *animi dissimulans* ("concealing [his] resentment"); 1.8.1: *populi unius corpus* ("a single body politic"). On Romulus and his actions in relation to ensuring Rome's future, see Ch. 2.
60 Liv. 1.57.1-5.
61 On the relationship between official Roman sacerdotal colleges and sacred sodalities and those fraternal associations which in the early republican period appear to have been identified with various families (*gentes*), see Kloppenborg and Wilson (1996: 17).
62 Liv. 1.57.6: *forte … incidit de uxoribus mentio.*
63 On the one hand, Roman historiography presupposes the existence of the past which it claims the authority to present. Complementarily, the particular category of historical writing within which Livy's AUC may be situated represents a literary amalgam of annalistic (and therefore discursive) and narrative (in other words, descriptive; or, in a structural sense, quasi-fictional) historiography. While these methodological and conceptual elements impose self-evident tensions, at the same time one of the rewarding by-products of reading a

literary composition like AUC history that incorporates notions of truth-telling and storytelling is discovering how such a work reflects and reinterprets the world around it. In this light, Livy's representation of men and women – what might be termed gendered historiography – can be understood (and will be characterised in the present study) as *mimetic*. On mimesis as a strategy for representing reality in Western literature, see Auerbach (1953); on tragedy and history as mimetic genres indebted to epic, see Rutherford (2010).

64 Liv. 1.57.7.
65 Liv. 1.57.9; cf. Columella, *Rust.* 12.9 (which represents female disdain for supervising wool working as a moral failing; Juv. 6.287-91 (idealising the industry associated with Lucretia's hands, hardened by Tuscan wool); Suet. *Aug.* 64.2 (which links the concepts of *pudicitia* and *lanificium*); Plut. *Quaest. Rom.* 30 (recalling a bronze image of Gaia Caecilia with sandals and a distaff, signifying her industry and her domestic duty); *CIL*1².1211 = *ILS* 8403: *domum servavit, lanam fecit* ("[Claudia] looked after the home and she made wool"); *CIL* VI 10230 l.28: *modestia probitate pudicitia opsequio lanificio diligentia fide* ("in modesty, decency, chastity, obedience, woolworking, diligence and loyalty"); *CIL* 6 1527: *domestica bona pudicitiae obsequi comitatis facilitates lanificiis tuis adsiduitatis cur memorem* ("Why should I mention your domestic virtues: modesty, obedience, affability, good nature, industry in woolwork?"). For the significance of wool working, see Dixon (2001: 117–119) and Chrystal (2017: 20–21).
66 According to this outcome – and as the competition is designed to satisfy the needs of elite male rivalry – it is legitimate under the rules established by the drunken young soldiers to regard the husband of the most exemplary wife as the *victor* of the contest.
67 By naming Helen and outlining the post-siege histories of Aeneas and Antenor in the opening sentences of his AUC narrative, Livy has made explicit the link between his account of Rome's foundation and the Greek epic cycle. Livy's association between Troy and Rome allows the reader to draw a connection between this element of Lucretia's story and the episode of the contest of wives (Aphrodite, Hera, and Athena) for the prize of a golden apple addressed "To the Fairest."
68 *Pudicitia*. On *pudicitia*'s association with married women, public display, and the negotiation of the boundaries of social status, and its role as a key civic virtue of Roman men, see Langlands (2006). *Regni cupido*. See Liv. 1.4-6 for the conflict between Romulus and Remus over the site of Rome, the foundational episode relating to "that ancestral vice, greed for monarchy" (1.4.3: *avitum malum, regni cupido*).
69 Livy's representation of Sextus Tarquinius reflects the historian's ongoing concern with the moral aspects of political issues. Like his father before him, so, by his words and deeds, the king's son illuminates the corrupting effect of individual or civic power and the decline of political and social institutions. On moral historiography in Sallust, Livy, Tacitus, and Ammianus Marcellinus, see Mellor (1999: 196–198).
70 Liv. 1.59.
71 Liv. 1.58.5. For analysis of the *iudicium domesticum* to clarify if its jurisdiction, restricted to the domestic sphere, reflected whether it was a true court or an advisory body within the family, see Bosch (2011); on the evidence for the existence of a domestic court in the republican period, see Winkel (2015: 16).
72 Liv. 1.58.7.
73 Liv. 1.58.7-8.
74 Liv. 1.58.11.

75 Liv. 1.58.10.
76 Liv. 1.58.7-8, 10-11.
77 Liv. 1.58.10: *nec ulla deinde inpudica Lucretiae exempio vivet.*
78 Liv. 1.57.9: *regias nurus.*
79 According to Dionysius Halicarnassus (*Ant. Rom.* 2.12) and Pomponius (*Dig.* 1.2.2.15), the *tribunus celerum* was the commander of the Celeres, the king's bodyguard.
80 See Fig. 1.2.14.
81 Liv. 1.7.8-9 (Carmenta); 1.19.5 (Egeria); see Fig. 1.2 (nos. 6 and 10, respectively).
82 Val. Max. 1.2.1; Ov. *Fast.* 3.154; 4.669; *Met.* 15.482; Verg. *Aen.* 7.763, 775; Juv. 3.12.
83 Liv. 1.19.1: *[Numa] iure eam legibusque ac moribus de integro condere parat.*
84 Liv. 1.19.5: *qui cum descendere ad animos sine aliquo commento miraculin non posset, simulat sibi cum dea Egeria congressus nocturnos esse; eius se monitu, quae acceptissima diis essent sacra instituere, sacerdotes suos cuique deorum praeficere.*
85 Liv. 1.7.8: *venerabilis vir miraculo litterarum, rei novae inter rudes artium homines, venerabilior divinitate credita Carmentae matris, quam fatiloquam ante Sibyllae in Italiam adventum miratae eae gentes fuerant.*
86 Liv. 1.7.7.
87 Other references to Carmenta: Ov. *Fast.* 461–542; Plut. *Quaest. Rom.* 56 (= *Mor.* 278); Serv. *Aen.* 8.51; Solin. 1.10.13; Hyg. *Fab.* 277.
88 Aetiological items: Egeria – Numa's religious reforms, including the institution of the *flamines* and the appointment of Vestal Virgins; Carmenta – the establishment of the cult of Hercules at the Ara Maxima.
89 Liv. 1.19.6-20.7.
90 Liv. 1.21.3: *lucus erat, quem medium ex opaco specu fons perenni rigabat aqua. quo quia se persaepe Numa sine arbitris velut ad congressum deae inferebat, Camenis eum lucum sacravit, quod earum ibi concilia cum coniuge sua Egeria essent.* On the Camenae as Muses, see Liv. Andron. ap. Gell. *NA* 18.9.5; Hor. *Carm. Saec.* 62; Verg. *Ecl.* 3.59, 7.19; Hor. *Carm.* 2.16.38; Columella, *Rust.* 2.2.7; on the grove Numa devoted to the Muses in the vicinity of Rome before the Porta Capena, see Vitruv. 8.3.1; for a temple in the same place, see Plin. 34.5.10.
91 The myth of Hercules and Cacus (Liv. 1.7.4-14): Evander, the king of Pallantium, stands in judgement over Hercules, who clubbed to death Cacus, a shepherd so taken by the beauty of the cattle the hero had pastured nearby that he stole them. Cacus' fellow shepherds accuse Hercules of murder, but Evander recognizes Hercules as a great hero and decrees that the people must worship him, whereupon Hercules builds an altar for that purpose. In Livy's version of the story, it is only the intervention of the king that turns Hercules from a murderer into a hero, and Cacus is a rustler of cattle who sets the stage for the state's imposition of civilised law and order. Here Livy's historiographical strategy establishes a potential threat to the stability of Pallantine society (accusation of murder levelled against Hercules by the uncivilized neighbouring pastoral community), which can only be resolved by Evander (respected widely due to his kinship with Carmenta). Acknowledging his mother's prophecy foretelling that Hercules should be added to the number of the gods, and that an altar should be dedicated to him in the place which the nation one day to be the most powerful on earth should call the Greatest Altar, Evander delivers the conditions by which Rome's eventual foundation is assured.
92 Romulus' constitutional measures: magisterial emblems (Liv. 1.8.1-3); right of asylum (Liv. 1.8.4-6); creation of the Senate (Liv. 1.8.5-7).

93 Numa's reforms: adjustment of the ritual calendar (Liv. 1.19.6-7); appointment of the *flamines* to maintain newly instituted cults (Liv. 1.20.1-2); recruitment of six virgins to supervise the cult of Vesta and maintenance of the sacred fire (Liv. 1.20.3); inception of the priestly college of the *Salii* (Liv. 1.20.4); creation of the pontificate (Liv. 1.20.5-6); installation of an altar to Jupiter Elicius (Liv. 1.20.7); foundation of shrines to Fides and Egeria (Liv. 1.21.3-4); and introduction of the rite of the Argei (Liv. 1.21.5).

94 Liv. 24.4.1-7.12; 21.1-26.16.

95 Liv. 24.4.3: *huic consilio eius summa ope obstitere filiae, nomen regium penes puerum futurum ratae, regimen rerum omnium penes se virosque suous Adranodorum et Zoippum, qui tutorum primi relinquebantur.*

96 Liv. 24.22.8: *inflata adhuc regiis animis ac muliebri spiritu.*

97 Liv. 24.22.8-10.

98 Liv. 24.22.8, 11.

99 Liv. 24.24.2: *nunc illud esse tempus occupandi res, dum turbata omnia nova atque incondite libertate essent, dum regiis stipendiis pastus obversaretur miles, dum ab Hannibale missi duces adsueti militibus iuvare possent incepta.*

100 Liv. 24.25.1-7.

101 Liv. 24.25.6: *qui cum ordine omnia edocuisset: principium coniurationis factun ab Harmoniae Gelonis filiae nuptiis.*

102 Liv. 24.25.8-9: *ea natura multitudinis est: aut servit humiliter aut superbe dominator; libertatem, quae media est, nec suscipere modice nec habere sciunt; et non ferme desunt irarum indulgentes ministry, qui avidos atque intemperantes suppliciorum animos ad sanguinem et caedes.*

103 Liv. 23.30.11-12.

104 Liv. 24.4.1-4.

105 Liv. 24.4.5-5.14.

106 Examples of non-Roman women portrayed by Livy in negative terms include: *scortum* from Campana (Liv. 26.12.16-20); young woman (*muliercula*) from Tarentum (27.15.9-11); wife of Nabis (Liv. 32.10); Theoxena (Liv. 40.4).

107 Liv. 24.22.8: *sed evocatum eum ab legatis Damarata uxor, filia Hieronis, inflata adhuc regiis animis ac muliebri spiritu, admonet saepe usurpatae Dionysi tyranni vocis, qua pedibus tractum, non insidentem equo relinquere tyrannidem dixerit debere.*

108 End of the royal family of Hiero (Liv. 24.25–26); Sack of Syracuse (Liv. 25.31).

109 On the origin and construction of AUC history: Wille (1973); Ampolo (1983); Forsythe (1999). On Livy's literary style: Burck (1934); Walsh (1963); Luce (1977).

2

GENDERED COLLECTIVES
IN LIVY

The *agmen mulierum* and independent
female demonstrations in AUC history

2.1 Hortensia, the demonstration of 43
BCE, and the extent of matronal authority in
Roman public life and patriarchal culture

On 27 November 43 BCE one of Rome's plebeian tribunes, P. Titius, held
an assembly of the people, at which he proposed and carried a law through
which a board of three for the establishment of the state (*triumviri reipublicae constituendae*) was formally put in place. This triumvirate comprised
M. Aemilius Lepidus, M. Antonius, and C. Iulius Caesar Octavianus and the
law promulgated that day confirmed what had been agreed earlier on a small
island in the midst of a river near Bononia: that they should together hold
consular *imperium* and appoint magistrates for a period of 5 years.[1] The
triumvirs also instituted what are known as proscriptions, identifying, and
officially condemning declared enemies of the state, with a list of 130 names
of those to be killed being posted on the night following the passing of the
lex Titia, to be followed shortly afterwards by another 150.[2] According to
our sources for the initial period of the proscriptions,[3] the *triumviri* were
required to supply the deficiency in monies raised from the morally circumscribed, ill-attended, and unprofitable auctions of proscribed property. To
do so, they saw fit to publish an edict demanding that 1400 wealthy *matronae* declare the value of their properties and contribute whatever proportion
the triumvirs might designate. Any false declaration was to be punished by
a fine, and rewards were promised to informers. It would seem that this
widespread and compulsory property valuation and individually assessed
contribution to the expenses of civil war did not find favour with the targets
of the triumviral edict. We are told that the women concerned decided to
appeal to the female relatives of the triumvirs; specifically, Octavia, Julia and
Fulvia, Octavianus's sister, and Antonius's mother and wife.

It is easy to locate in this episode symmetries of situation and cultural
frame distinguishing the contexts of these women and the experiences of
certain women in *Ab Urbe Condita* (AUC) history;[4] not to mention of a
woman whose story is memorialised on the funeral inscription known as the
laudatio "Turiae."[5] Indeed, it is tempting to identify in Livy's representation

of collective female action in Books 1, 2, and 24 the ghosts of women who, according to Appian, transgressed significant structural and ideological protocols[6] by pushing their way to the magistrates' tribunal in the forum to have their case heard through their chosen spokeswoman Hortensia.

Here, I do not think that it matters as much if we regard Appian's narrative of these events, our sole surviving source of any historical quality, as the product of excerption or critical reproduction. In the same way that Livy relies on particular sources that only survive today in fragmentary form in his own or other historical texts, Appian is thought to have grounded his account of the proscriptions in the lost histories of C. Asinius Pollio, which treated the period from 60 BCE to the battle of Philippi in 42 BCE. This provides an encouraging degree of surety to his claims for the number, position, motivation, conduct, and relations of these Roman women. Born in Alexandria in the last years of the 1st century CE and reaching the highest distinction in his native city, Appian must have been a member of the privileged Greek possessing class. But his predilection for more social and economic material than most historiographers suggests that this talented and well-connected man would have been aware not just of the varied roles played by Roman women in the city where he practised law and eventually gained the *dignitas* of procurator under Antoninus Pius. The influence and marital uses of women at the Ptolemaic court[7] and of the Roman period up until the middle of the 2nd century CE[8] would have been known to him, and we may assume that his consciousness of and experiences with the lives of women in a culturally heterogeneous social environment like Alexandria permitted him to represent the protesting Roman *matronae* of 43 BCE in a distinctive context.

Dwelling on those factors which underscore Appian's capacity to provide a plausible account of this episode speaks favourably to the probability that Livy – a contemporary of the events of 43 BCE – had access to first hand testimony of what transpired.[9] In his brief biographical profile of the historian, Ogilvie asserts that Livy was "predisposed to a narrow minded and somewhat *bourgeois* detachment from the political struggles of his time."[10] But the fact that Livy is known to have enjoyed a relationship with a former triumvir – the princeps Augustus himself, no less, who designated him a *Pompeianus*, suggesting a forthright and healthy freedom of thought – and encouraged a young Claudius to write history,[11] casts an instructive light on the discriminating and knowledgeable eye Livy could bring to bear on episodes similar to the matronal demonstration led by Hortensia and the vigour and integrity with which he will have sought to compose his account of such events.

In relation to the events of 43 BCE, Appian's narrative clearly draws out the adverse reaction of the triumvirs to assertive women challenging magisterial authority and subverting conventional decision-making protocols by making public speeches and questioning the actions of the government. But it also makes very clear the strongly voiced support of the people assembled in the forum. On the face of the evidence, this comprised at the very least popular displeasure at the dismissive attitude of the individuals recently elected to refit the state and their endorsement of rough treatment of elite female citizens of that state. In the context of Hortensia's passionate appeal, we may infer popular disapproval at summary rejection by the triumvirs of a reasonable argument based on normative principles of family, character, and feminine nature against the imposition of a proscriptive tax on women's property. We learn that Lepidus, Antonius, and Octavianus deferred the question of elite Roman women paying taxes for a civil war and thereafter redistributed the ambit of property valuation across a far more heterogeneous population of Roman citizens, as well as foreigners, freedmen, or priests of any nation. This reaction lends some credence to the claim of Octavianus in the opening verses of his very public declaration of achievements and expenses: "Wars, both civil and foreign, I undertook throughout the world, on sea and lead, and when victorious I spared all citizens who sued for pardon."[12] In the same light as Hortensia making terms with the 20-year-old heir to Caesar from a position of relative strength, so it is easier to imagine the vivid point of reference on which Livy could focus as he drafted narrative episodes about elite, influential women, accompanied by large numbers of other women of similar status and social condition, negotiating with powerful, authoritative men.

This clarifies the observation of Hemelrijk that the all-female demonstration in Appian's narrative and others of its type reflected "an independent status hierarchy of women, comparable to that of upper-class men but obtained by different means."[13] Their actions may comprise an expression of class- as opposed to gender-consciousness implicit to their defence of a traditional elite female right: exemption from state taxation. Nonetheless, by compelling the triumvirs to deflect the bulk of the tax burden to the possessing component of the male population, these Roman *matronae* exert significant authority on their own behalf. It would seem that one did not necessarily need to share the honours, military commands, or government of a male-prominent society to evince comparable influence. Nor was one condemned merely to share vicariously in the *dignitas* of significant male others when pursuing a commitment to a particular status and family structure. In the latter regard, Daube identifies the kind of civil disobedience shown by the *matronae* as belonging to a type "committed entirely with a view to the welfare of those who are being obeyed."[14] Yet the subtle shift in the disequilibrium of social relations accomplished by the non-normative interactions and self-possessed intentions of these women[15] should not be re-appropriated solely by patriarchal interests. Quintilian reported that the speech of Hortensia delivered in the presence of the triumvirs had been published and read not only in praise of her sex.[16] So we may infer that the independent stand taken by "Hortensius's daughter" (the Quintilianic formulation) and the multitude of female demonstrators for whom she spoke encompassed more than the reinforcement of social differentiation and male *dignitas*. Here, it will be instructive to consider the extent to which Livy formulates his depictions of elite Roman women in similar episodes of public confrontation and negotiation with politically powerful men according to the conditions under which women in late republican times engaged in expressions of civil disobedience.

That adoption by elite Roman women of a pattern of activity associated with the competitive politics of male identity was not exceptional is suggested by the degree of affront occasioned by Fulvia's rejection of their appeal and the triumviral reaction to their public demonstrations.[17] The women pursued a conventional channel of dialogue and submitted their case to other women of like status perceived as exercising influence in matters pertaining to the responsibilities of governance administered by male kin. Only after another woman abrogated the process of submission and negotiation did the *matronae* seek redress in a less traditional manner. It is interesting to note that Appian's narrative paints an analogous relationship between the joint nature of triumviral rule and the need for consensus of opinion and activity among their female relatives. Winning support from Octavianus's sister and Antonius's mother was still inadequate in achieving a reassessment of the property valuation decision without Fulvia's agreement. Appian's attribution of resentment as the catalyst for the women's transgression of bounded magisterial space enhances the mimetic parallelism of the exchange. The repercussions for the Roman state of aggravated affective and social relations among aristocratic males like Lepidus, Antonius, and Octavianus reflect the comparability of male and female interventions in public space in response to personal indignity.

However, while this notion provides important contextual understanding in relation to Livy's depiction of matronal demonstrations in his early history of Rome's foundation and during the mid-republican period of military conflict and expansion in the Mediterranean, the thwarted attempt under orders from the triumvirs by the lictors to clear the *matronae* from the tribunal reminds us that the similarities between incidents of male and female civil disruption only extended so far.[18] In other words, it may have been acceptable for elite women to apply for remedy by way of other influential women equivalent in status, but clearly this kind of access to avenues of decision-making did not extend to blatant overstepping of spatial and ideological boundaries. Threatening physical ill-treatment of the *matronae* emphasises the problematic aspects of civil disobedience by elite Roman *matresfamiliae*. What otherwise would have remained strategically private – the existence of an alternative, interdependent hierarchy of status, identity, and influence explicitly gendered and radically effective – had spilled over into the heterogeneous and far less strictly stratified streets of the city. Any remaining pretence of male claims for sole resort to the discourse of power relations was now extinguished, or at the very least severely compromised. Just as the *matronae* resented Fulvia's dismissive attitude (her *hubris*)[19] to their circumstances, so the triumvirs were angered by a public display of that assured, declamatory, and emphatic female behaviour well-known to them but usually delimited to contexts less open to the popular gaze.[20]

Though they might have assumed a supreme authority overarching consuls, provincial governors, and even the law, the triumvirs suspended normal apparitorial process in ordering their lictors to remove married women from the spaces around Caesar's *rostra* at the western end of the *forum Romanum*.[21] Imagining 36 attendants, each wielding bundles of rods[22] against 1400 women inured to the vicissitudes of civil conflict and vigorously disposed to assert their claims for consideration affords us a glimpse of the thin line between outrage and insecurity underpinning the action of the triumvirs. It was a moment of clarity so much more visceral to a contemporary popular audience and a conceptual awareness that would have resonated with similarly particular force, one can only imagine, when reading in Livy's contemporary account of AUC history about how elite Roman women contested traditional male actions.

The other mark of Roman society's structural fragility revealed by the forcible removal of *matronae* from the Forum is the conceptual equivalent of the psychological uncertainty already inferred: magisterial *potestas* over against matronal *auctoritas*. The reason for the latter's demonstration of disaffected solidarity was as much as anything else Fulvia's unexpected disregard for elite female influence and prestige in the expression of viewpoint, intention or desire. What we are privy to, in a moment of grave misjudgement verging on panic, is the highly inappropriate contestation of official male legal power and unofficial female aristocratic validity – a confrontation resulting in abuse of the law and extraordinary exercise of customary persuasion. Instructively, this response is very far removed from the episodes where Livy represents similarly fraught civil exchanges: the intercession of Sabine women on the battlefield between military forces of Roman and Sabine men, the delegation of Veturia-Volumnia (or Volumnia-Vergilia) to Cn. Marcius Coriolanus at the head of a Volscian army, and opposition to the *lex Oppia*.[23]

At this point, it will repay our attention to consider the oblique narrative and explicit rhetorical references in Appian's account to specific social relations expressed in gender in distinct spatial contexts within the city. Here, to employ a conceptual framework, we can compare the integration of categories of gender into urban space, along with other multiplicities of men and women's lives.[24] Appian tells us that the women affected by the edict of 43 BCE "resolved to appeal to the female relatives of the triumvirs."[25] In the words assigned to Hortensia, the *matronae* followed this course "as was appropriate for women of our rank who wished to make an appeal to you [i.e., to important state officials like the *triumuiri*]."[26] Taking this testimony at face value, we may attempt to draw a parallel between the role of the Roman aristocratic house in formal and informal male political activity[27] and the strategies deployed by the *matronae* within the same spaces.

We must first consider the manner in which the citizen population of Rome became aware of the proposition. If the triumvirs followed the same procedure which saw their intention to instigate a series of proscriptions passed into law, they will have put their proposal to a vote of the tribal assembly of the people (*comitia populi tributa*). This would imply that the *populus* was summoned by formal right of convocation (*ius agendi cum populo*) possessed by the triumvirs to gather in the inaugurated space of the forum known as the *comitium*. Presumably, this special convocation took place on a day when citizens could vote on political or criminal matters (*dies comitialis*), after auspices had been taken. Thus, even before pronouncement of the legislation to the assembly, news of an impending legal enactment would have circulated through constituent voting channels. Such news must have alarmed those members of the *populus* most at risk in the wake of the initial round of poorly subscribed auctions. Of course, we may not wish to place all of the *matronae* at the place of assembly. Nonetheless, it would have been very difficult indeed for them not to have learned of the import of the single item of legislation to be determined by the vote of the urban tribal group. This was especially so when the intervening period of 27 days between initial and final announcements of the assembly is taken into account. We know that the resolution of the *comitia* on this matter was not subject to formal ratification by whatever patrician senators remained in Rome before it became law.[28] Therefore, we may assume that the edict and the names of those women explicitly targeted by the triumvirs were then published in the forum and posted like the lists of the proscribed in many places in the city.[29]

In this context of extraordinary assembly and wildfire confirmation of financial exactions, we may reasonably situate Hortensia and an uncertain number of the 1400 women to be assessed under the provisions of the edict. Though impossible to confirm, the spokeswoman representing elite female interests in this regard may still have resided in or near the house of her deceased father Q. Hortensius Hortalus, now reasonably identified as the dwelling generally known as the house of Livia.[30] As the *mons Palatinus* was favoured as a place of residence for the possessing classes, we can safely locate a number of *matronae* under threat of property assessment in the same district. The buildings of the Imperial period may have fundamentally altered the road system of the Palatine and blotted out the remains of private houses in and around the hill. Still, we can expect communications among the affected female constituency of the Palatine community to be direct and easily facilitated.

Moreover, it would not have surprised the female relatives of the triumvirs mentioned in the sources to receive a deputation about the edict. Octavia, married at this time to C. Claudius Marcellus,[31] may be assumed to live in the same district as that in which she was born – if we locate her childhood in the same house in which Octavianus was born and where he lived for some time: "Ox Heads."[32] This was certainly a suitable accommodation for the sister of a triumvir and wife of an ex-consul. By the same token, Fulvia resided in the home of M. Antonius. Wherever Julia lived at this time,[33] we may again conjecture that she was not too far distant from the elite district of the city. Therefore, we may posit a month in which to contemplate, discuss, and prepare for a piece of legislation squarely aimed at their independent property interests. We may also adjust this to accommodate the immediate aftermath of the edict's publication and strategic notification of its target population. It is not too difficult to imagine a representative female legation traversing the north and west slopes of the Palatine, receiving a sympathetic hearing from Octavia and Julia, but turned away from Fulvia's door.[34]

In these negotiations among females of equal or nearly equal standing, we may recognise the practices of aristocratic competition and the role of patronage within Roman political relations usually allocated to the elite male population. This is not to say that the potential for elite women to exert influence through men did not exist until this point in time. In a late 21th-century synthesis of evidence regarding women in the Roman Empire, King argues that "[ancient Roman women's] political exclusion meant less after the decline in the roles of senate and assemblies."[35] This view would appear to explain the extant historiographical perspectives on the events of 42 BCE. With respect to the 2nd century CE Greek historian Appian, his long acquaintance with the importance of the Imperial family in the political sphere would have underwritten his perceptions about the level of female influence in earlier periods. This awareness is similarly apposite to the assessment of Valerius Maximus, whose prefacing remarks to his item on Hortensia's speech at first sight express his abhorrence at an apparently recent trend toward radical female intervention in the sphere of public assemblies. I suggest, however, that the phenomenon of women's influence[36] both in general terms and in the more specific realm of political relations impinged on male consciousness and compelled problematic tensions in male-authored discourses, especially in formulating responses to evidence for its enacted protocols and jurisdictions. These tensions and ambiguities may be seen to arise not so much due to the comparative rarity of female influence insofar as Valerius Maximus's Tiberian compendium of memorable deeds and sayings may imply, or its relatively late normalisation by the Severan period in the account of Appianus. Their existence can rather be traced to the transgression of customary boundaries differentiating the exercise of informal though in some cases equally effectual influence and formal, usually visible, and almost always male-prominent power.

Interestingly enough, and as a corollary, we may address the common observation that the representations of women who take a public role in sources on Roman history tend to be accompanied by allusions to female spite, treachery, or lack of self-control, like Valerius Maximus, or was intended to discredit the men associated with them, like Appian's, and even more so, Dio's portrayal of Fulvia, reinforcing by implication his view of Antonius.[37] Though apt, this viewpoint in no way discounts the fact of women's political action. Nor does it prevent us from considering this particular episode in Roman history as a manifestation of a pre-existing condition of Roman gender and class relations erupting momentarily to the surface during a period of historical discontinuity. In this regard, Livy's very early historiographical preoccupation with episodes of female intervention – over half a century prior to the publication of *factorum ac dictorum memorabilium libri XI*[38] – charted similar concerns about overt movements across well-established structural and ideological divides, whether in relation to military conflict between Rome and the Sabines, the threat of the city under siege by a Volscian army led by a Roman commander in exile, or the repeal of frumentary legislation prejudicial to the public status of Roman *matronae*. It is possible to determine from Livy's narrative that Roman society blurred the distinction between domestic and public spheres. The flexibility of *res publica* as a signifier of the state sufficiently illumines this notion. For Livy and, by implication, the weight of his readership, the dichotomy between female/domestic and male/public realms was discerned as of special interest. While it is difficult to ascertain the extent to which the historian identified distinctions between the desired/idealised and behavioural/normative values ascribed to social and political activity, the usefulness of the intervening space or female-prominent episode as a device for explicating and reinterpreting problematic elements of the received historical and cultural tradition is beyond question.

As an adjunct to this critical or reflexive quality of Livy's history, it is instructive to note the manner in which he questions or distorts specific personality types conventionally invoked as either portraying recognisable female traits or as performing the subordinate part of illustrating male virtues. The desire to reconfigure the revelation of female influence over realities other than the strictly domestic simply emphasises the general nature of the phenomenon. In the manner of a cybernetic feedback loop, this pretextual condition – the *feminarum auctoritas* in generations preceding late Republican representations – informed Livy's focus on legendary female interpositions, mediations, and negotiations. This focus in turn reflected male insecurities about social transformations in general and those previously regulated and unregulated social relations in particular.

Thus, Appian's comparatively positive standpoint on matronal demonstration may highlight the fact of Roman men behaving badly. But the manner in which the female relatives of the triumvirs are shown to admit or not other eminent women strongly suggests that the protocols of patronage, especially those of protection and prestige, were not the exclusive prerogative of important Roman men. And it was at this point that the informally assembled *matronae* would have realised that nothing short of radical intervention in the instrumentality of the state had the least chance of diverting the savage demands of the triumvirs from their thresholds. Fulvia's support for the acquisitive policy of her husband – implicit or otherwise, and apparent in her gesture of dismissal to the delegation of fellow-elite married women – effectively determined their next move. In a manner similar to the earlier foreshadowing of the assembly of the previous month, but perhaps far more urgent this time, word of Fulvia's response and its implications would have spread. By way of collaborating dependents and domestic slaves, not to mention direct exchange of information and intentions among peers, news may be imagined to have travelled throughout the Palatine community. Its dissemination should also be envisaged among the affected and sympathetic households in neighbouring districts, as well as those temporarily in residence on the fringes of the *suburbium*.

As we have seen, the *matronae* met with the 24-year-old Octavia and the 53-year-old Julia L. f.[39] and suffered exclusion from Fulvia's household. These meetings were more than likely prepared for over the period of three *nundinae* before the *comitia* ratifying the edict and took place in the days immediately following the decision and publication of the enactment and the associated catalogue of wealthy women. In the case of Antonius's mother and Octavianus's sister, the discussions took place in one or other of the flexible spaces comprising those areas of the late Republican aristocratic home given over to social interactions among men and women. Here we can see clearly that time and space, gender and status, constitute related categories of context and explanation underpinning any analysis of female participation in the domestic environments of late Republican Rome. To these, we may add what Livy often refers to as an *agmen* or *frequentia mulierum*, proceeding in this instance in concourse with an associated retinue of relatives, sympathetic acquaintances, dependent *clientelae*, and personal slaves – several thousand at the very least. This substantial throng can be imagined as descending to the Velabrum[40] or to the *sacra via*[41] and thence to the forum. Given the nature of festival activity in the urban environment, a female presence on the streets of Rome would have not been regarded as unusual.[42] But one as large and diverse as this must have provoked some comment as it made its way purposefully toward the heart of male-prominent space near the tribunal, and will almost certainly have resonated sufficiently in the civil memory of the city to provide the writer of AUC history with a contemporary *comparandum* by which to measure, negotiate, and articulate his representations of women coming up hard against male conduct in military and political contexts outside the traditional bounds of female intervention.

Unlike the approach taken in this chapter the analysis of episodes in AUC history incorporating representation of groups of women undertaking civil action of one kind or another will follow the chronological order set out according to Livy's annalistic structure. This variation in order aims to demonstrate the proposition aired in the introductory discussion: namely, the extent to which knowledge of historical personalities and events contemporary to the composition of the AUC – in this instance, the demonstration of Hortensia and Rome's *matronae* in 43 BCE – informed the content and representational strategies Livy employs to depict similar interventions of women in traditionally male-exclusive contexts in foundational and later republican Roman history. In addition, this chapter's chronological survey of Livy's gendered accounts of collective female demonstrations – the Sabine women in the midst of military action between Roman and Sabine forces; the mother and wife of the exiled general Coriolanus prior to the Volscian siege of Rome, and Rome's *matronae* advocating for repeal of the *lex Oppia* in 195 BCE – will follow the compositional trajectory adopted by Livy in order to bring to the surface the historiographical process of retrojection and how this might have been informed by contemporary historical episodes. In other words, while AUC history may be viewed (and was certainly composed) as a linear progression of cause and effect, and the historical "truth" observed and represented in the AUC is understood (unless expressly questioned) to have a corresponding factual reference extracted from literary, documentary, or epigraphic sources, Livy's annalistic monument is also a counter-time product or fabrication of a later literary retrojection. Therefore, setting out in chronological order each of the episodes where elite Roman (or qua-si-Roman, in the case of the Sabine) women intervene in the male world of politics and the battlefield will not only reinforce the structural paradigm of gendered Livian historiography already identified but also provide a sense of the impact which events of the late republic have on Livy's representation of women in early Roman history.

2.2 The Sabine women: defenders of the patriarchal order?

The section of narrative immediately prior to Livy's depiction of the Sabine women treats Rome's destiny as a history of the body in various guises. Romulus can only unite the people into a single body under the rule of law if he venerates his own body by adopting emblems of authority. The body of the community is united through sacral transformation of the *conditor*.

> Romulus called his people to a council. As nothing could unit them into one political body but the observance of common laws and customs, he gave them a body of laws … and he called into his service twelve lictors … a class of public officers … borrowed from the same people from whom the *sella curulis* and the *toga praetexta* were adopted.[43]

This body history may be rendered in schematic fashion (Table 2.1).

Noteworthy in this regard is the fact that Romulus' personal status – and the greatness of the city he has founded – is markedly differentiated from the nature of the *unius corpus*.[44]

> [Romulus'] next care was to secure an addition to the population that the size of the city might not be a source of weakness. It had been the ancient policy of the founders of cities to get together a

Table 2.1 The corpus of *res Romana*

Body of the FOUNDER
(lictores duodecim, sella curulis, toga praetexta).
>
Body of the CITY
  Liv. 1.8.4: "the city was growing by the extension of its walls in various
  directions" *(crescebat interim urbs munitionibus alia atque alia adpetendo)*
>
Body of the COMMUNITY
  Liv. 1.8.4-5: "in anticipation of its future population ... [Romulus] opened a place
  of refuge" (*in spem futurae multitudinis ... asylum aperit*)
>
Body POLITIC
  Liv. 1.8.7: "[Romulus] created a hundred senators ... who were called 'fathers' ...
  and their descendants were called 'patricians'" (*centum creat senatores ... qui
  creari patres ... patriciique progenies ... appellati*)

> multitude of people of obscure and low origin and then to spread
> the fiction that they were the children of the earth. In accordance
> with this policy, Romulus opened a place of refuge on the spot
> where, as you go down from the Capitol, you find an enclosed space
> between two groves. A promiscuous crowd of freemen and slaves,
> eager for change, fled thither from the neighbouring states. This was
> the first accession of strength to the nascent greatness of the city.[45]

Livy characterises the people as "rustic" in kind, "miscellaneous" in degree,
and "without distinction of bond or free." This "obscure and lowly multitude" requires an imposition of order (legislative and narrative). Equally
problematic is the reminder of falsification or invention associated with
autochthonous foundation.[46] Juxtaposed with the reality of Rome's aborigi-
nal population,[47] the premeditated ruse leading to the capture of the Sabine
women seems intended as a structural parallel. Here a question arises.
Livy's purpose would appear to include a representation of the nascent *urbs
condita* (divinely sanctioned and legally constituted) which emphasises its
humilitas and *muliebritas*, that is, "abject" unification and "feminine" *concordia*. Thus, narrative tensions are firmly in place before the intersection of
gendered historiographical criteria is initiated.

To set the scene, Livy establishes that the prolongation of the Roman state
is conditional on the presence or want of women.

> The Roman State had now become so strong that it was a match
> for any of its neighbours in war, but its greatness threatened to last
> for only one generation, since through the absence of women there
> was no hope of offspring, and there was no right of intermarriage
> with their neighbours.[48]

72

Only by the provision of offspring in the context of intermarriage (*conubium*) will Rome achieve continuity and alliance. Posterity through regional affinity and military association is uppermost in the minds of Romulus and his designated senate. Confusion and impatience ensue. Ambiguity arises from the solicitation of envoys sent to seek the privilege of *conubium*.

> As to the origin of Rome, it was well known that whilst it had received divine assistance, courage and self-reliance were not wanting. There should, therefore, be no reluctance for men to mingle their blood with their fellow-men.[49]

By acknowledging Romulus' divine lineage as authentic and equating this "fact" with the *virtus* of Roman origins, the king's messengers disavow any claim that Rhea Silvia might have to parenthood. However, this implicit reinforcement of the Vestal's absence stresses the transmundane nature of Rome, engendering distrust and fear.

Strangely enough, the suggestion that the new city had opened a sanctuary for women as well as for men earns the ire of Rome's young men.

> Nowhere did the envoys meet with a favourable reception. Whilst their proposals were treated with abuse, there was at the same time a general feeling of alarm at the power so rapidly growing in their midst. Usually they were dismissed with the question, "whether they had opened an asylum for women, for nothing short of that would secure for them inter-marriage on equal terms." The Roman youth could hardly tolerate such insults, and matters began to look like an appeal to force.[50]

It is difficult to understand at first why this imputation embodies an insult so demeaning that the state would undoubtedly begin to see violence. Perhaps it is incompatible (in Livy's eyes) that the perpetuation of Roman lineage should be contingent on a *conubium* between equals; that is, just as the city's male composition is defined as "lowliest beginnings,"[51] so Rome's neighbours infer that those given asylum should propagate among their own kind. Here, Livy squarely addresses the ambivalent tradition of *nobilitas* in the archaic AUC context. Only a partial reconciliation of origins and exposition is possible. The reality of *origines Romanae* is exposed without dissimulation, but the narrator focusses attention on the counterpoint between the rationale underpinning rejection of Rome's requests by her neighbours and the aggravated response of an aggrieved population of young adults.

The disturbing ramifications of a marriage between equals of lowly status are left unexplored at this stage. Nonetheless, they simmer below the textual surface, only to erupt at equally problematic sites of gendered tension. One such moment is the premeditated attack on Sabine families gathered at Rome for the festival of the Consualia.[52]

> When the hour for the games had come, and their eyes and minds were alike riveted on the spectacle before them, the predetermined signal was given and the Roman youth dashed in all directions to carry off the maidens who were present. The larger parts were carried off indiscriminately, but some particularly beautiful girls, who had been marked out for the leading patricians, were carried to their houses by plebeians who had been given the task.[53]

It is readily apparent that this act of seizure and rape performs a variety of functions and reveals very particular narrative interests. Aimed specifically at girls of marriageable age (*virgines*),[54] the process of selection is random, and conforms to possession by theft.[55] So, too, in the same way as the allocation of spoils reflects a retrojected social hierarchy, the choice associates male status, and female appearance.[56] And, in keeping with the discursive purposes of AUC history, the episode is partially aetiological in intent, providing the origins of the so-called wedding cry (*nuptialis vox*), "For Thalassius!"[57]

In every respect, therefore, the objectification of the female is paramount and total. The young Sabine women are reified as the means to an end. They are property to be plundered and their experience is depicted in such a way that it becomes the exterior site of an interior hierarchy: namely, the body politic inscribed on the female corpus and an explanation of male-dominant customary origins.

> Alarm and consternation broke up the games, and the parents of the maidens fled, distracted with grief, uttering bitter reproaches on the violators of the laws of hospitality and appealing to the god to whose solemn games they had come, only to be the victims of impious perfidy.[58]

At the same time, however, the shameful nature of this deception is indirectly acknowledged by parental accusations. In this regard, Livy represents the Romans as perpetrators of a criminal act that violates the traditionally inviolable hospitality of guest-friendship (*violati hospitii scelus*) – a fraudulent lie reviling divine law and conventional loyalties (*per fas ac fidem*).

Here Livy is careful to identify the Romans' culpable behaviour from the Sabine viewpoint, depicting the raped women as despondent and indignant.[59] This narrative tactic allows him to relate the justifiable anger and sense of futility felt by the *raptae* themselves[60] without necessarily imputing responsibility. This is vital, because there exists a potential for seeing the parents' indictment and the emotional responses of the abducted maidens as confirmation of the regional perception that the Roman men are inferior even to the unmarried children of their neighbours. This would be an extraordinary position to advocate explicitly and explains the considerable artistry beneath which Livy, like Romulus, conceals his mind (*animi dissimulans*).[61]

Indeed, it can be suggested that the historian dissembles in much the same way as his archetypal *conditor*. The latter is author of a deception whereby young women are carried off with a view to ensuring historical and social continuity; the former, author of a similar fraud by which the annalistic tradition might be "abducted" to effect a modification of the received record, replacing relational certitude with gendered ambiguity.

> Romulus, however, went around in person, and pointed out to them that it was all owing to the pride of their parents in denying right of intermarriage to their neighbours. They would live in honourable wedlock, and share all their property and civil rights, and – dearest of all to human nature – would be the mothers of freeborn men.[62]

It is instructive of Livy's rhetorical diversion that he places rationalisation of the attack and theft – paternal pride implicit in refusing *conubium* to the Roman state[63] – in the care of Romulus. The man who opened the sanctuary to human miscellany and who formalised deception as state policy is entrusted with an argument designed to alleviate Sabine indignation.[64] No less revealing is the manner in which Livy locates pride squarely as a quality of the neighbouring elders (*patrum superbia*). What is most surprising in this context is that Romulus concedes the disposition of *societas* to the young women.[65]

Association between male and female (in terms of property, citizenship, and children) is registered as the responsibility of the captured *virgines*. Taking the Roman king's instruction on face value is dangerous. A direct formulation of matrimonial reciprocity (as fellowship between individuals of coeval status) would not have been construed favourably (or even recognised as such) by an Augustan audience. It may be permissible to view such a radical statement of conjugal parity as exemplary of the gendered tension already prefigured in the narrative. Even though Livy is at pains to valorise reproduction as a privileged function of marriage,[66] it is difficult to jettison the associated benefits of social affiliation, material wealth, and membership of the state.

To delimit the impact of his radical rhetoric, Livy must reinstate the signifier which least problematises the relational condition his text is exploring. Thus, we return to "woman" as object, acted upon rather than interacting. As Romulus declares, "only let (the maidens) moderate their anger and give their hearts to those to whom fortune had given their bodies."[67] It would seem that the captured women possess the ability to temper the ambit of their emotional investment. But control of the female body itself resides in the accidental allocation of female to male previously identified as *magna pars forte* ("to a great extent by chance").[68]

However, the certainty of female agency confined to affective expression is modified in two ways. First, by Romulus' argument that, if the women were to "soften" their sense of injury and demonstrate a more favourable emotional stance, then their captors would reciprocate in like manner. The partiality of feelings echoes the more stereotypical economy of exchange emblematic of the marriage relationship.[69] Second, "the blandishments of the men added (to Romulus' explanation), justifying their deed by reason of passion and love – the most effective entreaties to a woman's nature."[70] Here, we find the distillation of Livy's narrative ambiguity. On the one hand, the men employ strategies usually associated (at least in AUC history) with the alien or the marginal elements in Roman society, whether civil or imperial. Further, they acknowledge an explicit link between the affective and the effective, the impulse and the act.[71] On the other, the distinguishing site of female identity – the essential nature of "woman" – is reduced to an inescapable reflexive emotional appeal. It is hard not to conclude from this that Livy did not so much seek to resolve the gendered problem as to underline and represent its disturbing tensions.

The battle to win over the hearts and minds of the captured women would appear at least partially successful. Livy uses this notional victory to set the stage for the military conflict between Rome and her affronted neighbouring states (Caeninenses, Antemnates, Crustuminians, and Sabines). To be sure, the mimetic rivalry of regional warfare – the exclusive privilege of kings, enemy commanders, armed soldiers, and army champions – modifies the civil/domestic dispute previously discussed in at least one significant detail. If a state wilfully indulges in conflict to satisfy an emotional imperative, let it do so at its own peril. For instance, Livy characterises the impetuosity of Caenina, Crustumium, and Antemnae as *iniuriae pars*: extension and confirmation of the exhortatory grief of the Sabine parents. The deliberate narrative artistry Livy displays here is easily overlooked, but a pervasive reminder of the figural nature of the received tradition. As Wiseman notes, "the delay of the Sabines was, of course, artistically necessary in order to allow their daughters to have given birth to Roman children before the showdown came."[72] This is a significant authorial intervention, given the pivotal position of *liberi* (legitimate offspring) in Livy's discourse of exchange. In any event, the intensely felt anger of the Caeninenses is redefined by Romulus as an illusory substitute for military strength.[73] So, too, the opportunistic hostility of the Antemnates is subverted by swift disciplined retaliation. Last of all, the desire of the Crustuminians is abated only in the face of their neighbours' losses.[74]

This rhetorically cumulative depiction of the inefficacy of emotional intensity when deprived of rational consideration highlights the radical ambivalence of Livy's exposition of the civic and domestic interplay between Roman men and Sabine women. It is offered in part as a defining corollary. Women are shown as susceptible to the arguments of a rational man (*Romulus docebat*) and the appeals of passionate men (*blanditiae virorum*). But Livy is careful to privilege the latter as the most significant indicator of the "seat" of the female self (*muliebris ingenium*). This identification is comparable to the *indoles* of Lavinia, the prophetic ability of Carmenta, and may also be likened to Hersilia's psychologically judicious manipulation of Romulus.[75] In other words, Livy's exposition of "woman" may be seen as part of a representational economy, encoding certain problematic elements of the annalistic tradition as gendered, and investing their reconstruction with a figural rather than referential significance.[76] This perspective would also help to explain the narrative tension underpinning Tarpeia's treachery, especially when viewed in the frame of a contextual comparison between the Romans and Sabines at the moment of their initial climactic confrontation.[77]

Livy represents this conflict as the "most serious" test of Rome's originary development. The reason for this is in line with the previous argument. Because "nothing was done in passion or impatience," the Sabines are free of the kind of emotional baggage which saw their neighbouring states defeated.[78] Livy regards this lack of passion as a formidable element of the Sabine threat, precisely because it mirrors Rome's single-minded purpose in pursuing expansionary goals under Romulus' reasoned leadership. That the Sabines do not parade war before they make it is considered an example of prudent judgement (consilio).[79] The fact that Livy then complicates his assessment by adding deception to the Sabines' list of attributes is a pivotal support to the contention of a gendered historiographical rhetoric. The absence of rage or greed (i.e., passion) is identified as a positive martial quality; whereas artifice (dolus) is used as a weapon more suited to a female arena of combat. Certainly, Tarpeia is reviled for her treachery and betrayal as much by the deceivers as the deceived.[80] To this, we must add the subsequent goading of the Roman army into a strategically disadvantageous position. The ploy is successful only because the ousted defenders of the citadel are wholly given over to the very passions absent in their erstwhile enemy. As such, it is only through the valour or "reckless courage" (audacia) displayed by the princeps Hostius Hostilius – and the pious entreaty vouchsafed by Romulus in the midst of his army's headlong retreat – that the Roman disorder is halted, and the tide of battle turned in their favour.[81]

It is in this contextual frame that Livy places the Sabine women. They exist at the centre of the physical and emotional field of conflict.

> Then it was that the Sabine women, whose wrongs had led to the war, throwing off all womanish fears in their distress, went boldly into the midst of the flying missiles with dishevelled hair and rent garments. Running across the space between the two armies they tried to stop any further fighting and calm the excited passions by appealing to their fathers in the one army and their husbands in the other not to bring upon themselves a curse by staining their hands with the blood of a father-in-law or a son-in-law, nor upon their posterity the taint of parricide.[82]

First and foremost, it is their fault that this war is being fought. Somehow, the sense of injury and resentment felt by the captured women (and only partially mitigated by Romulean reason and masculine blandishment) has transformed into a wrong perpetrated by rather than against them.[83] In a sense, Romulus' argument that injury often gives way to affection has been reified by the narrative in the same way that the text is mirrored syntactically.[84] If they are guilty, it is logical for them to appear so: with loosened hair and torn garments.[85] The interior transformation is externalised in a typical rhetorical embellishment.[86]

The intensity of their acceptance of responsibility for the war is inscribed on their bodies as the species of culpability, which comprises both likeness and artistic representation. This is depicted in such a way that another aspect of their *muliebris ingenium* – in this case, feminine anxiety or dread (*muliebris pavor*) – is overcome by their misdeeds. It is guilt, not valour, which allows the women to dare the site of hostility and anger. At this point psychological imperative rather than physical courage impels the narrative forward.[87] The purpose fuelling their decision to enter the fray and divide the rival forces is similarly affective. They seek to disarm the hostile forces of their anger through supplication.[88] This signifies a two-fold function of the narrative: Livy's encoding of the women's action as mimetic display of male engagement in battle, and his account of the war between Sabine and Roman as constitutive of imitative domestic rivalry.

Most salient of all, the women appeal to sacrificial reason and the pervasive economy of exchange which underlies the sacral transformation of female flesh.

> "If," they cried, "you are weary of these ties of kindred, these marriage-bonds, then turn your anger upon us; it is we who are the cause of the war, it is we who have wounded and slain our husbands and fathers. Better for us to perish rather than live without one or the other of you, as widows or as orphans."[89]

This investiture of personal duty in the face of potential collective pollution not only reflects their exterior image but is rendered more poignant through the implicit acknowledgement of altered status. Simply put, the women are now Roman *matronae*, no longer Sabine *virgines*. They identify the combatants as *patres*, *soceri*, *viri* and *generi*, their children as *nepotes* and *liberi*, and themselves as possible *viduae* and *orbae*. The saturation of familial denomination is unavoidable, and serves to link the public discourse of voluntary, self-willed ritual offering and the private sphere of nuptial alliance. The mutual affinities of community and domestic *societas*, *adfinitas* and *conubium* are thus ratified.

In the same way that Rhea Silvia became the author of blame, the Sabine women assume the mantle of guilt.[90] Unlike Romulus and Remus's Vestal mother, however, they invite (or rather, command) their kinsmen and husbands to channel their inappropriate passion through them, even if this means their death. As Romulus, in the heat of exultation after defeated the

Antemnates, acceded to Hersilia's plea to pardon the abducted women's parents and receive them into citizenship, so the prayer of the Sabine *matronae* stirs the soldiers and leaders alike in the thick of battle.

> The armies and their leaders were alike moved by this appeal. There was a sudden hush and silence. Then the generals advanced to arrange the terms of a treaty. It was not only peace that was made, the two nations were united into one state, the royal power was shared between them, and the seat of government for both nations was Rome.[91]

In this regard, the women perform a unifying function on a variety of levels, though in each degree acting as a catalyst for male resolution: political alliance, civic expansion, domestic peace, and social order.[92] Given this list of ostensible and valued achievements – appropriated by men, inspired by women – it is instructive to observe how Livy defines the position of *muliebris ingenium* in relation to the aftermath of potentially destructive internecine strife.

> The joyful peace, which put an abrupt close to such a deplorable war, made the Sabine women still dearer to their husbands and fathers, and most of all to Romulus himself.[93]

The historian resorts to the rhetoric of objectification. The reader apprehends an echo of the third of Romulus' promises – "that they would be the mothers of freeborn men" – should the women enter affectively into Roman marriage.[94] They are rendered "more precious" (*cariores*) still to their husbands, parents, and before all Romulus himself. There is no mention of shared property rights, no offer of reciprocal suffrage or franchise, only the valorisation associated with reproductive legitimation. The politics of exchange are explicated at the hermeneutic level of curial division, and a patriarchal civil ideology is propagated through the promise of free children.[95]

In other words, Livy's annalistic reconstruction of the received tradition regarding the theft, assimilation, and intervention of the Sabine women represents a deliberate articulation of the ways in which the characteristics of women were subordinated to male purposes, in turn reinforcing and expanding a partial insight into the process of regional Tyrrhenian expansion in archaic Roman history.[96] Harmonising this interpretation with the structural centrality of the women's role in the narrative is possible if one recognises the semantic equilibrium Livy generates in his attempted resolution of expository tensions.

This is especially so of the narrative movements from separation to reunion, hostility to reconciliation; and of the topological shifts regarding personal and civic status, from independence to assimilation, and from victim of male appropriation to object of male respect. Livy is cognizant of the contradictory imperatives which underpin human relations, be they domestic or socio-political, personal, or public. His reiteration of the theft allows him to explicate the ambiguities and difficulties implicit in such traditional male spheres of action as the city and the battlefield by positioning them in relation to contexts which require an exploration of non-conventional or incongruous emotions, arguments and actions.

In relation to the overarching narrative approach of AUC history to episodes incorporating the representation of women, Livy's historiographical frame may be seen to isolate and identify those factors integral to the resolution of political and military conflict in general, and, in this episode, between Rome and the neighbouring territories. In the face of a serious threat to the early stability of Rome's political constitution and the continuity of the state's military order, Livy depicts Rome and the Sabines arranging the terms of a treaty, declaring an end to their war, and uniting to become a single state – all in large part as a result of the intervention of a group of women on the battlefield. To paraphrase Miles, the narrative of abduction, rape, and intercession characterising the episode of the Sabine women illuminates those strategies by which the dominant social and political discourse of the Roman state sought "to domesticate a potentially disruptive outsider," be it Sabine woman or regional state.[97]

2.3 Veturia and Volumnia: reconstructing a tradition

Readers of the AUC next encounter collective female activity in a preeminently male context in relation to the story of Cn. Marcius Coriolanus. Coriolanus received his epithet for his deeds of heroism in the capture of Corioli, a town in the territory of the Volsci located south of Rome, in 493 BCE.[98] Coriolanus was a young patrician during Rome's wars against the Antiates in the early 5th century when he distinguished himself in this way, but he was also a member of the senate, who, not too many months later, stood at the head of the oligarchic faction. At this time there was a famine, and, in contradiction to the plebeian statement that they had not been guilty of pillage, it was now said that the land had been devastated by them. Fruitless attempts were made to procure corn. Money was sent to Sicily to buy some, but the Greek king returned the money, and gave the corn as a present. When the question of what should be done with this corn was discussed in the senate, Coriolanus proposed that it should neither be sold nor distributed, unless the plebeians renounced their newly acquired rights.[99] Another proposition only marginally less prejudicial to the plebeians was that the grain should be sold to them as if they were a collective entity, thereby compelling individuals to buy it second-hand. This plan, by which the patricians recuperated double the primary cost of the grain, was adopted. As might be expected, following through on the implications of the proposal excited considerable plebeian exasperation. At the same time, it also transpired that Coriolanus had insisted on making use of the opportunity to do away with plebeian privileges. The unyielding patrician's proposal to exploit a famine in order to render the plebeians submissive resulted in the tribunes bringing a charge of breaking the peace against Coriolanus and to his banishment in 491 BCE.[100]

According to the general account, Coriolanus withdrew from Rome and took himself to the Volscians, whom, it is said, he induced to hazard war against Rome once more. At the head of the Volsci enemy, he conquered town after town: first Cerceii, then those lying to the south of the Appian Way (Satricum, Longula, Polusca, and Corioli, towns which the Romans had recently acquired), then those on the Latin road (Lavinium, Corbio, Vetellia, Trebium Labici, and Pedum), until at last he advanced against Rome itself.[101] It is at this point in the story, when Coriolanus is on the Roman frontier five miles from the city and the Romans send embassies to him, first ten senators and then the fetial priests, that Livy scrutinises Roman society in crisis through a gendered narrative lens.[102]

As outlined above, the episode is prefaced by an outline of the attack conducted by Coriolanus. Heroic combatant, conservative ideologue, embittered exile, Coriolanus is a disturbing figure, where the commonplaces of external threat and internal disorder intersect – of the Roman elite by birth, a vigorous commander by display, and violently disposed to the plebeians by dint of his hostile proposition during a recent grain crisis. The assault not only poses a threat to Rome externally, it represents a challenge to the traditional pieties of family, household and gods, emphasised by the failure of senators and priests to negotiate a settlement.[103]

Given that Coriolanus marched on Rome at the head of a Volsci army to a large extent because of the confrontation between the patricians and plebeians that began in 494 BCE with the foundation of the people's tribunate, the manner in which each of the so-called orders – the relatively homogenous patriciate and the far more socially and economically fragmented plebeians – responded to the threat provides a clue to the strategy that will result in the eventual restoration of civil stability.

> These [dissensions among plebeians and patricians] certainly would have arisen – to such a fever-pitch were the tribunes exciting the plebs by their attacks on the chief men of the state – had not the fear of the enemy outside – the strongest bond of union – brought men together in spite of their mutual suspicions and aversion. On one point they disagreed: the senate and the consuls placed their hopes solely in arms, the plebeians preferred anything to war.[104]

In the same light, the resolution of a potentially disastrous confrontation is directly ascribed to the active role of elite Roman wives and mothers, who pursue a negotiated resolution very much according to the plebeian view. These women are the matronal descendants of the women who prevented the war between their fathers and husbands, and inheritors of the Sabine example of transgressive intervention. In this context, the representational economy Livy's historical narrative displayed in the intervention of the Sabine women prescribes an objectification of this determinative function in the figures of Veturia and Volumnia (respectively, Coriolanus' mother and wife).

The creation of a sense of familiarity (with which Livy hopes to make his past recognisable) requires the deployment of conventional rhetorical elements; in this case, the inclusion of formulaic language traditionally adhering to the action of women in a masculine sphere.

> Then the matrons went in a body to Veturia, the mother of Coriolanus, and Volumnia his wife. Whether this was in consequence of a decree of the senate, or simply the prompting of womanly fear, I am unable to ascertain, but at all events they succeeded in inducing the aged Veturia to go with Volumnia and her two little sons to the enemies' camp. As men were powerless to protect the City by their arms, the women sought to do so by their tears and prayers.[105]

Livy intervenes at the outset of his account to cite his inability to uncover the cause of the gathering of *matronae* at Veturia's house.[106] *Timor* is modified by *muliebris* in a context which contrasts the rational deliberation of male citizens with the undesirable fear of women.[107] The repeated association of the action and effort of the women with prayers and tears demarks the rationalised ritual activity of *matronae* usually confined to an officially defined domain of influence.[108] Their expression of unbridled grief in a situation beyond the sanctioned limits of sacral female space contravenes the public-spirited decorum of matronal grief.[109]

> On their arrival at the camp a message was sent to Coriolanus that a large body of women were present. He had remained unmoved by the majesty of the state in the persons of its ambassadors, and by the appeal made to his eyes and mind in the persons of its priests; he was still more hard-hearted to the tears of the women. Then one of his friends, who had recognised Veturia, standing between her daughter-in-law and her grandsons, and conspicuous amongst them all in the greatness of her grief, said to him. "Unless my eyes deceive me, your mother and wife and children are here."

The arrival of Veturia, Volumnia and their children at the head of a great company of women and Coriolanus' recognition of his mother may be identified as a classic example of a *peripeteia* (reversal of situation) and its accompanying *anagorisis* (change from ignorance to knowledge). Livy's use of dramatic patterns characteristic of Aristotelian tragic structure will have reinforced his readership's familiarity with recurrent thematic motifs already encountered in gendered episodes like this by associating such lexical *topoi* with the equally recognisable formulation of stage-productions. If there is any truth in the possibility of connections between performances on the Roman stage and the development of Roman historical traditions – namely that, in a society in which literacy was not widespread, public spectacles at annual festivals or which accompanied triumphs, temple dedications, and aristocratic funerals constituted an important medium for creating, adapting, and propagating popular traditions, and in some instances these traditions were taken over by Roman historians and woven into the literary historical tradition of the Roman state – what better environment for Livy to inaugurate the questioning or modification of the received tradition regarding the story of Coriolanus than the paradigmatic environment of tragedy in accordance with the Greek model.[110]

> Before I admit your embrace suffer me to know whether it is to an enemy or a son that I have come, whether it is as your prisoner or as your mother that I am in your camp. Has a long life and an unhappy old age brought me to this, that I have to see you an exile and from that an enemy? Had you the heart to ravage this land, which has borne and nourished you? However hostile and menacing the spirit in which you came, did not your anger subside as you entered its borders? Did you not say to yourself when your eye rested on Rome, "Within those walls are my home, my household gods, my mother, my wife, my children?" Must it then be that, had I remained childless, no attack would have been made on Rome; had I never had a son, I should have ended my days a free woman in a free country? But there is nothing which I can suffer now that will not bring more disgrace to you than wretchedness to me; whatever unhappiness awaits me it will not be for long. Look to these, whom, if you persist me your present course, an untimely death awaits, or a long life of bondage.[111]

Livy recounts that *matronae* first went in a body to Veturia and convinced her and Coriolanus' wife Volumnia to band together with their children and go to the Volsci encampment near the Marrana canal so as to safeguard with their prayers and tears the city that arms could not defend.[112] As the undeniable figurehead of the third (and, following the previously unsuccessful senators and priests, final) delegation, Livy's Veturia urges Coriolanus to consider his actions through a succession of rhetorical questions, comparing her son to an enemy, albeit a *hostis* (enemy of the state), rather than an *inimicus* (personal political foe); and, in a noteworthy statement, relating what is politically important with what is most suitable for a family and its feelings. For Veturia's speech not only stresses the psychological distress her son's behaviour has triggered personally but also foregrounds her son's emotional relationships and responsibilities to herself and other family members, mentioning her son's wife and sons.

Additionally, by designating Rome itself as having conceived and provided for her son, Livy's Veturia invites Coriolanus to consider his native land equivalent to his mother, thereby representing it as his *matria*. To be sure, by declaring that she is somehow responsible for Rome's tribulations (because she gave birth to her son), Livy represents Veturia as hostile, aggressive, and argumentative. But Coriolanus' scandalous political actions justify her strategy – and Veturia accomplishes what senators and priests have failed to do: getting her son to do what she – and Rome – wants.

> When she ceased, his wife and children embraced him, and all the women wept and bewailed their own and their country's fate. At last his resolution gave way. He embraced his family and dismissed them and moved his camp away from the City.[113]

The attribution of *materna auctoritas* as the motivating factor behind Coriolanus' personal irresolution and military withdrawal – in conjunction with the visceral techniques of effective persuasion (physical embraces of wife and children, collective lamentation of the *agmen mulierum*) – draws attention to the transgression of normative boundaries involved in restoring social stability and to the unpolitical influence attached to Veturia.[114] It should be noted that the aggregate address voiced on the battlefield by the Sabine women[115] is effectively inverted by Livy in his treatment of Veturia and the Roman *matronae*. In both instances, however, it is the restoration of *civitas* which initiates and governs the female intervention of masculine space.[116]

> After withdrawing his legions from the Roman territory, he is said to have fallen a victim to the resentment which his action aroused, but as to the time and circumstances of his death the traditions vary. ... The Roman husbands did not grudge their wives the glory they had won, so completely were their lives free from the spirit of detraction and envy. A temple was built and dedicated to Fortuna Muliebris, to serve as a memorial of their deed.[117]

The successive citation of Coriolanus' death and the lasting memorial to the women's glory performs a two-fold function. It associates the symbolic eradication of inordinate desire[118] with the foundation of a cult embodying ritual female activity.[119] Additionally, it juxtaposes the constructive and social dimensions of unofficial female activity with the destructive and martial influences of approved masculine endeavour.[120]

All in all, while purely gentilicial, symbolic or linguistic approaches to the composition of the story of Coriolanus' attack on Rome, his capitulation and ignominious death, fail to find a more general explanation for its meanings and functions in the broader historiographical context, it is clear that the very presence of female activity in a prescriptively masculine space – the public domain of senatorial, sacerdotal and military engagements – provides the clue and encompasses the authorial intention. Namely, to encourage interrogation of women's appointed roles and spheres of action in the AUC tradition, and to stimulate interest in the constitution of the *agmen mulierum*, the relationship between the members of the community, and the designated strategies and otherwise insensible influence of their actions.

Immediately after collective female intervention averts the threatened assault on the city, Rome faces a serious internal challenge: the suspicion that one of the elected patrician consuls, Spurius Cassius Vicellinus, aimed at monarchy. In line with the now-familiar narrative paradigm, Livy's interposition of his gendered episode between Coriolanus' attempt on the city from outside and Sp. Cassius' projected coup highlights the problematic nature of a liberty which accommodates the subordination of humanity to the legislated principles of normative behaviour.[121] In other words, by distorting the perimeters of acceptable practice through his representation of female activity – to the extent that a quasi-parity is implied by virtue of the celebrated merit of such an intervention[122] – Livy renders problematic the typical Roman understanding of the concept of *libertas*. This historiographical tactic will have certainly brought into sharper focus to Livy's readership the ways in which the concept was understood during the last period of the Republic – in political terms, the relation between the liberty of the citizen and the power of the commonwealth; when applied to Roman society more broadly, freedom from the mastery of another – and how it might be reconceived under the newly constituted and developing framework of the Augustan principate.[123]

2.4 Cato and the *frequentia mulierum*: a crux of social legislation

> Amid the anxieties of great wars, either scarcely finished or soon to come, an incident occurred, trivial to relate, but which, by reason of the passions it aroused, developed into a violent contention.[124]

Livy's devotion of over an eighth of a book to an explicitly designated matter of little consequence – his account of the action to repeal the *lex Oppia*,[125] a frumentary law carried in the heat of the second Punic war that restricted the weight of gold a woman could display, the kind of garment she could wear, and the mode of transport she could use within a mile of the city of Rome or any other town (except on the occasion of a religious festival)[126] – represents a drawing-together of a variety of linguistic and semantic threads associated with his deployment of gendered historical incidents.

The annalist's interposition of a *res parva* (ostensibly relating to domestic affairs) between crucial external developments in the history of Rome conforms to the structural conventions of AUC historiography. The events which preface Livy's debate are T. Quinctius Flamininus' settlement of Greece after the defeat of Philip V at Cynoscephalae in Thessaly and Hannibal's flight to Antiochus III of Syria (who was planning war against the Romans). The *bella imminentia*, then, refer to the wars in Spain and with Antiochus.[127] But his choice of a full-scale debate set against the background of a collective demonstration by a multitude of women (*frequentia mulierum*), drawn from elite urban families and the communities of the rural tribes, suggests a conscious manipulation of the accepted narrative frame, a rhetorical strategy that situates external military success together with internal social disorder for contrasting effect.

In this regard, if we accept Kraus' characterisation of the process underpinning the elaboration of a rhetorical superstructure of history – the artificial "alternation of annalistic notices with mimetic episode"[128] – then Livy's introduction to his literal and structural intervention should be read as confirmation of his intention to address the matter of social history which consistently expresses itself in such contexts. In this instance, his purpose is achieved by juxtaposing violent rhetorical contention, articulated in the speeches of the consul M. Porcius Cato and tribune L. Valerius, against an evocative account of male-female interaction in the public sphere, located in the streets and approaches to the Forum, on the slopes of the Capitoline, and at the home of the plebeian tribunes.[129]

To this end, the striking and powerful debate delineated by Livy charts the oppositional socio-political and ideological currents running through the entire community.[130] Certainly, the law finds support in the persons of the tribunes M. and P. Iunius Brutus and the consuls Cato and L. Valerius Flaccus,[131] and equally vociferous antagonism from the tribune Valerius and the crowd of women. But it should not be overlooked that the aristocracy of Rome was clearly divided over the issue; and this discord among the city's well-known elite was shared by a representative proportion of the community at large, from a roster of distinguished men who came forward to speak for *and* against the proposed repeal to crowds of supporters and opponents of the bill, including the *frequentia mulierum*.[132] In addition, while it is evident that the female collective comprises a percentage of women from the communities of Roman citizens lacking a full municipal organisation (*ex oppidis conciliabulisque*), the implication is that the motivating impulse propelling the demonstration resides with the wealthier elite, the *matronae*.[133] As such, any consideration of this so-called "trivial incident" must avoid simplistic appeals to anachronistically gendered explanation.

At the same time, the prominence allotted to female activity which unequivocally transgresses normative socio-political protocols – whether of the early 2nd century BCE (the historical context) or the early years of the Augustan principate (the historiographical milieu) – can only be viewed as a deliberate emphasis designed to frame the reader's evaluation of the arguments propounded by Cato and Valerius. Consequently, Livy's representation of the ideas and events interweaving the repeal of the *lex Oppia* in 195 BCE provides us with an overview of a society in the grip of a crisis of consciousness. Notably, this transgressive activity impinges on domestic privileges and preconceptions – "the *matronae* could not be kept at home by advice or modesty or their husbands' orders" – and the environs of public and political space – "they blocked all the streets and approaches to the Forum," "they dared even to approach and appeal to the consuls, the praetors, and the other officials," and "an even greater crowd of women appeared in public, and all of them as a body beset the doors of the Bruti."[134]

In the end, the tensions and ambiguities which are exposed by Livy in the course of his consecutive speeches are not resolved by the episode's abrupt periodic coda: "The law was repealed twenty years after it was passed."[135] In fact, the historian's oblique admission – that the speeches purporting to rework the views of Cato and Valerius are the product of free composition[136] – suggests that each instance of direct speech (*oratio recta*) contains *in extenso* Livy's formulation of the problematic issues confronting Roman society in the wake of tumultuous domestic and regional upheaval. To this end, and in the hope that such a rhetorical exposition of moral and prudential argument – mirroring the more obvious (if less satisfying) exercise of fitting the occasion and evoking the style of each speaker – might evoke a critical interpretation of larger historical problems, Livy maps out a range of interdependent concerns (Table 2.2).[137]

Given this overview, it seems reasonably clear that the issue of female behaviour is one of a number of matters pertinent to the general interest of the Roman community. Without question, attribution of derogatory and praiseworthy qualities to women may be located in both speeches and range from disparaging and diminishing attributions – expressions of

Table 2.2 Comparison of subject-matter in the speeches of M. Porcius Cato and L. Valerius

Cato	Valerius
2.5-3.2: the liability to moral harm vested in exposure to female conduct.	5.4-13: reply to Cato's claim that the behaviour of women is unprecedented.
3.3-5: the function of law in upholding the common good.	6.1-18: reply to the argument that repeal of the law entails the invalidation of all laws.
3.6-9: the "real" motives of the women.	7.1-10: the injustice of debarring women from enjoyment of luxury when others are permitted.
4.1-11: the dangers adhering to the morbid pathology of *avaritia* and *luxuria*.	7.11-15: the unlikelihood of male *auctoritas* suffering diminishment from female activity.
4.12.30: the condition of the *res publica* subsequent to abrogation of the *lex Oppia*.	

consternation and alarm (*consternatio*), ungovernable and irrational conduct (*indomitum animus*), presumptive lack of restraint (*licentia*), inordinate and willful inclination to satisfy sensual desire (*libido*), and general
want of spirit or courage (*infirmitas*) – to attributes deserving admiration
and approval – dignified and honourable character (*maiestas*), a general
sense of modesty and propriety (*pudor*), and personal integrity (*sanctitas*).
The characterisation of female action is similarly conventional, if extreme,
referring to political insurrection (*secessio*), civil discord (*seditio*), and sub-
jection (*servitum*).[138] But the overriding concern of both speeches is to elicit
an understanding of this overt (and clearly disturbing) behaviour by comparison with the past, analysis of the present, and contemplation of the
future, with a view to reconstituting or maintaining the perceived demarca-
tions of customary practice.

Thus, Cato's evaluation of the dangers inherent in the female violation of
patriarchal authority – whether individually in the context of a husband's
rights (*ius viri*) or collectively in the public space of political assembly –
is measured in relation to ancestral custom (*maiores nostri*). In turn, the
opposition of contemporary intervention in public affairs (*rem publicam
capessere*) and the traditional exercise of familial *potestas* underpins the
consul's foreshadowing of wholesale invalidation of legal imperatives.[139]
Similarly, the motif of moral corruption caused by private wealth and conspicuous consumption (*avaritia et luxuria*) – regarded as the tokens of danger threatening the continuity of the *res publica*[140] – is historicised with
pointed reference to the contrast between foreign influence imported by
Roman generals and the acceptable stringencies of the *leges Licinia* and
Cincia.[141]

Valerius, too, repudiates Cato's warrant to the claim that the women's
actions were unprecedented. He invokes the matronal interventions in the
wars against the Sabines and with the Volscians under Coriolanus; in addition, he cites the ransoming of the city after the Gallic capture, the contribution to a severely depleted treasury during the second Punic war and the
reception of the Magna Mater by the *matronae primores* in 207 BCE.[142]
Contemplating the praiseworthy consequences of women's actions in the
recent and legendary past, the tribune questions the unbending, authoritarian and single-minded dismissal of independent female intervention.

> But what no one wonders that all, men and women alike, have done
> in matters that concern them, do we wonder that the women have
> done in a case peculiarly their own? What now have they done?[143]

This interrogation eventually supports Valerius' argument that all members
of the Roman governing class should enjoy the benefits of national peace
and stability.[144]

Of particular interest are the explicitly inclusive references which pepper
both speeches, despite the ostensible rationale that each is addressed to the

matter of a piece of sumptuary legislation directed solely against female display.

> And I can scarcely decide in my own mind whether the act itself or the precedent it sets is worse; the act concerns us consuls and other magistrates; the example, citizens, rather concerns you.[145]

Livy's Cato might place his animadversions on private conduct in the context of a decline of old virtue, but he does not limit the danger accruing to permissiveness to the activity of a particular segment of society. Indeed, his complaints encompass the register of gender and status.

> You have often heard me complaining of the extravagance of the women and often of the men, both private citizens and magistrates even, and lamenting that the state is suffering from those two opposing evils, avarice and luxury, which have been the destruction of every great empire.[146]

As such, he views the law as universally applicable.

Likewise, the historian invests Valerius with an inclusive socio-political perspective. In arguing the case for admitting the petitions of respectable women (*honestis feminis*), he sanctions the precedent by appealing to the just claim of all to a hearing in matters which concern them.

> All other orders, all men, will feel the change for the better in the state; shall our wives alone get no enjoyment from national peace and tranquillity?[147]

As previously noted, he openly advocates a broadly-based parity before the law and in the general interest. Of course, it cannot be overlooked that Valerius qualifies the equitable thrust of his *tractatio* by contextualising his arguments in relation to the exercise of *potestas*, and by suggesting that the women are content to accept the judgement of men to whom they are subject.

> They prefer to have their finery under your control and not the law's; you too should keep them in control and guardianship and not in slavery and should prefer the name of father or husband to that of master. ... The greater the authority you exercise, the greater the self-restraint with which you should use your power.[148]

If this reading of the emphasis placed by Livy on the repeal of the *lex Oppia* is plausible, then it follows that the historian is not so much concerned with the ability of the women to organise their own demonstration or with the implications of a new way of life imported from the East. Rather, he has elaborated a hard core of authentic data – the legislative abrogation itself, subsequent to a preliminary *contio* noted for its irregularity, and dating to the consulship of M. Porcius Cato and Valerius Flaccus – with the narrative superstructure of supposition. To achieve this, Livy produces a pair of speeches which fulfil the requirements of rhetorical characterisation, but with a view to attributing typical extant attitudes in a likely setting, in addition to the criteria of composition and content, to provide the most historiographically satisfying exposition of the social ramifications inherent in the unfolding of *res Romana*. In sum, Livy introduces the figure of Cato, mentioned only incidentally before this, to contextualise his circumstantial account.[149] The historian's Cato may be seen as illustrative of certain ideological precepts familiar to his audience – notably, the decline of the Roman character caused by foreign influence.[150] While the authenticity of his speech is not at issue,[151] insertion of such a seminal figure into a vivid representation of problematic events must be regarded as part of the process of "putting past events into an interpretative framework that not only explains but also legitimates them."[152] As such, since the schematic division of the paired speeches illustrates the overriding preoccupations of the episode – law, legality, legitimacy or, more generally, authority – it seems appropriate to categorise the attention paid to the subjects of the *lex Oppia* as evocative of the larger historiographical questions; namely, of the social system and the law which sustains it, the authority of this law and its justification, and threats to the law.[153] To paraphrase the chiastic formulation which sets the agenda for Cato's conservative programme, the elected officials of hegemonic discourse should concern themselves with the *exemplum*, and the people as a whole with the *res*.[154]

In this light, Cato's argument in defence of the continued existence of the law and Valerius' speech for its repeal constitute an historiographical pretext, allowing Livy to treat the general issues of social freedom and civic function.[155]

> As it is, our liberty, destroyed at home by female violence, even here in the Forum is crushed and trodden underfoot, and because we have not kept them individually under control, we dread them collectively.[156]

On the one hand, the non-violent opposition represented by the collective action of a politically subordinate group is portrayed as an unequivocal threat to the domestic and political freedom of the governing class.

> Hear how often they have done it and always, indeed, for the general good.[157]

On the other, the historical record of crucial socio-political intercessions – Sabine mediation, Punic contribution, Idaean piety[158] – reflects a public identity committed to the common weal. The reconstruction of these ostensibly irreconcilable assessments of women's social definition enables Livy to depict in intellectual terms what his narrative frame exhibits through the particularity of plausible events. Specifically, this episode in AUC history illuminates the intersection of inflexible, institutionalised tradition (favouring obedience to authority and with one purpose in view) and the challenging, unpredictable, and potentially transformative principle of historical change. This latter force is embodied in the transgressive alterity of the *mundus muliebris*, the "woman's world."[159]

> "That we may glitter with gold and purple," says one [woman], "that we may ride in carriages on holidays and ordinary days, that we may be borne through the city as if in triumph over the conquered and vanquished law and over the votes which we have captured and wrested from you; that there may be no limits to our spending and our luxury."[160]

For Cato, the issue of female adornment lies at the heart of the calamitous inversion of Roman tradition.

> What else do they lay aside in times of mourning than purple and jewellery? What do they put on when they have finished their time of mourning? What do they add save more splendid jewels in times of congratulation and thanksgiving?[161]

For Valerius, public display constitutes the indelible lineament of female acquiescence to the patriarchal order. That both regard Roman women as different from and inferior to Roman men is clear.

> Give loose rein to their uncontrollable nature and to this untamed creature and expect that they will themselves set bounds to their licence.[162]

Cato voices the traditional evaluation of the female as uncontrollable and untamed, the reverse of the rational, civilised masculine principle.

> A thing like this would hurt the feelings even of men: what do you think is its effect upon weak women, whom even little things disturb?[163]

Valerius conforms to the reductive conceptual pattern by envisaging women as diminished beings overwhelmed by the most trivial of considerations. Yet Livy explicitly overturns the discursive logic which unites the superficially divergent arguments of his paired speeches by depicting the *frequentia mulierum* as successfully engaging a political system adamantly espoused by both speakers as the repository of male authority. If, to cite another historian of Rome, it is true that "the idiosyncracy of an author is best penetrated through his inventions," Livy's rendition of the debate concerning the Oppian law could be read as a moralising discourse on "the exercise by women of some limited power and self-expression in the public domain of the Roman world."[164] However, the annalist incorporates his contrasting recitation of hierarchical values concerning female behaviour within a narrative which specifically addresses the widespread and indisputably successful nature of the women's protest.

The key to this dilemma resides in the ambit of the law under discussion. Conceding that Livy betrays a genuine interest by iterating a theme self-consciously styled as *res parva*, then there is something more than mere rhetoric in the enunciation of circumstances pertinent to the repeal of simple sumptuary legislation. The *lex Oppia* is directed exclusively at ostentatious female display, and the law is repealed as a consequence of collective female pressure brought to bear in the decisive veto of dissenting tribunes.[165] The focus of legal regulation lies squarely on the activity of upper-class women; and it is through the effective transaction of female influence in a traditional political context that confrontation is resolved. If the historian wished to problematise the intervention in itself, then surely the independent organisation and constructive involvement of the *maior frequentia mulierum* would warrant a more precise condemnation. Assuming that Livy's inclusion of this incident in AUC history is designed and written for a specific purpose, the reader is directed to study the disruptive impact exerted on conventional social divisions by the revelation of already existing incongruities in the perceived hierarchies of gender and status. In other words, Livy is not so much interested in condemning the degree to which a group of women was prepared to defend public privileges; that is, their material possessions in money or gold and their right to wear purple clothing and ride in carriages. Rather, he seeks to illuminate the extent to which socio-political conventions can be blurred in response to the considerable pressures of irresistible historical change.

From this standpoint, Livy's rhetorical articulation of female image and disposition falls flat in the face of the reported behaviour of the Roman *matronae*. Not only do they fail to resort to the traditional female strategies in situations of transgressive action (prayers, tears, and pleading), but their decisive and confident resolve against notable resistance belies any stereotypical appeal to subordinate status and infirmity of character – at least as ascribed to women by Cato and Valerius. Apart from anything else, the demonstration is in aid of a restoration of "former distinctions."[166] This citation recognises the extent to which female participation in public affairs had benefitted the state in the past and reflects the prior toleration of public display.[167] Therefore, if Livy is taking any particular attitude toward the subject under discussion, it is not so much directed against the protection and confirmation of traditional female privileges as the disintegration of gender and class boundaries. After all, we have already noted the explicit involvement of a broad cross-section of Roman society in the preliminary informal debate. To this, we can add the implicit prerogative of *dignitas*: the symbolic expression of competitive familial rivalry and hierarchical status through mimetic external display. Historicised in the context of a desire to use wealth in the acquisition of power and influence, such diffusion of reputation and class transcends any superficial resentment of conspicuous consumption by women. Its exposition highlights, in Livy's eyes, the degree to which Roman tradition has been challenged by the intersecting currents of social and political history – and, as Milnor observes, what Livy represents in relation to the debate over the repeal of the *lex Oppia* and the provocative actions of Roman women in public life "resonates profoundly with the social, spatial, and historical messages embedded in the Augustan social legislation."[168]

In sum, the exemplary value of Livy's gendered retailing of the repeal of the *lex Oppia* cannot simply be limited to imitation or avoidance in the conduct of one's personal life and public career. Instead, it should be considered in the broader setting of his historiographical propensity to provide ambivalent precedents. This is especially so in relation to Roman society's engagement with issues of gender and the law during the period contemporary with the composition of the AUC – issues brought very much to the surface by virtue of the Augustan regime's scrutiny of women, the family, and the home. In this light, the mere upholding of law and order or of favourable conditions for the pursuit of economic ends must confront the indefinable complexity of human behaviour if the *res Romana* is to be truly representative. In contradiction to the view that "Roman republican historians never seem to have had critical enquiry and objective analysis as their primary purpose in composing history," the evolution and characteristics of Livian historiography outlined above suggest that the chronicler of this incident contemplated an account which allowed for far more subtle manipulation of traditional methods and themes.[169]

2.5 Conclusion

Cooperative undertakings by female collectives, unfettered by social, legal, or political restrictions, are visible occasionally in literary accounts of Roman history, legend, and myth. Livy's AUC is no exception in this regard. Despite the fact that their objectives may not have been the same, they give the impression that women as a group could and did have the capacity to express their attitudes and opinions about civil matters through non-violent demonstration. Given the fact that these public expressions of disapproval or objection invariably succeed in accomplishing their intended aims, it is reasonable to conjecture that they articulated a necessary remedy to counteract behaviour, legislation, or institutions harmful to Roman society in general or women – and invariably elite female citizens – in particular. Or that, from another viewpoint, such actions, although taken on by women in numbers, appeared reasonable and believable to the readers of AUC history. As noted, certainly a factor integral to the attainment of their goals was the social condition and influence of the women who took part in the collective enterprise and the high regard they were accorded as *matronae*. So, too, whether on the battlefield, at the gates of a city under siege, or contesting civil legislation in social and political contexts reserved for male discourse and action, the women Livy represents in episodes of collective female demonstration show that boldness, fearlessness, and strength were considered to be important, ultimately beneficial characteristics of the elite Roman female. In brief, Livy's gendered historiography of collective female demonstrations supports the view that Roman women possessed the necessary relationships and abilities to organise, initiate, and bring to successful conclusion wide-ranging and far-reaching civil actions.

All that remains is to revisit the subject of this chapter's introduction: the relationship between the matronal interventions depicted in the AUC and the collective female action led by Hortensia in 43 BCE. In this regard, it is possible to discern more or less clearly the outlines of the episode recounted by Appian in relation to each of Livy's female interventions. First, the historian depicts women coming together in various ways to address issues that affect them personally and collectively. They seek out each other – in Book 1 of the AUC, the Sabine women, whose collective identity was forged in the shared moment of abduction and rape at the Consualia and reflected in their communal uniform of loosened hair and torn garments, are seen already together as they rush onto the battleground in the midst of the city; and in Book 34, the Roman *matronae* aggregate in large numbers in the city streets, the Roman Forum, and on the Capitoline Hill in order that by their actions they might effect a political decision to repeal the *lex* Oppia. They also seek out other women to act as leaders of the collective action – in Book 2, the married women gathered in large numbers at the house of Veturia and Volumnia to put the case for cessation of military action to Coriolanus. And in relation to the matronal demonstration contemporary with the lifetime of the young historian, they seek out other women as representatives of the cause – during the proscriptions of the late 40s BCE Hortensia spoke to Fulvia, Antonius' wife, on behalf of 1400 of the richest women required by the triumviral edict to make valuations of their properties and to contribute to the state treasury such amounts as the triumvirs might determine.

It is also plausible to identify a connection between the claims made by the male protagonists in each episode. The abduction, rape, and marriage of the Sabine women and the subsequent wars with the Caeninenses, Antemnates, and Crustimini which characterise Rome's relations with her Latin neighbours hinge on the foundational rationale of Rome's greatness, both as a physical entity and as a world power. The reason for Coriolanus' march on Rome in the 6th century BCE at the head of a Volsci army is easy to understand: the disgruntled aristocrat, driven into exile by adverse political circumstances and admitted to a position of leadership by his country's enemies, wished to secure what he perceived as just retribution for being expelled from his order and his *patria*. For the consul M. Porcius Cato and plebeian tribunes M. Iunius Brutus and P. Iunius Brutus, the line of argument in opposition to M. Fundanius, L. Valerius, Cato's consular colleague L. Valerius Flaccus and the extraordinary public demonstrations of women relies on culturally traditional views about women in general and elite Roman women in particular. To those who resisted the repeal of a law decreed primarily as an economic measure in response to serious financial issues during a war that ended 20 years earlier, the *lex Oppia* removed the shame of poverty because it made all women dress to an equivalent standard, restrained a woman's desire to spend money by placing a limit on expenditure, and held back the tide of female extravagance and love of luxury that threatened to corrupt Roman society. Displaying the same elite male logic – namely, placing a political impost on a category of person (for the early Romans, the Latin nations; for Coriolanus, the plebeian order; for Cato, Rome's *matronae*) – the triumvirs Antonius, Octavian, and Lepidus justify the edict on matronal wealth as the means to fund action against the assassins of Julius Caesar, ensuring that they might bring an end to ongoing civil strife and that the state (and Octavian in particular) might achieve justice for the murder of Rome's perpetual dictator.

Finally, it is important not to forget the fact that each collective female action (historical and contemporary) oversteps the traditional limits of male-exclusive space to achieve their respective aims: the battlefield, between the Palatine and Capitoline hills, where hostile Roman and Sabine armies are compelled to desist from fighting when the Sabine women rush between them to part the forces, quell their anger, and negotiate a settlement; the Volsci camp, site of male-exclusive political and religious embassies, potential launching point for a fully-fledged assault on the city of Rome, and finally female negotiations with Coriolanus; the Palatine hill and the Roman Forum, site of political, legal, and social dialogue between elite Roman women and the official representatives of the second triumvirate in the wake of Caesar's assassination.

Livy's narrative manifests the shifting Roman consciousness regarding traditional personal relations, constituted in symbolic terms so as to resonate with the ideological tensions of late republican realities and institutional roles. It documents a recognition and investigation of the problematic assumptions residing in the prevailing social system. Chapter 3 examines the annalist's rhetorical treatment of episodes that introduce into AUC history representations of non-Roman women, how these episodes bring order to critical or potentially catastrophic moments in Roman history, and to what extent this approach confirms or complicates Livy's historiographical focus.

Notes

1 Aug. *RG* 1 and 7; Plut. *Cic.* 46, *Ant.* 18-19; Suet. *Aug.* 96.1; App. *B Civ* 4.2-3.
2 Modern scholarship estimates that only (!) 520 individuals perished under Sulla and around 300 under the triumvirs; as opposed to Appian's respective totals of about 1600 and 2300. Francois Hinard's prosopographical catalogues of the proscribed for 82 (the first of the category of proscription involving execution and confiscation of property, under Sulla) and 43 give 75 and 160 names respectively. Although he is more concerned with the body politic, Hinard (1985: 326) observes that the proscriptions of the freeborn elite Roman population left "une marque indélébile dans le mémoire collective," perhaps even to the extent of exercising "un role déterminent dans l'évolution des mentalités." This assignation of a definitive significance to "les proscriptions de la Rome republicaine" echoes Syme's notice on the reconstitutive power of civil war over the Roman people: Syme (1939: 388), citing Lucr. *ND* 5.1145-7 on the fragmenting effects of civil disorder. It is an effect also articulated by M. le Glay (1978: 67): "They [the social war and the civil war] had profound effect on both the moral climate and the social structure of the Roman Republic."
3 For the proscriptions in general, see App. *B Civ.* 4.1-52 and Cass. Dio 47.1.19; for specific reference to the female "demonstrations" discussed below, see Val. Max. 8.3.3 and App. *B Civ.* 4.32-4.
4 Historical or otherwise: the Sabine women (Livy 1.9.13; Dion. Hal. *Ant. Rom.* 2.45-7; Plut. *Rom.* 14.20, *Quaest. Rom.* 85); the delegation of Coriolanus' mother and wife (Livy 2.40; Dion. Hal. *Ant. Rom.* 8.39-56; Plur. *Cor.* 33-7; Val. Max. 8.2.1, 4.1); opposition to the *lex Oppia* (Livy 34.1-8; Dio Cass. 18 [= Zonaras 8.17]; Val. Max. 9.1.3; Tac. *Ann.* 3.33-4; Oros. 4.20.5; cf. Plaut. *Aul.* 498–502, 528–537; *Op.* 223–236.
5 For a useful comparison of "Turia" and Hortensia, see de Arena (1986). For a thorough account of the inscription's history and provenance, execution, and relation to the rhetorical tradition of the *oratio* – including a discussion of prosopographical difficulties, chronological questions, and indications of status and ideological attitude – see Horsfall (1983). Regarding its length, Horsfall (1983: 96n.1) estimates – contra Durry (1950: li); after Costa (1915: 10) – that 41% of the text in column 1 survives and 61.5% of that in column 2, leaving us with a text that most probably ran to 180–190 lines of commemorative prose. That the *laudatio* "Turiae" and the contemporary *laudatio* Murdiae record after the event funeral speeches delivered at or near the burial place of two Roman women of the possessing class is well discussed by Durry (1950: xvi ff, lxxviii); see also, e.g., Cutolo (1983–1984: 34); Kierdorf (1980: 35n.80); Koenen (1970: 251ff); Crawford (1941: 17ff). Horsfall (1983: 89–91, with n.43) neatly surveys the material. For recent treatments of this inscription, see Keegan (2014: 87–122) and Osgood (2014).
6 Such transgressive behaviour was especially problematic for the wives of outlaws risking the danger of identification. of explicitly Greek values: Arsinoe II (*Syll*.434-5); participating in crises of political power: Arsinoe.
7 For example, projecting an image of concern for and patronage III and Agathokleia (Polybius 15.27.1-2; 29.8-30.1; 33.7-12); owning and controlling in their own right considerable landed and other property in Egypt: Berenike, daughter of Ptolemy III (*P. Teub.* III.720); occupying the post of priestess in the Greek ruler cult: see de Cenival (1977: 29–30); Rowlandson (1998: 55–62); not to mention the extraordinary biography of Kleopatra VII. For an extended consideration of the role, resources and relations of queens in Hellenistic Egypt, see Pomeroy (1984: 3–40).

8 From the legislated regulation of status, marriage and inheritance set down in the so-called Gnomon of the Idios Logos – *BGU* V.1210; BL II.2.25-6, III.18, IV.7, VI.15, VII.19, VIII.43; see S. Riccobono (1950) and Rowlandson (1998: 55, 175–177) – to the exercise of direct control over and disposal of agricultural land – buying or selling, inheriting, and leasing arable land: e.g., women of the Julio-Claudian imperial family like Antonia; see Kokkinos (1992) – and non-agricultural property – houses and parts of houses, or other assets in real or movable property like personal possession and money, plots of ground, ships, camels, slaves and revenue producing enterprises like potteries, fulleries, even religious precincts; see Rowlandson (1998: 245f).

9 While the sources confirm that Livy resided in Rome, from when and for how long must remain a matter of speculation. That said, what is far more certain, though, again, only confirmed second hand, is the historian's personal knowledge, and in all likelihood, experience in his twenties, of the impact of the civil wars on his birthplace of Padua (Cic. *Phil.* 12.10; Macrob. 1.11.22).

10 Ogilvie (1963: 2).

11 Acquaintance with Augustus: Tac. *Ann.* 4.24; described as *Pompeianus*: Sen. *Controv.* 10 pr. 5; encouragement of Claudius: Suet. *Claud.* 41.1.

12 *RG* 3.1: *bella terra et mari civilia externaque toto in orbe terrarum suscepi victorque omnibus veniam petentibus civibus peperci.*

13 Hemelrijk (1987: 232).

14 Daube (1972: 26).

15 Behaviour and aims, moreover, which seem to have been regarded with concern by men and women alike.

16 *Inst.* 1.1.6: *Hortensiae Q. filiae oratio apud triumuiros habita legitur non tantum in sexus honorem.*

17 An affront exacerbated perhaps by Fulvia's recent resort to a similar tactic of public confrontation, in relation to senatorial measures aimed at declaring Antonius an enemy of the state. According to Appian (3.51), Julia and Fulvia, accompanied by Antonius' son (either M. Antonius "Antyllus" or an otherwise unrecorded son of his previous marriage to his cousin Antonia), negotiated with "the influential" throughout the evening preceding the all-important tribunician vote; and "when day broke they accosted senators on their way to the meeting, threw themselves wailing and lamenting at their feet, and stood by the doors clad in black and crying out." *Despite* Cicero's defence of the measure against – and *with* L. Calpurnius Piso Caesoninus' defence of – Antonius, the advocacy of mother and wife would seem to have proved useful in ameliorating the senate's motion; contra the observation of Virlouvet (2001: 74): "[Fulvia's] action had no impact on the senate's decision."

18 App. *B Civ.* 4.34.

19 By identifying Fulvia's refusal to hear the petition of the *matronae* as hubristic, Appian associates her conduct with the logic of honour, insult, humiliation, and revenge usually applied to public or private male-male relations in agonistic Greek or Roman society. Her response certainly encompasses the kind of abuse which deliberately humiliated or insulted another man. Appian's portrayal of Fulvia more generally – as a participant in the depredations of the triumviral proscriptions (4.29), as a passionate accomplice in the political stratagems of civil unrest (5.19-21), as a crucial adviser in the military deployments of the Perusine siege (5.33) – accords with this identification. Cf. e.g., Dem. *Meid.* 21.46, where the orator claims that to a *free person* there is absolutely nothing more unbearable than an act of *hubris*; and Arist. *Pol.* 1267b39, where, acc. to Hippodamus's theory of law, the only three things about which *men* litigate are death, damage, and *hubris*. For a discussion of *hubris* in relation to verbal

abuse and physical and sexual violence in the classical Athenian community, see Cohen (1995: 119–162).

20 App. *B Civ.* 4.34.

21 App. *B Civ.* 4.34 provides the detail. Val. Max. 2.1.5, 5.2.1, Sen. *Contr.* 1.2.3, 6.8, Plut. *Rom.* 20.3 and Festus 142L inform us of the prohibition against touching a Vestal or a *matrona*, even at a judicial summons; cf. Mommsen (1887: 1.376-377). Cic. *Verr.* 5.167 expresses the notion that Roman magistrates were forestalled from abusing their *auctoritas* and their apparitorial attendants *et legum et existimationis periculo*; and avers the collective Roman animadversion towards the use of lictors to damage the physical integrity of a citizen (160–169).

22 Approximately 1.5 metres long, of elm or birchwood, and held together by red thongs; by common consent, the *fasces* did not possess the single-headed axehead within the *pomerium* of Rome. For a close consideration of the *fasces* in Roman *res publica*, see Marshall (1984).

23 See Note 4, above.

24 For an analysis of the festival environment of Rome as an instance of permeable gender boundaries in Rome's urban spaces, see Keegan (2014: 198–248).

25 App. *B Civ.* 4.32.

26 App. *B Civ.* 4.32.

27 Especially as the level of aristocratic competition increased in the last century of the Republic: cf. e.g., Harris (1979: 17–34); Wiseman (1985: 3–20); Wallace-Hadrill (1983).

28 A *lex Publilia* of 339 BCE (Livy 8.12) had established that the so-called *patrum auctoritas* must be given to new laws *before* the voting of *comitia*.

29 Cf. App. *B Civ.* 4.7.

30 This was eventually to serve as Augustus's house (Suet. *Aug.* 72; cf. 29). For discussion of the circumstances and issues pertinent to identifying the house – variously linked to the Casa di Livia (Tomm, Degrassi, and Lugli), the remains situated to the south of the same structure (Royo), or the Casa di Grifi (Castagnoli) – see Papi (1995b).

31 Marcellus would not seem to have been part of the dissessions of 44–42 BCE.

32 Suet. *Aug.* 5: *ad capita bubula*.

33 In the home of her disgraced husband P. Cornelius Lentulus Sura; or that of her father, L. Iulius Caesar; or of her son, M. Antonius; or in her own home.

34 App. *B Civ.* 4.32.

35 King (1995: 1263).

36 This is discussed in more theoretical terms in chapter 4.2.

37 Val. Max. 8.3.1-3; App. *B Civ.* 4.32; Cass. Dio 47.8.4.

38 If we accept 31 CE as the date for the release of Valerius Maximus's handbook, and 31 BCE for Books 1–5 of Livy's *ab urbe condita*.

39 For convenience, I have inserted the youngest possible ages of Octavia and Fulvia. In Octavia's case, if we imagine her as 12 on her marriage to C. Claudius Marcellus by 54 BCE, then the daughter of C. Octavius and Atia was born ca. 66. Regarding Fulvia, if her son by M. Antonius Creticus was born in 83 BCE, then at the earliest she was born in 95.

40 This route begins on the western side of the *mons Palatinus*, and then proceeds along the *cliuus Victoriae*, and through the *porta Romana*.

41 Here the *frequentia mulierum* would descend the so-called "*cliuus Palatinus*," then approach the Forum Romanum via the *porta Mugonia* on the northern side of the hill near the temple of Jupiter Stator.

42 For a detailed analysis of this activity, see Chapter 5 of the present study.

43 Liv. 1.8.1-3: *vocatque ad Concilium multitudine, quae coalescere in populi unius corpus nulla re praeterquam legibus poterat, iura dedit ... lictoribus*

duodecim sumptis fecit … apparitores hoc genus … unde sella curulis, unde toga praetexta sumpta est.

44 Liv. 1.8.2: "an uncivilized race of men" (*generi hominum agresti*), 6: "an undifferentiated crowd of freedmen and slaves" (*turba omnis sine discrimine liber an servus*); 7: "to the nascent greatness (of the city)" (*ad coeptam magnitudinem*).

45 Liv. 1.8.4-6: *crescebat interim urbs minitionibus alia atque alia adpetendo loca, cum in spem magis futurae multitudinis quam ad id quod tum hominum erat munirent. deinde, ne vana urbis magnitude esset, adiciendae multitudinis causa vetere consilio condentium urbes, qui obscuram atque humilem conciendo ad se multitudinem natam e terra sibi prolem ementiebantur, locum qui nunc saeptus escendentibus inter duos lucos est, asylum aperit. Eo ex finitimis populis tuba omnis, since discrimine liber an servus esset, avida Novarum rerum perfugit, idque primum ad coeptam magnitudinem roboris fuit.*

46 Liv. 1.8.5: "The founders of cities … spread the fiction that they were the children of the earth" (*condentium urbes … natam e terra sibi prolem ementiebantur*).

47 Liv. 1.8.5: "A multitude of people of obscure and low origin" (*obscuram atque humilem … multitudinem*).

48 Liv. 1.9.1: *iam res Romana adeo erat valida ut cuilibet finitimarum civitatum bello par esset; sed penuria mulierum hominis aetatem duratura magnitudo erat, quippe quibus nec domi spes prolis nec cum finitimis conubia essent.*

49 Liv. 1.9.4: *satis scire, origini Romanae et deos adfuisse et non defuturam virtutem; proinde ne gravarentur homines cum hominibus sanguinem ac genus miscere.*

50 Liv. 1.9.5-6: *nusquam benigne legatio audita est: adeo simul spernebant, simul tantam in medio crescentem molem sibi ac posteris suis metuebant. ac plerisque rogitantibus dimissi ecquod feminis quoque asylum aperuissent; id enim demum compar conubium fore. aegre id Romana pubes passa et haud dubie ad vim spectare res coepit.*

51 Liv. 1.9.3: *ex infimo nasci.*

52 Liv. 1.9.7-11. The Consualia is a festival in honour of Consus, the tutelary deity of the harvest and stored grain.

53 Liv. 1.9.10-11: *Ubi spectaculi tempus venit deditaeque eo mentes cum oculis erant, tum ex composito orta vis signoque dato iuventus Romana ad rapiendas virgines discurrit. Magna pars forte in quem quaeque inciderat raptae: quasdam forma excellentes, primoribus patrum destinatas, ex plebe homines quibus datum negotium erat domos deferebant.*

54 Cf. Liv. 1.9.9: *Sabinorum omnis multitudo cum liberis ac coniugibus venit.*

55 Liv. 1.9.11: *magna pars forte … raptae.* Hemker (1985: 42–43) cites Livy's foregrounding of chance (*fors*) as a narrative strategy whereby any guilt accruing to the deceitful plan is diverted to a "non-human agency" (as opposed to Romulus and his men); *fors* is later identified as the "actor" responsible for having given the women's bodies to the Roman men (1.9.15). Cf. the women's later explicit confession of *causa belli* and Livy's condemnation of *iniuria* (1.13.1, 3). See also Miles (1993: 166): "[T]he element of theft also emphasizes the passive role of women … objects transferred from one male to another."

56 Liv. 1.9.11: *forma excellentes … primoribus patrum*; 12: *unam longe ante alias specie ac pulchritudine insignem a globo Thalassii.*

57 Liv. 1.9.12.

58 Liv. 1.9.13: *turbato per metum ludicro maesti parentes virginum profugiunt, incusantes violati hospitii foedus deumque invocantes cuius ad sollemne ludosque per fas ac fidem decepti venissent.*

59 Liv. 1.9.14: *nec raptis aut spes de se melior aut indignatio est minor.*

60 Liv. 1.9.14: *aut spes de se melior aut indignatio est minor.*

61 Liv. 1.9.6.

62 Liv. 1.9.14: *sed ipse Romulus circumibat docebatque patrum id superbia factum qui conubium finitimis negassent; illas tamen in matrimonio, in societate fortunarum omnium civitatisque et quo nihil carius humano generi sit liberum fore.*

63 Liv. 1.9.14-15: *patrum id* (= *qui conubium finitimis negassent*) *superbia factum.*

64 Brown (1995: 297) draws attention to the fact that Livy devotes "almost as much space to the conciliation of the women as to their abduction." It is significant in terms of structural arrangement that the historian differentiates between the stylistic characteristics of the twin appeals and accentuates their thematic importance by "framing" them between a chiastic referential pattern of parental and daughterly emotion. Such rhetorical contrivance – *amplificatio* and (*ex*)*ornatio* – confirms Livy's conscious historiographical distortion of the tradition, esp. with a view to legitimising a potentially radical argument.

65 Miles (1993: 179) considers the function which Romulus assigns to legitimate children as a reflection of the role that their mothers will later perform: "(Women and children) will be the mutually valuable object that will bring parties (mother and father, husbands and blood relatives) together."

66 As the historian frames the proposition, to the extent of balancing the syntactical framework and its semantic emphasis. Liv. 1.9.14: *illas tamen in matrimonio, in societate fortunarum omnium civitatisque et quo nihil carius humano generi sit liberum fore.*

67 Liv. 1.9.15: *mollirent modo iras et quibus fors corpora dedisset darent animos.*

68 It may be more appropriate to regard the radical nature of Romulus' formula as addressed to the women rather than to the reader. If so, Romulus appeals to *muliebris animus* "with the voice of male authority" (Miles 1993: 180), stressing alliance for mutual interest and sentimental associations of kinship and community. In this regard, viewing his argument as rhetorical (in the forensic sense) classifies his offer as feigned rather than authentic; cf. the *blanditiae* and *preces* of the abducting men.

69 This exhortatory admonition combines with the instructional reference to associate Romulus with the pedagogy of authoritarian rule. Brown (1995: 298) compares the formality of his argument with the men's intimacy.

70 Liv. 1.9.16: *accedebant blanditiae virorum factum purgantium cupiditate atque amore quae maxime ad muliebre ingenium efficaces preces sunt.*

71 Miles (1993: 184) notes that, if the men display authentic feelings towards the women, such emotional motivation casts them in a mould similar to those identified as signifiers of qualitative passion (e.g., Tarpeia, the Latin communities), and therefore brands them as "unreliable members of the community." Though applied in a different context, one might incorporate Brown's (1995: 299) observation that such a display of emotion subverts the pragmatism of Roman decorum, which "frowned upon a man's private desires influencing his public actions."

72 Wiseman (1983: 447).

73 Liv. 1.10.3: *pro ardore ira*; 4: *vanam sine viribus iram esse.*

74 Liv. 1.11.1: *raptim et ad hos Romana legio ducta*; 11.3-4: *quod alienis cladibus ceciderant animi.*

75 For discussion of Carmenta, see Chapter 1.3; for Hersilia, Chapter 3.2; and for Lavinia, Chapter 4.2. In each of these instances, the woman is regarded as possessing certain qualities favourable to the operation of the state and worthy of recognition by men. Of especial interest is Hersilia's influence over her rational husband at the moment when he is overwhelmed by strong positive emotion. Cf. Liv. 1.11.2: *duplicique victoria ovantem Romulum.*

76 Cf. Halperin (1990: 113–151, esp. 148–151).
77 Liv. 1.11.5-9; for discussion of Tarpeia, see Chapter 3.2. Brown (1995: 300) sees Livy's reconstruction as a paradigm of "male and female nature in conflict and complementarity ... an illustration of the interaction of men and women, a playing out ... of their essential differences." His essentialist claim can be disputed. Instead, his concept may be redefined as a representational exploration of male territories of power configured as the structural *inventio* of gendered relations. The blurring of clear-cut distinctions which Brown sees as operative between male and female, powerful and weak, becomes explicable as an epideictic dissection of the praise- and blameworthy in male activity alone.
78 Liv. 1.11.5: *novissimum ab Sabinis bellum ortum multoque id* maximum *fuit; nihil enim per iram aut cupiditatem actum est, nec ostenderunt bellum prius quam intulerunt.*
79 Liv. 1.11.5: *nec ostenderunt bellum prius quam intulerunt.*
80 For Tarpeia, see Chapter 3.2.
81 Roman passions: *quam ira et cupiditate* (Liv. 1.12.1); Hostilius' valour: *audacia sustinebat* (Liv. 1.12.2); Romulus' entreaty: *deme terrorem Romanis fugamque foedam siste* (Liv. 1.12.5); tide of battle turned: *sed res Romana erat superior* (Liv. 1.12.10).
82 Liv. 1.13.1-2: *tum Sabinae mulieres, quarum ex iniuria bellum ortum erat, crinibus passis scissaque veste, victo malis muliebri pavore, ausae se inter tela volantia inferre, ex transverso impetu facto dirimere infestas acies, dirimere iras, hinc patres, hinc viros orantes, ne sanguine se nefando soceri generique respergerent, ne parricidio maculaent partus suos, nepotum illi, hi liberum progeniem.*
83 Liv. 1.13.1: *quarum ex iniuria bellum ortum erat.*
84 Liv. 1.9.15: *saepe ex iniuria postmodum gratiam ortam.*
85 Liv. 1.13.1: *crinibus passis scissaque veste.*
86 Hemker (1985: 43) draws attention to Livy's "plethora of detail" by which he "dramatizes the women's intervention."
87 Brown (1995: 308) characterises the abducted women's intervention as the suppression of "one aspect of their nature {*muliebris pavor*} in order to give expression to other even more fundamental aspects (peacefulness and familial loyalty)." This view ignores Livy's explicit internalisation of guilt and the externalisation of the masculine requisite of sacrificial exchange. Brown sees Livy's insistence on "the relevance of gender to the dynamics of the action" as a "readjustment of conventional assumptions." True enough, "rhetoric lines up with physical situation and personal relationship" (309). But the annalist's emphasis on the women's integration into the ideological paradigm of a male representational economy takes the reader further. Livy allows his audience to explore the limits of appropriate and effective male behaviour, mediated through the agency of the Sabine women.
88 Just as they beset Hersilia with entreaties: *precibus raptarum fatigata* (Liv. 1.11.2; see Ch. 3.2 for the detail).
89 Liv. 1.13.3: *si adfinitatis inter vos, si conubii piget, in nos vertite iras; nos causa belli, nos volnerum ac caedium viris ac parentibus sumus; melius peribimus quam sine alteris vestrum viduae aut orbae vivemus.*
90 For discussion of Rhea Silvia as the ambiguous emblem of divinely polluted, humanly regulated sacral flesh, see Chapter 4.2.
91 Liv. 1.13.4: *movet res cum multitudinem tum duces; silentium et repentina fit quies; inde ad foedus faciendum duces prodeunt. nec pacem modo sed civitatem unam ex duabus faciunt. regnum consociant: imperium omne conferunt Romam.*

92 Alliance: *ad foedus faciendum duces prodeunt nee pacem modo sed civitatem unam ... regnum consociant* (Liv. 1.13.5); expansion: *geminata urbe* (Liv. 1.13.5); peace: *laeta ... pax* (Liv. 1.13.6); order: *nomina earum curiis inposuit* (Liv. 1.13.7).

93 Liv. 1.13.6: *ex bello tam tristi laeta repente pax cariores Sabinas viris ac parentibus et ante omnes Romulo ipsi fecit.*

94 Liv. 1.9.15: *quo nihil carius humano generi sit liberum fore.*

95 Hemker (1985: 43) condenses the semantic thrust of Livy's rhetorical hermeneutic in this way: "The Roman soldiers' control over the forces of reproduction ensures the strength of the Roman state." While the subsequent breakdown of *societas* between Roman and Sabine might in part support her additional contention that the "state's militaristic policies" effectively victimise the reproducers and the reproduced – that is, the women and children ("potential warriors") – this interpretation seems ancillary to Livy's chief intent: the problematic representation of gendered relations. Hemker's "tragic possibility" – that a woman's reproductive capacity places her at risk of intolerable violence, the effects which may well pass down to the next generation – is not a theme specific to the seizure of the Sabine women. Cf. the exemplary justice meted out by fathers to sons in the name of *disciplina* (e.g., Liv. 2.5.5-10).

96 Brown (1995: 312) sees "an alternation based on the male versus female orientation of episodes" as emblematic of "a development ... which charts the evolution of (women's) psychology and their status and importance within the community." Equally plausible is the view that Livy's successive registration of the women (*virgines, raptae, mulieres*) – in the context of their transformation from outsiders to *matronae* – is an articulation of acculturation to the dominant ideology. In fact, given Livy's careful artistic reconstruction of the episode, it is possible to see the unification of Roman and Sabine and the marriage of abductors and hostages as coeval images of the one discourse. It reflects the achievement of a sociopolitical ideal transcending gender.

97 Miles (1993: 163).

98 Liv. 2.33.5.

99 Political rights for plebeians formally recognised prior to 491 BCE include the creation of the offices of plebeian tribune and plebeian aedile and the legitimacy of the plebeian curiate assembly (*consilium plebis*), which elected the plebeian tribunes and aediles, and passed legislation (*plebescita*) that applied only to the plebeians. See Forsythe (2006: 157–183).

100 Liv. 2.34.

101 Liv. 2.39.1-4.

102 Liv. 2.40.1-12; Dion. Hal. *Ant. Rom.* 8.39.1-54.5, 55.3.

103 Liv. 2.39.9-12.

104 Liv. 2.39.7-8: *quae profecto orta esset – adeo tribuni iam ferocem per se plebem criminando in primores civitatis instigabant – sed externus timor, maximum concordiae vinculum, quamvis suspectos infensosque inter se iungebat animos. Id modo non conveniebat quod senatus consulesque nusquam alibi spem quam in armis ponebant, plebes omnia quam bellum malebat.*

105 Liv. 2.40.1-2: *tum matronae ad Veturiam matrem Coriolani Volumniamque uxorem frequentes coeunt. id publicum consilium an muliebris timor fuerit, parum invenio: pervicere certe, ut et Veturia, magno natu mulier, et Volumnia duos parvos ex Marcio ferens filios secum in castra hostium irent et, quoniam armis viri defendere urbem non possent, mulieres precibus lacrimisque defenderent.*

106 Liv. 2.40.1: *id publicum consilium an muliebris timor fuerit parum invenio.*

107 Cf. Liv. 1.13.1: the *pavor* of the Sabine women.

108 Liv. 2.40.3: *mulieres precibus lacrimisque*; 4: *lacrimas muliebres*; 9: *fletusque ab omni turba mulierum ortus et comploratio sui patriaeque*. Cf. Tabulae XII.10.3, 6-7, restricting the congregation of female mourners and providing statutory regulation of burial practice in general.

109 Cf., e.g., Liv. 2.7.4: *decus publica fuit maestitia ... matronae*; Liv. 2.16.5: *luxere matronae ut Brutum*.

110 Cf. Wiseman (1994: Ch. 1), for a discussion of the likelihood that Roman historians of the earlier second century BCE were strongly influenced by dramatic performances. See also Ogilvie's (1963: 334) discussion of the possible resonances between 2.40.3-5 and the language of Greek tragedy (Aesch. *Sept.* 580–583; Eur. *Hec.* 550–553; [Sen.], *Phoenissae* 446).

111 Liv. 2.40.5-9: *sine, priusquam complexum accipio, sciam, inquit, ad hostem an ad filium venerim, captiva materne in castris tuis sim. in hoc me longa vita et infelix senecta traxit ut exsulem te deinde hostem viderem? potuisti populari hanc terram quae te genuit atque aluit? non tibi, quamvis infesto animo et minaci perveneras, ingredienti fines ira cecidit? non, cum in conspectu Roma fuit, succurrit: intra illa moenia domus ac penates mei sunt, mater coniunx liberique? ergo ego nisi peperissem, Roma non oppugnaretur; nisi filium haberem, libera in libera patria mortua essem. sed ego mihi miserius nihil iam pati nec tibi turpius usquam possum, nec ut sum miserrima, diu futura sum: de his videris, quos, si pergis, aut immatura mors aut longa servitus manet.*

112 Liv. 2.40.1-2.

113 Liv. 2.40.9: *uxor deinde ac liberi amplexi, fletusque ab omni turba mulierum ortus et comploratio sui patriaeque fregere tandem virum. complexus inde suos dimittit: ipse retro ab urbe castra movit.*

114 Cf. Asc. p23 Strangl., referring to that personal quality of a Roman matron which expressed a moral authority thought by others as improper to question.

115 Liv. 1.13.3-4. NB This follows Hersilia's oblique representation to her husband Romulus on their behalf (Liv. 1.11.2); see also Chapter 3.2.

116 Cf, Mustakallio (1990: 130): "[t]his was not the first time when ... a group of women bearing their children ... defended such an order which would bind the members of families together and thus put them into their proper places and roles in society."

117 Liv. 2.40.10-11: *abductis deinde legionibus ex agro Romano, invidia rei oppressum perisse tradunt, alii alio leto. ... non inviderunt laude sua mulieribus viri Romani – adeo sine obtrectatione gloriae alienae vivebatur – monumento quoque quod esset, templum Fortunae muliebri aedificatum dedicatumque est.*

118 Liv. 2.40.10: *invidia res oppressum perisse.*

119 Liv. 2.40.12: *monumentoque quod esset templum Fortunae muliebri aedificatum dedicatumque est.* Cf. the alleviation of the threat posed by Lars Porsenna through the heroic virtue of Cloelia, commemorated by the erection of an equestrian statue in honour of her glorious deeds.

120 Contra L'Hoir (1992: 81), as displaying the antithesis of order in a republic based on that virtue.

121 Cf. 2.1.1-2: *liberi iam hinc populi Romani ... imperiaque legum potentiora quam hominum*; see also [Sallust], *Ep. ad Caesarem* 2.5.3: *nullius potentia super leges orat.*

122 Liv. 2.40.11-12: *non inviderunt laude sua muliebribus viri Romani adeo sine obtrectatione gloriae alienae vivebatur.*

123 Livy's notion of *libertas* under the Augustan principate in general and as applied to Augustus in particular – and its conceptualisation by readers of AUC history – will have been informed first and foremost by the princeps' own statement at the opening of the record of his achievements and expenses which

he left to be set up before his mausoleum. At the opening of his *Res Gestae* Augustus states: "I championed into liberty the state oppressed by the arbitrary rule of a faction" (*RG* 1.1: *a domination factionis oppressam in libertatem vindicavi*). For a discussion of the relationship between *principatus* and *libertas*, see Hammond (1963).

124 Liv. 34.1.1: *inter bellorum magnorum aut vixdum finitorum aut imminentium curas intercessit res parva dictu, sed quae studiis in magnum certamen excesserit.*

125 Liv. 34.1-8.3.

126 Liv. 34.1.3: Weight of gold: no more than half an ounce (*semiuncia*); type of clothing: variegated in colour (particularly when trimmed with purple) (*versicolor*); category of transport: a wheeled carriage (*vehiculo*).

127 War in Spain: cf. Liv. 33.21.6-9; war with Antiochus: cf. 33.45.1-5.

128 Kraus (1993: 13); cf. Cicero, *de orat.* 2.63. See also White (1987: 6-9).

129 Speeches: Cato (Liv. 34.2-4) and Valerius (Liv. 34.5-7); male-female interaction: Liv. 34.1.5-7, 8.1-2. According to Briscoe (1981: 43–44), the Valerius speaking on behalf of the repeal of the *lex Oppia* is probably L. Valerius Tappo (pr. 192, iiivir 190, 189 BCE). On the rhetorical ploy of using topography, real or imagined, and the relationship between depictions of urban space and gendered action, see the introductory discussion in this chapter (Chapter 2.1) of the matronal demonstration of 43 BCE.

130 The debate is initiated by the proposal of the tribunes M. Fundanius and L. Valerius to abrogate a law carried in the midst of the Second Punic War 20 years prior to this.

131 Liv. 33.43.1. Rriscoe (1981: 44) notes that "there can be little doubt that Flaccus supported Cato."

132 Liv. 34.1.4.

133 Liv. 34.1.6. Cf. Sherwin-White (1978: 74–75).

134 Privileges and preconceptions. 34.1.5: *matronae nulla nec auctoritate nec verecundia nec imperio virorum*). Public and political space. 34.1.5: *omnes vias urbis aditusque in forum obsidebant viros descendentes ad forum orantes*; 7: *et consules praetoresque et alios magistratus adire et rogare audebant*; 8.1-2: *maior frequentia mulierum … in publicum effudit unoque agmine omnes Brutorum ianuas obsederunt.*

135 34.8.3: *viginti annis post abrogata est quam lata.*

136 As Briscoe (1981: 39–40) observes, insertion of an extant speech would amount to plagiarism; and, conversely, invention of an available original speech would be absurd.

137 Following Briscoe (1981: 43); contra Ullmann (1927: 140–143).

138 Qualities: (a) derogatory – *consternatio* (Liv. 34.2.6, 3.6), *indomitum animus* (Liv. 34.2.13), *licentia* Liv. 34.2.13, 14, 3.1), *libido* (Liv. 34.4.3, 6.10), *infirmitas* (Liv. 34.7.14); (b) praiseworthy – *maiestas* (Liv. 34.2.8), *pudor* Liv. 34.2.8, 10, 4.12, 13, 16, 6.8), *sanctitas* Liv. 34.6.8). Actions: *secession* (Liv. 34.2.7, 5.4, 7.14), *seditio* (Liv. 34.2.7, 3.8, 5.5, 7.14), *servitus* (Liv. 34.7.12, 13).

139 Cf. Briscoe (1981: 47) on Livy's confusion of the limits to the control of women *sui iuris* and married with *manus*. See Liv. 34.2.11: "Our ancestors permitted no woman to conduct even personal business without a guardian to intervene on her behalf; they wished them to be under the control of fathers, brothers, husbands" (*maiores nostri nullam, ne privatam quidem rem agree feminas sine tutore auctore voluerunt, in manu esse parentium, fratrum, virorum*).

140 Liv. 34.4.3: "'the more I fear that these things will capture us than we them. Dangerous signs, believe me …'" (*eo plus horreo ne illae magis rei nos ceperint quam nos illas. infesta mihi credite signa*).

141 For example, the statues taken by Marcellus after the capture of Syracuse in 212 BCE (Liv. 25.40.1; 26.21.8); cf. the return of the army that fought against Antiochus (Liv. 39.6.7) (discussed in Chapter 3.1).

142 Liv. 34.7.1: "'All other orders, all men, will feel the change for the better in the state; shall our wives alone get no enjoyment from national peace and tranquility?'" (*omnes alii ordines omnes homines mutationem in meliorem statum rei publicae sentient ad coniuges tantum nostras pacis et tranquillitatis publicae fructus non perveniet*). On the matronal interventions in the wars against the Sabines and with the Volscians under Coriolanus, see this chapter (Chapter 2.2 and 2.3, respectively); for the ransoming of the city after the Gallic capture, the contribution to a severely depleted treasury during the second Punic war and the reception of the Magna Mater by the *matronae primores* in 207 BCE, see the relevant items in Figs. 1 and 2 (nos. 33, 45, 50), and 3.

143 Liv. 34.5.12: *ceterum quod in rebus ad omnes pariter uiros feminas pertinentibus fecisse eas nemo miratus est, in causa proprie ad ipsas pertinente miramur fecisse? quid autem fecerunt?*

144 Cf. Pomeroy (1994: 177–178); Hemelrijk (1987: 221).

145 Liv. 34.2.4: *atque ego uix statuere apud animum meum possum utrum peior ipsa res an peiore exemplo agatur; quorum alterum ad nos consules reliquosque magistratus, alterum ad vos.*

146 Liv. 34.4.1: *saepe me querentem de feminarum saepe de virorum nee de privatorum moda sed etiam magistratuum sumptibus audistis, diversisque duobus uitiis, avaritia et luxuria, ciuitatem laborare, quae pestes omnia magna imperia everterunt.* Cf. (on *luxuria*) Liv. 39.44.1-3; Plut. *Cato* 18.2; Nepos, *Cato* 2.3; (on women) *de agri cultura* 143; Gell. *NA* 10.22, 17.6; Plut. *Cato* 9.6.

147 Liv. 34.7.1: *omnes alii ordines, omnes homines mutationem in meliorem statum rei publicae sentient: ad coniuges tantum nostras pacis et tranquillitatis publicae fructus non perveniet?* Cf. Liv. 34.5.12 (above, n. 143): *ceterum quod in rebus ad omnes pariter viros feminas pertinentibus fecisse.*

148 Liv. 34.7.13: *in vestro arbitrio suum ornatum quam in legis malunt esse; et vos in manu et tutela, non in servitio debetis habere eas et malle patres vos aut viros quam dominos dici.* Liv. 34.7.15: *quo plus potestis eo moderatius imperio uti debetis.*

149 Liv. 24.25.10; 32.7.13, 8.5, 27.3.

150 From exposure to Hellenistic literature – cf. Williams (1968: 608–619) – to the introduction of *ploutos* at Rome (Fabius Pictor fr. 20P) and the commonplaces of Sallust (*BC* 2.3-6, 5.8) and Horace (e.g., *Od.* 3.24).

151 Although Ennius, *Ann.* fr 352V, might well intimate that Cato participated in a debate before a formal vote was taken – and it is similarly conceivable that Livy might have been familiar with a speech ascribed to Cato in one or more of the (no longer) extant annalistic tradition (e.g., Valerius Antias or Claudius Quadrigarius) – it is the presentation of attitude and character which occupies Livy's interest.

152 Kraus (1994: 6).

153 Cf. White (1987: 11–14 and 18–20) on the moralising imperative of self-conscious historiography.

154 See Liv. 34.2.4 (above, n. 145).

155 Cf. Liv. 34.3.8: "What pretext, respectable even to mention, is now given for this insurrection of women?" (*quid honestum dictu saltem seditioni praetenditur muliebri*).

156 Liv. 34.2.2: *nunc domi victa libertas nostra impotentia muliebri hic quoque in foro obteritur et calcatur, et quia singulas sustinere non potuimus universas horremus.*

157 Liv. 34.5.8: *accipe quotiens id fecerint et quidem semper bono publico.*
158 For the references, see above, n. 142.
159 Liv. 34.7.9: "These [elegance of appearance, adornment, and apparel] our ancestors called the woman's world" (*hunc mundum muliebrem appellarunt maiores nostri*).
160 Liv. 34.3.9: "*ut auro et purpura fulgamus,*" inquit, "*ut carpentis festis profestisque diebus, velut triumphantes de lege victa et abrogata et captis ereptis suffragiis vestris, per urbem vectemur: ne ullus modus sumptibus, ne luxuriae sit.*" For Livy's Cato, these are the patriarchal prerogatives of law and franchise.
161 Liv. 34.7.9: *quid aliud in luctu quam purpuram atque aurum deponunt? quid cum eluxerunt sumunt? quid in gratulationibus supplicationibusque nisi excellentiorem ornatum adiciunt?*
162 Liv. 34.2.13: *date frenos impotenti naturae et indomito animali et sperate ipsas modum licentiae facturas.*
163 Liv. 34.7.7: *virorum hoc animos vulnerare posset; quid muliercularum censetis quas etiam parva movent.*
164 Syme (1968: 4), citing the "cardinal virtue" of *orationes* in Greek and Roman historians; Wyke (1994: 141), on the adornment and display of the surface of the female body as a signifier of social definition).
165 Ostentatious female display: *ne qua mulier ... veheretur* (Liv. 34.1.3). Collective female pressure: *matronis ... pristinum ornatum reddi paterentur* (Liv. 34.1.5). Decision: Liv. 34.6.21.
166 Liv. 34.1.5: *matronis quoque pristinum ornatum redid paterentur.*
167 Cf. Liv. 5.25.8-9, regarding the privilege of riding in carriages (awarded to women in recognition of their voluntary contributions).
168 Milnor (2005: 158).
169 Toher (1990: 150).

3

THE RHETORIC OF THE UNFAMILIAR OTHER

Non-Roman women in AUC history

3.1 Stereotypes and *personae*: representing non-Roman female identity

Examining depictions of who people were in the ancient Roman world – how they thought about themselves, how others viewed them, and their defining characteristics – introduces conceptual and practical matters that require careful thought. Life in the 21 century comprises a variety of identities. Individuals and social groups are defined according to whether or not they: have or share common, distinctive cultures, religions, languages, and the like (ethnicity); demonstrate a legal relationship with a formally constituted political entity or state (nationality); possess particular physical characteristics (race); distinguish themselves as male, female, or other in relation to social and cultural sexual differences (gender), display basic attitudes, beliefs, or feelings with respect to social or cultural constructions of sexual preference (orientation), are divided systemically based on perceived social or economic status (class), profess a set of beliefs concerning the cause, nature, and purpose of existence (religion), and so on. The daily lives of men and women living under Roman rule were similarly complex, sustaining many identities, some easily seen and others kept out of sight, some established and secure and others more malleable depending on the circumstances. The rapidly evolving nature of contemporary society has resulted in widespread discussion of identities and in turn provided a range of intellectual tools for examining, explaining, and interpreting them.[1] Of course, ancient Roman society was different from modern contexts, and ancient languages did not afford the same breadth of vocabulary used in relation to the subject of self; but, in spite of this perceived limitation, those who communicated with one another using Latin or Greek terminology understood that identities are made up of many elements that can relate to one another in complicated ways.

In this regard, the Romans appropriated the Greek terminology of asymmetrical identity, applied to groups speaking foreign languages (i.e., *not* Latin or Greek), the so-called "invention of the barbarian" (Gk. *barbaros*; Ln. *barbarus*).[2] What is important to note is that, while views transmitted in literary

107

texts of and about nations and persons other than Roman conformed to a uniform linguistic code, this perspective did not follow a homogeneous representational template: indeed, it has been demonstrated that writers of Latin literature adopted a multitude of registers in which representations of ethnic others were articulated in Roman texts.[3] Even more interesting in the present context is the fact that – apart from one significant exception, namely, the Germani – Livy appears to have avoided the convention, well-established by the mid-1st century BCE, for Roman writers to incorporate ethnographic excurses into historical works.[4] Of course, like his fellow Roman annalists, Livy maintained a consistently pro-Roman outlook in his *Ab Urbe Condita* (AUC) history – at least in the portions that survive from antiquity – creating and elaborating on versions of the Roman past that emphasised Rome's grandeur and courage.[5] When viewed through the lens of ethnic identity, this outlook is especially evident in the historian's representation of Roman imperialism as it pertains to Hannibal and the Carthaginians.[6]

How and why Livy wrote about non-Roman women – as opposed to women from his own social milieu – are questions that intersect with the representation of ethnic or cultural identity in Latin literature in general and AUC history in particular. As we have seen, Livy's depiction of Roman women (Egeria, Carmenta, and the Vestal Virgins; Lucretia; the *frequentia mulierum* of 195 BCE) follows what modern scholarship designates as a key rule of gendered narrative representation: whether mythological, legendary, and historical, Livy's women are shown as simultaneously "other" (different from Roman men as a category of person) and yet "same" (praiseworthy for sharing publicly displayed traits and qualities with their male kinsmen).[7] In the same light, Livy's representation of non-Roman women (Helen; Veturia, Volumnia, and the Sabine women; Damarata, Harmonia, and Heraclia) incorporates a similarly binary approach. However, at least in the examples considered to this point, determining the degree to which Livy's description of women in gendered AUC episodes depends on the ethnic or cultural identity of individual or collective female historical agents or participants is far from straightforward.[8]

To consider the question, therefore, attention will be paid in this chapter to representations of women belonging to societal groups whose national or cultural traditions are other than Roman. In order that the historiographical approach adopted by Livy to describing this category of female is examined in sufficient depth and breadth, the analysis that follows comprises two sections: a detailed examination of a single important historical episode dating to the early 2nd century BCE, the Bacchanalian conspiracy, which involves a number of women belonging to elite and non-elite social strata; and integrated study of nine brief gendered incidents, featuring particular Roman and non-Roman women (Hersilia, Tarpeia, Cloelia, a woman from Pandosia, Busa, the wife of Mandonius and the fiancé of Allucius, Sophonisba, and Theoxena), drawn from books across the extant corpus of the *AUC*. The first section will explore the rhetorical strategies Livy deploys in relation to a narrative where women cross social and political boundaries, inhabit personal and official spaces, and are situated in the foreground of an episode that integrates authentic historical information and a romantic literary story. The second section follows the trajectory of Roman and non-Roman female representation across a range of gendered vignettes depicting Roman, Italian, and foreign women over the course of almost 500 years of AUC history (from the 8th to the early 2nd centuries BCE).

3.2 The Bacchanalia: a fictive history or historical romance of gender relations?[9]

That Livy embellishes the hard core of authentic historical data available to him in order to further the critical purpose of his historiographical project is particularly evident in his retelling of the Bacchanalian affair of 186 BCE.[10] At the outset, the irrelevance of approaching Livy's account of Bacchic persecution in the subjective footprints of *Quellenforscher* should be stressed.[11] Let us accept that Livy modifies the transmitted story of earlier sources without agonising unduly over the putative origins of the final narrative superstructure.

What should prove instructive is a contextual analysis of Livy's elaborated account in the light of official information which confirms certain salient details of his report. Apposition of the letter containing a decree of the senate on the Bacchanalia allows the modem reader to accept the episode as historical, and to ponder (along with his ancient audience) the significance underlying the historian's integration of official senatorial policy with the techniques and devices associated with his historiographical treatment of critical moments in *res Romana*.[12]

The overwhelming scholarly consensus regarding the approach adopted by Livy in his account of the suppression of Bacchanalian cult activities in 186 BCE relegates the textual treatment of plot and characterisation to the stylised realm of Hellenistic and Roman New Comedy.[13] Certainly, his readers would have been familiar with the diction, incidental narrative stratagems, stereotypical characterisations, and paradigmatic structure expected of New Comedy writing. As such, Livy's deployment of formulaic language attached to the commonplace motifs of romantic or comic convention may be explained as another means of creating a recognisable past "quite detached and different from everyday life ... beyond that of its manifestations in particular events of individual tales."[14] In other words, Livy is attempting to make sense of the arbitrary extant *datum* of the *Senatus Consultum de Bacchanalibus* by shaping it to a recognisable pattern already known to his audience.[15]

However, we have previously observed the variety of ploys Livy adopts to subvert his superficial textual conformity to the production and reinforcement of culturally prejudicial historiographical material – and this episode is no exception to that "rule." Thus, the names in Livy's account and the insertion of certain senatorial directives argue for the verisimilitude of historicity.[16]

So, too, the romanticised nature of his "domestic drama" seeks to establish the intertextual dynamic of recognition and acceptance.[17] Nonetheless, the experienced reader would need to respond critically to at least two atypical elements of the narrative: the patent exaggeration and hyperbole associated with the allegations which formulate the Livian picture of Dionysiac ritual and its participants; and the deliberate disruption of the structural development conventionally expected of performative comic patterning.[18]

To illustrate the consciously elaborated literary nature of this episode, consider the following discussion in relation to a simplified visual representation of Livy's dramatic arrangement of the episode's narrative and discursive structure (Table 3.1).

The narrative and discursive elements outlined in Table 3.1.1-2 are easily summarised. The Bacchanalian conspiracy was a foreign ecstatic cult that a disreputable Greek had introduced into Italy. The cult gained many followers among women and marginalised social groups. The cult's secret initiation rites were unseemly and immoral. Cult members performed criminal acts in order to amass funds and influence. An informer brought the cult to the attention of the Roman authorities. In 186 BCE, the Roman Senate outlawed the cult, sought out and punished its followers, and placed harsh controls on its scattered survivors. Throughout, Livy's gendered historiographical method is on display – how he deploys the representation of women and their relations with each other, with men, and with the customs of civil Roman society to tell this important story in a memorable way, to transmit information about a recorded historical episode and the aetiology of particular processes and practices, and to foreground the significance of events that frame the affair and what is required of individuals and society to recognise the causative factors and address their effects (Table 3.1.3).

Livy introduces his account in a very particular way.

> The following year diverted the consuls Spurius Postumius Albinus and Quintus Marcius Philippus from the army and the administration of wars and provinces to the suppression of an internal conspiracy.[19]

If a modern student of literary-critical theory were to regard the introductory sentence of Livy's retelling of the Bacchanalia in a semantic as well as purely narrative sense, then the agenda underpinning the structure of this initial historiographical period might read something like this.[20] On the expository level, the historian alerts his readers to an unconventional diversion of consular prerogative – from the responsibilities of military and provincial administration to dealing punitively with a civil conspiracy. On the semantic plane, Livy is signalling his intention to turn away from the traditional textual rhythm of annalistic arrangement in order to arrogate and restore to prominence the significance of the domestic plot in his vision of AUC history.[21]

Table 3.1 Livy's account of the Bacchanalian conspiracy (Liv. 39.8-18)

Livy, Book 39	Section	Content	
1 *The romanticised and embellished tale (narrative)*			
8	Preface	Arrival and early development of the Bacchic cult in Etruria	Origins of the *coniuratio*
9.1-4	Chapter One	Spread of the cult to Rome and a description of the pressures placed on Aebutius by his mother and stepfather to undergo initiation	Origins of domestic tensions
9.5-10.9	Chapter Two	Introduction of Hispala Faecenia and her role in persuading Aebutius to refuse initiation	Origins of the relationship between the innocent and victimised youth and the warm-hearted courtesan
11.1-7	Chapter Three	Expulsion, wandering and refuge of Aebutius; verification of his allegations	Origins of Aebutius' decision to report the affair
12.1-14.3	Chapter Four	Confrontation, compulsion, and confession of Hispala	Origins of Hispala's decision to reveal information about the Bacchic rites and cult devotees
2 *The insertion of credible information designed to convey historical exactitude (discursive)*			
15.2-5	Introduction	Description of the reasons for the use of the regular formula of prayer prior to the address of a consul to the Roman people	Origins of Roman and non-Roman ritual practices
15.6-9	Proposition	Description of the history of the Bacchic cult, the number of women involved, their role, and the impact of cult practices on male devotees	Origins of female and male degeneracy
15.10-11		Description of the dangers posed by the Bacchic cult	Origins of the role of the popular assembly in times of civil crisis (military and political)
15.10-16.9		Description of the negative effects of the Bacchic cult on individual and civil *mores*	Origins of the application of senatorial decrees to address criminal acts in urban and regional locations (political and religious)

(Continued)

Table 3.1 Livy's account of the Bacchanalian conspiracy (Liv. 39.8-18) (*Continued*)

Livy, Book 39	Section	Content	
15.12	Discussion	Description of consular investigation of the Bacchic cult	Origins of extraordinary magisterial roles in times of civil crisis
16.1-3		Description of criminal conspiracy of members of the Bacchic cult	Origins of state control of private action
16.10-13	Conclusion	Description of the impact of the civil investigation of the Bacchic cult on worship of the gods, the *res publica*, and public/ private conduct.	Origins of magisterial and popular vigilance in times of civil crisis
(14.4-17.3)		*senatus consulta* (cf. 14.5-7)	

3 *The integration and conversion of disharmonious structural and thematic ambiguities*

The resolution of political action and domestic tension

Clearly, such an interpretation of the prelude to Livy's narrative proper would only trigger recognition in the ancient reader on the level of explanation. But the latter emphasis on a transformative understanding of style and purpose betrays the manner in which the arrangement, expression, and resolution of historical content intersects with the artefacts of social consciousness normally buried beneath linguistic and cultural custom. Viewed in this way, Livy's structural organisation reflects an architectonic logic. While normally the distinctive formal structure of Livy's kind of historiography is mirrored in the narrative interplay of external success and internal disorder, the historian is here clearly manipulating the formulaic boundaries of structure and content.[22]

In keeping with the framing paradigm of gendered AUC history, therefore, the events which encompass the Bacchic conspiracy (*coniuratio*) only serve the highlight its profoundly disturbing social and political implications. The problematic triumph of Cn. Manlius Volso and the notorious rout of Q. Marcius Phillipus by the Ligurian Apuani parenthesise the extensive internal episode in such a way as to foreshadow and confirm the dysfunctional interdependence of civil and military affairs.[23]

Specifically, Livy prefaces his account of the arrival and early development of the Bacchic cult in Etruria with a scarcely veiled reference to the commonplace historical thesis regarding Rome's moral decline.

> Yet those things which were then looked upon as remarkable were hardly even the germs of the luxury to come.[24]

112

This is couched in his description of Cn. Manlius' ostentatious triumph.[25] After the cult's effective demise, Livy marks the transition from *res internae* to his account of warfare in northern Italy and Spain with a surprisingly frank account of the humiliation and losses suffered in Q. Marcius' encounter with the provincial Ligurian force.[26] The twin tensions exposed by these select annalistic citations could only strike the late 1st century BCE reader as parallel manifestations of the internal disorder so dramatically evoked between triumph and defeat.[27]

In this regard, the annalistic citations which bracket Livy's account of the Bacchanalian affair neatly exhibit the twin tensions inherent in this kind of transaction: the explicit threat to aristocratic Roman tradition and the challenge represented by continuing provincial hostility to the stability of the *res publica*. The former is embodied in the corrupting importation of foreign excess (*luxuria peregrina*); the latter, by the perverse permissiveness denoted by a failure of military discipline (*indisciplina militaris*). Both are regarded as debilitating and insidious influences potentially and referentially harmful to the continuity of *res Romana*. In this regard, it must surely be more than incidental that the reprimands, criticism, and systematic opposition directed towards *luxuria* and *cupido* – whether the extravagance of ostentatious wealth publicly displayed or the aspirations of men for excessive power – find their focus in the rhetorical or melodramatic episodes of Livy's fourth decade. Specifically, I would cite as instructive the linking figure of that eminent *novus homo*, M. Porcius Cato, whom we encountered in Chapter 2. Three aspects of his career find resonance here: his condemnatory opposition to repeal of the *lex Oppia* (as consul in 195 BCE, accompanied by his influential patrician sponsor, L. Valerius Flaccus); his sedulous prompting of impeachments against P. and L. Scipio (relating to charges of embezzlement and peculation, including the accusation of misappropriating the first of Antiochus III's payments of the indemnity imposed after Magnesia); and his placement of crushing taxes on women's jewellery and clothing (as well as the purchase of young slaves and the ownership of expensive carriages).[28] Each action either directly implicates the transgression of domestic and public space by the female body, or obliquely frames episodes which perform the same function. If we extend the suspension of disbelief in coincidence a stage further, regard the following juxtaposition of Livy's Sallustian panegyric on behalf of Cato[29] – which places the previously identified faults of self-inflation, naked ambition, and virulent attacks on Africanus[30] in a generous and measured light – and, if you are disposed to believe Valerius Antias,[31] the diligent termination of L. Postumius' praetorian investigations into the Bacchanalia. This comparison emphasises a certain syncrony of *mores* elevated and *coniurationes* extinguished.

By now, it should be clear that Livy's pursuit of literary effect is designed not only to engender plausibility but to expose inconsistency. Any attempt to mine his narrative for an accurate estimation of the Bacchic cult is immediately confronted by a vein of misinformation, distortion, and invention. If we compare the focus of the senate's directives with that of the alleged activities denounced by the heroine of Livy's tale, Hispala Faecenia, her lover Aebutius, and the historian himself, it becomes clear that the official document "takes no note of criminal offences and private vices assigned by Livy to the Bacchants."[32] Be that as it may, what message was the contemporary witness to this reported wickedness and excess to take from Livy's relentlessly hostile portrayal of such insidious and pervasive private corruption?[33] Indeed – in concert with the ancient reader of this instalment in the ongoing publication of AUC history – how are we to reconcile such disparate substantive and symbolic features of the narrative as: the strikingly uncharacteristic hostility toward a foreign religion; the exceptional establishment of a *quaestio extraordinaria* to investigate, interrogate, judge, and prosecute the adherents of this *externa religio*; the equally notable interference in the local concerns of Italy;[34] the widespread nature of the persecution and the severity of its penalties; and its sensational and melodramatic stylistic characteristics?[35]

We must decide if it is enough to stigmatise the affair by resorting to political conjecture. True, labelling the incident as an extended example of *coniuratio* enables it to be categorised as a signpost to the emergence of (and official reaction to) a contestation of civic order. Equally, it may be possible to relegate the incident's ambiguities to a manifest distrust and apprehension of disquieting cultic practices or unfamiliar belief-systems. In this regard, such concern can be seen to express itself in the unequivocal echoes of suspicion, intolerance, hostility, and wholesale eradication which pervade Livy's account. Simply put, are we justified in ascribing to the reconstituted Rome of Livian 2nd century BCE history such socio-cultural, political, and/ or ideological explanations for Livy's comic distortions and the aristocracy's unprecedented reactions as religious prejudice, philhellenic xenophobia, class suppression, or moral regulation?

To answer this, we must confront the startlingly prominent discourse of gender relations through which Livy illuminates his internal theme. Again, a graphic depiction of the interpenetrations of character which inform the greater proportion of Livy's account should help (Table 3.2).

In this respect, although it might be asserted that diagrammatic arrangement of discursive and narrative material unnecessarily simplifies or omits useful interpretative detail, the orientation and distribution of male and female participants, in relation to the story's dramatic structure, provides the reader with a significant critical point of departure. Male involvement in those scenes which forward the narrative development of the overall episode is described or enacted in close proximity and sympathetic response to a female catalyst. Of itself, this could be regarded as simply the logical requirement of a story which unfolds in a private context. But, if taken in concert with the graphic image of Livy's structural intentions, the intellectual purpose binding plot and character may be seen in a clearer light.

Table 3.2 The characters of the Bacchanalian conspiracy (Liv. 39.8-18)

Minor protagonists	Major protagonists
Duronia, mother of P. Aebutius (9.2)	**Hispala Faecenia**, freedwoman and noble courtesan (9.5; 11.2; 12.1-2; 13.8; 14.2, 6; 19.3,5)
T. Sempronius Rutilius, father of P. Aebutius and *eques equo publico* (9.3)	Sp. Postumius Albinus, consul and colleague of Q. Marcius Philippus (6.1; 8.1; 9.1; 11.3; 13.3; 14.3; 19.1; 23.1,3; 45.2,5,8)
Paculla Annia, mother of Minius and Herrenius Cerrinus (13.9)	P. Aebutius, lover and tutor of Hispala Faecenia (9.2,6; 11.6; 12.1; 13.1,3,4; 14.3, 6; 19.3,4)
Minius Cerrinus, one of the chief priests and founders of the Bacchic cult (17.6; 19.2)	**Aebutia**, sister of Duronia, aunt of P. Aebutius, and virtuous woman (*proba femina*) (11.3,4,5; 12.1)
	Sulpicia, mother-in-law of P. Aebutius and eminent woman (*gravis femina*) (11.4,6; 12.3; 13.1,3,6)

In essence, the final part of the historian's comic structure, which serves to precipitate unequivocal political action, is also the nexus of characterisation in Livy's account: Faecenia Hispala > Sp. Postumius Albinus > Sulpicia.[36] As such, the culmination of a radical stylistic paradigm (the comic strategy) impacts directly with the deliberative faculty and imperative mechanisms of Rome's policy-making body in a time of considerable civil disturbance.[37] This may be seen to offer the reader an often-sought but seldom-distinguished intersection of hard data and historiographical frame – all in the context of an undeniably gendered predicament.

To establish the pivotal nature of this section of the narrative, it need only be added that the situation is the most profoundly dramatic element of a highly charged scenario, and at the same time the least familiar in terms of established comic conventions. That is to say, the historian's structurally central exposition fails on every level to conform to the shape of the romantic story retailed by Livy to that point. It therefore compels critical attention.

Like the contextual historiographical frame for the episode – on the one hand, the triumph of Manlius; on the other, the defeat of Marcius – what Scafuro identifies as the "inner panel" of Livy's comic scenario is bracketed by the actions and interactions of individuals and groups qualitatively gendered and usually marginal to the scaffold of historical events.[38] To begin with, the introduction of the Bacchic cult and the dissemination of its practices are attached to an obscure Greek male, a petty sacrificial priest, and prophet.[39] Moreover, the effects of his instruction are explicitly associated with the debasement and inversion of what Livy clearly regards as normative behaviour patterns – secret ritual by night instead of open disclosure of

115

profession and teaching; the intermingling of men with women, and those of tender age with their elders (i.e., the indiscriminate debauchery of free-born boys and women); perjury, forgery, violence, and murder. In this way, Livy associates the deleterious impact of Dionysiac worship with the pronounced fraying of the social fabric. To adopt an analogy more apt to the historian's representation, the Bacchanalia is like a cancerous growth infecting the body of the Roman people.[40]

But the ascription of responsibility for establishing the medium – which Livy describes as the *officina* or "training ground"[41] – by which the *unius corpus* is infected changes with the telling.[42] The Greek, unknown/unnamed priests, Roman *matronae*, a Campanian woman (Annia Paculla), women as a collective, and a coterie of male conspirators – all are implicated, each one a presumably originary element in the Bacchanalian aetiology. Whether or not we minimise the narrative's propensity for confusion and assign a more likely sequence to this degenerative process is finally less important than recognising Livy's incorporation of a welter of characters and collective denominations remarkable for its diverse ethnicity, social status, and gender.

Identifying historical likelihood in this episode is, as noted, a difficult and ultimately frustrating assignment, especially given our reliance on the personal and conflicting witness of Hispala. If viewed as scrupulous, then her account to Aebutius can be explained as simply incomplete, its omissions rectified in the more formal report extracted by Postumius. If considered duplicitous, then neither story can be taken on face value (an especially invidious alternative). We must also bear in mind the less than categorical assignment of responsibility to the fraternal Atinii (plebeians), L. Opicernius (Faliscan), and M. Cerrinius (the son of Annia Paculla and brother of Herennius) by Livy – at least according to established reports.[43]

In any event, taken in association with the highly charged and pervasive nature of the Bacchic ritual's symptomatic pathology, it would seem logical to identify the unifying thread of Livy's account as the ease with which the continuity of social history can be disrupted – namely, darkness and secrecy, crime and sexual abuse, the permeability of male and female roles, and the breakdown of customarily defined social boundaries.[44] In other words, regardless of political, institutional, religious and cultural customs, and preconceptions, the training-ground which produces that contagious individual and social disequilibrium (exemplified so spectacularly in the character of this episode) often remains as undetected and just as easily asserts its malignant grasp as the plague of Bacchus afflicting 2nd century BCE Rome. In the same light, then, it can be seen to dwell within all sectors of society, and so transcend all official and conventional perimeters dividing class, race, creed, or gender.

This preoccupation is an integral component of the speech which Sp. Postumius addresses to a specially summoned *contio*. Indeed, the rhetorical core of this *oratio* emphasises the innate and universal challenge faced by the state: "there has never been so great an evil in the body politic involving more persons or more issues."[45] This threat to the security of the state[46] is measured by the enslavement of reason and the perversion of normative action.[47] The *res publica* is most susceptible to this identifiable danger by virtue of ignorance; namely, of reality.[48] The consul's thesis is relentless, and enumerates in no uncertain terms the very elements of the narrative which most resist conventional explanation: the functional ambiguity of gender,[49] the technical illegitimacy of the citizen-soldier, defender of *pudicitia* and *libertas*,[50] and in consequence the antithetical subversion of the *res publica*.[51] The transgressive impulse – whether a function of disposition or the result of imposition – is the existential, ideological, and referential tension which requires suppression.

Regardless of its ostensible form (debased religion, revolutionary assembly, shameful/dishonest action), the nature of Livy's enquiry concerns the definition and preservation of Roman identity. This would appear to be a matter of pivotal importance to the reconstruction of AUC history and an indispensable component, if not exclusive focus, of Livy's historiographical project.

Considering the stakes, it makes sense that the ensuing decrees, indictments, condemnations, and exactions of punishment are represented as the product of an inexorable compulsion of which "nothing in earlier Roman history provides a parallel."[52] If the price of subordination to such a disruptive principle is the loss of individual and civic (i.e., national) selfhood, the burden of survival becomes paramount. Selfhood – or, in this context, identity – may be understood as that ineffable yet intrinsic constellation of qualities by which one is known – and knows. Gruen sees the episode as a vehicle supplying "a means to declare state policy independent of and a restraint upon individual inclinations toward Hellenism." In other words, the dramatic measures adopted by the senate can be explained as symbolic of "the ongoing tension between Roman actions and Hellenic assimilation."[53] Certainly, the framing incident of Manlius' triumph emphasises the threat to Roman tradition posed by the cultural world of Greece.[54] However, I would extend this reading of symbolic significance to incorporate the congeries of attitudinal and behavioural traits invoked and absorbed by Livy's drama. Otherwise, interpretation of the affair is condemned to a naive and simplistic scenario, comprising discrete facets which lack explanatory cohesion.

In this way, by following a necessarily circuitous yet hopefully intelligible route, designed in part to echo Postumius' hesitant and oblique investigation, and certainly to traverse the path pursued by the historian's highly wrought narrative, the reader arrives at the structural heart of the narrative/thematic conspiracy. The account of Faecenia Hispala's meeting with the consul Postumius in the house of his mother-in-law Sulpicia – and the questions which arise in reading of the process by which the "noble prostitute" (*scortum nobile*) is eventually induced to inform – encompass the literary and sociological territory deliberately marked out by Livy as fertile ground for the exploration of issues ordinarily foreign to the male-prominent rhythms of forum and battlefield. Essentially, if the meeting is placed in its narrative context, it becomes clear that the preservation of Roman *mores* from abuse and transgressive violence (criminal or sexual, actual or symbolic) forms the all-inclusive field of Postumius' civil vision – as part of the personal investigation into secret conspiracies which is eventually to be assigned by decree to him and his fellow-consul (the ill-fated Q. Marcius Philippus) – and Livy's historiographical regard.[55]

Knowledge of Titus Sempronius Rutilus' implied misappropriation of part (at least) of Publius Aebutius' inheritance, and of the ubiquity of Bacchic corruption, sets the investigation in motion.[56] Further, while the chain of communication has many links, the ramifications of this disruptive activity (if widespread) clearly require urgent consideration and explicit confirmation.

It is at this crucial juncture of understanding and necessity that Livy's characterisation of Faecenia Hispala comes into play. Even the most cursory comparison between the source of information and the other significant participants in the domestic drama is suggestive. In terms of historiographical (and avowedly literary) conventions of exemplary typology, the reader is able to assign the following roles:

1 Sulpicia – the epitome of *decorum* and *dignitas* ("quintessence of *gravitas, pietas,* and *sapientia*").[57]
2 Postumius – model of magisterial *officium* (diligent, determined, and single-mindedly dutiful) and patriotic protector of civil order and social tradition (consul and *vindex*).
3 Aebutia – *exemplum* of honesty, simplicity, and religious scrupulosity (a Roman "of the old stamp").[58]
4 Aebutius – the naive yet reputable youth of "romance" (the innocent and mistreated *adulescens*).[59]

and, on the debit side of Livy's exemplary ledger,

5 Aebutius' wicked mother and stepfather, Duronia and Sempronius.[60]

But what of Hispala: "noble courtesan of the New Greek comedy, though lacking the poise of a Menandrian heroine"; "a slave of presumably Spanish origin (who) assumed the *nomen* Faecenia from her patron on emancipation"; "unselfish devoted mistress" of the romantic literary tradition and "a literary topos, the 'whore with the heart of gold' ... still a *scortum* and seducer of the young?"[61] The fact that Livy allows the character of his story's heroine to carry such an ambiguous narrative and thematic burden establishes Hispala as critical to any understanding of the episode. This textual weight should also alert the reader to avoid ascribing traditional stereotypical appellations or motivations to this most human of Livy's historiographical female representations.

The contradictions are legion. She is introduced as a member of a specific class (*libertina*) and the practitioner of a highly visible profession (*scortum*). Even if the modern reader fails to recognise the preconceptions and cultural assumptions associated with such terms as "freedwoman" and "whore,"

Hispala's subordinate status in the eyes of Livy's audience must be self-evident. The derogation adhering to any person earning money by commerce or trade – not to mention the dependency of a tutor-less ex-slave on the provision of law and the authorisation of state officials[62] – could only place Hispala in a context explicitly defined by biases of gender and class.

Yet, Livy is at pains to subvert these negative prejudices by allotting to her a worth dissimilar to that normally implied by her occupation.[63] This valorisation comprises an affective dimension which both avoids attaching blame to Aebutius and substitutes itself in place of his mother's unnatural greed.[64] In addition to the qualitative nuances of affectionate regard and unequivocal generosity, Hispala is characterised as a proponent of filial and religious piety.[65] But the reader also knows her to be a seducer and a participant in the very *officina* which presently threatens the domestic and civic Roman community.[66]

If this suspicion – that such complications of respectable and reprehensible *topoi* are deliberate and purposeful narrative inclusions – holds true, it is less surprising that Hispala's meeting with the consul reflects a corresponding degree of tension.[67] By now, the reason for this problematic alternation of intentions, compulsions, reactions, and perspectives is becoming transparent. Hispala exists within the disturbing landscape that marks the customary boundary between *res publica* and *privata*. She inhabits a territory left unexplored for the most part, and consequently generates conflicting attitudinal and intellectual responses. What Livy asks of his (a)historical/ historicised personage is nothing short of heroic: to transcend self- and socially-imposed normative limits of gender and status, to unite the domestic and civic spheres, and to initiate what Livy perceives and represents as the necessary reappraisal of *mores maiorum*.

All the more instructive that the historian consciously chooses to situate his exploration of the process underlying such inherently dramatic developments within archetypally conventional environs – the inner confines of the house of a consul's mother-in-law[68] – and that he symbolises its oscillating permutations as a confrontation between the socially marginalised and delimited Hispala and the composite weight of tradition embodied in Postumius and Sulpicia. No wonder the freedwoman from the Aventine is alarmed and almost faints; no surprise that she is seized by such panic and trembling that she is struck speechless. All the recognisable rhetorical motifs are brought to bear, simultaneously affording the tentative reader a modicum of narrative familiarity and alerting the more critical interpreter to the approach of an historiographical *locus*.[69]

And what is so traumatic that Hispala must run the gamut of strategies designed to repudiate her involvement in this affair? Just that! Engagement with the imperatives of civic responsibility, and the subordination of private concerns to public duty pose a dual challenge to the individual in Roman society who places a greater value on emotional satisfaction and personal security. On the one hand, the Bacchantes may be seen to represent those who permit loyalty to self and the dictates of inordinate desire to outweigh the ideological impulse to service and to maintenance of the state. On the other, the custodians of the social order (i.e., the aristocratic oligarchy) are depicted as obligated to submit the manifestations of that activity (impinging on the common weal) to scrutiny and public regulation.[70]

This apposition of collective interest and individual excess – and the apprehension it is capable of engendering – is exemplified in the dilemma faced (and eventually resolved) by the senators after Postumius' report.[71] Clearly, the *patres* invest similar concern for the interests of the state and the ramifications of familial involvement in the conspiracy at the private level. But they eventually side with the installation of a *quaestio extraordinaria* and the arrogation of exceptional public authority, emphatically distinguishing social restraint from individual aspiration. What Livy manages to inject into his exposition is the reality of self-abnegation – its cost in human terms. The consul, his mother-in-law, the Aebutii and the senators would naturally apprehend the necessities of social order. In the cyclic narrative of traditional AUC history, they internalise its prerogatives.[72] So, too, the *exempli mali* would always embody submission to base instinct and the susceptibility of irrational character to presumption and desire.

Hispala is outside the mould, cast adrift of the reassuring literary patterns which would normally reconcile articulations of marginal status and socio-political circumstance through separate strategies. Instead, Livy deploys a socially disadvantaged woman as the focus of his carefully constructed composition. Through her, he is able to explore the problematic issues arising from his depiction of conflicting loyalty, if only because Hispala inhabits a space exterior to the requirements of normative behaviour, and therefore of the conventional limitations of historiographical narrative. Thus, on the one hand Sulpicia fulfils the role adhering to the aristocratic female who has the ear of a *vir fortis*, namely as supporter of another woman struck low by difficult times and as mollifier of the "great man's" passion in the face of unexpected circumstance.[73] On the other hand, Hispala must confront the knowledge of her subordinate status, the infidelity of her lover,[74] the implications of her impiety and the threat to her person following on from her revelations – all in a context of intimidation and urgent expectation. She is Livy's formulation of the ordinary human condition, that flawed, inconsistent social being wherein mind and heart interact in unpredictable and irregular fashion. In essence, she is the historicised configuration of the non-elite, quasi-Roman woman, at one and the same time antithetical to the elite male value system which superordinates such concepts as *dignitas, civitas*, and *virtus*, yet representative of culturally desirable qualities and abilities like *munificentia*.[75]

Like the rift in the social fabric embodied in the nightly ritual of the Bacchanalia, this characterisation of experiences and attitudes common to males and females of indeterminate status and ethnic affiliation must be reconstituted. If the audience is to accept the historian's invitation to explore the implications of such a radical notion, then Livy will be required to resolve the problematic elements of his artistic elaboration in the same way that the outcome of his broader historiographical subject is restored to a temporary equilibrium. In other words, just as Rome's permeation by the alarming contagion of the Bacchic cult provides the catalyst for a reaffirmation of senatorial prominence in the affairs of state, so Hispala's unorthodox integration into public life sets into motion the reassertion of authority and the reclamation of responsibility for the security of the state. Hispala's reintegration is portrayed here as a frightening disruption of the status quo: resisted and denied by Hispala herself; compelled and encouraged by Postumius and Sulpicia. In the process of civil transformation, Hispala cannot remain outside the normative requisites of either literary or social expectations. Otherwise, her character would take on the decidedly orthodox but contextually inexpedient representative function ascribed to women by polemic and invective, namely, the "other" which threatens male control – in this case, the combined *auctoritas* of author and of patriarchal Rome. So Livy provides Hispala with the necessary accoutrement adhering to the legitimate display of qualities usually assigned to elite men (and women) in unconventional or transcendent historical circumstances.[76] She is sequestered under Sulpicia's care at the request of the consuls and emerges from protective custody – albeit now as the subject of Livy's elaborated senatorial decree – enfranchised beyond her manumitted status and designated inviolable under state auspices. In order, Hispala is assigned an apartment above Sulpicia's house, named as the beneficiary by official pronouncement of certain rights (bestowal and withdrawal of resources, marriage outside her gens, personal status of guardian) normally legitimised by the will of a deceased *vir*, and designated as subject to the duties of patronage and safe-conduct, to be monitored and enforced by present and future consuls or praetors.[77]

In essence, the subordination of private interests and relationships to the concerns of the larger political community is signalled by senatorial recognition of civic service, which resolves the tensions of socially transgressive action. The irreconcilable conceptual complementarity of Hispala as identifiably expressive of the alterity and inferiority commonly associated with the socially marginal by virtue of gender, status, or ethnicity – and yet responsible for confirming the need to act at a critical historical moment – is eradicated by the male-sanctioned and recommended change of symbolic standing in the community: from a prostitute of some note to a legally competent, equivalent-elite Roman woman.

3.3 From Hersilia to Theoxena: mirrors of male reality?

In order that this discussion might be viewed in perspective, the chapter will conclude with a brief itinerary illustrative of Livy's representations of the female. The intention is to apply the tentative conclusions of the preceding analysis to a cross-section of discrete examples which covers the breadth of extant text. Hopefully, this will provide a useful catalogue of gendered traits, contextualised so as to determine more precisely to what extent women in AUC history – and non-Roman women in particular – can be regarded simply as models of specific personality types, and to what degree Livy employs stereotypical constructions as part of a more elaborate historiographical project.

3.3.1 Hersilia

Consider, first, Hersilia, the wife of Romulus.[78] As her husband was exulting in his double victory over neighbouring tribal communities, Hersilia – beset with entreaties by the captive Sabine women – begged Romulus to forgive his enemies, the women's parents, and receive them into the state, which would in any case gain strength by such harmony. Rome's first king readily granted her request.[79]

In this momentary vignette, the reader sees Hersilia as an agent in her own right, acting on behalf of a captive female collective.[80] What is equally apparent is that her plea, coincident with Romulus' celebration of his triumphs over the Caeninenses and Antemnates, smacks of psychological strategy. It is the explicit action of a woman who recognises an opportunity to extract a concession from her jubilant spouse, and who responds to the needs of concerned individuals reasonably and directly.[81] More than this, the fact that Livy implicitly stresses Hersilia's recognition of the causal link between Romulus' satisfaction of the Sabine women's entreaties (*preces*) and the conceptual fortification of the city through harmonious relations (*concordia*) reflects a sense of higher purpose associated with her intimate prayer. Simply, Hersilia embodies the desire to mollify the disequilibrium between Tyrrhenian nations through remission and assimilation.[82]

It is interesting that the captured women recognise Hersilia's potential for influence over Romulus, just as she intuits the propitious nature of his exultation as a chance for judicious suggestion. Of course, all is contingent on the king's acquiescence. The fragility of female influence is tangibly expressed by the casual brevity of Livy's conclusion to the oblique exchange between husband and wife: "[Hersilia's request] was obtained easily" (*facile impetratum*).

3.3.2 Tarpeia

Hersilia's intervention is positioned in close proximity to the incident of Tarpeia's treachery.[83] According to the surviving accounts, Tarpeia, daughter of Spurius Tarpeius, commander of the Capitol garrison, fell in love with Tatius, and/or was greedy for the gold bracelets worn by the Sabine warriors. She therefore offered to betray the Capitoline Hill to the Sabines if she would give her what they had on their left arms (which may have been either bracelets or shields), and she did so, but was rewarded by being crushed to death by the Sabines' shields.

Tarpeia is unnamed in Livy's account. She is identified as *filia* and *virgo* (a daughter of marriageable age), denominations acquired in relation to the commander of the Roman citadel, Sp. Tarpeius. But her signification is further defined in the course of the citation. She is a traitor and betrayer (*proditor*), susceptible to the appeal of material gain and reward without merit.[84] In a sense, Tarpeia encompasses a profile of treachery (*fraus*) in response to deception (*dolus*). As such, she may be seen to personify the anathema of betrayal from within, the ignominy of seductive materialism and the naivete of impetuous, untutored youth. From one angle, then, Tarpeia is the duplicitous object of the Sabine king's prudent deception.[85] Alternatively, she embodies the *exemplum* of decisive treachery abnegated as much by the deceivers as the deceived.[86] In the latter case, the ancillary legendary variants appended by Livy draws the reader's attention to her *cupiditas*. This is an emotion specifically denied the Sabine besiegers, thereby casting Tarpeia as beneath even the Roman attackers' contempt.[87]

Notably, Livy's account of these events fails to mention the variety of representations of Tarpeia – her motivations, actions, and legacy – depicted in the source tradition available to him. In the other extent narrative dealing with these events – the lengthier episode recorded in the *Antiquitates Romanae*, a narrative drawing on material provided in the now lost works of Fabius Pictor, L. Cincius Alimentus, and L. Calpurnius Piso Frugi – Dionysius of Halicarnassus describes the young woman's negotiations with the Sabines as "inspired by the desire of performing a noble deed"; and, more importantly, that "she was honoured with a monument in the place where she fell and lies buried on the most sacred hill of the city and the Romans every year perform libations to her."[88] While Dionysius notes contradictions between the version of events which he eventually follows (Piso) and observations by Fabius as to the reason why Tarpeia falls beneath the shields of the Sabines, he expresses his willingness to rely more on the historical reliability of Piso's account due to the fact that, if she had died in betraying her country to the enemy, it was unimaginable that she would have received any of the honours accorded her.[89]

What this means, of course, is that Livy made particular choices in crafting his representation of Tarpeia – choices which, again, may be reasonably associated with the historical and legendary events framing the episode. The preceding vignette which recalls Hersilia as the person who mediated between the Romans and the Sabines stands in sharp counterpoint to Livy's account of Tarpeia's treachery. While providing a logical aetiology for the name of the Tarpeian rock – which marks the site for the execution of convicted traitors in later Roman history – the historian sets his tale of the treacherous *virgo* between twin myths of heroism in the face of national crisis: Hersilia on the one hand; and that of the bravery of the Sabine champion Mettius Curtius, who defeated Rome's appointed defender Hostius

Hostilius prior to the final assault of the Sabines, but was put to flight not far from the Palatine gate by a band of gallant youths led on by Romulus.[90]

In addition to the relationship between framing stories of exemplary courage (Roman and non-Roman) and an internal episode depicting an act of unqualified duplicity governed by personal desire, Livy's historical narrative at this early point in Book 1 situates Tarpeia's treacherous bargain between twin episodes marking Rome's victorious trajectory in establishing itself as a militarily secure, politically stable, and socially ordered community – the end of the wars with the Caninenses, the Sabines, and Rome's nearest rivals, Fidenae and Veii;[91] the organisation of the people into 30 *curiae* and 3 tribes; the apotheosis of Romulus, the city's founder, and, following a brief *interregnum*, the continuation of monarchical rule under Numa Pompilius, Rome's second king.[92] As a reflection of contemporary Augustan discourse, Tarpeia's story brings to the surface and places under scrutiny the relationship between private and public and how, in contrast to explicitly virtuous (i.e., male – Romulus; Hostius Hostilius; Mettius Curtius – or quasi-masculine – Hersilia) conduct and expression, stereotypically female behaviour (i.e., Tarpeia's excess, indulgence, and debauchery) places the public good (in other words, the *res publica*) in jeopardy.[93]

3.3.3 Cloelia

Now when courage had been thus distinguished, even the women were inspired to deeds of patriotism.[94]

As part of the treaty which ended the war between Rome and Clusium in 508 BCE, Roman hostages were taken by Lars Porsenna. One of the hostages, a young woman named Cloelia – an unmarried girl, vulnerable with regard to her place in patriarchal Roman society, and perceived as lacking physical strength (though capable of swimming a reasonable distance) – fled the Clusian camp, leading away a group of unmarried Roman maidens.[95] According to Valerius Maximus, she mounted a horse and, crossing the river Tiber, "freed not only herself from the condition of a hostage but her country from fear"; Livy does not mention a horse, describing instead Cloelia swimming the Tiber at the head of the band of girls under a rain of hostile darts.[96] In contrast to the *exempla* of Hersilia and Tarpeia, and despite his failure to mention a steed, Livy's representations of Cloelia's dramatic and daring rescue of young hostages from the Etruscan king Porsenna earns for this heroic *virgo* an equestrian statue, set up on the summit of the via Sacra in gratitude for her deeds.[97] The reason for the provision of this "new kind of honour" is the pivotal role which Cloelia plays in establishing peace between the Etruscans and the Romans.[98] It should be noted that Livy prefaces his story with the statement that it was the demonstration of *virtus* that inspired Cloelia's extraordinary patriotism.[99] In other words, this courage – "new in a woman" – is dependent on and imitative of the virtues of masculine bravery and moral excellence.[100] For his part, Porsenna reflects Roman admiration for her display of *virtus* by counting her deeds superior to those of Horatius Cocles and Mucius Scaevola and arrogating to her the choice of hostages to be returned in pledge of peace. For hers, Cloelia combines wisdom and nurture in selecting for rescue those children of an age which particularly exposed them to injury – masculine sagacity, because she chooses the *impubes* most in danger of being outraged (i.e., *muliebria pati*); feminine care, because she allows her emotional sensitivity to forestall any misinterpretation of the rationale underlying her choice.[101] Thus, it is Cloelia's signal manifestation of masculinity which attracts the gift of the Roman people;[102] and her exhibition of national devotion, courageous virtue, and integrity which demonstrates that a Roman woman, in the eyes of the writer of AUC history and his audience, could express more authentic fervour for the *res publica* than any non-Roman male (i.e., Lars Porsenna).

3.3.4 Woman from Pandosia

[A] solitary woman, exposing herself to the inhuman savagery of the raging crowd, besought them to forbear a little, and with many tears declared that her husband and children were prisoners in the hands of the enemy, and that she hoped that with the body of the king, however much disfigured, she might redeem them. this ended the mutilation. what was left of the corpse was cremated at Consentia by the care of none other than the woman, and the bones sent back to Metapontum, to the enemy; whence they were conveyed by ship to Epirus, to his wife Cleopatra and his sister Olympias.[103]

Part of a narrative digression between his record of the years 327 and 326 BCE, Livy describes the exploits and death in Italy of Alexander of Epirus. After suffering defeat near Pandosia in Bruttium, and in flight after breaking through a Lucanian blockade, Alexander was transfixed by a javelin while crossing the river Acheros. According to Livy, his body was "barbarously mangled" (*foeda laceratio corporis*): cut into two, half sent to Consentia, the other half kept for the Lucanians' "sport" (*retenta ad ludibrium*).[104]

At this point in the account, a lone woman from Pandosia – originally a Greek settlement but later overrun by the Bruttians – intervenes. Standing between the Epirote king's brutalised remains and the violence of an enraged crowd (*saevienti turbae*), the woman's steadfast intercession in the face of a display of madness beyond what one would have thought credible for human anger is notable. Like the interposition of the Sabine women on the battlefield, though lacking the support of Veturia and Volumnia's familial and communal networks, Livy situates this lone woman (*mulier una*) outside traditionally female social and civil contexts: well beyond the security of the household, in danger of suffering injury of the kind normally confined to military action. Even more remarkable given the emotional intensity of those who had endured the depredations of Alexander's campaign, she mollifies the crowd's animalistic passion by appealing successfully to their humanity and acceptance of recognised cultural protocols: proper treatment of the deceased king's corpse (cessation of bodily mutilation and cremation); return of Alexander's bones to his wife and sister; return of her husband and children, hostages of the Epirote forces.

Livy's representation of this Italian woman – singularly self-possessed and profoundly courageous in a time of civil distress when confronted by the worst extremes of human savagery; highly moral and steeped in the responsibilities and privileges of rightly performed customary practice; committed to preserving the social bonds of family – stands out starkly as a still point of civilised behaviour amid the turbulent perturbations of Rome's Neapolitan and Sabine wars. Once more Livy inserts a very particular depiction of female behaviour – in this instance, that of an otherwise unknown non-Roman woman – between ongoing seismic political and military events in 4th century BCE Roman history.

3.3.5 Busa

> Those who escaped to Canusium were aided by an Apulian woman of birth and fortune named Busa. The townspeople had merely afforded them the protection of the walls and shelter, but she provided them with corn, clothing, and money for the way, in return for which munificence she was afterwards, on the conclusion of the war, voted honours by the senate.[105]

Livy's mention of Busa takes us from the regional conflicts of a nascent Latium to the desperate struggle of a Mediterranean power against a seemingly implacable foreign nemesis. Her citation is abrupt, terse, but suggestive in context. Following the disastrous rout of the Roman forces at Cannae in 216 BCE – marking the ignominious aftermath of Hannibalic victory and the nadir of Roman fortunes in the war against Carthage – those survivors who flee the field and reach Canusium are provided with protection, shelter, food, clothing, and money for their return to Rome, through the munificence of Busa, a wealthy Apulian woman of good family. For this splendid generosity, she is formally honoured after the war – reminiscent on a considerably larger scale of Hispala's provision for Aebutius.

Busa's *munificentia* marks a deliberate counterpoint to Livy's demoralising itinerary of surrender, ransom, despoliation, and retreat – and embraces the preservation of the military tribunes Ap. Claudius Pulcher and P. Cornelius Scipio.[106] So, too, awareness of the services a women from an Apulian city (Canusium) under Roman rule since 318 BCE[107] – Busa's courtesies and kindnesses (*officiis*) to as many as 10,000 men – provides to the surviving Roman soldiers an exemplary model of right action for the people of

Venusium, where four and a half thousand of Rome's defeated cavalry and infantry had fled to join the consul C. Terentius Varro.[108]

Again, Livy places a woman at the intersection of the socio-political tensions between external threat and internal dysfunction. In accordance with those structural and thematic principles already associated with Livy's gendered historiography, Busa's critical intervention is followed by Scipio's unhesitating confrontation of the crisis. It is the *vir fortis* destined to lead the Roman armies against the Carthaginian menace who acts while the woman who saved him disappears from the narrative altogether and all around are reduced to a kind of numbed stupor of incredulity.[109]

3.3.6 Wife of Mandonius and fiancé of Allucius

Livy allocates the concluding part of Book 26 to Scipio Africanus' victory over New Carthage and the consequences of his triumphant attack.[110] Following the city's defeat, the Romans obtained jurisdiction over the captive Carthaginians, important representatives of local communities. According to Livy's account, the hostages were managed in a particular order, each section providing a larger part of the overall picture but reproduced separately for close study. With respect to the first and most substantial group, Scipio ascertained their homelands and dispatched emissaries to these locations so that the prisoners could be brought home by their own people. Those lucky enough to have ambassadors from their communities close by were handed over at once; otherwise the remainder were assigned to the *quaestor* C. Flaminius.

The second group comprised young women under the care of the wife of Mandonius, who Livy depicts in typically vivid fashion.[111]

> [O]ut of the midst of the crowd of hostages came an elderly woman, the wife of Mandonius, who was the brother of Indibilis, prince of the Ilergetes, and weeping she fell at the feet of the general and began to implore him to charge the guards more strictly with the care and comfort of the women.[112]

What particularly concerns this stalwart Spanish woman – a venerable female who in another context would almost assuredly have been identified as a *matrona*; so much so that Africanus accords her and those elite women standing with her, the designation[113] – is the exemplary virtue of chastity. Deeply ingrained in the Roman concept of the ideal woman, the sexual integrity of unmarried elite young women reflected cultural meanings with economic, political, and social significance: the agricultural fertility on which Roman society depended, the physical integrity of the body politic, and the cohesion of marital bonds among elite citizens on which the social structure of Rome relied. It is no accident, therefore, that Livy represents the elderly Spanish matron surrounded by the daughters of Indibilis (her husband's brother) and other young women of similar social position, "all of whom paid her the honour due a parent."[114] Moved by this exemplary display of elite female decorum, Africanus assures the women that they will be accorded every gesture of respect appropriate to their status. Noting that it is in no small part due to their clear demonstration of *matrona*-like courage and dignity that they need not fear any threat of sexual violence, the Roman commander assigns them – in the same way as guardianship was formally understood as an aspect of *potestas* and a right exercised in the interest of the protected person under Roman law[115] – to the care of "a man of proven uprightness."[116]

Last of all, brought to Africanus after dealing with the wife of Mandonius, was "a maiden so extraordinarily beautiful that, wherever she went, she drew the eyes of everyone."[117] The story of this unmarried woman, betrothed to a leading man of the Celtiberians named Allucius, bears many of the rhetorical and thematic hallmarks of Lucretia's tale.[118] In contradistinction to Tarquinius' rape and Lucretia's suicide, Africanus, learning about her fiancé, summons Allucius and his parents and hands the maiden over to them, untouched. The young woman's parents, upon hearing this news, offer the Roman commander a lavish gift of gold, explaining that they had originally assembled it as the ransom for their captive daughter. Africanus accepts the treasure only to present it to the young couple as his wedding gift to them. The local Celtiberians are so impressed by their conqueror's moderation and liberality that they side with Rome, providing Africanus with a critical strategic aid in his eventual victory against Carthage.

Livy's account of the story is so much more sympathetic than that of his precursor Polybius, which sketched Scipio as an opportunist who cultivated a supernatural persona – though he is shown to have returned the daughter to her father, which secured for him the approval of his soldiers.[119] In contrast, Livy presents him as the supreme moral exemplar. In doing so Livy embellishes some details, such as giving the young woman a nobleman fiancé named Allucius. The historian also puts into Africanus' mouth a speech to Allucius, in which he defines his action as done in duty to Rome and emphasises his sexual continence. Unlike his depiction of the wife of Mandonius, Livy's representation of the unmarried maiden betrothed to Allucius is limited to her role as the exemplary token of male exchange: the beautiful, chaste, youthful (and, by implication, fertile), elite chattel of arranged marriage, seen but never heard. Spoken about in the course of Africanus' one-sided conversation with Allucius, the young woman's worth is instrumental, dependent on her social position and reproductive capability; and her portrayal is purely conceptual, spoken about (never spoken to, and never speaking) in exemplary ideological terms.

3.3.7 Sophonisba

Livy's record of the last years in the life of Sophonisba, one of the Carthaginian general Hasdrubal's daughters, is divided between Books 29 and 30.[120]

In 206 BCE, Sophonisba had been betrothed to Masinissa, a leader of the Massylii or eastern Numidians who served along with Gisco against Rome in Hispania, in order to conclude the diplomatic alliance between Carthage and the Massylii. However, the Carthaginian Senate prohibited the wedding and ordered Sophonisba to marry Syphax, chieftain of the western Massylii, who up to that point had been allied to Rome. Cassius Dio suggests that this was because Syphax was considered a better ally, while Appian tells Syphax was in love with Sophonisba and actively pressed for the marriage, harassing Carthage with revolts and threatening attacks alongside Roman forces until they conceded. In any case, Sophonisba married Syphax in 206 BCE, turning him into Carthage's greatest ally in African terrain. Meanwhile Masinissa, disgruntled by the circumstances, secretly allied himself with Scipio Africanus and returned to his lands.[121]

Some believe those accounts might be embellished, as Livy implies Masinissa met her for the first time after the Battle of Cirta, but this is not entirely incompatible with what has already been reported. What is clear from the earliest reference in AUC history is that Livy's Sophonisba belongs to a world explicitly characterised as barbarian. When Hasdrubal visits Syphax to clarify details for the Massylian king's marriage to his daughter, the Carthaginian general cannot help but observe Syphax's desire for Sophonisba, noting in passing that "the Numidians are of all barbarians the most ardent lovers."[122] At the same time, while drawing up a treaty between Carthage and Massylia and ratifying it on oath, Hasrubal is also reported to have thought any alliance based on marriage would not last if Scipio Africanus were to land in Africa, if nothing else due to his familiarity with the "capricious and fickle nature of the barbarians."[123]

Classical chroniclers praise Sophonisba for her virtues and skill. Diodorus Siculus called her "comely in appearance, a woman of many varied moods, and one gifted with the ability to bind men to her service," while Cassius Dio states she had a high education in music and literature and was "clever, ingratiating, and altogether so charming that the mere sight of her or even the sound of her voice sufficed to vanquish everyone, even the most indifferent."[124] Polybius also emphasises her youth, calling her a "child" bride, something which Diodorus also mentions.[125] Livy's representation of Sophonisba emphasises the degree to which her sexual allure determined the ongoing strength or potential dissolution of the alliance between Carthage and Massylia. As he notes when describing Scipio Africanus' operations in Africa relating to the siege of Utica in 204 BCE, the Roman general had not lost sight of his purpose to win over Syphax "in case his (i.e., Syphax's) passion for his wife should have cooled through unstinted enjoyment."[126]

Loyal to her city, Sophonisba managed to convince Syphax to join forces with Hasdrubal and face Scipio and Masinissa in the battle of the Great Plains on the Bagrades, but the Punic force ended up ultimately defeated. It is difficult at this point in Livy's narrative to avoid the perjorative overtones embedded in his characterisation of Sophonisba's machinations in aid of continuing support for Carthage.

> He was urged on by his wife, who did not now trust to the endearments and caresses with which she had formerly swayed her lover, but with prayers and piteous appeals and eyes bathed in tears she conjured him not to betray her father and her country, or allow Carthage to be devastated by the flames which had consumed his camp.[127]

Sophonisba is portrayed here in quintessentially gendered terms. Reliant on sexual manipulation until such time as her impact on Syphax's physical desire diminishes, she resorts to psychological persuasion – prayers, appeals, tears – and emotional argument – familial betrayal, national dissolution. Livy reinforces this stereotypical view of Sophonisba as personally exploitative, emotionally controlling, and deliberatively influential, noting that, even while Syphax's garrisons were expelled and he was confined within the limits of his former kingdoms, Sophonisba continued to goad her love-sick husband on.[128]

Despite all her efforts, Syphax was defeated and captured in 203 BCE in the battle of Cirta. In the same way that he had shown how Sophonisba influenced Syphax, so now in the wake of Syphax's capitulation Livy depicts her using her physical attractiveness, sexual ploys, emotive argument, and gentle flattery to ensnare Masinissa. Thus, when Sophonisba falls into Masinissa's hands, he frees her and marries her, accepting that she had been forced to marry Syphax against her will. As before, Masinissa is unable to deny his innate barbarian nature: "a slave to passion like all his countrymen, the victor at once fell in love with his captive."[129]

Livy reinforces his gendered representation of elite non-Roman men (Syphax, Masinissa) and women (Sophonisba) through his report of the captured Syphax's address to Africanus.

> He first exhibited his folly, his utter disregard of all private ties and public obligations, when he admitted a Carthaginian bride into his house. The torches which illuminated these nuptials had set his palace in a blaze. That fury of a woman, that scourge, had used every endearment to alienate and warp his feelings, and would not rest till she had with her own impious hands armed him against his host and friend.[130]

Through the course of this carefully crafted *oratio obliqua* Livy distils the essential conditions by which a Numidian man surrendered himself to the influence of a Carthaginian woman. Here, the historian assigns his formulation of deviant gender relations – deviant, that is, as regards depictions of normative conduct between men and women in antiquity – to a very specific context outside customary Roman practice. That said, certain discursive triggers familiar from previous gendered historical episodes involving non-Roman and Roman men and women recur. In particular, Livy identifies the rejection of traditional *mores* – the social ties of guest friendship (*privata hospitia*) and the political bonds of contracted alliance (*publica foedera*) – as the causative factors leading to a fundamental diminishment of male *potestas*. As for Sophonisba, Livy deliberately raises awareness of her affective female strategies, likening how she uses her body and her mind (namely, her physical charms and psychological blandishments) to something akin to a whip (*furiam*) or disease (*pestem*). In other words, this dangerous non-Roman woman is shown to employ qualities which Livy's readership would recognise as identifiably feminine so as to bend a vulnerable man's desires and intentions to her design. In this situation, although "broken and ruined," Syphax consoles himself in his misery with the knowledge that Masinissa ("his bitterest foe") will now admit Sophonisba ("that pestilential fury") into his household.[131]

However, after hearing claims (confirmed by C. Laelius' inquiries) that Syphax had acted against Rome under the influence of Sophonisba, Africanus refused to agree to this arrangement, fearing she would turn Masinissa against him as well.[132] He insisted on the immediate surrender of the princess so that she could be taken to Rome and appears in the triumphal parade.[133] As an elite Roman male and a military commander who, though young when he fought in Spain, was never swayed by any captive girl's beauty, Africanus articulates what defines proper male action in appropriate spheres of conduct – establishing political alliances, winning personal glory in military victories – and how virtuous Roman men should resist the kind of feminine wiles that Sophonisba exerted – namely by maintaining one's socio-political integrity and controlling one's personal feelings.[134]

Although Masinissa loved Sophonisba, he accepted Africanus' advice that he leaves her before being declared an enemy to Rome and went to Sophonisba. He told her that he could not free her from captivity or shields her from Roman wrath, and so he asked her to die like a true Carthaginian princess. With great composure, she drank a cup of poison that he offered her and died. While Livy reports that Sophonisba berated Masinissa for making their marriage short and bitter – "I should have died more happily had not my marriage bed stood so near my grave" – he rounds off his representation of the Carthaginian queen by ascribing to her possession of a fierce and courageous spirit, though using the comparative form of the adjective *ferox*, associated with wild animals and barbarians. The last we hear of Sophonisba in this episode relates to her fearless disposition, allowing her to drink the poison without the slightest sign of trepidation.

In keeping with the overarching structural paradigm reflected in episodes where women are represented, the expository and exemplary role Livy assigns to Africanus' words and actions – as they reflect on Sophonisba and her relationships with Syphax and Masinissa – explains the historiographical frame used by the historian. Prior to the marriage Hasdrubal arranged between Syphax and his daughter, Livy recounts Africanus' blockade of Utica and his triumph over Carthaginian and Numidian forces. Then, after Sophonisba took her own life with poison and her body handed over to Rome by Masinissa, we read that the Carthaginian assembly accepted terms for the secession of conflict with Rome, ordering Hannibal and Hanno to end the Italian campaign and return to Africa. Notably, while Hannibal pressed for peace, Rome found the terms he proposed unacceptable; whereupon negotiations broke off, resulting in the decisive battle of Zama Regia and Carthaginian defeat. Livy's comparative juxtaposition of fictional narrative – the political disorder, military defeat, and social dysfunction resulting from internecine Numidian rivalry caused in large part (and advocated for) by a beautiful, manipulative, corrupting Carthaginian princess – and historical account – the relentless series of Roman triumphs in the aftermath of catastrophic military defeat at Cannae under the command of the ideal elite Roman general P. Cornelius Scipio Africanus – confirms in form and function the template of gendered historiography as applied to incidents in the *AUC* incorporating Roman *and* non-Roman women.

3.3.8 Theoxena

To complete this brief overview of representations of Roman and non-Roman women in AUC history, consider the tragic account of Theoxena's murder of her extended family in relation to Livy's preoccupation with defining and enlivening the underlying causes of Philip V's downfall.[135] Once again, Livy provides his readers with a character understood in specifically gendered terms. Theoxena is depicted as daughter of Herodicus (a leading man or *princeps* in Thessaly),[136] wife of her father's son-in-law, and mother of a son. Like Cornelia, mother of the Gracchi, Theoxena had many suitors after the execution of her father and husband, but scorned marriage.[137] Like Octavia minor, sister of the *princeps* Augustus, she rears another woman's children by her own hands.[138] Like Lucretia, she is threatened by a scion of royal blood with the possibility of insulting or outrageous treatment.[139] Like Chiomara, wife of the Tectosagi chieftain Orgiagon (38.24), she will likely be subject to the lust of her guards.[140] Like Medea, she lends her mind to a monstrous deed – the murder of her son and her sister's sons by her own will rather than the edict of Philip.[141]

In the latter context, it is hard not to observe that Theoxena is credited with possessing the kind of courage normally attributed to the male warrior.[142] She is prepared to venture a deed which her husband finds abhorrent even to contemplate.[143] This preparedness to act boldly translates into the fierce-spirited defiance of a woman willing to perpetrate a savage outrage unhesitatingly.[144] Further, Poris is depicted as successively loathe to pursue such a course, as willing to accept exile in the face of Philip's all-consuming suspicion, as hopeful of divine intervention when circumstances conspire against his planned crossing to Euboea, and finally as acquiescent to his wife's fatal wishes (40.4.7-15). On the other hand, Theoxena subscribes to the familiar (and inflexible) behavioural tricolon of thought-word-deed, although here she embodies the affection and intellection usually distributed among a variable catalogue of incidental and crucial participants.[145]

Taking a broader perspective, Livy's deployment of Theoxena's tragedy seems integral to his historiographical project and reflects the emblematic structural and thematic roles such gendered history plays in his reconstructed AUC tradition.[146] As Walsh notes, Livy "skilfully adapts this dramatic account to his annalistic presentation."[147] In this case, the reader may discern the tragic pattern which underpins the historian's source-author Polybius' depiction of the final years of Philip V. The grisly calamity afflicting a single household (*unius domus clades fecit*, 40.4.1) is treated by Livy as almost the turning-point in the tragic action pertaining to the typical Aristotelian "hero."[148] As such, the reader is invited to compare Theoxena's self-assertive high-spiritedness (*ferox femina*) with Philip's violent and savage nature, inflamed by the curses levelled against him by the dispossessed citizen-body and families of coastal Paeonia.[149] Contemplation of the aftermath of Theoxena's performance as death's promoter is also warranted: namely, inflammation of the existing hatred directed against Philip, which results in divine acknowledgement of the common folk's curses and the effecting of personal violence by the king against his own flesh and blood.[150]

According to the epitomator's summary, Livy's conflation of what appears to have been Polybius' first two of Fortune's punishments exacted from Philip is filtered through Theoxena's extremity to preface the third of his chief protagonist's errors.[151] In this, the reader would be remiss to ignore the suggestive typology applied to the agent of conflict in the royal Macedonian household. Perseus is portrayed as possessing an "effeminate mind" (*muliebri ... animo*, 40.5.3). This quality expresses itself through such stereotypical manifestations as criminal hope, ambivalent suggestion and deceit – like Tarpeia, like Demarata, like Tullia.[152]

If the story of Theoxena's murder of her stepchildren and her own child – and her suicide (shared with Poris) – is, as Walsh (1996: 14) observes, "one of [Livy's] stories of female heroism which act as watersheds in the history of a nation," his use of a derogative gendered appellation in describing a chief figure in his larger, dramatic historiographical design of aggressive war against Rome might be seen as a lexical reminder of the puzzling meanings associated with previous actors in the AUC panorama – bearing the similar stigmata of *invidia* for family or peers.

3.4 Conclusion

The narrative thread and historical discourse of briefer episodes representing women in times of conflict and crisis are not only far easier to discern and less problematic to interpret than more extended episodes; they also serve to reinforce rather than question the prevailing symbolic order. Indeed,

Table 3.3 The structural template of Livy's gendered AUC history

Narrative element	Thematic element
1 Threat	Perceived or actual
2 Intervention	Beneficent or malign
3 Response	Variably conducive to the re-establishment of social order

whether the sprawling comic tale of the Bacchanalian affair or the select miscellany of vignettes scattered throughout AUC history, each incident may be seen to align with the framing paradigm already established as integral to Livy's gendered annalist history. In addition, it is possible to superimpose a related, undoubtedly deliberate, historiographical arrangement.[153]

The schema shown in Table 3.3 corresponds to the notion that Livy's interposition of stories which accord prominence to women acts to co-opt the functional reconstruction of Rome's past. In this respect, the historian's insertion of stereotypical or nuanced gendered *personae* provides a familiar space within which he might ratify a particular element of AUC ideology.

What this chapter has also shown is that Livy's choice to incorporate into critical historical episodes women who are not ethnically Roman, who do not possess Roman citizenship, or who are otherwise unassimilated into the fabric of Roman society, complements rather than complicates his overarching literary method and historiographical objective. Whether these women play crucial or incidental roles in any particular account, whether the historian's use of his gendered narratives featuring foreign women are more or less integral to his larger historiographical project, and whether the depiction of such women exemplifies culturally positive or negative models of individual or collective behaviour – Livy's representation of foreign women conveys particular messages to a Roman readership that align with stereotypical constructions of non-Roman characters, externalise corrupting practices emblematic of uncivilised cultural values, and support his broader desire to foreground desirable moral virtues. As such, the extended narrative dealing with the suppression of the Bacchanalian affair reflects social anxieties of gender and status and restores traditional distinctions between men and women; Hersilia and Sophonisba's stories address the spectrum of acceptable to destabilising female influence on men who possess important political and/or military roles in elite society; Tarpeia and Cloelia's/the wife of Mandonius' antithetical tales of treachery and courage in circumstances threatening the security of the city – either in terms of invasion and occupation of the urban fabric or the disestablishment of fragile contractual alliance – reflect the ideological extremes of female nature: on the one hand, duplicity and betrayal when exposed to the temptations of excess and luxury; and on the other, the ideal display of fortitude, resourcefulness, and honour when the reproductive continuity of future generations are at stake; despite the temptation to acquiesce to local factional or wider national imperatives – whether the polarising extremes of loyalty and rebellion or of ritual piety and bodily defilement – the local aristocrat Busa and the otherwise unknown woman of Pandosia's acts of selfless generosity address the twin moral compass points of benefaction, magnanimity, and compliance with right burial practice when confronted by the poor hospitality or communal antipathy of fellow townspeople; and the fiancé of Allucius and Theoxena's episodes illuminate those accounts in AUC history which most explicitly comprise the injection of fictional material in service to the provision of exemplary narrative action – either the archetypal models of marriage as the conduit for male exchange or of the death of self and children to avoid falling into the hands of and be abused by dishonourable men.

It is essential at this point to consider two final, interdependent elements of AUC history: the extent to which the roles assigned by Livy reflect a traditional or revisionist interpretation of gender; and the degree to which Livy's narrative framework represents a complex amalgam of authentic historical data and secondary oral-literary superstructure. By examining a variety of rhetorical instruments used with episodes involving significant women in the foundation history, the next chapter will explore the link between the *topoi* used by Livy in his depiction of female engagement in the process of history and key terms which signal those moments of change. With respect to the historicity of the *AUC*, Chapter 4 will argue that throwing a spotlight on the gendered lens Livy overlays on particular crucial events in Rome's foundation narrative afford his readers opportunities to test the degrees of correspondence between points of historical tension in his overarching annalistic reconstruction.

Notes

1 Collins (2015).
2 On the origins of the Greek word *barbaros*, the pejorative cultural uses of the concept, and Rome's late republican revision of the idea of barbarism from a monolithic and unsophisticated view of the world as divided between Greeks and nations that do not speak Greek to a more complex perspective which understood the concept as a societal trait susceptible to change, see Jensen (2018: 1–22).
3 On Roman views of foreigners, see, e.g., Sherwin-White (1967) and Balsdon (1979); for an introduction to the ancient ethnographic tradition, esp, in historical works, see Rives (1999: 11–21).
4 The summary of the lost Book 104 of *Ab Urbe Condita* opens with the statement that "the first part of this book contains an account of the country and customs of Germania" (*Periochae* 104.1: *prima pars libri situm Germaniae moresque continet*). First century BCE ethnographic excurses include: Caes. *BG* 6.11-28 (Gauls and Germani); Sall. *Jug.* 17–19 (Africani).
5 For an explicit justification of Roman imperialism, see, e.g., Liv. 5.27.
6 For a transparent expression of Pro-Roman/anti-Carthaginian views, see, e.g., Liv. 22.13. On Carthaginians as: untrustworthy (Liv. 21.4.9); lacking established rules for post-war conduct (Liv. 22.6.12); dishonest in regard to accepting terms for peace (Liv. 30.16.10-11).

7   On the interdependency of the designations "same" and "other" in relation to depictions of elite Roman women, see Hallett (1989).

8   Whether or not the women depicted in AUC history are ethnically or culturally Roman, it cannot be emphasised enough that Livy's female characters are far from what Smethurst (1959: 80) regards as "one-dimensional"; nor should they be understood, in the view argued by Santoro L'Hoir (1992: 77), as "shadowy impersonations of womanhood, subordinated to the males who are themselves ancillary to the virtues and vices that form the woof on the loom of Roman history."

9   See Syme (1991) for a typically erudite definition of these overlapping literary genres.

10 Liv. 39.8-18; see Table 1.2 no. 54.

11 Gelzer (1936); Fronza (1947); Tarditi (1954).

12 For the decree, see *CIL* I2, 581; *ILS* I, 278; and *ILLRP*, 511. Walsh (1994: 5) thinks that the second section of Livy's account [Liv. 39.14.3-19] "must be accorded respectful weight" because it is "based ultimately on senatorial records." I would ask whether such a judgement denotes an elision of the very criteria by which such a decision is reached. With due regard to certain elaborated elements of the AUC account, the historicity of the affair may be regarded as assured: inasmuch as the *senatus consultum* authorising detailed directives on sanctions and control of Bacchants (despatched to Roman foederati in Italy) corresponds to sections of Livy's narrative; and albeit with minor discrepancies (omissions or abbreviations) that may be ascribed to difference in genres and conflation of senatorial resolutions in revised consular letters. Livy deploys a range of approaches in constructing his version of the Bacchanalian affair, including figurative, dramatic, characterological, rhetorical, expository and ideological techniques and devices.

13 For example, Fraenkel (1932: 386), "die Novellenmotive"; Meautis (1940: 477), "roman-feuilletou"; Tarditi (1954: 283, "la fabula di Ebuzio e di Fecenia"); Cova (1974: 95–96), "L'introduzione del romanzo diventa inevitabile"; Scafuro (1989: esp. 125–127); Gruen (1990: esp. 62).

14 Bettini (1991: 288 n.25).

15 White (1978: 81–100).

16 For a study of the plausibility and provenance of the non-Roman characters and citizen families depicted in Livy's received account, see Rousselle (1989: 35–54).

17 Cf. Walsh (1994: 5): "unique in Livy's pages in its approximation to a dramatic performance." It can be argued that the first, characterising 'act' of the Licinian-Sextian rogations (legislative proposals) – the domestic *invidia* of Fabia Ambustus – is a romanticised reflection of Lucretia's story. Although it lacks the oppressed characterisation and the tragic ramifications, that episode conforms thematically and stylistically to comic structure (at least initially).

18 By this point in the published AUC record (if we accept the conventional wisdom), Livy's audience would have enjoyed the fruits of 13 or so years of his historiographical rhetoric.

19 Liv. 39.8.1: *insequens annus Sp. Postumium Albinum et Q. Marcium Philippum consules ab exercitu bellorumque et provinciarum cura ad intestinae coniurationis vindictam avertit.*

20 *Historia comica > oratio et consulta > conclusio*; cf. Table 3.1.1-3.

21 The record of the state at peace, which frames the narrative of a foreign campaign, is a stylistic elaboration of the archival material corresponding to the annual changes to which the state was subject (elections and assignment of military commands).

22 While the basic unit of Livian history (the year) is divided into *res internae* and *res externae* and framed by the magisterial protocol of year-opening and unelaborated documentary material of year-end, here we see Livy counterpoint the inhibition of domestic trouble with external fear. For the theory of *metus hostilis*, see Luce (1977: 271–273); Harris (1979), s.v. *metus hostilis*.

23 *Volso's triumph*: over the Gauls in Asia at the close of the year in early March; *Philippus' defeat*: in which 4000 soldiers were lost, and three standards of the second legion (together with 11 ensigns of the allied and Latin contingents) fell into enemy hands.

24 Liv. 39.6.9: *vix tamen illa, quae tum conspiciebantur, semina erant futurae luxuriae* (= the seeds of the extravagance to follow). Cf. Polybius 6.57.3, 31.25.3; Sallust, *Cat.* 11.4-7, *Jug.* 41, *Hist.* fr 10M.

25 Liv. 39.7.1-5 (postponed until a late date so that the *triumphator* might avoid falling under the ambit of the retiring magistrates' indictment of L. Scipio).

26 Liv. 39.20.5-10 (which includes the description of the consul's posting of several detachments of his demoralised army in pacified territory to conceal the extent of his losses).

27 For *luxuria* as illustrative of Rome's moral decline with reference to the transgression of domestic and public space, cf. e.g. Sall. *Cat.* 1-16 (general discussion of the corruption pervasive at Rome); Cic. *Rosc. Am.* 14.39 (Roscius' devotion to a simple life in the country should be viewed as an indication of probity), 75 (on the consequences of abundance, arrogance and weakness); *Leg. agr.* 2.97 (*luxuria* coupled with *superbia* results in *scelus* and *flagitium*); *Orat.* 2.171 (moral decay associated with luxury); and Liv. 1.pr. 11 (*avaritia* and *luxuria* contrasted with *paupertas* and *parsimonia*), Liv. 1.57.9 (Lucretia contrasted with the other officers' wives, feasting *in convivio luxuque*), Liv. 7.25.9 (senators worried about raising a large army in a situation where they had resolved that *divitias* and *luxuria* were the only things toward which they strove), Liv. 34.4.1-2 (Cato speaking in the debate over the *Lex Oppia*). For reviews of the tradition ascribing the political failure of the republic to moral corruption derived from wealth and foreign conquest – a tradition arising from the propaganda of the Gracchan period – see, e.g., Lind (1972); Spawforth (2012: 14–18). For a lucid and methodical analysis of the technical problems and proposed solutions adhering to any discussion of the Bacchanalia, see Gruen (1990). For a useful precis of the pertinent religious and historical issues, see North (1979).

28 Liv. 34.2-4 (186 BCE: support for continued impost of the lex Oppia); 38.54 (187 BCE: support for prosecution of the Scipiones); 39.44.2 (184 BCE: censorial imposition of taxation on women's jewellery, clothing, slaves, and carriages).

29 Liv. 39.40.3-12.

30 Liv. 34.15.9; 37.57.13; 38.54.1.

31 Liv. 39.41.6: *si Antiati Valerio credere libet*.

32 Hispala Faecenia: Liv. 39.10.5-9; 13.8-14; Aebutius: Liv. 39.11.3-4; Livy himself: Liv. 39.8.3-8. Gruen (1990: 62). The offences and vices enumerated by Livy include indiscriminate debauchery (Liv. 39.8.7: *stupra promiscua*), perjury by witnesses (Liv. 8.7: *falsi testes*), forgery (Liv. 8.8: *falsa signa testamenta*), poisonings (Liv. 8.8: *venena*), domestic slaughter (Liv. 8.8: *intestinae caedes*), and murder of unwilling initiates (Liv. 39.13.3: *raptos ... abripiant eos ... notuerint*).

33 The Augustan reader, tolerant of historiographical distortion and certainly oblivious to any deliberate misrepresentation of historical materials.

34 Especially the jurisdictional prerogatives and judicial procedures of the municipalities and rural regions of the peninsula.

35 Regarded by Walsh (1994: 4) as "unsatisfactory in the sense that it concentrates largely on the alleged human aspects by which the 'conspiracy' was detected."

36 Liv. 39.12.1-14.3; 14.4-17.3. The account of Hispala Faecenia's summons to the house of the consul Postumius (at the request of his mother-in-law Sulpicia), her interrogation by that custodian of civil order, and her eventual confirmation of widespread and subversive Bacchanalian activity.

37 Postumius' rhetorical exhortation and the resultant senatorial proclamations.

38 Liv. 39.12.1-14.3. Scafuro (1989: 13 and *passim*).

39 Liv. 39.8.3: *Graecus ignobilis ... sacrificulus et vates.*

40 Cf. Liv. 39.9.1: "The destructive power of this evil spread from Etruria to Rome like the contagion of a pestilence." (*huius mali labes ex Etruria Romam veluti contagione morbi penetravit*).

41 Liv. 39.8.7-8: *nec unum genus noxae ... ex eadem officina exibant*; 10.6: *scire corruptelarum omnis generis earn officinam esse.*

42 Livy himself: "a nameless Greek" (Liv. 39.8.3: *Graecus ignobilis*); Hispala, to Aebutius: "a sort of victim for the priests" (Liv. 39.10.7: *velut victimam tradi sacerdotibus*); Hispala, to Postumius: "it was a ritual for women, and it was the custom that no man should be admitted to it" (Liv. 39.13.8: *primo sacrarium id feminarum fuisse nec quemquam eo virum admitti solitum*); "Paculla Annia, a Campanian ... when priestess ... had been the first to initiate men, her sons" (9: *Pacullam Anniam Campanam sacerdotem ... et viros eam primam filios suos initiasse*); Postumius, to a gathering of citizens: "a great part of them are women, and they are the source of this mischief" (Liv. 39.15.9: *mulierum magna pars ... fons mali huiusce fuit*); Livy again: "But the heads of the conspiracy, it was clear, were M. and C. Atinius of the Roman *plebs*, and the Faliscan L. Opicernius and the Campanian M. Cerrinius: they were the source of all wickedness and wrongdoing, so the story went, and they were the supreme priests and the founders of the cult" (Liv. 39.17.6-7: *capita autem coniurationis constabat esse M. et C. Atinios de plebe Romana et Faliscum L. Opicernium et Minium Cerrinium Campanum: ab his omnia facinora et flagitia orta, eos maximos sacerdotes conditoresque eius sacri esse*).

43 Liv. 39.17.6: *dicebantur, constabat.*

44 Cf. Liv. 39.8.5-8; 10.6-9; 13.10-14; 15.8-9; 16.3,5.

45 Liv. 39.16.2: *nunquam tantum malum in re publica fuit nec ad plures nec ad plura pertinens.*

46 Liv. 39.16.3: "But the evil increases and spreads daily; it is already too great for the private ranks of life to contain it and aims its sights at the body of the state" (*crescit et serpit quotidie malum. iam maius est, quam ut capere id privata fortuna possit: ad summam rem publicam spectat*).

47 Liv. 39.15.3: "nor those gods who would drive our enthralled minds with vile and alien rites, as by the scourges of the Furies, to every crime and every lust" (*non illos [deos] pravis et externis religionibus captas mentes velut furialibus stimulis ad omne scelus et ad omnem libidinem agerent*); cf. 13.11: "Men, as if insane, with fanatic tossings of their bodies, would utter prophecies" (*viros velut mente capta cum iactatione fanatica corporis vaticinari*).

48 Liv. 39.15.6: "But I feel sure that you do not know what this thing is" (*certum habeo ceterum quae ea res sit ignorare*).

49 Liv. 39.15.9: *simillimi feminis mares.* Cf. L'Hoir (1992: 97): "*feminis/mares,* vague indicators of gender regularly applied to animals and infants of indeterminate sex"; see also Packard (1968), s.v. *mas.*

50 Liv. 39.15.13-14: "Do you think, citizens, that youths initiated by this oath should be made soldiers? That arms should be entrusted to men mustered from this foul shrine? Will men debased by their own debauchery and that of

others fight to the death on behalf of the chastity of your wives and children?" (*hoc sacramento initiatos iuvenes milites faciendos censetis, Quirites? his ex obsceno sacrario eductis arma committenda? hi cooperti stupris suis alienisque pro pudicitia coniugum ac liberorum vestrorum ferro decernent?*); cf. 15.13: "meetings of men and women in common" (*[coetus] promiscuos mulierum ac virorum*); 13.10: "men mingling with women" (*permixti viri feminis*).

51 Liv. 39.16.4: "as we hold this meeting in the day-time, summoned by a consul, in accordance with law" (*huic diurnae legitime ab consule vocatae par nocturna contio esse poterit*); cf. 13.14: "almost constituting a second state" (*alterum iam prope populum esse*).

52 Gruen (1990: 46).

53 Gruen (1990: 78, 76).

54 Cf. the equally rich display of Scipio Asiaticus (Liv. 37.59).

55 Liv. 39.8.3.

56 Liv. 39.9.3: "his stepfather [T. Sempronius Rufus], who had so administered his guardianship that he could not render an accounting" (*vitricus quia tutelam ita gesserat ut rationem reddere non posset*). Aebutius' inheritance was likely to have been considerable – an inference adduced by Livy's citation of the young man's biological father as having served in the cavalry-elite and been issued with a horse by the state (Liv. 39.9.2: *cuius pater publico equo stipendia fecerat*). It is interesting to dwell here on Livy's use of *officina* and *stuprum* as *exempla* of transgressive activity, especially his portrayal of the influence of Bacchic corruption (central to the narrative of the Bacchanalian affair) as transgressing hierarchical boundaries of class and decorum. In this regard, consider Hispala's disclosure to Aebutius that she accompanied her mistress to the *officina* of moral deterioration implicates the enslaved and slave-owners in the process of exposure and spread of infection; that is, initiation and participation in further enrolment. If we understand *stuprum* to apply regularly to the rape of unmarried women and boys, then Hispala's reference *to per vim stuprum*, inflicted on unwilling initiates no older that twenty (Liv. 39.10.7: *biennio constare neminem initiatum*) ascribes to the Bacchanalia contravention of the two-sided moral coin, *pudicitia-virtus*, gendered signifiers of the patriarchal behavioural code. In regard to the legal concept of *stuprum*, see Gardner (1986: 121–127).

57 L'Hoir (1992: 93). Sulpicia is the *matrona* par excellence (Liv. 39.11.4: *gravem feminam*; 12.2: *tam nobilem et gravem feminam*; 12.4: *tali femina*; 13.3: *gravissimae feminae*).

58 Liv. 39.11.5: *probam et antiqui moris feminam* (an indubitable assessment, given that it represents Sulpicia's opinion). Cf. Aebutia's pious interjection (11.7: *di propitii essent*), excusing her description of the rites (as reported to her) to Sulpicia as *obscenis sacris*.

59 Liv. 39.9.6: *adulescentis aut rei aut famae damnosa*; 10.4: *pudicitiam famam spem vitamque tuam perditum*; 11.7: *probus adulescens*; cf. 12.1: *non vanum auctorem*. These citations are offered in contradistinction to Aebutius' association with Hispala and his broken promise (albeit compelled) to keep her knowledge of Bacchic initiation secret.

60 Duronia and T. Sempronius Rutilus are explicit instances of *exempli mali*. On the one hand, Duronia is completely under the thrall of her husband (Liv. 39.9.3: *mater dedita viro erat*; cf. *dedo*, in its perjorative figurative sense of giving oneself wholly to another, or of giving oneself entirely up to wickedness or pleasure, i.e., addiction as opposed to devotion); and she is willing to further through deception or protect through dispossession the interests of criminal propinquity by marriage over the rights of familial consanguinity by birth (Liv. 39.9.4; 10.2-3; cf. 11.7: *eiectus a matre*). On the other, T. Sempronius Rutilus

is a wicked guardian and misappropriating steward; and the instigator of his ward's likely loss of virtue, reputation and future prospects (Liv. 39.9.3: *vitricus … cupiebat*, 10.4-5: *vitricus … properat*; cf. 11.7: *spoliatus … oporteret*).

61 Ways of seeing Hispala. 1. Noble courtesan. Smethurst (1959: 82); cf. Balsdon (1962: 37): "courtesan of distinction." 2. Spanish slave. Rousselle (1989: 61). 3. Devoted mistress. Gruen (1990: 64); cf. Walsh (1994: 119): "[Hispala] bears a close resemblance to the decent courtesans of Roman comedy" (e.g., Thais and Bacchus in Terence's *Eunuchus* and *Hecyra*). 4. Literary topos. L'Hoir (1992: 91, 93).

62 The *lex Atilia* of 210 BCE; the praetor and a majority of tribunes. Cf. Gardner (1986: 14–22).

63 Liv. 39.9.5: "not worthy of the occupation to which, while still a mere slave, she had accustomed herself" (*non digna quaestu cui ancillula adsuerat*).

64 Liv. 39.9.6: "for he had been loved and sought out without any effort on his part, and, since his own relatives made provision for all his needs on a very small scale, he was maintained by the generosity of the courtesan" (*amatus appetitusque erat et maligne omnia praebentibus suis meretriculae munificentia sustinebatur*). According to L'Hoir (1992: 92), *meretrix* is "the genteel term for the followers of that venerable profession." This reflects Livy's authorial contrast with the *infamia* attaching to his earlier use of *scortum*. Of course, the etymological link between *meretrix* and *merere* (to earn) should not be ignored. It is an association that cannot wholly obviate the expression of an aristocratic Roman aversion to commercial practice.

65 Liv. 39.10.4: "for perhaps it is not right to accuse your mother" (*matrem enim insimulare forsitan fas non sit*), 5: "beseeching gods and goddesses for peace" (*pacem veniamque precata deorum dearumque*).

66 Liv. 39.9.6: "for he had been loved and sought out without any effort on his part" (*ultro enim amatus appetitusque erat et maligne omnia*); 10.5: "she told him that while she was a slave she had accompanied her mistress to that shrine" (*ancillam se ait dominae comitem id sacrarium intrasse*).

67 Interestingly, L'Hoir (1992: 93) identifies Hispala as a resident of the Aventine, a district noted for its admixture of "plebeian families, foreign merchants (and their cults), freedmen, runaway slaves, and other *quisquilia* [odds and ends, waste, refuse]." Her association with an identifiably pluralist neighbourhood outside the *pomoerium* – open space within and without the city walls sacred from habitations and from culture – resonates neatly with the complex and supraliminal nature of her character.

68 Liv. 39.12.3: *in interiorem partem aedium abductam*.

69 Liv. 39.12.2: *perturbata* (confused, disturbed, and thrown into disorder in response to the summons of so prominent and august a lady as Sulpicia); 3: *exanimata* (weakened and fatigued when confronted by the unexpected sight of the lictors, the consul's retinue and Postumius himself); 5: "such fear and trembling seized her in all her limbs" (*tantus pavor tremorque omnium membrorum*).

70 Cf. Gruen (1990: esp. 65–78), who considers the episode as the vehicle by which the senate as an institution sought to assert its "collective ascendancy" (78). In other words, the worshippers of Dionysus should be considered an excuse for a shift in the emphasis of Roman foreign policy and victims of the senate's assertion of aggregate authority. As Gruen would have it, "the *coniuratio* was not that of the Bacchants, but of those who sought to make an example of them" (65). I accept this as a valid interpretation of Livy's account, based on comparative analysis, and argued with meticulous logic. There is much which I find attractive in the thesis, especially the reasoning which posits Livy's depiction of the Bacchic cult and its participants as part of a campaign

(mounted by the historian through the persons in his narrative) to justify its suppression.

71 Liv. 39.14.4: *cum publico nomine ... privatim.*

72 For a discussion of the view that Roman identity may be preserved indefinitely through successive re-enactments of an historical cycle, and the argument that Livy systematically selects and reshapes traditional material so as to elaborate this view, see Miles (1986).

73 Liv. 39.13.3: "at the same time (Sulpicia) encouraged her and mollified the anger of her son-in-law" (*simul eam adhortari simul iram generi lenire*); cf. Hersilia (see Section 2 of this chapter).

74 Beneficiary of her financial support (maintained ironically through her earnings as a prostitute).

75 For an excursus on the view that elite Roman men conceived of the female sex as a bipartite one, see Hallett (1989).

76 See the discussion of this phenomenon (in relation to Cloelia and Busa) in Section 2 of this chapter.

77 Liv. 39.14.1-3; 19.5, 6. It should be noted that Aebutius is similarly embraced and rewarded by the state. He is ordered to move into the house of a consular dependent (Liv. 39.14.3) and finds himself a qualified candidate for the first Servian property-class and exempt from military service (Liv. 39.19.4). The sum of 100,000 sesterces signifies restitution of that property lost through T. Sempronius Rutilus' depredations, and pronunciation of service performed reflects the weight of civic duty placed on his report to the consul.

78 Liv. 1.11.2; see Table 1.2 no. 8.

79 Liv. 1.11.2-3: "Whilst Romulus was exulting over this double victory, his wife, Hersilia, moved by the entreaties of the abducted maidens, implored him to pardon their parents and receive them into citizenship, for so the State would increase in unity and strength. [3] He readily granted her request" (*duplicique victoria ovantem Romulum Hersilia coniunx precibus raptarum fatigata orat ut parentibus earum det veniam et in civitatem accipiat ita rem coalescere concordia posse. facile impetratum*). Cf. Eur., *Supp.* 286–331 (Aethra > Theseus > Theban women).

80 It should be noted that Hersilia's agency is qualified by the signifier *coniunx*. Cf. Liv. 2.40.1-2 (Veturia and Volumnia > Coriolanus > Roman women – *matronae*, *mulieres*). See Chapter 2.3 for an analysis of the mediating role of women in times of civil crisis.

81 Wiseman (1983: 449) draws attention to the possible association between the etymological derivation of Hersilia's name (from *orare*; cf. Plut. *Quaest. Rom.* 46) and "the activities attributed to Hersilia and the women in the story of her intervention." Cf. Ogilvie (1963: 73), who suggests that Hersilia is the personification of Hora Quirini ("the power of Quirinus"). If so, the reader is entitled to read in Livy's depiction of Hersilia an aetiological rationalisation of the ability of mortal Romulus-divine Quirinus; in this instance, the ability to reconcile enemies.

82 Brown (1995: 302–303) regards Livy's attribution of the policy of extending citizen-rights to the initiative of a woman – in concert with her originary articulation of the concept of *concordia* – as part of his narrative strategy to enhance the figural role of women as representative of forgiveness and harmony. However, one might just as reasonably interpret Hersilia's role as embedded within the transitional context of Roman marriage (she is, after all, now a *matrona*, though nominally Sabine), with its implications of exchange and assimilation of value-systems. In this regard, the reader is entitled to ask whether Hersilia is speaking as representative of Sabine desires or as conduit of the functional Roman notion of *societas*.

83 Liv. 1.11.5-9; Dion. Hal. *Ant. Rom.* 2.38.2-40.3; Prop. 4.4; Ov. *Fast.* 1.261; Plut. *Rom.* 17.5, 6; see Table 1.2 no. 9.

84 Liv. 1.11.6: "bribed with gold by Tatius" (*auro corrumpit Tatius*); 9: "she forfeited her life to the bargain she herself had struck" (*sua ipsam peremptam mercede*).

85 Liv. 1.11.6: "To their prudence they even added deception" (*consilio* [= Tatius' prudence] *etiam additus dolus* [= Tarpeia"s deception]).

86 Cf. Liv. 1.12.4: "The fortress is already bought by a crime and in the possession of the Sabines" (*arcem iam scelere emptam Sabini habent*). Romulus' designation of Tatius' *dolus* and Tarpeia's *fraus* is significant for the way in which it accentuates the successful application of deceptive practice by the leaders of men – an allusion to Romulus' *dissimulans* (Liv. 1.9.3) is arguable – and the susceptibility of unreliable or inferior individuals to such stratagems – the unattached and vulnerable *virgo* as comparable to the inferentially inferior neighbours of divinely-favoured, virtue-endowed Rome (Liv. 1.9.6). It is the display of moral pliability, regardless of its textual embodiment, which interests Livy.

87 It may not be accidental that Livy positions two exemplary expositions of what might be construed as *muliebris dolus* in such proximity: on the one hand, Hersilia's conjugal application; on the other, Tarpeia's virginal abuse. Each is potentially an offshoot of a shared propensity: the disposition to manipulate a situation within the parameters of one's personal sphere of influence. Cf. Brown (1995: 305), who argues that Tarpeia is an "antitype" and represents the antithesis to the Sabine women's (and therefore Hersilia's) loyalty.

88 Dion. Hal. *Ant. Rom.* 2.38.3, 2.40.3.

89 Dion. Hal. *Ant. Rom.* 2.40.3. It is interesting to note that, while referring to "others writing about Tarpeia," Plutarch (*Rom.* 17.5) recalls that the Greek author of a history of Italy named Antigonos represented Tarpeia as the daughter of Tatius: consequently, she was depicted as innocent of treachery and instead a model of filial virtue, betraying Rome to her father. This favourable version of Tarpeia's story aligns with that of Piso preserved in the *Antiquitates Romanae* and lends credence to the interpretation of the line in a poem by Propertius – "famous for the virtue of Tarpeia" (1.16.2: *ianua Tarpeiae nota pudicitiae*). On Tarpeia's *pudicitia* in Propertius 1.16 in relation to the accounts of the early Roman historians, see Cairns (2011).

90 Liv. 12.2-13.5.

91 Liv. 1.10, 13.5, 14.4-15.

92 Liv. 1.3.6-8, 1.16-17, 1.18-21.

93 Berg (2002: 39–40); cf. Claassen (1998: 84–85).

94 Liv. 2.13.6: *ergo ita honorata virtute, feminae quoque ad publica decora excitatae*.

95 Liv. 2.13.6-11; Dion. Hal. *Ant. Rom.* 5.32.3-35; Virg. *Aen.* 8.651; Flor. 1.10.7; Val. Max. 3.2.2; Sen. *Cons. ad Marc.* 16.2; Juv. 8.265; Plut. *Poplicola* 19.2; *de Mul. Virt.* 14; Polyaenus 8.31; Serv. *ad Aen.* 8.646; Oros. 2.5.3; see Table 1.2 no. 16.

96 Val. Max. 3.2.2: *non solum obsidio se sed etiam metu patriam solvit*; Liv. 2.13.6: *dux agminis virginum inter tela hostium Tiberim tranavit*.

97 Liv. 2.13.11.

98 Liv. 2.13.11: *novo genere honoris*. The roots of the conflict between Rome and the Etruscans lay in the insidious amalgam of advice and entreaty rendered to the king of Clusium by the exiled Tarquinii (Liv. 2.9.1-3).

99 The virtuous display inspiring Cloelia is provided by the unquestionably noble actions of Horatius Cocles (Liv. 1.10.1-13: the provision of a statue, land and

gifts denoting the thankful consensus of *civitas* and *private*) and C. Mucius Scaevola Liv. (1.12.1-16: the bestowal of a field across the Tiber).

100 Liv. 2.13.11: "in a woman with a new kind of honour" (*novam in femina virtutem*). Cf. Sen. *Cons. ad Marc.* 16.2: "We virtually enrolled [Cloelia] as a man because of her outstanding courage" (*ob insignem audaciam tantum non in viros transcripsimus*).

101 Liv. 2.13.10: *virginitati decorum*.

102 Liv. 2.13.11: *Romani ... donavere*.

103 Liv. 8.24.16-17: *mulier una ultra humanarum irarum fidem saevienti turbae immixta, ut parumper sustinerent precata, flens ait virum sibi liberosque captos apud hostes esse; sperare corpore regio utcumque mulcato se suos redempturam. is finis laceratione fuit, sepultumque Consentiae quod membrorum reliquum fuit cura mulieris unius, ossaque Metapontum ad hostes remissa, inde Epirum devecta ad Cleopatram uxorem sororemque Olympiadem*; see Table 1.2 no. 37.

104 Liv. 8.24.14.

105 Liv. 22.52.7: *eos qui Canusium perfugerant mulier Apula nomine Busa, genere clara ac divitiis, moenibus tantum tectisque a Canusinis acceptos, frumento, veste, viatico etiam iuvit, pro qua ei munificentia postea bello perfecto ab senatu honores habiti sunt*; see Table 1.2 no. 42.

106 Ap. Claudius Pulcher: to be *praetor* and *propraetor* in Sicily from 215 BCE (including the murderous expression of popular feeling against the Syracusan monarchy in 214 BCE); P. Cornelus Scipio: architect of the crucial African campaign and associate in effective command against the great king Antiochus III.

107 Liv. 9.26.

108 Liv. 22.54.3-4: "In all other matters, too, they dealt hospitably by them, both as a town and as individuals, in their zeal that the people of Venusia should not lag behind a Canusian woman in friendly offices. But the great multitude was beginning to be too heavy a burden upon Busa — and indeed there were now as many as ten thousand men ..." (*ceteraque publice ac privatim hospitaliter facta certatumque ne a muliere Canusina populus Venusinus officiis vinceretur. Sed gravius onus Busae multitudo faciebat; et iam ad decem milia hominum erant*).

109 Liv. 22.53.13: *haud secus pavidi quam si victorem Hannibalem cernerent, iurant omnes custodiendosque semet ipsos Scipioni tradunt.* Cf. legendary individuals like Brutus (Liv. 1.59.1), Verginius (Liv. 2.41.7), and Valerius and Horatius (Liv. 3.53.2); as well as historical figures such as C. Licinius and L. Sextus (Liv. 3.35.8; 36.10-37; 39.5-12), M. Porcius Cato (Liv. 34.2-4), and Sp. Postumius (Liv. 39.15.2-16.13).

110 Liv. 26.41.1-51.14.

111 Polyb. 10.18.7-14; Liv. 26.49.11-16; see Table 1.2 no. 48a.

112 Liv. 26.49.11: *e media turba obsidum mulier magno natu, Mandonii uxor, qui frater Indibilis Ilergetum reguli erant, flens ad pedes imperatoris procubuit obtestarique coepit ut curam cultumque feminarum impensius custodibus commendaret.*

113 Liv. 26.49.15: "I am moved to an even stricter care in that respect by the courage and dignity of you women also, who even in misfortune have not forgotten what is seemly for a matron" (*nunc ut id curem impensius, vestra quoque virtus dignitasque facit quae ne in malis quidem oblitae decoris matronalis estis*).

114 Liv. 26.49.13: "and in the bloom of youth and beauty the daughters of Indibilis were standing about her, and others of no less rank, all of whom paid her the honour due a parent" (*et aetate et forma florentes circa eam Indibilis filiae erant aliaeque nobilitate pari, quae omnes eam pro parente colebant*).

115 Gardner (1998: 241–247).

116 Liv. 29.49.15 (n. 112, above).
117 Liv. 26.50.1: *captiva deinde a militibus adducitur ad eum adulta virgo, adeo eximia forma ut quacumque incedebat converteret omnium oculos.*
118 Polyb. 10.19.3-7; Liv. 26.50.1-14; Sil. *Pun.* 15.268-85; Dio fr. 57.43; Val. Max. 4.3.1; Gell. *NA* 7.8.6; Frontin. *Str.* 2.11.5; Polyaenus, *Strat.* 8.16.6; *Vir. Ill.* 49.8; Amm. Marc. 24.4.27; Zonar. 9.8.5; see Table 1.2 no. 48b.
119 Polyb.10.19.6-7; cf. Gell. *NA* 7.8.6, which records the otherwise unattested version of the fiancé's story where she was not returned to her father but kept by Africanus and used for sex.
120 Polyb. 14.1.7; Liv. 29.23.3-6; 30.3.4; 30.7.8-9; 30.11.3; 30.12-15; App. *Pun.* 27; Dio Cass. 57.51; Plut. *Scip.* 29; Zonar. 9.11, 12, 13; see Table 1.2 no. 52.
121 App. *Pun.* 2.10-11.
122 Liv. 29.23.4: *et sunt ante omnes barbaros Numidae effusi in Venerem.*
123 Liv. 29.23.6: *vana et mutabilia barbarorum ingenia.*
124 Diod. Sic. 27.7; Dio Cass. 17.51-52.
125 Polyb. 14.1.7.
126 Liv. 30.3.4: *si forte iam satias amoris in uxore ex multa copia eum cepisset.*
127 Liv. 30.7.8-9: *cum uxor non iam ut ante blanditiis, satis potentibus ad animum amantis, sed precibus et misericordia valuisset, plena lacrimarum obtestans ne patrem suum patriamque proderet iisdemque flammis Carthaginem quibus castra conflagrassent absumi sineret.*
128 Liv. 30.11.3: *stimulabat aegrum amore uxor.*
129 Liv. 30.12.18: *ut est genus Numidarum in Venerem praeceps, amore captivae victor captus.*
130 Liv. 30.13.11-12: *tum hospitia privata et publica foedera omnia ex animo eiecisse cum Carthaginiensem matronam domum acceperit. illis nuptialibus facibus regiam conflagrasse suam; illam furiam pestemque omnibus delenimentis animum suum avertisse atque alienasse, nec conquiesse donec ipsa manibus suis nefaria sibi arma adversus hospitem atque amicum induerit.*
131 Liv. 30.13.13: *perdito tamen atque adflicto sibi hoc in miseriis solatii esse quod in omnium hominum inimicissimi sibi domum ac penates eandem pestem ac furiam transisse videat.*
132 Liv. 30.14.2-11; cf. App. *Pun.* 5.27; Diod. Sic. 27.7.
133 Again, we may note the choices Livy made in composing this episode. For instance, Plutarch (*Scip.* 29) considers Africanus asked for Sophonisba's delivery for safety reasons, fearing Masinissa could torment her in revenge for her marriage to Syphax.
134 Liv. 30.14.2 (Spanish campaign), 5 (continence and control of passions), 7 (self-control and subjugation of seductive pleasures), 11 (control of feelings).
135 Liv. 40.4.1-15; see Table 1.2 no. 59.
136 Liv. 40.4.2: *principem Thessalorum.*
137 Liv. 40.4.3: *multis petentibus aspernata nuptias est.*
138 Instead of the offspring of her husband by a previous marriage (Octavia cared for Fulvia's children by M. Antonius), Theoxena married her deceased sister Archo's husband Poris (Liv. 40.4.3: *longe principi gentis Aenianum*), devoting the same care to her sister's sons as to her own child (Liv. 40.4.5: *ut in suis manibus liberi sororis educarentur ... et tamquam omnes ipsa enixa foret <suum> sororisque filios in eadem habebat cura*). For the portrait of Theoxena as an instance of contemporary allusion in AUC history, see Appendix 2.4.
139 Liv. 40.4.6: *ludibrio ... regis.*
140 Liv. 40.4.6: *custodum ... libidini.* For attributions of Chiomara's name, see Polyb. 21.38; Plut. *De mul. vir.* 22; for the chieftain's name: Ortiagon (Polybius), Orgiagon (Livy), Ortiagon (Plutarch). It is clear that Livy avoids the particularly complex characterisation invested by Euripides in his fictional creation.

Theoxena's (and Archo's) children are legitimate; Medea's are not (cf. Aristotle's *Athenian Constitution* regarding foreign status and its implications for citizenship and inheritance). Theoxena's persona is coherent, consistent and resolute, regardless of circumstance; Medea's off-stage lamentations contradict her visible engagement in the conclusion of agreements, the swearing of oaths and the practice of forensic rhetoric. Theoxena's activity is depicted as conforming to the traditional ideology of hegemonic discourse; Medea destroys four *oikoi* (her own, Helios', Creon's and Jason's) and transgresses the boundaries of male space. Finally, Theoxena displays a fierce-spirited rationality; Medea is irrational passion embodied, that destructive nature which turns the ordered world created by men upside-down. What is interesting in conducting such a comparison is Medea's awareness of the consequence of infanticide and the requisite need to justify her actions. This is a problematic consciousness absent from Livy's incarnation of Theoxena.

141 Theoxena's actions lack the tortuous and reflexive moral ambiguities adhering to Medea's spumed proxy of Jason's manipulation and self-serving socio-political alliances. See Appendix 1.1 for Theoxena as the obverse of a famous *exemplum malus*. Of course, what she does nonetheless results in condemning the children of previously executed enemies of the Macedonian king to arrest and probable death.

142 Liv. 40.4.7: *ausaque est dicere.*

143 Liv. 40.4.8: *abominatus mentionem tam foedi facinoris.*

144 Liv. 40.4.13: *ferox ... femina*; 14: *auctor mortis*; Liv. 40.5.1: *atrocitas facinoris.*

145 Here, the reader should note the sense of *abominatus*, which implies seeking to avert an by thought (Liv. 40.4.13: *ad multo ante praecognitatum revoluta facinus*); word (14: *mors inquit una vindicta est*) – Theoxena's exhortation to suicide by sword or poison, so that her children might escape the king's arrogance (*effugite superbiam regiam*); and deed (the annihilation of her household).

146 Kampen (1992: 235) notes the importance of non-Roman women on imperial monuments, suggesting that "the barbarian woman with babe in arms signals the depth of defeat suffered by her society just as Livia, beneath her divine spouse and next to her ruling son, is the crucial link in the chain of enduring dynastic power." Zanker (2000: 173) has explored violent images of captive non-Roman women and children on the Column of Marcus Aurelius, claiming that these women represent the eternal sorrow of conquered non-Romans. He concludes that on the Column the enslavement of women and the separation of their children from them is a visual sign of the destruction of the last traces of social unity among the defeated non-Romans.

147 Walsh (1996: 15).

148 Poetics 1453a: "not eminently good or just, but highly renowned and prosperous ... whose misfortune is the outcome of some error or frailty."

149 Liv. 40.3.5-6: *execrationesque in agminibus ... vincente odio metum ... his ferox animus.*

150 Liv. 40.5.1: *ut saeviret ipse in suum sanguinem effecerunt.*

151 Philip's initial errors: his misguided decision to tranter populations; and his arrest of the children of executed opponents. His last mistake: countenancing the murder of his son Demetrius (Liv. 40.23.10) – a situation lent impetus by the Romans.

152 Liv. 40.5.7 *speciem ipsius*; 3: *sermonibus perplexis*; 5: *fraude.*

153 Cf. Figure 5.1: the historiographical periodisation of crisis and/or revolution.

4

TOPOI, TROPES, AND THE FEMALE

The rhetorical memory of the annalist tradition[1]

This chapter recalls one of the key statements Livy made in the Preface to the opening pentad, which articulates in large part the entire subject and purpose of the *Ab Urbe Condita* (AUC):

> There is this exceptionally beneficial and fruitful advantage to be derived from the study of the past, that you see, set in the clear light of historical truth, examples of every possible type. From these you may select for yourself and your country what to imitate, and also what, as being mischievous in its inception and disastrous in its issues, you are to avoid.[2]

What is so striking about these words, and why it makes good sense to revisit them at the start of this final consideration of how Livy represents women in Rome's foundation narrative, is the deep relationship they imply between the writing of history and the theme of memory. Drawing on the recent bibliography of classical scholarship dealing with the extent to which episodes, locations, and people in antiquity are important to creating and preserving memories of the past, Di Fazio states that, "[i]n order to be fixed in a group's memory, a truth must present itself in the concrete form of an event, a place, a person."[3] Equally important to the current study, this conceptualisation of historical memory, generated as a rhetorical product of Livy's historiographical project, not only ensures that a very specific version of the past is remembered ("set in the clear light of historical truth") but also plays a relevant role in legitimating the social order ("for yourself and your country") contemporary to the writer, familiar to his readership, and desirable to the key stakeholders in the Roman state ("what to imitate ... what to avoid").[4]

To this point, it is clear that Livy's version of history from the foundation of the city organises the subject matter of Rome's past so that the reader is guided toward ways of thinking about (and, one should imagine, acting in relation to) contemporary political topics, social situations, and cultural contexts. And, in line with the paradigm identified as essential to the explicitly gendered composition of AUC history, this reconfiguration of

Rome's collective or social memory – albeit in competition with, and with due regard for, divergent records of the past – inserts representations of mythological, legendary, and historical women in order to shape particular moments in historical time and urban space according to a desired or intended narrative.

4.1 The commonplace topics of gendered AUC history

In line with this view of historical memory as a cultural product – namely, how knowledge of the past is recollected and reconstituted in narrative performances – it is important to consider the extent to which the roles assigned by Livy to the women who constitute important participants, belonging to or occupying particular spaces, at key moments in Rome's past, reflect a traditional or revisionist interpretation of gender in foundation history. With all cautions set in place, this first section of this chapter will begin with an examination of a variety of rhetorical instruments used with episodes involving two significant women: Horatia and Verginia. Of special interest in this regard will be the possibility of identifying a link between the focal *topoi* used by Livy in his depiction of female engagement in the process of history and key terms which signal those moments of change.

4.1.1 Horatia

A useful starting-point is the problematic episode involving the sororicide Horatius.[5] Here, the reader cannot fail to address the structural and thematic echoes of the equally contentious fratricide which heralds the beginning of *Ab Urbe Condita* (AUC) history: Remus' death at his brother's hands.[6] These resonances provide comparative access to the gendered representational economy that Livy brings to bear on his historiographical reconstruction of annalistic events.

First, consider the evidence which testifies to an intentional doubling of narrative structure.

It seems unlikely that Livy would invest such *repetitio* into episodes which deal so unflinchingly with the transgressive act of kin-slaying without purpose. It is possible that the intellectual resonances which he sets in motion by a technique of historiographical rhetoric impinge on his gendered discourse about the evolving body politic.

Livy is an historian of the social imperative. For him, promulgation of generational continuity is a quintessential strategy whereby the socio-political mechanism is maintained. Paramount in this schema of rhetorically conceived historical reality is the paradigm of exemplary experience. If the annalist is able to characterise the facets of qualitative exposition which foster this sociological goal, then it may well be possible to influence the desirable course of future history – that is, the re-founding of the city as historiographical parallel to Augustan imperial policy. In this context, the

147

Table 4.1 Narrative reference-points in episodes of fratricide and sororicide

(1)	
The twins (esp. the fratricide Romulus) are instrumental in restoring their grandfather to his rightful place as king of Alba Longa.	The triplets (esp. the sororicide Horatius) secure victory over the Alban Curiatii, giving Rome dominion enforced by fetial treaty.

In each instance, a valuable service is performed on behalf of the city: restitution and preservation of *regnum*.

(2)	
The twins, seized with the desire to found a city,[7] manifest the characterological flaw of covetous desire (*regni cupido*), and engage in a morally disgraceful rivalry over augural precedence (*foedam certamen*).	Horatius, overwhelmed with rage at his (unnamed) sister's display of grief for her slain betrothed,[8] rebukes Horatia for her violent complaint and public display of lamentation over the death of a fallen enemy.[9]

In both episodes, Livy is careful to identify a weakness of disposition (a psychological disorder, if you will), as the cause of the friction between kin.[10]

Romulus' anger impels him to strike Remus down, calling out, "Thus hereafter whosoever other who shall leap over my walls."[11]	The enraged Horatius drives his sword through his sister, crying, "Thus perish every Roman woman who mourns a foe!"[12]

The killing of brother and sister is marked by an admonitory apophthegm: intransigent and lacking remorse.[13]

---

reader must question Livy's problematic renditions of Romulus' act of foundation and Horatius' heroic preservation of that heritage.

It is possible to adduce that the historian's introduction of a character flaw lies at the structural and semantic heart of this tension and holds the key to its solution (Table 4.1). The founding twins' *cupido* can be worthwhile or destructive, depending on its object. The act of building a city is productive, whereas the exercise of dominion is prone to the vagaries of despotic rule. The former is incorporative and binding; the latter, divisive and authoritarian. Horatius *ferox* is similarly ambivalent in nature. The display of daring on the battlefield is admirable, but the surrender to presumption can only be labelled headstrong. The one is an offshoot of that audacious courage valued most highly in time of war; the other is a disturbing loss of that self-discipline equally valorised by martial society. In Horatius' case, the constructive pole of his high-spiritedness is activated by his engagement with the Curiatii.

Ferox in the negative sense is the result of a sister's lamentation.[14] In other words, Horatia is objectified as the cause of a debilitating psychological defect. In the same way that the Sabine women identify themselves as *causa belli*, so Horatia is made to serve a similarly dysfunctional purpose.[15] She becomes the generator of social disorder. Given that her father, Publius Horatius, originally intended that she perform a far more traditional social role, it is ironic that her public affection for her betrothed precipitates a

148

potential rift in the internal socio-political structure at the hand of the unifier of rival communities.

Thus, Horatia is introduced as a girl of marriageable age and promised to one of the Curiatii. Without question, this occurs on the instigation of her *paterfamilias*; no doubt, with a view to promoting the *societas* advocated by Romulus and temporarily achieved in part due to the Sabine women. The fact that Livy delineates a compensatory affiliation between the agent of problematic violence and the male community represented by that agent is pertinent. Here, the difficulty which the socio-political hierarchy (*rex, patres*, and *plebs*) finds in coming-to-terms with Horatius' act is another example of Livy's figural hermeneutic. From one angle, it is an intellectual exploration and rationalisation of a deed at one and the same time fierce, shocking, and intolerable, yet perfectly in tune with a nature previously enumerated as savage and ungovernable (*ferox*).[16] Here, Livy juxtaposes appearance and reality to resolve the impasse: the deed seemed revolting (*atrox visum*), in contrast to the verifiable performance of his recent victory on the battlefield.[17] However, what is at stake is not the shameful murder of a defenceless and understandably emotional young girl;[18] rather, the narrative emphasises the flouting of invested state dispensation.[19] Concern is focused exclusively on the social reality, namely male usurpation of a function of the state: treason.

Why not a charge of *parricidium sororis* (murder of a sister)? Watson sees the king (Tullus Hostilius) resorting to *perduellio* and the appointment of *duoviri* as a reflection of political expediency in the face of an insurmountable tension between "the treatment merited by the hero Horatius and that deserved by the savage Horatius." It seems reasonable to concur with his view that this approach recommends itself on the principle of "psychological verisimilitude."[20] But his line of reasoning may be extended to include the clarity with which Livy examines male responsibility and the devolution of "competing jurisdictions":[21] regal authority, duumviral pronouncement, popular advocacy, and the *potestas* of Horatius' (and Horatia's) *paterfamilias*. Tullus Hostilius refuses to cast judgement;[22] the magistrates appointed by the king pronounce sentence in the same casuistical breath as denying Horatius' guilt;[23] his father asserts the justice of Horatia's death by denying his son's punishment;[24] and the people's council accede to Horatius' *provocatio* and his father's appeal.[25] "Man" is acquitted by male rationalisation, and "woman" is pronounced guilty without charge or hearing.[26] Watson wonders why the *duoviri* "voluntarily and unnecessarily interpreted the statute as not giving them power to absolve," but their abuse of magisterial jurisdiction can be seen as symptomatic of the paradigm of overlapping male expiation.[27] The crime? Apparent murder, redefined as treason.[28] The punishment? Piacular sacrifices (by the father) and symbolic purification of bloodguilt (by the son). The victim? Named only in death and objectified in perpetuity as the signifier of an ornamental tomb.[29] Regardless of how we view Horatius' slaying of his sister, the status of the female is constant. In other words, while Horatius's condition may be interrogated in relation to the public crime of murder (*parricidium*), as well as to the killing of a person subject to one's own *paterfamilias*, or the breach of a particular duty of obligation (*perduellio*), Horatia's status remains static. She is, therefore, the catalyst of male thought and action, forever trans-fixed by the instrument of man's penetrating reason, and doomed to suffer a sacralised death in order that history learns its lesson.[30]

In addition, the episode of Horatia – and particularly its agonistic redistri-bution of responsibility and jurisdiction – seems in part designed to address the resonant silence which greets the earlier archetypal incident of blood guilt, Romulus' slaying of Remus. Perhaps the foundation tradition proved resistant to Livy's rhetorical ministrations, for all the reader is left with is the incontrovertible facts of Remus' death and Romulus' consequent acqui-sition of sole *imperium*. It might be that the originary *conditor* of the *urbs sacratissima* could not be exposed to the epideictic analysis a lesser hero would expect. In any event, Horatius' cleansing of the pollutions of blood and battle-fever should be viewed as Livy's way of dwelling on the absence of absolute clarity and on the complexity of the male moral imagination in matters of the public good.

Here, it is possible to extrapolate the commonality of meaning underpin-ning both episodes. Livy wishes his audience to understand the ambiguities of male experience, appreciate the manifold lessons which these examples offer, and apply the outcomes of this historiographical pedagogy to the real-ity of their lives and the history of their remaking.[31] As Solodow states, "Livy's main engagement is not so much with the records of the Roman past as with the mind of his reader."[32] In other words, Livy's silence regard-ing Romulus, in part resolved by Horatius' appeal to the people, is another stratagem whereby the annalist explores "man" in order that the body pol-itic might develop the instrumentality with which to consolidate and justify its evolutionary imperative, its historical mandate.

To put this in context, the accomplishment of the archetypal *patrator* (the signifier of effective male society, Romulus the founder) must be weighed against the avid *interfector* (inaugural fratricide and savage defender of the *urbs condita*). So, too, Horatius' superordination of state over self will remain problematic if applied unreservedly to every sphere of the *res pub-lica*, martial or civil. In the foundation narrative, Livy cautions his readers against the ancestral evil of *regni cupido*.[33] The Horatius episode contains a similarly objectified threat to the social order: "woman" as betrayer of love of city for love of enemy. Horatia – Tarpeia in another rhetorical disguise – is the personification of the will to blur the necessary distinctions between private and public good. Thus, Horatius' father sheds tears only for his son, exemplar of steadfast courage in any situation, and the people exonerate his guilt by reason of his *virtus*, not the foundation of law or morality.[34] Solodow believes that Livy suspends judgement altogether in the case of Horatius, but it seems clear that, while he might refuse "either to condemn or to approve," the argument is explicit and the treatment of Horatia illus-trative rather than referential.[35]

4.1.2 Verginia

The profoundly disturbing pathology of *libido* casts its morally contemptible shadow over the workings of a pivotal *res interna* turning on the death of Verginia.[36] In summary, the irruption of a self-serving oligarchy of decemvirs – who, while appointed to govern the state with consular powers and to continue to draft a code of laws, began to behave tyrannically and refused to stand down at the end of their term – provokes a crisis which prompts, in turn: a *secessio* of the plebs, the overthrow of the second Decemvirate (and the suicide of its leader), the restoration of the old constitution, and a settlement framed in a series of enactments (proposed by L. Valerius Potitus and M. Horatius Barbatus), the so-called Valerio-Horatian laws. The catalyst aggravating this turning-point in the formative process of Rome's sociopolitical development is (again) a tyrant's lust, in this case for a chaste young maiden.

There is no need at this point to enter into the scholarly debate that arises from an examination of the detailed problems associated with the historical reconstruction of such a complex series of events.[37] That said, it is clear that certain episodes in the narrative should be viewed as subject to secondary elaboration.[38] With that in mind, the reader can identify obvious analogies between the stories of Verginia and Lucretia.[39] Livy compels his audience to consider the results of what happened in the context of how and why those events transpired.[40] For example, the reader is immediately drawn by force of Livy's artistry to the following commonplaces of gendered historiography:

1 The recurrent topology of *regnum*, embodied in the extravagant character portrait of Ap. Claudius.[41]
2 The reflexive background of military disaster, representing the interpenetration of *res interna* and *externa*, and signalling the renewal of mimetic interrelationships.[42]
3 The murderous duplicity of those inheriting the pedigree of violent opportunism.[43]
4 The overwhelmingly corrupting influence of the desire to transgress traditionally inviolable social boundaries.[44]

The parallelism is undeniable.

In addition to the points of comparison shown in Table 4.2, it is possible to discern strikingly similar expostulations of lust for a female nominally (and customarily) protected by normative barriers of decorum and respect.[45] Both Sextus Tarquinius and Appius Claudius display a distraction bordering on madness.[46] This condition arises from the attraction of physical appearance and resolute purity;[47] and is responsible for the compulsion to perform trickery when faced with an otherwise immovable moral tenacity.[48]

While there is room to extend the itinerary of similarities, it is useful to dwell for a time on the intriguing variants Livy has inserted in the later

Table 4.2 Similarities between the episodes of Lucretia and Verginia

Lucretia	Verginia
The last of the Tarquinii	Ap. Claudius and the decemvirs
The siege of Ardea	Decemviral incompetence in Sabine territory
Composite depictions of tyrannical *dominatio* and civilian *servitio*	
Lucius' and Sextus' deceptive ruse to win Gabii	The decemvirs' murder by proxy of L. Siccius

episode.[49] For a start, Verginia is condemned by the historian to a stony silence as the chain of events unravels relentlessly around her. Even though Sextus compelled Lucretia to voiceless submission, Livy still enabled her to address her summoned kin and their friends. Significantly, Verginia is rendered immutably passive, regardless of circumstance. She is subject to the desperate wishes of the male protagonists who intersect with her life-way – to a large extent because of another narratively imposed silence.

Consider the extenuating tensions brought to bear on this *virgo adulta*, arrayed in the recognisable garment of personal and social female identity (*pudicitia*).[50] Verginia is embodied as the promised object in marriage, a figure of unparalleled beauty, and the substantive effect sparking Claudius' *libido*.[51] In addition, Livy portrays her as the representation of familial status, especially male reputation in the community.[52] Moreover, she is the cause of advocacy before the decemvir's tribunal.[53] Throughout, she is conceived of as the "thing" which is contested or pronounced over.[54] For some, she may be understood as the qualitative measure of *libertas* and appropriated symbol of plebeian *virtus*.[55] For others, if all other contingencies fail, Verginia becomes the means by which contesting male wills signal the transfer from mimetic to actual rivalry.[56]

Given the explicit representative role assigned to Verginia, Livy begs the question. Why consign his "supreme example of the virtue of *pudicitia*, a supreme condemnation of *libido*," to the mute vacuum of objectified space, while allowing Lucretia a significant and determinative voice in the unfolding (albeit the closing chapter) of her (and her community's) destiny?[57]

It may be enough to assume that the prophetic utterance assigned to Lucretia is made to bear fruit – and, in a sense, to pronounce justification – through the exemplary *virtus* of a father's protective dispensation.[58] If so, the reader is required to accept the voiceless submission of a female figure lacking all but the semblance of reality as the logical progression of Livy's historiographical perspective on the inclusion of women in the received tradition.[59] Following Ogilvie, "the hazards and dangers attending liberty" exert a conscious and persistent pressure on the narrative exposition within the space of a fictively gendered discourse.[60] The structural, intellectual, and ideological tensions generated by these concerns appear to coincide in this episode. Each is expressly signalled as meaningful by the historian and arranged in such a way that the contextual environment proffers a further avenue of critical interpretation.

First, Livy draws attention to the connections between the stories of Lucretia and Verginia. It is not sufficient that the reader makes the obvious comparisons. There is a didactic mind at work behind the introduction to this historiographical period. What cannot be avoided in even the most cursory reading of Livy's prologue is the definitive association of Tarquinian and decemviral expulsion.[61]

Second, Livy draws attention to himself: as historiographer and historian (characteristic interventions as author and recorder of *res Romana*), and as person (a rare and tantalising glimpse of his own interpretation of contemporary social consciousness).

The allusion to historiographical *libertas* is suitably and subtly couched in the narrator's elucidation of Ap. and M. Claudius' concocted juridical scenario.[62] Taking into account Livy's avowed intention to surpass the efforts of his annalistic predecessors, the astute and practiced reader of AUC history would recognise the tell-tale signature of the supremely confident historiographer.[63] Its inscription encodes the process which forges the narrative superstructure of his composition as part of the working-out of a similar conceit invented by historicised characters.[64] More explicitly, Livy intervenes in the role of assiduous chronicler to report the final judgement of Ap. Claudius over the fate of Verginia.

> It is possible that the ancient writers may have correctly stated some ground which he alleged for his decision, but I do not find one anywhere that would justify such an iniquitous decision. The one thing which can be propounded as being generally admitted is the judgment itself. His decision was that the girl was a slave.[65]

If we believe Cicero, this kind of authorial interference was an expected feature of ancient historiography.[66] The historian was required to pass judgement on his subject, rather than assume the critical distance of the "invisible" narrator. What is notable in this digressive insertion is the interplay of rival historiographical conventions.[67] Livy cites the existence of sources for Ap. Claudius' decree in the annalistic manner;[68] yet he dilutes the authorial *auctoritas* usually evoked by use of the third person by introducing signs of hesitation or doubt.[69] Further, while he notes that the unadorned content of the decree which he intends to set before his readers is verified by the available accounts, his first-person intrusion tends to diminish the certitude he appears to hold for his representation.[70] These tensions – narrative coherence and persuasive authority offset by doubts over the received tradition and implicit engagement of the reader in the critical process – recall a similar Livian interposition in the story of Lucretia.

By enumerating these and, I believe, other still more atrocious incidents which his keen sense of the present injustice suggested, but which it is not easy to give in detail, he goaded on the incensed multitude to strip the king of his sovereignty and pronounce a sentence of banishment against Tarquin with his wife and children.[71]

That there is a marked development in the force of Livy's interjection would seem to parallel the thematic and characterising variants already noted, and certainly aggravate the interpretative ambiguities implicitly raised by the circular figure of *res* as *fabula*.

Prima facie, the impression that Livy wishes his readership to consider the significance of this episode in all its complexity is emphatic and communicated on a variety of levels. The aspect of AUC history which forms such an integral part of the narrative is precisely that facet of Livy's treatment most readily apprehended yet most often underplayed or ignored. Simply, set in a gendered discourse and framed by human action, the relationship between male and female gives rise to the incident's structural premise and provides the core around which all argument and conflict revolve.

At this point, it is helpful to refer to the *pathetikos* attending the elevation of Verginia's corpse and its display before the people.[72]

> The matrons, who followed with angry cries, asked, "Was this the condition on which they were to rear children, was this the reward of modesty and purity?" with other manifestations of that womanly grief, which, owing to their keener sensibility, is more demonstrative, and so expresses itself in more moving and pitiful fashion. The men, and especially Icilius, talked of nothing but the abolition of the tribunician power and the right of appeal and loudly expressed their indignation at the condition of public affairs.[73]

This moment comprises the tragic climax of the historian's composition and a lucid example of Livy's rhetorical refinement of Greek (especially Hellenistic) historiographical practice.[74] Although Verginia is struck dumb throughout, Livy inserts a specifically thematic interrogation articulated by a cortege of loudly complaining *matronae*. The reader should not be surprised that these women are present. After all, they have accompanied and participated in the events surrounding Verginia in a variety of contexts.

> Verginius, in mourning garb, brought his daughter, similarly attired, and accompanied by a number of matrons, into the Forum. ... The women who accompanied [Icilius] made a profounder impression by their silent weeping than any words could have made. ... Whilst the man [M. Claudius] who claimed the maiden was being pushed back by the group of women and her supporters who stood round, the crier called for silence.[75]

What might be construed as unexpected is the manner in which Livy deploys this female collective. It can be discerned not so much in any radical or deviant sense, but rather in a most stylised and disproportionately traditional way – namely, as the chorus of archetypal tragedy.[76]

Whether introduced as escorts, affective communicants of revolutionary appeal, or tenacious defenders of beleaguered chastity, the crowd of women conforms to a familiar dramatic typology, providing a representative commentary on the action. If so, then Livy co-opts his female aggregate to support Verginius' claim of ownership, Icilius' surety of betrothal, and Verginia against M. Claudius' proximate assertions. Once again, Verginia is depicted as a substitute for male interests, this time by association with the express disposition of a body of women usually ascribed as possessing moral and/ or social *dignitas*: *matronae*. Therefore, the reader is aware of the rhetorical force informing the exprobations of these women regarding the outcome of Ap. Claudius' judgement.[77] But the remarks which follow these questions – artfully positioned between the act and the effect of threatened *dominatio* (Verginia's murder and civil disorder) – bear the striking imprimatur of authorial assessment. Livy provides his readers with a personal epitome of the underlying focus of this episode.

Consequently, any opinion which regards the signifying products of (or representative status expressed by) a woman's customary role in Roman society as subject to conditional affection or provisional advantage and distinction can only be viewed as the promptings of female (or effeminised) distress or vexation (*muliebris dolor*), itself the expression of weak character (*imbecillus animus*).[78] On the other hand, that outlook which grants undeviating priority to civic considerations must conform to the collective voice expressive of *virilis ingenium*.[79] The ideological line would seem to be drawn in no uncertain terms, and by the historian's own critical yardstick.

Yet the Livy who seeks to represent the existing density of AUC tradition in terms which at times render the constraining texture of the narrative decisively problematic cannot be far removed from such a site of intersecting structural and semantic tensions. If the female collective superficially register as inseparable from Verginia, but on closer scrutiny identify more readily with superordinate male interests, then the conventional devaluation of affective female behaviour (as the sign of an unhealthy or enfeebled disposition) may be seen to resonate ambiguously against the clear-sighted depiction of normative male rivalry. This is especially so with respect to that disturbing space – signified by the female *corpus* – which separates the socially-defined yet demonstrably unpoliced margins of gender.

Moreover, it seems logical to allow that Livy's developed sense of the complexity which interpenetrates and underpins human intellection and action could not help but recognise the imaginative inconsistency of this episode.[80] So the fixity of vision displayed as characteristic of resolute "man" might equally well degenerate into domination, injustice, and prescriptive injury.[81]

Following this reading, Verginius' clarion *in libertatem vindico* (3.48.5) becomes a two-edged linguistic call-to-arms. It may be taken as symptomatic of the ambiguity inherent in Livy's deployment of rhetorical antithesis and juxtaposition of opposites.[82] This is a feature of the patriarchal historiography equally evident in the story of Horatia. The skewed identity of Livy's *libertatis vindex* cannot represent a challenge to the prevailing phallogocentric symbolic order, in the same way that the style of AUC history (if not elements of content) cannot fail to admit of influence from a constellation of historiographical theorists (utopian to partisan) and practitioners (scientific to empathetic).[83] But its very ambivalence – aligned within gendered coordinates – suggests a carefully conceived invitation to the reader, formulated in the space of the code with which ancient historians made the past recognisable to their audience. One need only observe the relative ease with which the most elementary of stereotypical binarisms (male and female) may be subverted. Similarly, consider the fragile boundary which divides the tyrant from the liberator. Both oppositions straddle the problematic gulf between domestic order and social concord, household management and political constitution, the family and the state. Livy does not wish to rescind the ideology which explains and dictates the normative perceptions and behaviours of his milieu, but he fervently desires that his readership (in concert with the author) explores the previously hidden *desiderata* of social intercourse which play an integral role in determining the shape and substance of once and future Rome.

4.2 Fakes, forgeries, and historical fiction in the *Ab Urbe Condita*: the authenticity of gendered historiography

As this study moves toward an ending, and in the light of coming to terms with the value of gendered readings of Livy's monumental historiographical project, it is interesting to consider the relationship between the literary and historical undercurrents to the composition of AUC history and the syncretistic process – sometimes called *interpretatio romana* – reflecting direct contacts between Rome and Italy going back to the very beginning of the archaic period.[84] If we apply the principles of a process normally limited to the re-interpretation of the mythology and religion of other cultures in terms of Roman concepts, practices, and shared characteristics, it is possible to suppose that other aspects of socio-cultural character might be shown to resemble their equivalent phenomenal counterparts in the contemporary Roman world. In other words, over and above the structural logic which allows modern scholars to regard the rulers of Rome as the product of historical circumstances similar to those influencing the 6th century BCE *milieu*, one can postulate that the society of central Italy in the archaic period consciously set out to imitate amenable, attractive, or in some way congruent activities, customs, institutions, or intellectual traditions. According to this view, it is also possible to infer that the narrative framework, chronology, and substantive information contained within Livy's early annalistic history represents a complex amalgam of hard data and secondary oral/literary superstructure. Thus, for example, an episode attempting to treat a memory of the archaic period will reflect the conjectural, biased, mistaken, even dishonest filters applied to the core of authentic information.

Taking this brief excursus into account, a coincident and identifiable literary treatment of an episode like the tyrannical character of the later Roman kings might allow a modern audience to interpret Livy's model of kingship in a manner closer to his late republican intention. By exploring an extensive, historiographical period of archaic AUC history, it may be possible to address a crucial issue pervading scholarship of the recent age: the value of the annalistic record. More than this, highlighting Livy's conscious decision to apply a gendered narrative lens to the events of Rome's on-going foundation should help to determine the degree of correspondence between points of historical tension in his annalistic reconstruction – in this case, the problem of charismatic authority in conflict with the pathology of the governing class[85] – and relations between men and women.

If episodes found in books after the foundational first pentad give us some idea of Livy's ideological perspectives on issues of gender and on relational dynamics in private, public and mixed social conditions, it may be possible to adduce evidence which reveals if a particular view of female sexuality was implicit in the construction of women's social roles. Such a perspective should be discernible in the earliest instances of gendered AUC narrative.

4.2.1 Lavinia, Rhea Silvia, and Larentia

Consider the role of Lavinia in the foundation account. Subject to the arrival of refugees from the legendary siege of Troy, the king of the Latins gives his daughter in marriage to Aeneas, the Trojan leader. The economy of exchange is specific and formal: "there Latinus in the presence of the household gods added a domestic treaty to the public one."[86] The alliance between Aeneas and Latinus (*res publica*) is mirrored in the marriage between Aeneas and Lavinia (*res privata*). On the one hand, the text retails a pledge of personal *amicitia*, a treaty assigning public acceptance, and communal ratification by *salutatio* (a right of the collective male citizeny/soldiery); on the other, an offer of guest-friendship (*hospitium*), the exercise of *potestas* (*matrimonium* as social institution), and joint affirmation of Troy's hope (*Troianis spes*). Throughout, Lavinia is unnamed. Instead, she is rendered *filia* and *uxor*.[87] Her identity is depicted in relational terms, contingent on the superior status of the male (*pater* or *vir/maritus*). A consequence of civic and domestic alliance is the foundation of a town ("which Aeneas named Lavinium after his wife") and the conception of a child ("a male scion of the new marriage, to whom his parents gave the name of Ascanius").[88] In the former instance, Lavinium is named by Aeneas. It is a singular act, defining his position (status and reputation), reifying his authority (Trojan leader and independent ally of Latinus), and defining a broad sphere of influence (social and regional). In the latter case, Ascanius is named by his parents. This is a shared act which confers limited agency on Lavinia (over the child, not the father) and arrogates to her a limited sphere of influence (the household). These referential assignations of gendered activity find expression in a potent denominator. Latinus' unnamed daughter is only given identity in the act of foundation: a telling representation of the objectification of the female as gift and property.

Enter Tumus, king of the Rutilians: "to him Lavinia had been betrothed."[89] The complication is melodramatic; its signification is instructive. Lavinia (named for the first time) is again objectified, in relation to her father and the expectant partner in a solemn promise of marriage (*nuptialis sponsio*). More than this, she exists as a catalyst of conflict between rivals. Indignant that "a stranger should be preferred before him," Tumus attacks Aeneas and Latinus.[90] Through all this, Lavinia remains silent and passive. In a sense, Livy renders her "absolute," an abstraction freed from the restraint of reality. She is nothing more or less than a cause or reason, explaining (in narrative and intellectual terms) the death of Latinus, the alliance of mutual convenience between the Rutilians and Etruscans (under Tumus and Mezentius), the assimilation of Trojans under the Latin name, and the victory of the Latins and the death of Aeneas.

Our final encounter with Lavinia occurs in a context of tutelage and kingship: "under the maintenance of a woman (such was the profound ability in Lavinia) the Latin state and the kingdom (of his father and grandfather) stood for the boy."[91] Here, Lavinia embraces the role of guardian. But as protector of state and defender of sovereignty, she is invested with an authority (*imperium*) which is explicitly male in prerogative and agency. In addition, Livy cites possession of an inborn quality. This talented disposition (*tanta indoles*) allows Lavinia to maintain unimpaired rightful authority of Aeneas' son and heir. Given his previous adumbration of the female role in society, the reader is justified in asking whether Livy is bestowing deserved praise (reward for merit) or expressing justified surprise over Lavinia's *tutela muliebris* and *indoles*. The historian gives the clue to interpretation: "This Ascanius – no matter where born, or of what mother – founded a new city himself.[92] In the end, it does not matter if Ascanius was born in Ilium or Lavinium; neither is it apposite whether his mother was Creusa or Lavinia. As Livy asseverates in first-person intervention, "I shall not discuss the question, for who could affirm for certain so ancient a matter?"[93] The important thing is Ascanius is Aeneas' son, and he founded a new city himself.[94] His identity is agnate, reflexive and reproductive.

As such, the son is an originator, a founder, and in that sense the scion of his father's lineage; whereas the mother (or stepmother) is given the governance of Lavinium by Ascanius.[95] It is difficult not to associate the city's propitious circumstances as a bequest of the departing Ascanius, rather than the product of Lavinia's good government. This is confirmed by Livy's identification of the indomitable sphere of Latin influence as a consequence of Aeneas' defeat of the Etruscans "in spite of a woman's tutelage (or a boyish first apprenticeship of the kingdom)."[96]

In close proximity, Livy introduces Rhea Silvia.

> Adding crime to crime, he murdered his brother's sons and made the daughter, Rhea Silvia, a Vestal virgin; thus, under the pretence of honouring her, depriving her of all hopes of issue.[97]

Like Lavinia, this woman's identity is mediated through her relationship to a male relative (Numitor, her father), and her ability to bear children (*partus*). The context is again crucial. Numitor is the preferred inheritor of his father's *imperium* and *potestas*; as the eldest son, the bequest reflected his father's wishes (*voluntas patris*).[98] He is also portrayed as the natural elder agnate and repository of testamentary precedence (*verecundia aetatis*). Finally, he represents a superordinate bloodline (*stirpem fratris virilem*). These considerations greatly displease his younger brother, Amulius, who drives Numitor into exile and rules in his stead.

Consequently, Rhea Silvia's role is fixed by male thought and action. She is delimited as the *filia* of Amulius' violence (*vis*), the mimetic object of Amulius' crime (*scelus*) – here, the distinction between mother and stepmother seems almost immaterial (or at least inconsequential) – and a surrogate threat by virtue of her shared bloodline (*partus*).

From now on, as the historian notes (above), she is known only through Amulius' imposition of status (public) and sexual continence (private).

At this point, a difficulty intrudes. The received tradition speaks of twins, born of divine blood. But Livy has eschewed those poetic legends belonging to a time "before the city was founded."[99] His explicit declamation reads thus: "neither to affirm nor refute" (*ne adfirmare ne refellere*) the fabulous and the mythic. A solution offers, gendered and problematic, but nevertheless reasonable in context. The Vestal is raped (ostensibly by Mars) yet is seen to be blameworthy (*culpa*). Livy calls into question the veracity of the claim that Mars perpetrated the embracing violence of rape (*vi compressa*). He ascribes parentage of Romulus and Remus to Rhea Silvia's personal testimony. Her claim is further disputed as either the product of mistaken (or misguided) belief or of reflexive guilt over her debased status as mother and guardian priestess (*sacerdos*).[100] In this way, the text controverts the basis of Rome's divine origin by framing the contention through the testimony of a constituent element of the mythography. The effect of this secondary diffusion of critical commentary is to confer complicity on the narrative frame, Rhea Silvia. By doing so, the annalist excises himself from the historiographical conundrum of Rome's "doubtful offspring" (*incertae stirpis*). To paraphrase, he considers it more creditable (*honestior*) for a woman to be seen as the author of fault (*auctor culpae*) than the god or the omniscient narrator (*ita rata ... deus*). The fact that the *sacerdos*, manacled, and imprisoned – as

159

much by the implications of Livy's rhetoric as by the manipulative Amulius – disappears from the text (at the moment in which doubt of the tradition is inferred) seems propitious. Having been aired, the historian's ironic sublimation of Rome's dubious heritage may now be put to metaphorical rest. This allows *divinitus* (divine influence or literary inspiration) to again hold sway, and the tale to be told *sans* the stain of ravished motherhood.

The stigmatose pathology ascribed to female identity is not wholly eradicated. When the twin children of Rhea Silvia (and Mars?) – committed to the Tiber, fed by a she-wolf – are found by the shepherd Faustulus, they are given over to his wife's keeping.[101] It cannot be coincidence that Livy assigns to putative sources a singular etymological notion. Larentia, the royal shepherd's wife, is equated with the thirsty *lupa* of legend because of her reputation as a prostitute.

> Some writers think that Larentia, from her unchaste life, had got the nickname of "She-wolf" amongst the shepherds, and that this was the origin of the marvellous story.[102]

It seems just as reasonable to designate her as representative of the household, given the resonance of the collateral *lar* (hearth or dwelling place).[103] In any event, like Lavinia and Rhea Silvia, Larentia disappears from the narrative proper as soon as the particular semantic perturbation is exposed. Faustulus alone is associated with the twins' upbringing.

The clausulae *vulgato corpore* is suggestive. Foster translates it as "having been free with her favours."[104] It is a striking expression and can be taken another way: "the (female) body published." I would posit this singular statement as emblematic of Livy's approach in dealing with the problematic tensions and ambiguities of a foundation legend born of violence and conflict. In other words, the historian may be seen to have adopted a rhetorical strategy (*vulgato corpore*) to deal with any discursive rifts in the received tradition; that is, those moments of disequilibrium and alterity which fail to correspond to the normative constructs of annalistic historiography. *Vulgo* is a flexible copulative and may be used to explicate the nature of the author's engagement in the gendered episodes of AUC history.[105]

Hence, Livy "confounds himself with," "puts himself on a level with," or "divulges" the economies of exchange, the relational and contingent alliances, the objectified identities and mimetic rivalries "spread abroad" or mapped on the female body.[106]

4.2.2 *Tanaquil*

The lineage from which spring the tyrannical and agonistic instruments of political revolution in early Rome are illustrative not only of Livy's appreciation of evolutionary historical process but also of his rhetorical narrative economy. Demaratus, an exile and a stranger[107] – refugee from a violent

160

political upheaval in 7th century BCE Corinth – is father by an unmentioned woman of Etruscan Tarquinii to two sons, Lucumo and Arruns. Lucumo, an energetic man, and powerful by reason of the wealth inherited *in toto* from his fathers, is married to Tanaquil, herself born into the highest rank of the Tarquinian community.[108] Social expectations of an elite Etruscan *matrona* are identified as an essential component of Tanaquil's character, and as the basis of Lucumo's migration to Rome.

> The Etruscans looked down upon Lucumo as the son of a foreign refugee; she could not brook this indignity and, forgetting all ties of patriotism if only she could see her husband honoured, resolved to emigrate from Tarquinii.[109]

Specifically, as perceived through the eyes of her social and kinship groups, her husband's ignominious genealogy is an insufferable indignity; to the extent that she is willing to supplant love of country for honour of husband.

Here, the reader must carefully weigh the problematic of affective motivation if Livy's narrative purpose is to be accurately divined. On the one hand, the husband is an undeniably active man.[110] In ideological and socio-political terms, Lucumo is the ideal signifier of the masculine imperative: materially qualified and brave.[111] On the other, his judgements and desires are overtly fashioned by the expediency of his inherited estate, a condition enhanced by his marriage to a member of the Etruscan governing class.[112] Moreover, Lucumo is an ambitious man, eager for distinction, and consequently easily manipulated to identify Tanaquil's purposes as his own.[113]

The fact that Tanaquil not only harbours but succeeds in actualising a purpose of her own – to place her husband in an environment wherein his considerable merits might attract the recognition necessary to satisfy her social requisites[114] – is noteworthy in this context. She is presented as the mediating agent of the productive and destabilising principles constitutive of the nascent *res publica*, that formative community seen at this point in time as a meritocracy expeditious of ability and open to the material and intellectual vocabulary of like-minded individuals.[115] Through her agency, Lucumo's positive attributes – active ability, property, and bravery (i.e., *virtus*) – are promulgated and fostered under the auspices of potentially destructive emotional and intellectual denominators – desire, ambition, and vulnerability to persuasion. As such, the dramatically significant augural foreshadowing of Lucumo's socio-political ascendancy is rendered ambiguous by virtue of Tanaquil's two-fold intermediary status: a gendered conduit between the affective and effective elements of domestic and public relations; and an aetiological representation of Etruscan divination practice, identifier and interpreter of secular and divine relations.[116]

This association of human and transcendent contact with the conjunctive assimilation of female purpose and male expectation reflects a discursive recognition of the iterative hermeneutic already identified in the AUC narrative.[117] Lucius Tarquinius Priscus – the identity assumed by Lucumo as a subterfuge jointly published or given out with Tanaquil (*edidere nomen*)[118] – publicly pronounces ideas which echo the unspoken policy of his wife.[119] This can be seen not so much as the referential exposition of female influence as the representative evocation of the interactivity between the individual and social male self. Livy clarifies this disequilibrium between the seat of emotion and the faculty of reason by explicit articulation.

Tarquinius, excellent in all other respects, is governed by *ambitio*, and he is just as motivated by the impulse to personal empowerment as to civic expansion.

> Though in all other respects an excellent man, his ambition, which impelled him to seek the crown, followed him on to the throne; with the design of strengthening himself quite as much as of increasing the State, he made a hundred new senators.[120]

Ergo, the same qualities encouraged by Tanaquil before the migration are now internalised in the future king. This identification illuminates Tanaquil's intervention in the matter of the child Servius Tullius' portentous manifestation. Given her characterisation as the visceral link between the divine and temporal worlds, Livy deploys Tanaquil as the means by which ancestral destiny is foreshadowed.[121] More than this, she continues to perform that role earlier prefigured by Carmenta; namely, the guarantor of posterity. Tanaquil's hopeful interpretation of the child's burning head is a confirmation of unorthodox action in the face of uncertainty and confusion. Her advice is the crystallisation of that assurance needed if the constituent elements of the body politic are to continue.[122] In the same way, then, that he is deliberately constructing his discourse, Livy extols his audience to foster (publicly and in private) that subject-matter which is of momentous aptitude to personal enlightenment and civic protection.[123]

This is not to say that the female *personae* with whom Livy populates such seminal episodes in AUC history lack existence. Instead, it seems that the annalist uses them to represent qualities which may be taken as illustrative of responsible or dangerous socio-political strategies. Within this schema, "woman" (in her various guises) acts as a pivotal element in the figural superstructure of Livy's preferred civic ideology. To a certain extent, the structural core of this narrative framework is beside the point, at least with respect to the portion of AUC history which focuses exclusively on the birth of republican Rome.

Therefore, the agency Livy invests in Tanaquil (after the fatal attack mounted against Tarquinius by the sons of Ancus) is not as extraordinary an exposition of presumptive female influence as some might think. This is especially true if viewed in context with Livy's preceding depictions of *muliebris ingenium* and the roles played by women in the kinetic of relational history.

So we must view Tanaquil's advice to her husband in the same light as Hersilia's to the founder of Rome. After all, both women represent interests favourable to maintenance of the state; and each co-opts her spouse's agreement in the aftermath of male achievement – be it military victory or civic expansion and consolidation.[124] As well, the functional objectification of women is highlighted even in the moment of Tanaquil's apparent efficacy.

To subvert the alternative tradition that the etymological derivation of Servius Tullius' name arose from his birth to a slave woman, Livy personally intervenes to confirm the appropriateness of Tarquinius' conduct in betrothing his daughter to this boy looked upon as a son.[125] The way in which the annalist achieves this end is by the expedient of conferred status. Servius Tullius' credentials are bestowed by his parentage – he is the son of the wife of the chief man of the Latin town of Corniculum; she was the spoil of Tarquinius' martial triumph – and confirmed as the direct consequence of his mother's recognition by a woman of equal status, Tanaquil.[126]

In this regard, it is interesting to consider the extent to which the Romans of Livy's day may have been conscious of the shameful nature of a tradition which invested a king with an unrespectable pedigree (a servile origin and a lack of identifiable paternity).[127] The possibility exists that the historian's interposed and favoured legendary variant serves to confer legitimacy on a charismatic figure of obscure background in such a way that the threat of vertical mobility (discouraged by contemporary values of society) is averted, and that existing hierarchies are reinforced. Significantly, Livy complicates the major historiographical crux revolving around the origins of Servius Tullius (his ancestry, birth, and upbringing) by rationalising the tradition in gendered terms.[128] He integrates the unnamed mother's role as the face-saving vehicle by which the dignity of aristocratic birth might be conferred, and introduces Tanaquil's function as witness, bearer, engenderer, and rearer of the *natus*.[129] In a structural and ideological sense, the female is deployed as the surrogate of male agency: "she" is instrumental in the process of acceptable succession and the making of eligible monarchy. It is noteworthy that Livy emphasises the priority of specific affective manifestations as deeply enmeshed in this problem of relational legitimacy. The explicit quality of Tanaquil's "well-doing" – the value and degree of the kindness shown to Servius Tullius' mother – is identified as the cause of an augmenting intimacy between real and substitute protector and nurturer.[130] In concert with a burgeoning esteem and acknowledged preferment, it is also seen to initiate the investment of affection by the collective household in the shared subject of familiarity.[131] The growing friendship and native characteristics typically associated with the domestic or familial setting are promoted as necessary to the successful inception of Tullius as heir apparent to the office of king.

The renown to be associated with the gradual unfolding of AUC history is specifically gendered and likewise inextricably bound up in the overlapping interrelations of the domestic and public spheres.[132] As such, it should not be construed as coincidental that this episode adverts to Livy's perspective on the study of historical material. Each feature of the narrative – the marvellous event (*miraculum*) marking the early life of a future king of Rome, the significance of the customary practice of augural interpretation to the continuity of the city's destiny, the explicit focus on the critical role conferred on certain men in manifesting or contriving to affect the dynamics of future time, and the pivotal link between policy and prosperity – may be equated with the four-fold nature of *res Romana*:[133] Servius Tullius (*vita*), the *prodigium* (*mores*), Tarquinius (*vir*), and "the studies by which men are inspired to bear themselves greatly" (*artes*).[134] The fact that Livy embeds in a gendered context those questions to which he would have every reader give close attention is instructive and encouraging.

Livy places Tanaquil at the nexus of a social and ideological tumult. Assassinated at the instigation of the surviving legitimate sons of his predecessor, the king-who-reigns is replaced by the child fostered and promoted under Tanaquil's auspices. Not only is Servius Tullius an alien – a foreigner, and outside the patrician aristocracy (possibly even a slave's son) – but his election to power involves the subversion of those formalities adhered to in the earlier period of the monarchy. At the heart of this confluence of intellectually disturbing tensions (constitutional illegitimacy, charismatic authority, indefinable blood relationship, and populist *regnum*), Livy reconstitutes the figure of Tanaquil. She is cast as the imperative, prophetic kingmaker, embodying the legitimating strategies of political freedom, and representing the far-seeing inspiration of divine providence.

In the midst of the ambivalent and confused popular grasp of events,[135] Tanaquil takes charge in a succession of functionally and linguistically suggestive acts.

> In the midst of the confusion, Tanaquil ordered the palace to be cleared and the doors closed; she then carefully prepared medicaments for dressing the wound, should there be hopes of life; at the same time she decided on other precautions, should the case prove hopeless, and hastily summoned Servius. She showed him her husband at the point of death, and taking his hand, implored him not to leave his father-in-law's death unavenged, nor to allow his mother-in-law to become the sport of her enemies.[136]

First, she commands the palace to be closed. This order is given to royal attendants responsible to the king's directives. It is also applied to a signifier of the household (*regia*) which is suggestive of the roughly contiguous unified complex of buildings containing the king's residence and its associated household cults.[137] Second, she expels any and all individuals present who might potentially be regarded as eyewitnesses to the coming subterfuge and her explicit performative role in its successful inception. Third, she recognises the necessity for maintaining the pretence of hope in the eyes of those who remain. In this regard, she consciously provides for tending her husband's injury. Such a deliberate action seems calculated to emphasise the intentionality of her diligent preparation.[138] It may also be viewed as bearing a metaphorical implication of female usurpation of administrative authority, given the secondary reading of *curando volneri* as "taking charge of a (figurative) disaster" in state affairs.[139] Fourth, Tanaquil is realistic enough to set in motion other protections in the likelihood that the king's wound is fatal. Here, her recognizance is taken either for her own situation or with respect to the circumstances of political and social consequence. Fifth (and logically enough), these "fortifications" (*praesidia*)[140] require the presence of one fit to address the needs of the *res publica* and the *familia*; that is, the child-become-man, held in affection and esteem by biological and adoptive mothers and regarded with honour by patrician and plebeian alike, Servius Tullius. Sixth, Tanaquil responds with urgency to the exigent demand, summoning Servius to view the king's almost bloodless (and therefore powerless) body. In that moment of psychological stress and political hiatus, she holds fast to the young man's right hand, suggesting that she has him in her power and continues to manage public affairs through mastery of the moment. Not just this, but she also entreats Tullius that he might not suffer the death of his father-in-law to be unpunished or his mother-in-law to endure the mockery of enemies.[141] Altogether, it is difficult to avoid the centrality of Tanaquil's rational, affective, and physical involvement in the recognition, interpretation, evaluation, and application of strategies most efficacious in alleviating the problematic resonances of an unforeseen calamity to the household and the state.[142]

From a structural standpoint, the discrete clausal elements of Livy's historiographical period are designed to move the action forward. In this way, language and style reinforce the semantic emphasis. Livy is articulating Tanaquil as a founding figure, one of the "*protoi heuretai* (...) with which early Roman history abounds."[143] But his interest in identifying her as an "inventor" is not so much antiquarian as to trace the roots of contemporary practice. In other words, the historian establishes Tanaquil as a "founder" in her own right so that he might then question and modify the existing tradition. In this instance, Livy's aim of artistic composition is to reconstruct the second founding of Rome and in consequence its second founder.[144] Just as he drew out the implicit ambiguities of the city's exemplary *conditor* (the fratricide Romulus), Livy intends to radicalise the characterological significance of Etruscan Tanaquil beyond the prototypically Greek *femme fatale*.[145] To do so, he incorporates qualities of intellectual and emotional resource appropriate to (and necessary to encompass) a crisis of succession.

To further his argument, Livy apportions Tanaquil two speeches: an *oratio recta* (1.41.3-4), addressed in calculated, imperative terms to Servius, which succinctly analyses the nature of the historical event and characterises the interpenetrating roles of speaker and listener; and a sophisticated, indirect discourse to a crowd (1.41.5), an *oratio obliqua* which highlights the desired reaction of the population, clarifies the motivation of the queen as actor, and effectively focuses the reported nature of the scene. To Servius, the introductory taunt (1.41.3: *si vir es*), deliberately excited and unrefined, is overtly gendered to unsettle the authority of the formally composed speech and to disturb the conventionally unchallenged mimesis of the historian's own voice (the *sub oculos subiectio* of vivid narration).[146] This conforms to the contention that Livy seeks "the engagement of the reader in the histori-ographical project."[147] The purpose is at hand: to enumerate the profoundly desirable exemplum of one who deserves the denomination of "man." Conjoint with his recreation of Tanaquil as the intellectual focus of a textu-ally non-recurrent episode in his compendium of *res internae*, Livy encodes *vir* as rhetorically gendered – an emblematic identity quickened to existence by the representational progenitor of selfhood.

In a sense, Tanaquil fulfils the role of divine intermediary – *animus* (the spiritual principle of life or the rational soul) – by personifying the inspira-tional fire which testifies to the royal and super-temporal nature of Servius, heir to *regnum* and deserving of the epithet *clarus*. She identifies him as the chosen successor, and rouses him to excite his innate nature, pursue the gods as guides in any undertaking and bestir his true self in reality. This notional investiture is conditional on Servius becoming a "man" by virtue of authen-tic birth: self-aware, self-reckoned, and self-generated.[148]

Here, Livy's intricate intertextual net establishes a system of cross-references by which the direct, personal relationship between Tanaquil and Servius effectively mirrors that established between Livy and the reader through the narrative strategy of decentralised authorial voice.[149] Tanaquil speaks to Servius as Livy writes for an unidentified (almost certainly elite and masculine) "you." If the reader's task is to "observe closely (*intueri*) not only the results ... but also the workings of history," then reading Tanaquil's *oratio obliqua* to the *populus* should be as active a process as writing (or "making") history.[150] Of course, it is possible to see in her address from a palace window an aetiology of the porta Fenestella, evidence of the near-eastern "sacred marriage" ritual, and even late Hellenistic literary con-tamination.[151] But the cautious reader may also detect indications of a prag-matic historiographical agenda seeking to impart moral and ethical lessons through authorial persuasion and reader participation.

So we find a great number of people together, hardly able to keep in check impulsive, vehement passion. Inspired by the violence done to the state (in the body politic of the king) and characterised by loud din and furious motion,[152] the mob is assured that the cause of their disorder is unjustified and that the functions of the king – his physical and socio-political affects, inextricably connected in figural terms – would be sustained in appearance, both promised and surrogate. It is Tanaquil's achievement to bid the pop-ulation be safe and sound in mind and heart. She inspires confidence and restores order through blatant (yet justified?) duplicity and the assured com-mand of medical platitude. Equally significant is her ratification of Servius' superimposition as executor of the king's official duties.[153] At this point,

Tanaquil's words are transformed into visceral reality. The *imago* of Servius is brought forth – in a similar fashion to the process of continuous transformation to which Rome's history was subject as each generation commemorated its ancestors – and exhibited in the associative trappings of royalty.[154] Tanaquil hands him down to the people as if by tradition: bequeathed and propagated, "published" as exemplum reconstituted.

Such a transformation is symptomatic of the compositional economy implicit to Livy's approach to gendered narrative episodes.[155] It is also strikingly reminiscent of the ancient binarism between "word" and "deed" (*orationes ... facto*), which incidentally represents the contents of historiography; that is, speeches and narrative. Note in passing the resemblance between the signification of Tanaquil as the precursive embodiment of Servius – her words pre- and transfigure his actions – and the verbal interpositions of Hersilia, the Sabines, Lucretia, Veturia (and Volumnia), Fabia Ambustus (as we shall see), and so on. One might also remark on the tantalisingly suggestive word-play implicit in Livy's choice of *prodo*.[156] Its various connotations are all appropriate etymologies underscoring the rhetorical discourse deployed to further Livy's historiographical project.[157]

By this stage, it should be clear that Livy favours the deployment of parenthetical characterisation as a means of treating problematic historiographical elements.[158] Expected to pass judgement on his subject, Livy's need to query and to doubt (in an aporietic sense) manifests itself in those episodes which imitate the circumstantial particularity and rhetorical elaboration of

Table 4.3 The mirrored representations of Tarquinius Priscus and Servius Tullius

	Actions	
Marks of character	*Tarquin*	*Servius*
Prone to concealment and pretence	Sends the sons of Ancus away on a hunting expedition prior to the elective *comitia*	Keeps Tarquinius' death secret
Self-serving and politically ambitious	Canvasses votes and assays the people's favour	Strengthens his political resources
Populist and anti-aristocratic	Enlarges admission to the Curia to include members of *minores gentes*, and exhibits games on a larger scale than previously entertained	Redistributes wealth according to censorial rank and tribal division
Tyrannical by degrees	Creates a company of personal adherents by no means irresolute to the king	Surrounds himself with a strong guard and rules at first without the authorisation of the people (though having patrician consent).

his sources and the received tradition. His choice and meticulous infusion of diction, figures, and textual structures define the interpretative intentions of his programmatic historiographical articulation. Consider, for instance, the resemblances between Tarquinius Priscus and Servius Tullius: mimetic/ hypostatic doppelgangers of Tanaquil and (in a sense) the characterising equivalent of Livy's textual doublets (Table 4.3).

What is notable in this self-referential litany of qualities – pertinent to late archaic kingship, at least in its formative stages – is the common model and generative source of *regni ingenium natus*: Tanaquil, wife and adoptive mother-in-law. Unwilling to simplify the participatory interpretative complicity engendered by his mimetic narrative strategy, Livy instead continues to complicate the parameters of his history. He adds a substantive sense of dimension to both *topoi* and *personae*, an intertextual depth which disallows the conventional analysis of or expected theme associated with a traditionally paradigmatic annalistic space. If the voice of the *maiores* (ancestors, both historical and literary) depends on the activity of the reader, Livy is at pains to represent the familiar pattern of history as a complex artefact which combines the historiographical focus of particular events and individual tales in unexpected or dissonant ways. In other words, he strives for a rhetorical structure designed not simply to reinforce the archaic and republican expectations of the *annales* worldview but also to challenge and expose the reality of his contemporary historical milieu – on an institutional, social, and specifically human level. Thus, Livy plays with the biographical tradition associated with Servius Tullius. By interweaving his origins, accession, reign, and death with the problematic characters of Tanaquil and Tullia, the historian allows his readers to disentangle the multiplex echoes of authentic archaic kingship – lack of traditional legitimacy, appeal to charismatic authority and the protection and favour of the gods, and populist, anti-oligarchic rule – from the inescapable contemporary resonances – the transforming potential of uncivil discourse, the pathology of internecine rivalry among aristocratic dynastic fortunes, and the destructive fragmentation of social unrest.[159]

No clearer is Livy's intention to disturb the comfortable expectations of his readers than in his inversion of one of Rome's most accepted mores. This involves the subordination of deliberative counsel – the interpretative penetration and prudent judgement characteristic of household, judicial, curial, or military assemblies (met for the purpose of considered resolution and summoned or convened with the authority of the state or household) – to the pressures of destiny – the inevitable and urgent necessities regarded as the requirements of the eternal, immutable law of nature. At first, this appears to be a more typically Greek philosophical conundrum regarding the famously problematic relationship between *nomos* and *phusis*.[160] But Livy explicitly deflates Servius Tullius' adoption of Tanaquil's advice by rendering human wisdom incapable of breaking the adamant chains of fate.[161] In other words, the historian regards envy of sovereign rule (*invidia regni*) as epitomising the inescapable condition imposed on rational "man" by the "natural" universe.[162] Moreover, such control of the individual and social dimensions of the human condition is evidenced by all things faithless, treacherous, hostile, and troublesome.[163] These manifestations of the indomitable force of destiny are deployed as the antithesis of ostensible, undisturbed circumstance; that is, the favourable condition of the moment.[164] This distortion of secure order afflicts even the metonymical heart of the healthy state: the members of Servius' own family (*inter domesticos*).

It is easy to simplify Livy's intention here as wishing to evoke the identity of "woman" as ineluctably congruent with the "natural" (and therefore disturbed and disturbing) world.[165] This is particularly reasonable, given his concern to place Servius' arranged marriages of L. and Arruns Tarquinius to his daughters at the crux of his distinction between reason and the prophetic declaration of *invidia regni*. After all, he has already supplied his readers with the qualitative *exempla* of Tarpeia, Damarata, and Sophonisba (and we can look forward to his depiction of a similarly typical "philosophical" type as Tullia). However, it should be clear by now that Livy's historiographical programme admits a more sophisticated use of the stereotypical or topical commonplaces of the received tradition, particularly regarding women. Therefore, as an instance of the super-mundane grip of fate over the machinations of the rational faculty, his explanation of aristocratic ill-will implicates a rank or class of the *res publica* in the premonition of decline, rather than the entity or nature of "woman." In simple terms, the false and dangerous epiphenomena of that which threatens the status quo of desired existence may be defined more readily as socio-political than gendered realities, though one can naturally include the other.

4.2.3 *Tullia*

In this context, just as Livy draws our attention to the causes and outcomes of history (progress and process), so the reader is invited to read Tullia as a product of her domestic environment as much as the instigator of its inevitable collapse. In a sense, she is not simply the artefact of an essentialist biological female nature which, of necessity, obviates any blame or responsibility deferring to the male actors of her household tragedy; rather, she exists as a component in Quintilian's human chain of history.

> History does not so much demand full, rounded rhythms as a certain continuity of motion and connexion of style. For all its *cola* are closely linked together, while the fluidity of its style gives it great variety of movement; we may compare its motion to that of men, who link hands to steady their steps, and lend each other mutual support.[166]

Like the construction of an historiographical period, Livy's fabrication of Tullia as a discrete unit describing separate actions within a larger episodic event is dependent on previous and historically present subordinate causes. These motivating factors are arranged in a manner subject to semantic restraints and, to a lesser extent, historiographical conventions. They would also seem designed to move the story and critical interpretation of its premises and sources forward.

To complete the structural analogy, it is possible to regard Livy's use of the female figure as a continuative element within an interwoven pattern of meaning, to be deployed chiastically or interstitially, superimposed or sequentially arranged. AUC women are members of a textual architectonic which exploits varied thematic rhythms both for ornament and for point.

In this regard, Livy ensures that his audience is cognizant of the confluence of factors determining the shape of future history. First, he incriminates Servius Tullius for particular transgressions of acceptable *imperium*: exclusive use and enjoyment of sovereign power by dint of familiarity or practical experience; procurement of popular favour to secure unanimous election in response to L. Tarquinius' justified allusion to his rule as *iniussu populi*; and his conciliatory apportionment of land to the common people – an action in opposition to the will of the *patres*, whose initial support helped to secure his successful accession to power.[167]

Second, L. Tarquinius is invoked for parallel subversions of the normative code: manipulation of popular and patrician sentiment regarding Tarquinius' ignorance of the people's sovereignty and the aristocracy's policy on property distribution; self-serving approbation of the king's bestowal of land in the hope of expedient preferment; and the intense, burning nature of his rational will, mirroring his spiritual restlessness.[168]

Last, the historian delineates Tullia's complicity in the problematic historiographical schema by highlighting her vexatious and disturbing presence in the aristocratic household – a literary accretion of Attic tragedy modelled on the legendary fall of the houses of Atreus and Laius, fused with the anti-Catilinarian rhetorical exercises of Sallust and Cicero, thereby graphically extenuating the politics of late republican conspiracy.

> So it came about that the Roman palace afforded an instance of the crime which tragic poets have depicted.[169]

This achieves a two-fold aim: an allusive parallel between this event in the history of archaic Roman monarchy and other instances of wicked actions either represented in tragedy or of a tragic nature; and a foreshadowing of the consequences of a carefully delineated chain of psychological elements as promoting health and bearing fruit – the aim of Livy's project.[170]

Given this accumulation of interrelated contributing factors in the narrative, we need not regard Livy's exposition of this phase of the Roman monarchy as a purely literary phenomenon. It also embraces what might be termed a psychological portrait of Rome's socio-political growth. His composition addresses the sources and impact of affective and rational motivations by accommodating difference within a textual framework renowned for its inflexibility. Tradition and stability are forced to engage the oppositions, parallelisms, and intermediate spaces of human nature; a complexity which is reflected and demonstrated by Livy's varied (and at times difficult) style. As a guiding principle of productive and beneficial historical knowledge, such inconcinnity of characterisation is recognisable in the interweaving of *orationes rectae* attributed to Tanaquil and Tullia.

Significantly, Livy intervenes at this point to stress the ideological intersection of narrative elements. The permutations of destiny, so the historian avers, have conspired to arrange conditions most conducive to the coming of *libertas* and the ending of *regnum*; specifically, the prolongation of Servius' rule and the establishment of the state's traditions.[171]

It is interesting to note that Livy sees the overarching principle of fortune or chance as something which operates through (and in respect to) the Roman people.[172] This is so in order that the potent influences – innate to the modes of thought and peculiarities of disposition – owned by Tullia and L. Tarquinius might not be brought together.[173] Here we may identify the medium in which the *res publica* is formally conceived, and it is not due solely to the completion of Servius' constitutional reforms or despite the impetuous inclinations of aristocratic men or women or the collective will of the people. Instead, Livy conceives of the Republic as a consequence of circumstantial and intentional *concordia*: *unius corpus* personified.

> The fierce Tullia was annoyed that there was nothing in her husband for her to work on in the direction of either greed or ambition.[174]

None of this is to deny the potency of *ferox* Tullia. She is portrayed as headstrong, untameable, haughty, and insolent, and, by implication, the very stuff of the longing of desire unsatisfied and of the shamelessness of insolent presumption.[175]

> She despised her sister, because having a man for her husband she was not animated by the spirit of a woman.[176]

She cannot conceal her contempt for a sister whose acquisition of a "real" man has resulted in a failure to cultivate feminine intrepidity. Her essential nature is evil, destructive and injurious.[177]

> But it was the woman who was the originator of all the mischief.[178]

Importantly, Livy identifies her as the point of origin of L. Tarquinius' subsequent tendency to throw matters into disorder or confusion.[179]

In the latter instance, it is tempting to draw a link between Livy's emphatic reference to the axiomatic priority of Tullia as initiator of disturbance and the connotative resonances of *initium* (parentage, auspices, beginning of a

171

reign). The associative echoes of previous gendered episodes – e.g., Rhea Silvia, Lavinia, Egeria, Tanaquil – accrete and mutate in proximity to Livy's profile of such a *ferox femina*. One should also comment on his use of the gender term for "woman," identified by L'Hoir as "a component of Livian editorializing."[180] In light of the previous discussion, we might regard the inclusion of *femina* – as part of a moralising general statement concerning the adaptive quality of destructive inclinations – as a commentary on female behaviour in incorporative terms. Given the context and the frequency of male *exempla*, it is necessary to add that Livy is not so much highlighting the innate tendencies of "woman" (discursive or biological entity) as drawing attention to the qualities which complicate the human condition, and which can threaten (or support) social stability and order.

> She constantly held clandestine interviews with her sister's husband, to whom she unsparingly vilified alike her husband and her sister.[181]

To this portrait, Livy confers further criticism. Tullia, he recounts, is addicted to secret liaisons with the man belonging to her sister.[182] More than this, she is capable of heaping invective on her relations by blood and marriage. Interestingly, she appears disenfranchised and enfeebled by the inferiority and cowardice of others.

> She urged that it would have been more just for her to be unmarried and for him to lack a wife than for them to be united to their inferiors and be compelled to languish through the cowardice of others.[183]

Throughout, she is heedless of propriety or consequence.[184] This compelling and relentless agglutination of depreciatory appellations culminates in the murders of Arruns and the elder Tullia.[185]

Most conspicuous in Livy's exposition of the tragedy of Servius' reign is its setting: the *Romana regia* (regal household), divided upon itself into the figurative domains of daughter, father, and sons-in-law.[186] In this respect, it is useful to imagine the difficulty which Livy must have encountered in attempting to define or translate the amorphous, accretive, and socio-politically unique entity known as the *res publica*. An historiography which sought to espouse the redemptive quality of equilibrium and tradition would doubtless reflect the tensions and ambiguities arising from a consideration of the conventionally accepted yet ill-defined boundaries between public and private, government and society.[187] Taking this into account, Livy can be seen to highlight the effects on the social fabric of the *res publica* if the fragile *concordia* between public and private is fragmented or undermined, either from within or without. In this case, it is not only the characterology of Tullia but also the over-stepping of inferred, encouraged, and circumscribed customary boundaries that interests Livy.

So the tragedy, then, is indeed dynastic. Livy's focus resides on the breakdown of the aristocratic *familia*. The crime is overtly domestic: the distortion and inversion of social custom and precedent (*mores* and *exempla*). There is nothing more natural than for Livy to describe social behaviour in moral rather than institutional terms. This is especially so in the case of an institution which traditionally acted as a seat of intense emotions, ideals, and anxieties.[188]

Livy impresses upon his readers the decomposition of the household by reiterating the metonymical disturbance to the *paterfamilias* and emblem of *patria potestas*.[189]

> The woman began to look forward from one crime to another ... What she wanted, she said, was not a man who was only her husband in name, or with whom she was to live in uncomplaining servitude.[190]

Tullia is envisaged as the representation and agency of a distress inflicted on the core of Rome's social framework, father of the household and ruler of the state. In this, she is unlike Tanaquil, whose transferred *ambitio* never sought the overthrow of the conventional demarcation between fidelity to legitimate familial solidarity and the constitution of the *res publica*. Tullia's presumptive vision of effectual impiety transcends the prescriptive voice of the *maiores*. She turns away from the course of marital propriety, previously appropriated by Tanaquil in her encouragement of Tarquinius' political and social aspirations. Instead, Tullia estranges herself from the material and emotional bonds of the family relationship. This rejection of normative social virtue – at least those qualities which men hoped to find in women – is quantified by her want of duty and her unwillingness to accommodate the role of devoted servant.

> The man she needed was one who deemed himself worthy of a throne, who remembered that he was the son of Priscus Tarquinius, who preferred to wear a crown rather than live in hopes of it.[191]

Even more suggestive of Livy's determination to implicate Tullia as a signifier of social disruption is his depiction of her as an accomplished practitioner of rhetorical invective. In this regard, it is more than incidental that Tullia is seen to employ the kind of technique favoured especially by forensic or political orators, pamphleteers or apologiasts: that is, the projection of an image aimed at undermining the position of the opponent through accusation and derogation. L. Tarquinius is portrayed as lacking the self-esteem to rule, the self-possession which derives from his consanguine heritage, and the determination to achieve a desired goal. Such allegations conform to the claims of polemic rhetorical invective. Moreover, it is possible that Livy applied this variation of rhetorical style to Tullia in deliberate imitation of the projected images of powerful women found in contemporary Sallustian and Ciceronian writing.[192] These accusations have been seen as transmitting a representative view (that an active political role for women was undesirable) and as designed primarily to attack the politically potent male kin and associates of an otherwise superficial female target.[193] The contemporary oral and written devaluation of apparently prominent and influential women associated with or belonging to the late republican governing class bears a striking similarity to Livy's portrait of Tullia's character and interventionist role. By violating the boundaries of acceptable, aristocratic female behaviour and seizing the prerogative imperatives of male power, Tullia represents the source of the twin abusive *topoi* of clandestine female presence and alleged control too openly flaunted. Thus, L. Tarquinius is constituted by implication as subordinate to female influence. He is the mirror-image of Tullia's claim to superordinate will; a narrative ploy which effectively reinforces Livy's preoccupation with the dangerous ramifications of order unbalanced. Tarquinius' loss of *virtus* and Tullia's expression of *virilis audacia* underscore the narrative's representational inversion and sustain thematic integrity and continuity.

To apprehend the conscious design by which Livy encodes his subject-matter, it is instructive to superimpose the inspirational counsel of Tanaquil on the taunting declamation of Tullia, if only to recognise the extent to which the natural order of the *familia* (and, metonymically, the state) is under threat. In close order, then, we first see that Tanaquil's acerbic "if you are a man" (*si vir es*) is echoed by Tullia's "if you are the man to whom I thought I was married" (*si tu is es cui nuptam esse me arbitror*).[194] In each instance, the *virtus* of the husband is related to the exercise of *regnum*.[195] But it is the effect on Tullia, that is, the disappointing and purposeless nature of marriage to Tarquin, rather than on the well-being of civic order through the excision of tyrannical pretence, that is paramount in the latter's consideration.[196] In due course, Tanaquil's exhortations (*erige, sequere, expergiscere, reputa*) reflect her desire to enliven or quicken Servius' innate disposition to encompass the mantle of authority. Tullia's appeals (*quin accingeris, quid frustraris, sinis facesse, devolvere*) diminish Tarquin's capacity by focussing either on the animation of her adversative command or on his unproductive responses. In other words, the reader looks to one for inspiring principles; to the other for reductive abuse. Tanaquil's earnest recognition of Servius' divine and inherited right to rule as the combined expression and confirmation of his own identity[197] is subverted by Tullia's construction of piety, honour, authority, and pedigree as the external determinants of Tarquin's claim.

> Your father's household gods, your father's image, the royal palace, the kingly throne within it, the very name of Tarquin, all declare you king.[198]

Tarquin is represented as Tullia's creation from without, in opposition to Servius' culmination from within. Tanaquil is depicted as treating, arguing or pleading her case as an ambassador or advocate (*orat*), as if the matter still admitted of deliberation over advice or counsel (*consilia*).

> With taunts like these she urged on the young man.[199]

Tullia, on the other hand, pricks or goads her subject in such a way that inspiration becomes reproval, censure and rebuke. Rather than encouraged, Tarquin is upbraided, chided, and inveighed against. The persuasive effect and architectonic pattern of Livy's historiographical inquiry into the tragic disease afflicting archaic Roman social organisation, as well as its exemplary lessons for a late republican audience are refracted through reiteration of a unifying thematic link: jealousy.

> She, too, was perpetually haunted by the thought that while Tanaquil, a woman of foreign descent, had shown such spirit as to give the crown to her husband and her son-in-law in succession, she herself, though of royal descent, had no power either in giving it or taking it away.[200]

In the same way that *invidia regni* has been identified as the underlying impetus to disintegration of *regia* and *civitas*, Tullia is seen to demonstrate a similar resentment towards (and intolerance of) her mother's integral role in the double conferral of *regnum*. Her envy draws attention to the further distortion of expected behaviour by highlighting Tanaquil's foreign extraction and Tullia's aristocratic ancestry. Thus, in contrast to the purposeful, deliberative precision of Tanaquil's argument, Tarquin's emergence into the public sphere of political competition is the result of Tullia's impulsive, violent passion: "inspired by this woman's frenzy."[201] This ardent, maddened (and maddening) desire for power (*ambitio > regni cupido > invidia*) is an evocative indicator of the intensity of frenzied emotion overbalancing rational apprehension of the danger facing domestic relations and civil constitution.

It is interesting to note Livy's propensity to include the *peregrina mulier* (foreign woman) as often instrumental to *res Romana*, even if supernumerary to the larger narrative, either for good or ill.[202] Here, L'Hoir's observation that Tanaquil is stigmatised as an *exemplum* deficient in those female qualities idealised in the Augustan age – exclusive participation in domestic life, love of country, fidelity to ancestry, complementarity of status in marriage, and so on – requires qualification. Livy's explicit comparison of mother and daughter must be emphasised, especially his differentiation of each woman's rational and affective motivation, and of their contributing roles in the avoidance or exacerbation of disequilibrium.[203] The Virgilian echoes of the *virago*, the Horatian overtones of the *mulier peregrina*, or even the later Tacitean resonances of Livia – none of these overturn Livy's recognition and consequent problematic depiction of the productive role played by Tanaquil in securing the continuation of the institutional and organic development of the *urbs condita*.

In a similar context, Livy's ironic inclusion in Tarquin's harangue of the unconventional role Tanaquil performed in the unofficial ratification of her husband's accession to the kingship should also be mentioned.[204]

Given the pivotal involvement of his sister-in-law, lover, and wife in his ambitious assault on sovereign authority, the reader cannot help but adopt a more critical interpretation of the chain of events reported by *persona*, historical figure, and historian. Of equal importance is the growing inter-changeability of male and female protagonists in the structure of Livy's nar-rative. It is the susceptibility of either gender to the disruptive influences of the natural world (fate, destiny, fortune: *phusis*), objectified through the intensity of destructive affective impulses and its impact on the rational principle, which threatens social stability. In Livy's world, men or women display a supportive or fragmenting role in the growth or decline of *res Romana* and the *urbs condita*. While important to the establishment of traditional parameters of behaviour, any differences which might exist in gendered terms should be regarded as secondary to the depiction of human interaction with the various intersecting forces of history.[205]

The depth of Livy's historiographical intention – to dissect the extraor-dinary complexity of the received tradition without glossing its contentious or disquietening relational interactions or semantic overtones (regardless of superficial gendered commonplaces) – is revealed in his representa-tion of Tarquin's first day on the hustings. We may note particularly the Catilinarian echoes of Tarquin's manner: his demagoguery, inducements and bribes, polemic, and appeal to the support of armed personal depend-ents.[206] Contrast these resonances with the incontrovertible arguments he uses against the regime of Servius Tullius:[207] the tradition of an enslaved genealogy; his failure to observe the conventional *interregnum*, or to accede by sovereign election; and his populist redistribution of property, rank, and civic responsibility.[208] Servius' indignant expostulation in response to his opponent's *oratio obliqua* is delivered in lively and vigorous terms.[209] Toward this, Tarquin exhibits a familiar presumption. In this juxtaposi-tion of ruler and pretender, Livy establishes a mimetic rivalry between the spiritual fervour instilled by Tanaquil and the defiant haughtiness commu-nicated through Tullia. To complete the reiterative arrangement of structural elements, Livy positions his confrontation of ethical worldviews at the heart of public Rome and in the midst of a popular battlefield. We have moved from the clamour which greeted Tarquinius Priscus' assassination – and the shouting which prefaced Tanaquil's restorative address – to the cries of civil disorder consequent to the partisan division of the *res publica*.[210]

The circle is complete, and the reader should expect another significant death, reflecting the demise of *concordia civitatis*, preceding the intervention of a female protagonist, and culminating in a new phase of Rome's historical development.

It comes as no surprise to find Tarquin disposed by the pressure of destiny towards the ultimate display of audacity: physical assault on the person of the king and regicide by assassination.[211]

> It is believed – for it is quite in keeping with the rest of her wickedness – that this (Servius' murder) was done at Tullia's suggestion.[212]

Even less unexpected is the coda terminating this period of Livian narrative, which credits Tullia's clandestine influence as instrumental to the conception of regicide.

However, the tricolon of thought-word-deed we have seen Livy deploy in his exposition of Tanaquil's intervention is taken one step further. In this episode, Livy appends a portrait of the degree to which the boundaries of *mores maiorum* have been effectively redefined, and of the ethical consequences of such a drastic transgression. Based on the principle of characterological consistency – that the impious actions already catalogued as elements of Tullia's *res gestae* connote a reasonable probability of continued involvement – belief in Tullia's complicity in Servius' murder (born of unacceptable violation) becomes certainty.[213] In succession, she fails to stand in awe of the male assembly;[214] she exaggerates Tarquin's infringement against the dictates of constitutional law by summoning and ratifying her husband as king;[215] and she consolidates Tarquin's role in the assassination by adding blood-pollution to blood-guilt.

Stressing the significant historical development (or, rather, devolution) represented by these actions, Livy draws together the continuative elements of Servius' reign. First, he places Tullia in the centre of social disorder.[216] Second, he encodes her actions in terms of rhetorical commonplace and mythographical reference. Locating Tullia's brutal disfigurement of her father's corpse "at the top of the Vicus Cyprius where the shrine of Diana recently stood" links the act with Servius' role in establishing the cult of Diana in Rome.[217] By extension, this juxtaposition might suggest the consequences of actions designed to foster a spirit of hospitality and friendship (between the Latin communities and Rome) by the politically expedient means of religious mollification.[218] Ogilvie suggests that this new institution marked a Latin restoration at Rome and a transplantation of the sovereignty of Latium.[219] This supports the view that political and religious machinations underpinned the promotion of the cult of Diana of the Aventine as superior. It might also be adduced as evidence that the link between Servius' attempt to magnify the authority of the Roman state by following Tanaquil's suggested course of deliberative stratagem has foundered on the rocky undercurrents of treachery and hostility, the obverse of productive resolution.[220]

> Then, the tradition runs, a foul and unnatural crime was committed, the memory of which the place still bears, for they call it the Vicus Sceleratus. It is said that Tullia, goaded to madness by the

avenging spirits of her sister and her husband, drove right over her father's body, and carried back some of her father's blood with which the car and she herself were defiled to her own and her husband's household gods, through whose anger a reign which began in wickedness was soon brought to a close by a like cause.[221]

In terms of mythography, the allusion stresses Tullia's complicity in her father's violent death by invoking echoes and biographical details of the imported myth of Hippolytus. Finally, the extremity of her crime (and its impact on the *mores civitatis*) is registered in three interconnected ways. Its location is signified in aetiological terms as "the street of crime" (*Vicus Sceleratus*). Its commission is rendered in a superstitious accent by Livy's invocation of those murderous acts which originally contributed to the disruption of household and society (the kin-slaying of Arruns and her elder sister) as the incarnation of Tullia's contending internal passions and the recriminatory impetus inciting an act not befitting a human being. In the vocabulary of classical religion, Tullia's identity as a person and member of society is irremediably polluted by sacrificial blood spilled impiously.

Such defilement is stressed by the repetitive evocation of gore shed, smeared, and stained. In combination, Livy's thematic cola (punctuations) drive home the message that the breaking-up of the social fabric is akin to (and promulgated by) the fragmentation and subsumption of rational order to the vagaries and destructive impulses of affective aphasia.

Tullia is rendered insensible, frantic, and distracted by the extent of her transgression (*amens*), and it is her attraction to passion that marks the beginning and end of L. Tarquinius' coming reign (*quibus iratis malo regni*). As an adjunct to this, the prevalence of verbal resort to the received tradition (*traditur, vocant, fertur*)[222] sets up associations between the earlier reference to Tullia's instrumental role in the tyrannical usurpation of government (*per vis*) and her ultimate contamination of the guardian deities of the household and state.

In view of the preceding close reading of this episode, the conclusion to be drawn – from what might be loosely described as the narrative equivalent of the rhetorical *genus deliberatiuum*, where deliberative oratory unites those *topoi* from which one can deduce arguments that lead to a certain act or a general way of acting[223] – is vital, explicit, and consistent with Livy's overall project. In essence, the historian's appended apposition of Servius' equitable and lawful rule was to have culminated in abdication of sole authority and manumission of the country.[224] In conjunction with the agitation of civil and domestic crime, Livy puts the issue beyond reasonable doubt.[225]

4.2.4 Fabiae Ambusti

Livy's process of questioning traditional Roman social values and virtues in a characterising context is exemplified in the story of the sisters Fabiae, elder and younger.[226] The fact that Livy retrojects his own historiographical agenda through his decision to include and elaborate the anecdote is instructive and an appropriate end-point to the current examination of gendered AUC history.

Evidence for this intervention is contained in the narrative. Servius Sulpicius (husband of Fabia *maior*) is named as a consular tribune. This explicit allusion to plebeian eligibility for that office would seem to contradict the promise of the Fabiae story.[227] M. Fabius Ambustus' younger daughter's preoccupation with status – particularly the distressing condition of being tied to an inferior (C. Licinius Stolo), thereby "having married into a house into which neither political office nor influence could enter" – lacks legal foundation.[228]

Here, Livy's selective use of the *annales* reflects a narrative imperative superceding consistency. Given that the historian openly denotes the younger Fabia as the private catalyst of political change, we can assume that this incident has been chosen to reflect Livy's personal apprehension of the historical process and its socio-political components.[229] If we accept that the written *monumenta* of Livian historiography are the verbal representation of Roman *gesta*, the element of the major historical change exemplified by the domestic romance of Fabia *minor* should be decisive.[230]

The private misfortune attending the younger Fabia's jealousy towards her sister's social position, achieved through superior familial affiliation, sets in motion the increasing tension and powerful civil strife adhering to the contest over the Licinian-Sextian rogations, identified as "the heart of Livy's narrative plan."[231] In other words, Livy is interested in linking the reactions of the participants in this incident to specific causal factors as a way of exemplifying the generation of broader historical movements. These associations are most notable in relation to the historian's depiction of Fabia *minor*: she "grows pale," is "stirred up," "rankled," displays "regret," and is "stunned," responses encoded in her "ignorance" and "misguided judgement."[232] As Kraus notes, "Fabia's exaggerated response to a small thing is a microcosm of her story's effect in the narrative."[233]

In this regard, the reader becomes aware of a familiar authorial intervention (*credo*) which seeks to explain the significance underlying the younger Fabia's distress (her domestic *invidia*), and the manner in which Livy's presence intersects the equally formulaic manifestation of the reason for her distress (*causam doloris*).[234] Thus, the annalist can be seen to apply a gendered typology. The pejorative commonplace which identifies the female mind as inconstant is attached to the historian's traditional preoccupation with *causae*.[235] Livy interweaves the petty competitive principle of personal rivalry – which echoes the transgressive episodes of Romulus and Remus, Horatia and her brother, or the mimetic display adhering to the wife-contest in the Lucretia story – with the inner disturbance characterising Fabia's strong reaction.[236] He does this in order to provide an historiographical parallel (and prelude) to the upcoming social conflict.[237]

It is this interpenetration of style and theme – what Lipovsky refers to as "the relationship of literary technique to genuine historical judgement" – which helps to justify interpreting this episode as an integral dramatic and intellectual component of Livy's wider historiographical project.[238] Considering it in terms of genre and content, an imaginative refraction of Thucydidean clarity and perception can be located in the text: that is, the exposition of Roman history as a metaphorical autopsy afforded by literary memory.[239] If this is the case, then the reader should find echoes of Livy's preoccupation with the socio-political canvas, and especially of those recurrent indicators of change and development which he perceived as conducive to the exposition of the historical process (be it sudden shift or gradual development).

It is no surprise, then, that the striking and compelling accumulation of discursive similarities between the various story-types which unite the spheres of *res privata* and *publica* through a correspondence of (male) state and (female) body – the division of which threatens uncontrolled fragmentation of something which ideally functions as a corporeal entity – conflates Livy's persistent semantic binarisms (*libertas-regnum*, *potestas-dominatio*, *consilium-libido*). This is well portrayed in the composite allusions to Lucretia and Tullia during the final exposition of Fabia's narrative role. In the same way that the family and friends of Lucretia attempted to console her grief after her violation, so Fabius tells his daughter to be of good cheer.[240] Similarly, just as Tullia encouraged Tarquin to depose Servius Tullius [], so Fabia admits her distress at being tied to an inferior.[241] Finally, Fabius' consolatory words resonate alarmingly with Tullia's expostulations regarding the practical implications of deserved inheritance.[242]

The formulation and resolution of Fabia's story continues Livy's ongoing exploration of social complications, anchored in private and ordinary settings, and his recognition of the importance of the individual (female) predicament in the historiography of *res Romana*.

4.3 Conclusion

Throughout this chapter Livy's representation of women – legendary figures like Lavinia, Rea Silvia, Tanaquil, and Tullia; and quasi-historical characters like Horatia, Verginia, and the Fabiae sisters – reflects "what life and morals were like" during the period covered by his history. In addition, those narrative episodes examined here which comprise depictions of individual or collective female presence, participation, or agency articulate clearly the annalist's desire that the read should consider "how, with the gradual relaxation of discipline, morals first gave way, as it were, then sank lower and lower, and finally began the downward plunge which has brought us to the present time."[243] Given the stated benefit of historical writing as Livy understands it – namely, "that you behold the lessons of every kind of experience set forth as on a conspicuous monument; and from these you may choose for yourself and for your own state what to imitate and from these mark for avoidance what is shameful in the conception and shameful in the result"[244] – the commonplace figures that the historian incorporates into the narrative performances of his foundational *matronae*, priestesses, princesses, and queens, as well as his female relatives, unmarried lovers, betrothed virgins, and ambitious female elite, confirm his approach to crafting social or collective memory both as source and as subject. In other words, Livy uses gendered episodes not just as evidence of memory (what is remembered) but also about memory (how and why the past is remembered in one way and not another).

Of course, it is not solely those episodes of AUC history characterised as female-prominent which serve as conduits for selective remembrance and memorialisation. However, whenever Livy introduces women, especially those featured in the first decade of books dealing with the city's foundational narrative, he tasks his readership with the questions posed by Rome's earliest times and – what according to the historian is absolutely vital – the salutary effect which the study of ancient history in particular can have for his contemporaries. It is as much the use of these female figures as their representation that creates and makes memorable their characterisation, determines how they fit into the composition of Livy's received yet reconstructed tradition, and consequently shapes his readers' (and our) attempts at understanding them and the meaning of the events in which they are placed. Whether created as examples of personal or civic behaviour to be valued or rejected, Livy embeds women in consequential historical moments to achieve very particular historiographical objectives – establishing the jurisdiction of father and ruler over the individual and the state, the form of civic procedure and the right of popular appeal, the scope of criminal acts (*perduellio, parricidium*), and the use of sacral punishment (Horatia); denoting illegitimate uses of forms of public authority for the pursuit of private ends and the extent to which *regnum* reflects the political enslavement of Roman society (Verginia); confirming the capacity of a woman to act as regent without endangering the preservation of the state (Lavinia); demonstrating the vulnerability of women as scapegoats for male desire or scheming (Rhea Silvia); illuminating the productive role played by women in securing the continuation of the institutional and organic development of the *urbs condita* (Tanaquil); acknowledging the role of women in the tyrannical usurpation of government and the ultimate contamination of the guardian deities of the household and state (Tullia); contesting the conventions of familial aristocratic rivalry and how these play out in civil society (the Fabiae Ambusti). In doing so, Livy encodes female actors in the *Ab Urbe Condita* as emblematic narrative signifiers and integral historical elements of Rome's collective memory about the restitution and preservation of customary socio-political order, as expressions of the convergence of different traditions and historical contingencies, and as mediators of literary need.

181

Notes

1 The tropological conception of non-scientific discourse (and its usage by traditional poetics and modern language theory) is best articulated by White (1973: esp. 31–42).

2 Liv. 1 pr. 10. On this statement in relation to the tension between poetry and history when writing AUC history, see Chapter 1.1; for the original text, see Chapter 1, n.7.

3 Di Fazio (2018: 334); cf. Proietti (2012); Smith (2015).

4 Connerton (1989: 3).

5 Liv. 1.26.1-14; Dion. Hal. *Ant. Rom.* 3.21-22, 28–32; Flor. 1.3; see Table 1.2 no. 11.

6 Ogilvie (1963: 54) notes the contradiction between Romulus the fratricide and the *conditor urbis*, the bad man and the good. This contrast is emphasised by Livy's juxtaposition of a rationalist account and a *volgatior fama*; that is, the substitution of a political for a religious motive. Cf. Horace's attribution of the Civil Wars as a legacy of Romulus' act (*Epod.* 7.17-20).

7 Liv. 1.6.3: "Romulus and Remus were seized with the desire of building a city in the locality where they had been exposed" (*Romulum Remumque cupido cepit in iis locis ubi expositi ubique educati erant urbis condendae*).

8 One of the Curiatii, to whom she had been promised.

9 Liv. 1.26.2-3: "She recognised on her brother's shoulders the cloak of her betrothed, which she had made with her own hands; and bursting into tears she tore her hair and called her dead lover by name. The triumphant soldier was so enraged by his sister's outburst of grief in the midst of his own triumph and the public rejoicing that he drew his sword and stabbed the girl" (*cognitoque super umeros fratris paludamento sponsi quod ipsa confecerat, solvit crines et flebiliter nomine sponsum mortuum appellat. movet feroci iuveni animum comploratio sororis in victoria sua tantoque gaudio publico. stricto itaque gladio simul verbis increpans transfigit puellam*).

10 It is important to note that this natural flaw springs from a partially justifiable source, namely the reinforcing encouragement of an exultant community: in the first instance, the divided loyalties of Albans, Latins and pastoral refugees; in the latter, the celebratory rejoicing of a redeemed people.

11 Liv. 1.7.2: *sic deinde quicumque alius transiliet moenia mea*

12 Liv. 1.26.5: *sic eat quaecumque Romana lugebit hostem.*

13 Each statement comprises an aetiological imperative of self-justification which foreshadows future transgression of the most intimate social landscape, the *familia*. It is difficult not to see the eruptive fragmentation of late Republican/liminal Augustan civil distress as one focus of these fraught and bitter cries.

14 Solodow (1979: 253) notes that Livy's careful division of "the duel abroad and the trial at home" is amplified by a variety of such verbal echoes. This deliberate composition is intended to draw our attention to the problematic nature of Horatius' patriotic identity: his "subordination of self to the public good" (254).

15 Echoing Livy's appellation of *iniuria* (Liv. 1.13.1,3). This is a distinctly Roman application of the more celebrated Homeric *exemplum*, Helen – the woman first identified by name in AUC history Liv. (1.1.1). Cf. Hor. *Carm.* 3.3.25-26: *iam nec Lacaenae splendet adulterae/famosus hospes*. See also the discussion of Livy's treatment of Helen in the Foreword of this volume.

16 Liv. 1.26.5: *atrox visum id facinus.*

17 Liv. 1.26.2: "triple spoils" (*trigemina spolia*); 5: "recent service" (*recens meritum*). This alignment of the possible and actual may be compared with any number of similar valencies in foundation history: e.g., the union of Mars and

Rhea Silvia; the prostitution of Larentia; the celebration of the Consualia; the union of Numa and Egeria.

18 Liv. 1.26.4: "he drew his sword and stabbed the girl" (*itaque gladio simul verbis increpans transfigit puellam*). It should be noted that Horatia suffers the loss of three significant male others: her two brothers and her betrothed.

19 Liv. 1.26.5: (two *duumviri*) "who are to judge the treason of Horatius" (*qui Horatio perduellionem iudicent*).

20 Watson (1979: 441).

21 Watson (1979: 445).

22 Liv. 1.26.5: "To avoid responsibility for passing a harsh sentence, which would be repugnant to the populace, and then carrying it into execution, the king summoned an assembly of the people" (*rex ne ipse tam tristis ingratique ad volgus iudicii ac secundum iudicium supplicii auctor esset, consilio populi advocato*).

23 Liv. 1.26.7: "The duumvirs appointed under this law did not think that by its provisions they had the power to acquit even an innocent person." (*qui [= duumviri] se absolvere non rebantur ea lege ne innoxium quidem posse*).

24 Liv. 1.26.9: "Their decision was mainly influenced by Publius Horatius the father, who declared that his daughter had been justly slain" (*moti homines sunt in eo iudicio maxime P. Horatio patre proclamante se filiam iure caesam iudicare*).

25 Liv. 1.26.9: "The appeal was accordingly brought before the people" (*itaque provocatione certatum ad populum est*).

26 As per the duumviral law outlined in Liv. 1.26.5-6, even a person who was innocent might not be acquitted. Cf. n. 16.

27 Watson (1979: 447).

28 Liv. 1.26.12: "murder plain and simple" (*caedes manifesta*).

29 Liv. 1.26.14: "A tomb of hewn stone was constructed for Horatia on the spot where she was murdered" (*Horatiae sepulcrum quo loco corruerat icta constructum est saxo quadrato*). Cf. Liv. 1 pr 10: "you look on examples for a variety of experience set forth in a clear record" (*documenta in inlustri posita monumento intueri*).

30 I find it instructive that Ogilvie (1963: 114–115) finds Horatia guilty of *proditio* (mourning for an enemy), thereby enabling him to exonerate Horatius of *parricidium* by instead viewing him as "forestalling the due processes of the law by executing a criminal who had not yet been sentenced to death." In Ogilvie's words, if we focus too narrowly on the legal distinctions between murder and treason, all we do is "overlook the fact that Horatia was herself a criminal" (114).

31 A similar annalistic pedagogy can be adduced in the Lucretia story, in part adhering to the observation of Lipovsky (1984: 6–7, that "Livy was acutely aware of the 'kinetic' in history, the on-going processes of development which mark the history of a nation." In other words, he views Livy's exposition and explanation of AUC history as literary judgement, structurally designed to underscore and highlight his "dramatic and developmental" interpretation of key historical events. This line of reasoning provides implicit justification for seeing Livy's annalistic treatment of episodes incorporating women as illustrative of a representational hermeneutic. By dramatically emphasising episodes featuring gendered relations as exemplary of his historical thesis, Livy should not so much be regarded as perpetuating some kind of historiographical deception – by stressing problematic (and therefore diverting) incidents in order that other facts, embarrassing to his argument of the genealogy of *familia* or civitas be concealed – as an indication of his interpretation of the larger picture. As Lipovsky (1984: 13) states, "the presentation of the deeds has been

carefully molded and formed; from that process a larger historical interpretation emerges with clarity."

32 Solodow (1979: 259).

33 The evil to which Livy alludes is decidedly male: namely, *avitum* (of the grandsires). See Liv. 1.6.4: "These pleasant anticipations were disturbed by the ancestral curse – desire for royal authority" (*intervenit deinde his cogitationibus avitum malum regni cupido*). The historian's warning is timely indeed, given the tumult of contemporary Roman history. This is especially so regarding Livy's target audience, the political mainstream of late Republican patriarchy, possibly including the speculative object and model of rejuvenating Romulean destiny, Augustus himself.

34 Horatius' father's grief: "coming in triumph adorned with his enemy's spoils" (Liv. 1.26.10: *decoratum ovantemque victoria incedentem*); Horatio's exemplary courage: "a spirit equal to every danger" (Liv. 1.26.12: *parem in omni periculo animum*); the priority of *virtus* over law: "with admiration for his bravery rather than the justice of his cause" (Liv. 1.26.12: *admiratione magis virtutis quam iure causae*).

35 Liv. 1 pr. 7; cf. Solodow (1979: 260).

36 Liv. 3.44-49; see Table 1.2 no. 21.

37 To cite two of these problems by way of example: the purpose of the Decemvirate as an institution (a new kind of annual magistracy replacing patrician consuls and plebeian tribunes, or a provisional commission to draft a code of written laws); and the traditional contrast between the first (good) and second (bad) college (designed to explain the notorious ban on intermarriage in *Tabula* XI).

38 Of course, deciding which elements of the surviving story are fictitious (i.e., the product of conscious invention) or historical (i.e., based on authentic "fact" or the product of accepted conventions of historiographical reconstitution) remains an insoluble and intrinsically subjective exercise in speculative exposition.

39 Not to mention those of the beautiful plebeian *virgo* of Ardea (Liv. 4.9.4-10.7) and the *peregrina mulier* Theoxena (Liv. 40.4). On these episodes, see, e.g. Ogilvie (1962) and Claassen (1998: 94), on the maid of Ardea; Chapter 3.2 of this volume, on Theoxena.

40 The broad historical order of events comprises the production of the "document" known as the Twelve Tables, the restoration of the "old" system of privilege, protection and competition, and the settlement contingent on the overthrow of the despotic second Decemvirate – that is, a significant upheaval of the prevailing socio-political order. Cf. Cornell (1995: 274–275), who regards the more appropriate ambit of contextual investigation as encompassing a recognition of the historicity of the upheaval which occurred in the middle of the 5th century BCE and the evaluation of its quantitative results only.

41 On Livy's intentional use of the quasi-poetic traditions of the earliest days of Rome as a theoretical illustration of the interaction of personality and political power (esp. the crucial lesson of how a free state can be transformed into a dictatorship from within), see Vasaly (1987), esp. 212–222 (on Appius Claudius Decemvir).

42 The summary *clades* and deserved *flagitium* suffered by Roman armies against Sabine and Aequian forces, in turn threatening the very security of the city (Liv. 3.42.1, culminating in 9: *urbis oppugnandae*). These actions find mimetic counterpoint in the conflict between Horatius, Valerius and the decemvirs, represented by Ap. Claudius (Liv. 3.39-41). The president of the infamous second decemviral board of 450 BCE displays a similar qualitative typology. His

overweaning desire to retain the decemviral office, ostensibly through considerations of age and social standing – that is, private and public worth, *dignitas* and *honos*: "Ap. Claudius was very much aware of the possibility that he
might not be re-elected, in spite of his age and the honours he had enjoyed"
(Liv. 3.35.3: *in discrimen dignitas ea aetate iisque honoribus actis stimulabat
Ap. Claudium*] – clearly overrides the propriety incumbent on a prospective
senior magistrate: "as a man who was not so keen to resign office as to dis-
cover some way of prolonging it" (Liv. 3.35.6: *non tam properantis abire mag-
istratu quam viam ad continuandum magistratum quaerentis esse*. Similarly,
Claudius' propensity to manifest the qualities of a *tyrannus* is reflected in his
hypocritical and fraudulent dissembly: "(Claudius' colleagues) were convinced
that there was no sincerity about what he did"; "this was the end of Appius'
assumption of a part foreign to his nature" (Liv. 3.35.6: *apparere nihil sinceri
esse*; 36.1: *ille finis Appio alienae personae forendae fuit suo iam inde vivere
ingenio coepit*). These facets of Ap. Claudius' disposition embody the *superbia*
and *cupiditas* of the "natural-born" *tyrannus*. His despotic nature is confirmed
and reinforced by his reconstruction of his decemviral colleagues in his own
image: "he began to mould his new colleagues into the lines of his own character" (Liv. 3.36.1: *novosque colleges ... in suos mores formare*). This *inventio*
gives rise to the symptomatic efflorescence of oppressive absolutist traits such
as *impotentia consilia* (hatched *in secreto*, *libido*, and *crudelitas*), and inspires
intense popular feelings of terror and *metus* – all evocative of the archetype
of untrammelled *regnum*, the dynastic Tarquinii. Cf. Livy's overt connection
between the overthrow of Superbus and his family and the devolution of the
legislative college of ten: "they presented the appearance of ten kings"; (M.
Horatius Barbatus) called the decemvirs 'ten Tarquins'" (Liv. 3.36.5: *decem
regum species erat*; 39.3: *decem Tarquinios appellantem*).

43 The arranged killing of L. Siccius by men of his own command (Liv. 3.43).
44 Liv. 3.44.1: "a crime arising from desire" (*nefas ab libidine ortum*); cf. Liv.
3.47.4: "it was really madness rather than love that had clouded his judgement" (*tanta vis amentiae verius quam amoris mentem turbaverat*); Liv. 3.48.1:
"handing over his rational nature to desire" (*alienatus ad libidinem animo*).
45 Liv. 1.57.10: "Sextus Tarquinius, inflamed by the beauty and exemplary purity
of Lucretia, formed the vile intention to rape her by force" (*Sex. Tarquinium
mala libido Lucretiae per vim stuprandae capit*), Liv. 3.44.2: "Appius Claudius
raped a plebeian virgin, defiling her in lust" (*Ap. Claudium virginis plebeiae
stuprandae libido cepit*).
46 Liv. 1.58.2: "burning with love" (*amore ardens*); Liv. 3.44.4: "out of his senses
in love" (*amore amens*); cf. Liv. 3.47.4: "it was really madness rather than love
that had clouded his judgement" (*tanta vis amentiae verius quam amoris mentem turbaverat*).
47 Liv. 1.57.10-11: "inflamed by her beauty and exemplary purity" (*cum forma
tum spectata castitas incitat*); Liv. 3.44.4: "this virgin, now in the bloom of her
youth ... proof against all temptation" (*hanc virginem adultam forma excellentem ... omnia pudore saepta*).
48 Liv. 1.58.4: "When he saw that she was inflexible and not moved even by the
fear of death, he threatened to disgrace her" (*obstinatam videbat et ne mortis
quidem metu inclinari addit ad metum dedecus*); Liv. 3.44.4: "assaulting her
with presents and promises ... he resorted to unscrupulous and brutal force"
(*pretio ac spe perlicere adortus ... ad crudelem superbamque vim animum
convertit*). In this regard, three elements of female objectification in relation
to Livy's depiction of *forma* and *pudicitia* are pertinent: 'woman' as chattel,
status symbol, and extension of the male body. 1. 'Woman' as chattel. Cf. Liv.
1.58.4; 3.44.4 (see above). It is interesting to note that the dishonour visited

upon Lucretia is facilitated by Sextus' threat to "arrange her body" – elite, free, and of impeccable reputation – in proximity to that of a person in bondage. Similarly, the daughter of L. Verginius faces the accentuated ignominy of imposed servitude. The underlying discursive thread of the female as object and possession binds the narrative episodes through the paradoxical image of *matrona* or *virgo* as precious chattel of male wishes. Cf. the discussion in Joshel (1992: 125) of the assimilation of *matrona* and *virgo* to the status of the conquered and enslaved and the implications arising from this trend for the vulnerability or lack of physical integrity of the female. 2. "Woman" as status symbol. Liv. 3.44.8-9: "even if you have deprived us of the two citadels of our liberty ... let honour at least be safe" (*duas arces libertatis tuendae ademistis ... pudicitia saltem in tuto sit*). Here, Verginia's straitened situation is subordinated to the losses suffered (potentially) by Icilius (the surety of a betrothed's purity), already by the plebeian community (tribunician aid and the right of appeal), and similarly by Verginius if Appius' decision were to favour his client. This tricolon of female objectification is noted (but only in syntactical and legalistic terms) by Ogilvie (1963: 484): *ego, Verginius*; *pro sponsa, pro unica filia*; *omnes, pro ingenua* (the latter, a suggested interpolation which conforms to the appellative and semantic thrust of Icilius' *oratio recta*). Cf. Ap. Claudius' oblique recognition of Verginia's referential absence from the exigencies occasioned by his libido: "making a concession to the absent Verginius, to the name of father, and to liberty" (Liv. 3.46.3: *Verginio absenti et patrio nomini et libertati datum*). 3. "Woman" as extension of the male body. Liv. 3.48.5: "'In this the only way in which I can,' he said, 'I vindicate your freedom, my child'" (*hoc te uno quo possum ait modo filia in libertatem vindico*). This appellation fulfils the role foreshadowed by Livy – "They knew that the girl's safety turned upon her protector against lawlessness being present in time" (Liv. 3.46.6: *puellae salute si postero die vindex iniuriae ad tempus praesto esset*): namely, that the guardianship which Verginius affords his daughter (the preservation of well-being through protection against injury) amounts to his laying claim of legal right to deliver his dignity. This *dignitas* is a constraining necessity (Liv. 3.48.8: *necessitatem patris*), allied to the decemvir's crime (*scelus Appi*), implicitly viewed as inspired by Verginia's beauty (*puellae infelicem formam*). It is a requisite which Verginius ascribes (in his *oratio obliqua* as centurion of rank to a crowd of fellow soldiers) to compassion or mercy (Liv. 3.50.7: *misericordia*). But Livy is also careful to locate (again through the perpetrator of the act) this need in the interpenetrating space of male/female discourse (Liv. 3.50.9: *suum corpus vindicaturum quo vindicaverit filiae* – "my body, my daughter's body"; to protect the one, "defend" the "other").

49   Examples include the quasi-legal domestic court summoned by Lucretia and the specious "kangaroo court" convened by Ap. Claudius; the inflammatory speeches of Brutus and Icilius/Verginius; the visceral display of Lucretia's and Verginia's bodies.

50   Reflecting the moral rectitude of her father, which embraces all spheres of conventional male life (Liv. 3.44.2: *vir exempli recti domi militiaeque*). This quality of *pudicitia* is also inculcated by Verginius' (unnamed) wife, which implicitly delimits the ambit and role of the female to a subordinate level, fit only to instruct in the received tradition: "his wife had been brought up on equally high principles and their children were being brought up in the same way" (Liv. 3.44.3: *perinde uxor instituta fuerat liberique instituebantur*). Cf. Verginius' prescription on his daughter's role in society: "I have brought her up for marriage, not for outrage" (Liv. 3.47.7: *ad nuptias non ad stuprum educavi*).

51 Liv. 3.44.3: *desponderat filiam L. Icilio* (promised object in marriage). Liv. 3.44.4: *forma excellentem* (figure of beauty). Liv. 3.44.4: *hanc virginem adultam ... vim animum convertit* (stimulus of Claudius' desire).

52 Liv. 3.44.7: "The names of her father Verginius and her betrothed lover, Icilius, were held in high respect. Regard for them brought their friends, feelings of indignation brought the crowd to the maiden's support" (*Vergini patris sponsique Icili populare nomen celebrabatur notos gratia eorum turbam indignitas rei virgini conciliat*). This emphatically positions the name of father and betrothed – and the esteem with which they are regarded – as the driving forces behind the intervention of Roman citizens in Verginia's situation.

53 Liv. 3.44.8-9: "He cited the girl into court. Her supporters advised her to follow him" (*vocat puellam in ius. auctoribus qui aderant ut sequeretur*), 11: "the girl's advocates" (*advocati puellae*). The terms *auctor* and *advocatus* identify Verginia as the precedent or material instance of *causa liberalis* or *possessio* (whether M. Claudius' or Verginius'), to be supported or promoted before the movable platform of praetorial justice.

54 Cf. Liv. 45.1-3. Ap. Claudius argues that Verginia is either the slave of his client (M. Claudius) or under her father's control. This is regarded by the attendant crowd as an unjust decree (Liv. 3.45.4: *iniuriam decreti*); yet it is challenged only by L. Icilius, and on grounds which leave the substance of the decemvir's decree undisputed.

55 Liv. 3.44.8-9. For appropriated *virtus* as a signifier of female objectification, see above, n. 45.

56 Liv. 3.48.5 (see above, n.45).

57 Ogilvie (1963: 476–477).

58 Liv. 1.58.10: "No unchaste woman shall henceforth live and please Lucretia's example" (*nec ulla deinde inpudica Lucretiae exemplo vivet*).

59 Such logic configures Verginia as a rhetorical invention almost literally fulfilling the imperative of *vulgato corpore* (cf. Chapter 2.2); that is, an imaginatively rendered figment, a discursively constructed space to be acted upon (betrothed, seduced, claimed, protected, contested, judged, desired, pitied, killed, extolled, and revenged). In this regard, for a view of silence in Livy's stories of Lucretia and Verginia as a linguistic tool intended to erase the moment of violation by eradicating its subjective experience, see Joshel (1992: 126–127).

60 Ogilvie (1963: 478).

61 Liv. 3.44.1: "rising from lust ... the cause of their losing their power was the same in each case" (*ab libidine ortum ... causa etiam eadem imperii amittendi esset*).

62 In this instance, the reader may discern Livy exercising the accepted freedom to apply rhetorical colour to the jejune or insufficiently diverting *annales* of Roman history pertaining to the legal fiction that reconfigured Verginia's social and familial status: Liv. 3.44.9 (*notam iudici fabulam petitor quippe apud ipsum auctorem argumenti peragit*).

63 Liv. 1 pr 2: *aut in rebus certius ... aut scribendi arte ... superaturos.*

64 This is a reductively self-perpetuating and deliberately reflexive metaphor, which encloses Livy's methodological approach in the textual medium of aporietic discourse and neatly addresses the dilemma cited in the preface to Book 1 (Liv. 1 pr 6: *decora fabulis ... incorruptis rerum gestarum monumentis*). White (1973: 37) identifies this form of historical discourse as a "mode of thought which is radically self-critical with respect not only to a given characterisation of the world of experience but also to the very effort to capture adequately the truth of things in language." He labels this linguistic paradigm as the "trope of irony."

65 Liv. 3.47.5: *forsan aliquem verum auctores antiqui tradiderint: quia nusquam ullum in tanta foeditate decreti veri similem invenio, id quod constat nudum videtur proponendum, decresse vindicias secundum servitutem.*

66 Cic. *De or.* 2.63; *Fam.* 5.12.4.

67 Appropriately, the subject of this digression is discursive pretence (Liv. 3.47.5: *decreto sermonem praetenderit*).

68 Such citations are regularly incorporated to convey a reassuring authority. See Walsh (1970: 142); Develin (1983: 69–70, 79).

69 Cf. Woodman (1988: 16–23), on Thucydides. Re the introduction of hesitation and doubt: Liv. 3.47.5: *forsan*; the conditional *verum ... tradiderint* bracketing the cited sources (hesitation); *nusquam ... veri similem* (doubt).

70 Liv. 3.47.5: *quod constat nudum*, a familiar and eminently conventional formula juxtaposed with a substantive reference to the equally traditional practice of *exornatio*; cf. Liv. 39.47.5: *videtur proponendum*.

71 Liv. 1.59.11: *his atrocioribusque, credo, aliis, quae praesens rerum indignitas haudquaquam relatu scriptoribus facilia subicit, memoratis, incensam multitudinem perpulit ut imperium regi abrogaret exsulesque esse iuberet L. Tarquinium cum coniuge ac liberis.* In the earlier example, the admission of underlying supposition (*credo*) – and of Livy's complicity in the historiographical process of reconstituted narrative (*haudquaquam relatu scriptoribus facilia*) – can be taken as a strategy (oblique, but sympathetic to the reader's situation) of increasing trust. Cf. Quint. 9.2.19: *adfert aliquam fidem veritatis et dubitatio.* For the lessening of authorial conviction, cf. Quint. 2.5.19. Cf. Liv. 1.59.11. In this instance, Rome's liberator is found speaking to a gathering of men in the forum (as opposed to the libidinous decemvir before a crowd of men and women) and after the *matrona*'s suicide (instead of just prior to the *virgo*'s murder).

72 The kind of feeling engendered by Livy in this episode, a variety of suffering ideally produced in response to plausible, circumstantial and convincing narrative.

73 Liv. 3.48.8-9: *Sequentes clamitant matronae, eamne liberorum procreandorum condicionem, ea pudicitiae praemia esse? – cetera, quae in tali re muliebris dolor, quo est maestior imbecillo animo, eo miserabilia magis querentibus subicit. Virorum et maxime Icili vox tota tribuniciae potestatis ac provocationis ad populum ereptae publicarumque indignationum erat.*

74 See Walsh (1970), s.v. "Hellenistic historiography"; Walbank (1972: 34–39).

75 Liv. 3.47.1: *comitantibus aliquot matronis cum ingenti advocatione in forum*; 4: *comitatus muliebris plus tacito fletu quam ulla vox movebat*; 8: *cum repelleretur adserto virginis a globo mulierum circumstantiumque advocatorum.*

76 Cf. Davies (1986).

77 Liv. 3.48.8: *eamne liberorum procreandorum condicionem ea pudicitiae praemia esse.*

78 Customary roles include bringing children into existence and reifying purity of inheritance and mimetic *dignitas*. Provisional distinctions comprise, e.g., exclusion of female children from involvement by substitution in the contesting of male wills, the assignment of recompense by virtue of restraint, simplicity, and abstinence (unadorned conduct, if you will). Cf. the Ciceronian usage intimating passionate expression or rhetorical *pathos*: Cic. *Clu.* 13; *Scaur.* 9.

79 Such considerations depend on legitimate magisterial power adhering to tribunes of the people, right of appeal before a higher tribunal (taken away violently by decemviral edict), and the humiliation of *indignitas* suffered at the expense of the state (Liv. 3:48.9: *tribuniciae potestatis ac provocationis ad populum ereptae publicarumque indignationum*). Liv. 3.48.9: *virorum ... vox tota.*

80 An eminently feasible admission, given that the content of Livian historiography (chronology, topographical descriptions and, notably, analysis of causes

and character) not only complies with Cicero's historiographical curriculum (*De or.* 2.63) but reflects traditional elements found in other historians before and after (cf. Woodman (1988: 109n.77, 183–184)). If, as McDonald (1957: 163) claims, Livy "applied the accepted methods of historical composition" – and this programme incorporated even the most rudimentary psychological understanding (a lack of which Livy is not normally accused) – then it may be accepted that he apprehended the self-contradictory facets constituting Virginia's story.

81 The unified, implacable and exclusive discourse of legitimate authority, equity and justifiable resentment, asserted as the gendered antithesis to female vulnerability.

82 Hardie (1993: 34–35) refers to this phenomenon as "the collapse of distinctions that results from the play of literary models."

83 In no order of priority: Thucydides, Ennius, Cato, Claudius Quadrigarius, Sallust, Cicero, *et al.*

84 Tac. *Germ.* 43.3; cf. Plin. *HN* 2.5.15. On the Roman habit of replacing the name of a foreign deity with that of a Roman deity considered somehow comparable, see Rives (2012).

85 Especially such potentially disturbing actions as the expropriation and redistribution of oligarchic wealth, the challenge to political privilege, and the extension of civil rights to a wider interest group.

86 Liv. 1.1.9-10: *ibi Latinum apud penates deos domesticum publico adiunxisse foedus filia Aeneae in matrimonium data.*

87 Livy 1.1.9 (*filia*), 11 (*uxor*).

88 Liv. 1.1.11: *oppidum condunt Aeneas ab nomine uxoris Lavinium appellat. brevi stirpis quoque virilis ex novo matrimonio fuit cui Ascanium parentes dixere nomen.*

89 Liv. 1.2.1: *cui pacta Lavinia.*

90 Liv. 1.2.2: (Turnus) *praelatum sibi advenam aegre patiens ... Aeneae Latinoque bellum intulerat.*

91 Liv. 1.3.1: *tantisper tutela muliebri tanta indoles in Lavinia erat res Latina et regnum avitum paternumque puero stetit.*

92 Liv. 1.3.3: *is Ascanius ubicumque et quaecumque matre genitus ... novam ipse aliam ... condidit.*

93 Liv. 1.3.2: *haud ambigam quis enim rem tam veterem pro certo adfirmet.*

94 Liv. 1.3.3: *certe natum Aenea constat* (conferring the authority of tradition).

95 Liv. 1.3.3: (Ascanius) *opulentam urbem matri seu novercae reliquit.*

96 Liv. 1.3.4: *nec deinde inter muliebrem tutelam rudimetumque primum puerilis regni.*

97 Liv. 1.3.11: *Addit sceleri scelus: stirpem fratris virilem interemit, fratris filiae Reae Silviae per speciem honoris cum Vestalem eam legisset perpetua virginitate spem partus adimit.*

98 Liv. 1.3.10: "To Numitor ... he bequeathed the ancient throne of the Silvian house" (*Numitori ... regnum vetustum Silviae gentis legat.*

99 Liv. 1 pr 6: *ante conditam condendamve urbem.*

100 Liv. 1.4.2: *Vestalis ... seu ita rata seu quia deus auctor culpae honestior erat Martem incertae stirpis patrem nuncupat.*

101 Liv. 1.4.4-7.

102 Liv. 1.4.7: *sunt qui Larentiam vulgato corpore lupam inter pastores vocatam putent: inde locum fibulae ac miraculo datum.*

103 Ogilvie's explanation of Larentia's semantic/religious aetiology – as fostermother of the Lares par excellence, that is, Romulus and Remus, ancestors of the Roman people (1963: 50) – fails to adequately address the problematic implications of the 'natural' equation between assumption of a share in

the function of the wolf (*lupa*) and the subsequently developed tradition of the notorious whore (*meretrix*). The progressive substitution of the socially inferior and negatively gendered female (who earns money through her sexuality) for the wild animal (which suckles the emerging historical force in *res Romana*) is insidious and requires analysis and evaluation. This is especially true of the unexplained presuppositions linking each stage in the tradition.

104   Livy, *Ab Urbe Condita* 1, tr. Foster (1967: 19).

105   *OLD* (p. 2121, col. 3) s.v. *volgo*, *vulg-*: 1. To make available to the mass of the population, make common to all. b. to prostitute (one's body). Cf. Lewis, C.T. 1953. *A Latin Dictionary*. p. 1160, col. 3: 2a. to spread abroad, publish, divulge, circulate, report.

106   In line with the definitions noted above, the meaning assigned to Livy's gendered treatment of *res Romana* can be understood as a useful emblematic tool.

107   Liv. 1.34.5: *exsule advena*.

108   Lucumo. Liv. 1.34.1: "a diligent, powerful and wealthy man" (*vir impiger ac divitiis potens*); 3: "heir to all the property" (*omnium heredi bonorum*). Tanaquil. Liv. 1.34.4: "descended from one of the foremost families" (*summo loco nata*).

109   Liv. 1.34.5: *spernentibus Etruscis Lucumonem exsule advena ortum ferre indignitatem non potuit oblitaque ingenitae erga patriam caritatis dummodo virum honoratum videret consilium migrandi ab Tarquiniis cepit.*

110   Liv. 1.34.1: *impiger*; 1.34.6: *strenuo*.

111   Liv. 1.34.1: "powerful through wealth" (*divitiis potens*); 1.34.6: "brave" (*forti*).

112   Liv. 1.34.3-4: "[Lucumo] became elated by his wealth and his ambition was stimulated by his marriage with Tanaquil" (*cum divitiae iam animos facerent auxit ducta in matrimonium Tanaquil*).

113   Liv. 1.34.7: *cupido honorum*; *facile persuadet*.

114   Liv. 1.34.5: *consilium ... cepit*.

115   Liv. 1.34.6: "among a new people where all nobility is a thing of recent growth and won by personal merit" (*in novo populo ubi omnis repentina atque ex virtute nobilitas sit*).

116   Liv. 1.34.9: "Tanaquil, a woman who, like most Etruscans, was expert in interpreting celestial prodigies" (*Tanaquil perita ut vulgo Etrusci caelestium prodigiorum mulier*).

117   Liv. 1.34.9: "Embracing her husband she bade him look for a high and majestic destiny" (*excelsa et alta sperare complexa virum iubet*); 10: "Carrying these hopes and surmises with them they entered the city" (*has spes cogitationesque secum portantes urbem ingressi sunt*).

118   Liv. 1.34.10.

119   Cf. Liv. 1.34.6: *regnasse Tatium ... Numae esse*; 35.3-4: *et Tatium ... et Numam*.

120   Liv. 1.35.6: *virum cetera egregium secuta quam in petendo habuerat etiam regnantem ambitio est nec minus regni sui firmandi quam augendae rei publicae memor centum in patres legit.*

121   In addition to Evander's mother (Carmenta), it is instructive to consider Tanaquil's role in relation to the imaginary Egeria and Numa's appointment of *virgines Vestae*. For this, see Chapter 1.3.

122   The fabric of interstitial social relations, "our critical affairs ... our weakened royal house" (1.39.3: *rebus nostris dubiis ... regiae adflictae*).

123   This is a conscious paraphrase of the conclusion to Tanaquil's hortatory translation of the incandescent *prodigium*: "'Let us henceforth bring up with all care and indulgence one who will be the source of measureless glory to the state and to ourselves'" (Liv. 1.39.3: *proinde materiam ingentis publice*

privatimque decoris omni indulgentia nostra nutriamus). In addition to its literal meaning, *materia* can apply to the source, cause or design of some quantity or quality; that is, fuel for repairing or revitalising damaged structures or for blocking or consuming growth.

124 Tanaquil's inspiration is identified as beyond her will, and subject to the pleasure of the gods: "The task was an easy one, for it was carrying out the will of the gods" (Liv. 1.39.4: *evenit facile quod dis cordi esset*).

125 Livy's intervention – "I am personally inclined to believe" (Liv. 1.39.5: *magis sententiae sum*) confirms Tanaquil's action – "From this time forward the body began to be treated as their child" (Liv. 1.39.4: *puerum liberum loco coeptum haberi*).

126 Liv. 1.39.5: *cognita esset ob unicam nobilitatem ab regina Romana*.

127 Cf. the speech of Canuleius: "son of a war-captive from Corniculum, a man with nobody for his father and a slave for his mother" (Liv. 4.3.12: *captiva Corniculana natum patre nullo matre serva*).

128 Cf. Thomson (1980: esp. Ch. 3, 57–104).

129 Liv. 1:39.5: *cognita esset, ferunt, edidisse*; 6: *eductum*.

130 Liv. 1.39.6: "this kind treatment" (*tanto beneficio*).

131 Liv. 1.39.6: "strengthening familiar acquaintance between the women" (*inter mulieris familiaritatem auctam*) (intimacy); "as he was from infancy in the royal household held in affection and honour" (*ut in domo a parvo eductum in caritate atque honore fuisse* (affection, esteem, preferment).

132 Perhaps reflected in the structural amplification of semantic links between *educare* and *erudire*, household nurture and civic instruction. Cf. Liv. 1.39.3: *tam humili cultu educamus*; 4: *erudirique artibus ... cultum excitantur*.

133 Liv. 1 pr 9: "The subjects to which I would ask each of my readers to devote his earnest attention are these – the life and morals of the community; the men and the qualities by which through domestic policy and foreign war dominion was won and extended" (*ad illa mihi pro se quisque acriter intendat animum quae vita qui mores fuerint per quos viros quibusque artibus domi militiaeque et partum et auctum imperium sit*).

134 Liv. 1.39.4: "trained in those accomplishments by which characters are stimulated to the pursuit of a great destiny" (*erudirique artibus quibus ingenia ad magnae fortunae cultum excitantur*).

135 One voice (raised in a cry) and one movement (running or flocking together). This encapsulates a common intellectual response to the desperate attack of the shepherd-assassins: astonishment and amazement – "The shouting drew a crowd together, wondering what had happened" (Liv. 1.41.1: *clamor inde concursusque populi mirantium quid rei esset*).

136 Liv. 1.41.1-2: *Tanaquil inter tumultum claudi regiam iubet, arbitros eiecit. Simul quae curando volneri opus sunt, tamquam spes subesset, sedulo comparat, simul si destituat spes, alia praesidia molitur. Servio propere accito cum paene exsanguem virum ostendisset, dextram tenens orat ne inultam mortem soceri, ne socrum inimicis ludibrio esse sinat.*

137 For a radical revision of the topography of the upper Sacra Via, more traditionally allied to the palace of Numa, see Coarelli (1983: esp. Ch. 1, 56–78).

138 On a textual level this echoes the verisimilitude of reflexive discourse.

139 Liv. 1.41.1.

140 Liv. 1.41.1. The term *praesidia* confers/confirms Tanaquil's adoption/exertion of martial command in a situation demanding such leadership.

141 Tanaquil's entreaty echoes Hersilia's plea to Romulus at a psychologically propitious point in time.

142 Cf. 1.42.1: Servius' *emulatio* of Tanaquil's encapsulation and conflation of the boundaries between the public and private spheres of human activity: "Servius

consolidated his power as much by his private as by his public measures" (1.42.1: *iam publicis magis consiliis Servius quam privatis munire opes*). This completes the process of intellectual acceptance (and rational embodiment) of Tanaquil's concluding advice: "'If in this sudden emergency you are slow to resolve, then follow my counsels'" (Liv. 1.41.3: *si tua re subita consilia torpent at tu mea consilia sequere*). In other words, her design becomes his intention; her purpose, his determination; her stratagem, his wisdom. Cf. Wheeler (1988: 52–56)

143 Kraus (1994: 15).

144 Livy deploys *inventio* and *aemulatio* to recreate a compelling, affective past and an ethical interpretation of its formulaic episodes.

145 Cf. the picture of "a clever and unscrupulous woman" fostered by Ogilvie (1963: 143, 144, 161, 209).

146 This is the rhetorical figure variously called *evidentia, hypotyposis, ekphrasis*, or *subiectio sub oculos*: Cic. *De or.* 40.139; Quint. *Inst.* 9.2.40.

147 Kraus (1994: 13).

148 Liv. 1.41.3: "Think about yourself not in terms of where you came from, but who you are" (*qui sis non undo natus sis reputa*).

149 Liv. 1.41.3: *regnavimus* (the "we" who ruled); *mea consilia* (the wisdom, penetration, determination and resolution belonging to "me"); *tuum est ... regnum* (the kingdom which is "yours"); and *erige te ... expergiscere* (the "you" who must be aroused and excited). Cf. 1 pr 10 (cited in Chapter 1.1): *hoc illud ... omnis te exempli ... tibi tuaeque ... imitere capias ... quod vites.*

150 Kraus (1994: 14). Cf. Liv. 10.31.15; 31.1.1-5.

151 On the porta Fenestella, see Heurgon (1964), Ogilvie (1970: 778). On the "sacred marriage" ritual, see Kramer (1969), Cornell (1995: 146, 428n.80). On literary contamination, cf. the grafting of a motif from Hellenistic history, e.g. the ruse by which the death of Ptolemy Pholopater was concealed for a year (204–203) by Agathocles and Sosibius, or the death of Berenice by Euergetes in 246.

152 Liv. 1.41.1: "the shouting drew a crowd together" (*clamor inde concursusque populi*); 4: "the noise and impatience of the crowd" (*clamor impetusque multitudinis*). It is possible to read multitudes as implying the power of a "gang" or aristocratic threat. See Lintott (1968: 61, 83–85, 89–90).

153 Liv. 1.41.5: "he decided some cases and adjourned outhers under pretence of consulting the king" (*eum iura redditurum obiturumque alia regis munia esse*).

154 Liv. 1.41.6: "He appeared in his white tunic with purple stripes (*trabea*) with his lictors" (*cum trabea et lictoribus prodit*).

155 On this feature of Livy's literary composition – the method known as *einzelerzahlung* ("unit narration") – see the Foreword (n.9) of this study.

156 *OLD* (p. 1472. col.3) s.v. *prodo*: 2. To give birth to. b. to give rise to, produce (conditions). 5a. To hand down, transmit (tradition, custom). 6a. To publish in writing, record. 8a. To reveal the existence, character, etc., of.

157 Cf. Livy's earlier use of *volgo* – *OLD* p. 2121, col.3 (see this chapter, n.105 above) – in connection with the legendary status of Rhea Silvia, and the equally suitable semantic connotations of objectification as discursive strategy.

158 As Kraus (1994: 13) attests: "to show the seams of the text."

159 It is significant that Livy applies the commonplace of *invidia* (typically attracted by excellence) to a gendered subject, especially since the *invidia* attached to great *viri* was a declamatory topic. See Hellegouarc'h (1963: 196–199); Woodman (1988: 74). For a view of the intertextual links between Servius and Tarquin, especially in relation to Livy's exploration of the motives and products of aristocratic competition for status through his depiction of the fragmentation and reconstitution of traditional ideals in the late republican and proto-imperial Roman city, see Joshel (1992b: 114–115) and Kraus (1994: 9–17).

160 *Nomos*: "law," "custom," "convention," "inherited ideals," "received wisdom," "what we all acknowledge to be the case"; *phusis*: "nature," "the natural world," "reality." Cf. Herodotus 3.38.4: πάντων βασιλέα φήσας εἶναι ("Custom is lord of all").

161 Liv. 1.42.2: "Human counsels could not arrest the inevitable course of destiny" (*rupit tamen fati necessitatem humanis consiliis*).

162 Cf. Liv. 1.6.4: *regni cupido*, the character flaw of covetous desire noted as common to the narrative tensions underlying the tales of kin-slaying Romulus and Horatius. On this and the revisionist dimension of Livian historiography implicit in his approach to the commonplace difference between surface and reality, see Section 1 of this chapter.

163 Liv. 1.42.2: "general treachery and animosity" (*infida omnia atque infesta*).

164 Liv. 1.42.2: *praesentis quietem status*.

165 Cf. Aristotle's systematic descriptions of the observed existence and necessary principles of female relations with the male: Politics 1254b2-10; 1259a37-b17; 1260a9-24, 29-33; 1262a19-24; 1269612-70a31; 1277M8-25; 1313b32-9; 1335a7-17.

166 Quint. *Inst.* 9.4.129: *historia non tam finitos numeros quam orbem quendam contextumque desiderat. namque omnia eius membra connexa sunt ut homines qui manibus invicem apprehensis gradum firmant continent et continentur.*

167 Liv. 1.46.1: "He undoubtedly possessed royal authority by virtue of its use" (*usu haud dubie regnum possederat*) (sovereign power); "he was acclaimed as king by a unanimous vote such as no king before him had obtained (*consensu quanto haud quisquam alius ante rex est declaratus*) (popular vote); Liv. 1.46.2: "he granted land to the *plebs* in defiance of the senate" (*de agro plebis adversa patrum voluntate*) (conciliatory land distribution). Cf. Cornell (1995: 194–197). He reconstructs the Servian reforms as performing the function of minimising the power of locally dominant aristocratic clans and maximising the central power of the state. This reorganisation is comparable (and possibly inspired by) the contemporary developments of Cleisthenes' revision of the Attic tribes. Cf. Arist. *Ath. Pol.* 21.2, who notes that the aim of such a cross-sectioning of the whole community was to break up the old centres of local power by "mixing up" the citizens. The question of reducing the influence of the patricians by constitutional reform was surely a lively critical focus of late republican historiography. On the resonance of Augustan allusions in AUC history, see Chapter 1.1 for discussion; and n.19 for select bibliography.

168 Liv. 1.46.1: "He heard that the young Tarquin was boasting that he ruled without the assent of the people" (*iactari voces a iuvene Tarquinio audiebat se iniussu populi regnare*); 2: "traducing Servius and strengthening his own faction in the assembly" (*criminandi Servi apud patres crescendique in curia*) (popular and patrician manipulation); Liv. 1.46.2: "seizing the opportunity it afforded him" (*sibi occasionem datum ratus est*) (approbation of land distribution); Liv. 1.46.2: "He was a bold and inspiring youth" (*ipse iuvenis ardentis animi*) (personal will).

169 Liv. 1.46.3: *tulit enim et Romana regia sceleris tragici exemplum*.

170 Cf. Liv. 1 pr 10.

171 Liv. 1.46.3: "the loathing felt for kings hastened the advent of liberty and the crown won by villainy was the last that was worn" (*ut taedio regum maturior veniret libertas ultimumque regnum esset quod scelere partum foret*; Liv. 1.46.5: "in order that the reign of Servius might last long enough to allow the state to settle into its new constitution" (*quo diuturnius Servi regnum esset constituique civitatis mores possent*).

172 Roman historians frequently advert to a providential force, variously called *fatum, fortuna* or *sors*, that drives Rome on to her destiny, for good or for evil. As any precise philosophical influence remains unidentifiable, the intervention envisioned by Livy should relate to a more precise will; in this instance, characterological. See Levine (1993: 30–37).

173 Liv. 1.46.5: "It was, I believe, the good fortune of the Roman people which intervened to prevent two violent natures from being joined in marriage" (*forte ita inciderat ne duo violenta ingenia matrimonio iungerentur fortuna credo populi Romani*).

174 Liv. 1.46.6: *angebatur ferox Tullia nihil materiae in viro neque ad cupiditatem neque ad audaciam esse.*

175 Unlike her husband, whose inadequacies of *genius* represent for her the source of vexation verging on physical and mental pain.

176 Liv. 1.46.6: *spernere sororem quod virum nacta muliebri cessaret audacia.*

177 In like manner to her male foil, L. Tarquinius: "Likeness of character soon drew them together, as evil usually consorts best with evil" (Liv. 1.46.7: *contrabit celeriter similitude eos ut fere fit malum malo aptissimum*). The proverbial similarity between the two is introduced in asyndeton at the end of the argument to clinch the thematic point logically and linguistically.

178 Liv. 1.46.7: *sed initium turbandi omnia a femina ortum est.*

179 Cf. Sall. *Hist.* 1.77 (speech of Philippus in the Senate): *seditionibus omnia turbata sunt*, an expression which derives from 'civil war' language; cf. Vell. Pat. 74.3 (on Fulvia). Note its vividness and fullness, a characteristically Livian stylistic ploy to emphasize the inclusiveness of the description. Cf. Liv. 9.43.16; 21.11.6.

180 L'Hoir (1992: 92–93).

181 Liv. 1.46.7: *secretis viri alieni adsuefacta sermonibus nullis verborum contumeliis parcere de viro ad fratrem de sorore ad virum.*

182 Meeting in secrecy implies conspiracy; cf. *Lex XII Tabularum* 8.60; Sall. *Cat.* 20.1.

183 Liv. 1.46.7: *et se rectius viduam et illum caelibem futurum fuisse contendere quam cum inpari iungi ut elanguescendum aliena ignavia.*

184 Liv. 1.46.9: "She rapidly infected the young man with her own recklessness" (*celeriter adulescentem suae temeritatis implet*).

185 Liv. 1.47.1: *praeterita parricidia.*

186 Liv. 1.46.8: *domi se* (daughter); *apud patrem* (father); 1.46.9: *domos vacuas* (sons-in-law).

187 These interactions include the retention or display of confiscated property by military commanders; the relationship between religion and politics, the divine and secular (*auspicia > leges, fas/nefas*); the intellectual and practical mobility of bequeathed and acquired landholdings; the fluid mechanisms of a Reichstaat only distantly operating under the rule of law; the epitome of this unclear delimitation in the censor's public direction of private life; not to mention the undeniable fact of popular sovereignty as a myth constituted, fostered, and enforced by a senatorial minority of *nobiles* divided in turn into a distinguishable (and distinguished) hierarchy. This clique was dependent on the political theatre (competition, demagoguery and popular participation), and the daily spectacle of visually represented power (rituals, funerals, elections, games, magisterial attendants and regalia, triumphs, monuments, imagines, and eulogia) – all essential for social acquiescence, maintenance, and control.

188 For instance, *amicitia* (*hospitium, patronatus, collegium*), entailing a quantifiable hierarchy of social obligations described as friendship between equals; the social and moral expectations encompassed within the fundamental principle of inheritance; concern, responsible provision, and respect for the mechanisms comprising the life cycle; the conflict between the ideal of economic autarchy

and the *realia* of domestic inefficiencies and rural dependence; the sometimes contradictory commonplaces of emotional support, serial monogamy, and domestic virtues (cf. *ILS* 8402 = *CIL* VI 11602: *optima et pulcherrima lanifica pia pudica frugi casta domiseda*; Pliny, *Ep.* 4.19.2-4).

189 Liv. 1.47.1: "From that time the old age of Tullius became more embittered, his reign more unhappy." (*tum vero in dies infestior Tulli senectus infestius coepit regnum esse*).

190 Liv. 1.47.1: *ab scelere ad aliud spectare mulier scelus*; Liv. 1.47.2: *non sibi defuisse cui nupta diceretur nec cum quo tacita serviret*.

191 Liv. 1.47.2: *defuisse qui se regno dignum putaret qui meminisset se esse Prisci Tarquini filium qui habere quam sperare regnum mallet*.

192 For example, Chelidon, Pipa and Tertia (Cic. *Verr.* 2.1.136-37, 5.38-39; 3.77-78); Clodia (Cic. *Cael.* 1, 30–32, 36, 47–49, 78); Sempronia (Sall. *Cat.* 24.3-25.5; 40.5); Terentia (Ps.-Sall. *Invective against Tullius* 2.3).

193 Hillard (1989).

194 Liv. 1.41.3 (Tanaquil); 1.47.3 (Tullia).

195 Liv. 1.41.3: "The throne is yours, Servius" (*tuum est ... Servi ... regnum*); 1.47.3: "then I call you my husband and my king" (*et virum et regem appello*).

196 Liv. 1.47.3: "I have changed my condition for the worse" (*eo nunc peius mutata res est*).

197 Liv. 1.41.3: "Up! Follow the guidance of the gods" (*erige te deosque duces sequere*); "those who presaged the exaltation of that head round which fire once played" (*hoc fore caput divino quondam circumfuso igni portenderunt*); "let that heaven-sent flame now inspire you" (*nunc te illa caelestis excitet flamma*); "Do not think about where you came from, but who you are" (*qui sis non unde natus sis reputa*).

198 Liv. 1.47.4: *di te penates patriique et patris imago et domus regia et in domo regale solium et nomen Tarquinium creat vocatque regem*.

199 Liv. 1.47.6: *his aliisque increpando iuvenem instigat*.

200 Liv. 1.47.6: *cum Tanaquil, peregrina mulier, tantum moliri potuisset animo ut duo continua regna viro ac deinceps genero dedisset, ipsa regio semine orta nullum momentum in dando adimendoque regno faceret*.

201 Liv. 1.47.7: *his muliebribus instinctus furiis*; cf. Aesch. *Eum.* 46–54.

202 Examples of good character or behavior include: Busa (Liv. 22.52.7); the wife of Mandonius and sister-in-law of Indibilis (prince of the Ilergetes), Indibilis' daughters and *aliae nobilitate pari* [Liv. 26.49.11-15]; the wife of Mazaetullus, daughter of Hannibal's sister, wife of the king Oesalces (Liv. 29.29.12); the women of Argos, robbed by the wife of Nabis of Sparta (Liv. 32.40.10); and Theoxena (Liv. 40.4). Examples of bad character or behavior include the *mulier* Campana (Liv. 26.12.16-20); the *muliercula* of the captain of the citadel of Tarentum (Liv. 27.15.9-11); the *famosa mulier* from Placentia (Liv. 39.43.2); and Damarata (Liv. 24.4.1-7.12; 21.1-26.16). On this topic, see Chapter 3.

203 L'Hoir (1992: 89).

204 Liv. 1.47.10-11: "he seized the throne, a woman's gift" (*muliebri dono regnum occupasse*).

205 Normative or stereotypical representations provide the narrative protocol of historiographical familiarity; that is, the space within which the writer's code may be articulated for the benefit (and conform to the expectations) of his elite readership.

206 Cf. the Sabine leader Attus Clausus (Ap. Claudius), Cn. Marcius Coriolanus, and the patrician Fabii, not to mention the legendary warlords Aulus Vibenna, Lars Porsenna and Mastarna. See the useful discussion of the *clientes* or *sodales* associated with the aristocratic *condottieri* of central Italian society during the archaic period in Cornell (1995: 143–145).

207 Cf. Sall. *Cat.* 20.2-17.

208 It should be noted that Livy has previously intervened personally to reject the pedigree of servitude and unworthy parentage attached to Servius' family. As well, Tarquin's ambiguous assertion that Servius ruled *non auctoribus patribus* conflicts with the narrative's earlier construction: "Servius ruled … without opposition from the senate" (Liv. 1.41.6: *Servius … voluntate patrum regnavit*). Just as the line between approval and inclination is narrow, and that between slavery and aristocracy inversely broad, so Livy's reconstruction of Tullia's psychology (internalised in the nascent *tyrannus*, Tarquin) embraces the multiplex dimensions of *res gestae* historicised and reinterpreted for authorial and elite consideration.

209 Liv. 1.48.1-2. As Livy reports, "Servius exclaimed in a loud voice" (*excitatus … magna voce*), connoting strength kindled by inner anxiety.

210 Liv. 1.41.1: *clamor inde concursusque populi*; Liv. 1.41.4: *clamor impetusque multitudinis*; Liv. 1.48.2: *clamor oritur et concursus fiebat*. Cf. Sall. *Cat.* 45.3; Hor. *Sat.* 1.9.77-78: *clamor utrimque:/undique concursus sic me servavit Apollo* (= Hom. *Il.* 20.443).

211 Liv. 1.48.3: "Tarquin, forced by sheer necessity into proceeding to the final extremity" (*Tarquinius necessitate iam etiam ipsa cogente ultima audere*); "he seized Servius round the wait, and being a much younger and stronger man, carried him out of the senate-house and flung him down the steps into the forum below" (*medium arripit Servium elatumque e curia in inferiorem partem per gradus deiecit*), 4: "he (Servius) was killed by those sent by Tarquin" (*qui missi ab Tarquinio … interficitur*).

212 Liv. 1.48.5: *creditur quia non abhorret a cetero scelere admonitu Tulliae id factum*.

213 Liv. 1.48.5: "it is believed" (*creditur*); "it is generally agreed" (*id quod satis constat*).

214 Liv. 1.48.5: "unabashed by the presence of the assembly of men" (*nec reverita coetum virorum*).

215 Liv. 1.48.1: "'How dared you, with such insolence, convene the senate or sit in that chair while I am alive?'" (*qua tu audacia me vivo vocare ausus es patres aut in sede considere mea*); Liv. 1.48.6: "she called her husband out of the senate-house and was the first to salute him as king" (*evocavit virum e curia regemque prima appellavit*). Clearly, Tullia's action is an abrogation of *auctoribus patribus iussu populi* which even Tarquin appears to find beyond the pale. His reaction is instructive given his prior denunciation of Servius for ignoring curiate and patrician choice and the key institution of the *interregnum*.

216 Liv. 1.48.6: *tanto tumultu*.

217 Liv. 1.48.6: *ad summum Cyprium vicum ubi Dianium nuper fuit*.

218 Liv. 1.45.2: "Servius had been careful to form ties of hospitality and friendship with the chiefs of the Latin nation, and he used to speak in the highest praise of that cooperation and the common recognition of the same deity." (*eum consensum deosque consociatos laudare mire Servius inter proceres Latinorum cum quibus publice privatimque hospitia amicitiasque de industria iunxerat*).

219 Ogilvie (1963: 182).

220 Liv. 1.45.1: "(Servius) endeavoured to extend Rome's dominion by diplomacy" (*consilio augere imperium conatus est*).

221 Liv. 1.48.7: *foedum inhumanumque inde traditur scelus monumentoque locus est – Sceleratum vicum vocant – quo amens, agitantibus furiis sororis ac viri, Tullia per patris corpus carpentum egisse fertur, partemque sanguinis ac caedis paternae cruento vehiculo, contaminata ipsa respersaque, tulisse ad penates suos virique sui, quibus iratis malo regni principio similes propediem exitus sequerentur*.

222 Such repeated emphasis highlights the historiographical tradition's failure to provide a plausible story. Further, it could indicate Livy's unwillingness to vouch for the historicity of Tullia's act (despite the descriptions of her frenzy which follow immediately). In this way, by ironically subsuming his personal authority in the wider *auctoritas* of the narrative tradition, Livy gestures to the difficulties which arise in the space between the "real" and the "invented."

223 Quint. *Inst.* 3.8.6; cf. 3.8.36, 3.8.66.

224 Liv. 1.48.8-9: "With him perished all just and lawful kingship in Rome. Gentle and moderate as his sway had been, he had nevertheless, according to some authorities, formed the intention of laying it down, because it was vested in a single person, but this purpose of giving freedom to the state was cut short by that domestic crime" (*cum illo simul iusta ac legitima regna occiderunt. id ipsum tam mite ac tam moderatum imperium tamen, quia unius esset, deponere eum in animo habuisse quidam auctores sunt, ni scelus intestinum liberandae patriae consilia agitanti intervenisset*). Is this a sarcastic use of *iustus* ("lawful")? Cf. Liv. 10.8.9: "We have always heard the same objections raised – that the auspices were solely in your hands, that you alone enjoy the privileges and prerogatives of noble birth, that you alone can legitimately hold sovereign command and take the auspices either in peace or in war" (*semper ista audita sunt eadem, penes vos auspicial esse, vos solos gentem habere, vos solos iustum imperium et auspicium domi militiaeque*). In contrast to earlier references, Livy's citation of the tradition here (*auctores sunt*) seems to convey a reassuring authority.

225 Liv. 1.48.9: *scelus intestinum ... agitanti.*

226 Liv. 6.34.5-11. For a succinct analysis of the episode's structural, linguistic and thematic affinities with the Lucretia and Verginia narrative, see Kraus (1991); cf. Kraus (1994: 271–277).

227 Cf. Liv. 6.37.5, 8; 39.4

228 Liv. 6.34.9: *nupta in domo quam nec honos nec gratia intrare posset.* Cf. Livy's citations of the annalistic tradition which conflict with this crucial element of the narrative: the consular tribunate is open to the plebs from 445 BCE (Liv. 4.6.8); the first trib. mil. cons. pl. is elected in 400 BCE (Liv. 5.12.9).

229 Liv. 6.34.5: "an incident occurred which was slight in itself but, as is often the case, led to important results" (*parva ut plerumque solet rem ingentem moliundi causa intervenit*).

230 Liv. 1 pr 6; cf, e.g., Hor. *Carm.* 3.30.1.

231 Lipovsky (1984: 89).

232 Fabia's reactions: Liv. 6.34.6: *expavisset* (to grow pale); 7: *stimulas* (to stir up), *subdidit* (to rankle), *paenituisse* (to regret); 8: *confusam* (to stun). Causative factors: Liv. 6.34.6: *ignorare* (to be ignorant of); 7: *malo arbitrio* (owing to the misguided judgement).

233 Kraus (1994: 274).

234 Liv. 6.34.7: "in the mind of a woman easily excited by trifles" (*parvis mobili rebus animo muliebri*); "her father kindly but firmly insisted upon finding out, and she confessed the real cause of her anguish" (*elicuit comiter sciscitando ut fateretur eam esse causam doloris*).

235 Cf. Santoro L'Hoir (1992: 80–83); Fornara (1983: 76–90).

236 Liv. 6.34.8: "Her father happened to see her while she was still upset by this mortifying incident" (*confusam eam ex recenti morsu animi cum pater forte vidisset*).

237 Cf. Kraus (1991: 323): "a suitable mirror of the frustrations and annoyances suffered by both sides in the ten-year battle for plebeian consuls."

238 Lipovsky (1983: 25).

239 Thuc.1.1.3. For a discussion of narrative 'evidence' as an essential rhetorical component of ancient historiography Walsh (1970: 181–187).

240 Liv. 1.58.9: "They seek to comfort her, sick at heart as she was" (*consolantur aegram animi*) (Lucretia); Liv. 6.34.10: "Ambustus consoled his daughter and bade her keep up her spirits" (*consolans inde filiam Ambustus bonum animum habere iussit*) (Fabia).

241 Liv. 1.46.7: *se rectius viduam ... quam cum impari iungi* (Tullia); Liv. 6.34.9: "she was unwed to one who was her inferior in birth" (*iuncta impari esset parva, ut plerumque solet, rem ingentem moliundi)* Fabia).

242 Liv. 6.34.10: "She would very soon see in her own house the same honours which she saw at her sister's" (*eosdem propidiem domi visuram honores quos apud sororem videat*) (Fabius); Liv. 1.46.8: *si sibi cum quo Digna ... quod apud patrem vident* (Tullia).

243 Liv. 1 pr. 9. On the purpose of Livy's version of the existing historical tradition, see Chapter 1.1; for the original text, see Chapter 1, n.15.

244 Liv. 1 pr.10.

AFTERWORD
Final observations

What has been explored in the present study – the relationship between Livy's historiographical project and his gendered elucidation of Roman history; the extent to which his authorial choices regarding episodes that featured representations of individual women or female collectives (and, by implication, their male counterparts) consciously utilised the narrative conventions of traditional annalist history; how the historian's treatment of non-Roman women reflects or complicates the very particular discourse of gender representation deployed in service to the AUC project; whether the roles Livy assigned to women and men reflect an established or modified interpretation of Roman gender; and, in relation to the customary questions which must always be faced when assessing ancient literary texts (authorial intent, reliability, bias), the degree to which Livy's narrative fabric represents a sophisticated blend of historical detail and secondary oral-literary super-structure – will not require restatement or review. Rather than rehearse all that has gone before, a short series of final, related observations will follow, under three headings: conceptions of gender, distinctions of public and private, and conjunctions of literature and history.

Conceptions of gender

Livy's use of women appears representative of Roman society's (and, it should be added, his own) ideological perspectives towards issues of gender and relational dynamics in private, public, and mixed social conditions. His narrative can be interrogated to provide information about the existence of a particular view of female sexuality implicit in the construction of women's social roles. In particular, conceptions of sexuality in Livian historiography reflect the intersection of criteria adhering to gender, family, and civic function. Episodes involving women reflect the degeneration or revelation of male character, provide analogy to mimetic male rivalry, and comprise part of the record of the maintenance of male power. In some cases, women defend a patriarchal order which seeks to bind the members of families together, and thereby to put them in their "proper" places and roles in society.

According to this view, Livy will have consistently represented legendary, non-citizen, slave, ex-slave, freeborn, and elite women living in ancient Italy with respect to the socio-cultural relations of class, ethnicity, and gender. This, of course, requires that his historiographical project should comprise conventionally gendered objects of Graeco-Roman discourse and its deviant counterparts. Certain premises underpin this approach:

- The complex intersections of sexual subject positions with class or ethnic status.
- The projection of historical and social contingencies onto the template of Graeco-Roman sexuality.
- The comprehensive interaction between oral operations (presentation and hearing) and literary operations (reading and writing) in a "manuscript culture with high residual orality" – a process characteristic of a "rhetorical culture" like that of the first century BCE/CE Mediterranean.[1]

The episodes examined in *Livy's Women* reveal a network of horizontal social and sexual relationships.[2] As Table 1.2 (located in Chapter 1) reveals, this network oscillates among a variety of interpersonal, socially determined valencies centred on the idealised subject position of the virile male (*uir*), an individual's position as a member of Graeco-Roman society could be measured from one standpoint against a spectrum of normative descriptions and deviant prescriptions. Such normalcies and deviations revolve around the explicit or implied use of anatomical orifices: vagina, anus, and mouth. As a proficient user of the Graeco-Roman linguistic system, Livy deployed its gendered vocabulary in nuanced and sophisticated ways, differentiating between female penetration and the phallic agency of the male penetrator – the Sabine women; Lucretia; Verginia; the Ardean *virgo*, daughter of a plebeian family; the wife of the Clusian wine importer Arruns; Polycratia, wife of the Achaean Aratus; and, infrequently but emphatically, representations of male receptivity and the quasi-phallic activity of the female penetrator – Tullia; Cornelia, Sergia, and the other *matronae* responsible for poisoning Rome's leading male citizens; Damarata; Sophonisba; Apega, wife of the Spartan king Nabis.

As shown in Table A.1, this nexus of socio-linguistic designations is rendered more intricate by a complementary variety of vertical identifiers, *uir/homo* (man) and *femina/mulier* (woman). According to recent explorations of these terms in the canonical literature of Republic and Empire,[3] the Graeco-Roman reader was able to separate *uiri* from *homines*. The former category included celebrated men of senatorial rank, upper magistrates, notable *equites*, persons who participated in public life and were politically sound (i.e., the *boni*). It may also range from those who had distinguished themselves in their country's service either in the military or in the provinces and those whom the author wished to flatter. On the other hand, *homines*

Table A.1 Comparative sample of gendered AUC history in Livy

Book	Female representation	Reference in Livy and other sources + uses of *femina* and *mulier*	Related male representations
1	HELEN, wife of Menelaus and Paris	1.1.1	Aeneas and Antenor
	LAVINIA, daughter of Latinus and Amata; last wife of Aeneas	1.1.7, 9-11; 1.2.1-2; 1.3.1-4 *ab nomine uxoris* (1.1.11); *tutela muliebri* (1.2.2)	Turnus, Aeneas, Latinus and Ascanius
	CREUSA, daughter of Priam and Hecuba; first wife of Aeneas; mother of Ascanius	1.3.2-4	Ascanius (Iulus)
	RHEA SILVIA, Vestal Virgin	1.3.11; 4.1-4	Numitor, Amulius and Mars
	LARENTIA, wife of Faustulus; adoptive mother of Romulus and Remus (consort of Hercules; prostitute)	1.4.6-8	Faustulus, Romulus and Remus
	CARMENTA, prophetess and goddess of childbirth and prophecy	1.7.8-9; see also 5.47.2 (the temple of Carmentis/Carmenta); cf. 2:49.8; 24.47.15; 25.7.6; 27.37.11 (the Porta Carmentalis: Verg. *Aen.* 8.337-341; Dion. Hal. *Ant. Rom.* 1.32.3; Festus 450L; Solin, 1.13)	Evander and Hercules (the Politii and Pinarii)
	The SABINE WOMEN, brides, wives, and mothers	1.9.1-13.6 *penuria mulierum* (1.9.1); *muliebre ingenium* (1.9.16); *Sabinae mulieres* (1.13.1)	Titus Tatius and Romulus
	HERSILIA, wife of Romulus (wife of Hostus Hostilius; grandmother of Tullus Hostilius)	1.11.2 *Hersilia coniunx* (1.11.2)	Romulus
	TARPEIA, Vestal Virgin; daughter of Spurius Tarpeius	1.11.5-9	Sp. Tarpeius and Titus Tatius
	EGERIA, Nymph; consort and counselor of Numa Pompilius, second king of Rome	1.19.5	Romulus

(*Continued*)

Table A.1 Comparative sample of gendered AUC history in Livy (*Continued*)

Book	Female representation	Reference in Livy and other sources + uses of *femina* and *mulier*	Related male representations
	HORATIA, sister of the Horatii; betrothed to one of the Curiatii	1.26.1-14	Roman Horatii (esp. P. Horatius) and Volscan Curiatii
	TANAQUIL, mother; TARQUINIA, Tanaquil's daughter; and Tanaquil's granddaughters	1.34; 39; 41 *Tanaquil ... mulier* (1.34.9); *inter mulieris* (1.39.6)	Lucumo (L. Tarquinius Priscus) and Servius Tullius
	TULLIA MINOR, mother; TULLIA MAIOR; TARQUINIA, Tullia Minor's daughter	1.46.3-48.9; 59.13	L. Tarquinius Superbus
	LUCRETIA, daughter of Spurius Lucretius; wife of L. Tarquinius Collatinus	1.58-59	Sex. Tarquinius, L. Tarquinius Collatinus, Sp. Lucretius Tricipitinus and L. Iunius Brutus
2	VITELLIA, daughter of M. Porcius Cato Uticensis and Atilia; wife of M. Iunius Brutus	2.4	[Titus] Iunius Brutus, and [Tiberius] Iunius Brutus; Vitellii and Aquilii
	CLOELIA, hostage of Lars Porsenna	2.13.6-11 *in femina virtutem* (2.13.11)	Lars Porsenna
	VETURIA, *matrona*; mother of C. Marcius Coriolanus; VOLUMNIA, wife of Coriolanus	2.40	C. Marcius Coriolanus
	OPPIA, Vestal Virgin	2.42.11; cf. Dion. Hal. *Ant. Rom.* 8.89.4 (Opimia)	Caeso Fabius Ambustus; L. Aemilius and L. Valerius; Veii and the Volscians
3	Roman *matronae* (*stratae matres*)	3.7.8	Volscians, Aequi, Hernici, Latins
	RACILIA, wife of Cincinnatus	3.26.9	Sp. Nautius, L. Minucius and L. Quinctius Cincinnatus
	VERGINIA, daughter of L. Verginius, centurion; fiancé of L. Icilius, trib. pleb.	3.44, 49	Appius Claudius Decemvir, L. Verginius, L. Icilius and M. Claudius
4	The category of *femina* (the right of *connubium*)	4.4.10	C. Canuleius, M. Genucius, C. Curiatus
	The Ardean *virgo*	4.9.4-6	Tutor of *virgo sui iuris*

(*Continued*)

Table A.1 Comparative sample of gendered AUC history in Livy (*Continued*)

Book	Female representation	Reference in Livy and other sources + uses of *femina* and *mulier*	Related male representations
	POSTUMIA, Vestal Virgin	4.44.11-12; cf. Plut. *Mor.* 89e-f (*cap. inim. ut.* 6)	Sextus Pompilius and Antistius
5	Roman *matronae*	5.18.11	
	Women of Veii	5.21.10	Slaves
	JUNO REGINA, goddess, protector, and special counsellor of the Roman state	5.22.5-9	Youths selected from the army victorious over Veii
	Romanae matres	5.23.3	
	Ar(r)uns' wife	5.33.3	Ar(r)uns and Lucumo
	Soldiers' wives	5.38.5	Roman soldiers fleeing from the Gauls
	Vestal Virgins and Lucius Albinius' wife	5.40.10	L. Albinius, a plebeian
	Vestal Virgins	5.52.13-14	M. Furius Camillus (referring to the steadfastness of the Vestal Virgins in their duty to the state)
6	Roman *matronae*	6.4.2; cf. 5.50.7	M. Furius Camillus (reimbursing matronal contributions of gold)
	The FABIAE AMBUSTI, daughters of M. Fabius Ambustus; wives of Ser. Sulpicius and C. Livinius Stolo	6.34.5-11	M. Fabius Ambustus, Ser. Sulpicius (*tribunis militum*) and C. Licinius Stolo (distinguished plebeian)
8	MINUCIA, Vestal Virgin	8.15.7-8	*Pontifices*
	Woman from Pandosia; CLEOPATRA (Alexander's wife) and OLYMPIAS (Alexander's sister)	8.23.16-17 *mulier* (8.24.16); *cura mulieris* (8.24.17)	Alexander, king of Epirus, and crowd of men and women
	The *ancilla* and the 20 *matronae* accused of poisoning, incl. CORNELIA and SERGIA	8.18 *muliebri fraude* (8.18.6)	The *primores*, Q. Fabius Maximus (curule aedile, owner of the informer *ancilla*), Cn. Quinctilius (*dictator*), L. Valerius (*magister equitum*)

(*Continued*)

Table A.1 Comparative sample of gendered AUC history in Livy (*Continued*)

Book	Female representation	Reference in Livy and other sources + uses of *femina* and *mulier*	Related male representations
10	Roman *matronae*, VERGINIA, daughter of Aulus Verginius, wife of L. Volumnius (plebeian aedile) and the sacred spaces of *PUDICITIA PATRICIA* (*sacellum*) and *PLEBEIA* (*templum*)	10.23.1-10	Aulus Verginius, L. Volumnius, and the *viri in hac civitate*

NB Books 11–20 are no longer extant; brief summaries only exist

Book	Female representation	Reference	Related male representations
14	SEXTILIA, Vestal Virgin	*Per.* 14.7: *Sextilia, virgo Vestalis, damnata incesti viva defossa est*; cf. Oros. 4.2.8, Hieron. 126, Syncell. 522.19	
19	CLAUDIA, sister of P. Claudius Pulcher, cos. 249 BCE	*Per.* 19.5: Claudia, soror P. Claudi qui contemptis auspiciis male pugnauerat, a ludis reuertens cum turba premeretur, dixit: "utinam frater meus uiueret: iterum classem duceret." Ob eam causam multa ei dicta est; cf. Cic. *Nat. D.* 2.7, Val. Max. 1.4.3, 8.1. *damn.* 4; Suet. *Tib.* 2.2-3; Gell. 10.6.2-4; contra Polyb. 1.49.1-52.3	
20	TUCCIA, Vestal Virgin	*Per.* 20.4: *Tuccia, virgo Vestalis, incesti damnata est*; cf *MRR* 1.534-6	
22	BUSA	22.52.7; 22.54.4	Ap. Claudius Pulcher and P. Cornelius Scipio
24	Daughters of Hiero (DAMARATA and HERACLEA)	24.4.3	Hiero, Hieronymus, Adranodorus and Zoippus
	DAMARATA, HARMONIA (daughter of Gelon), and HERACLEA	24.4.3; 24.22.8; 24.25.11	Hiero, Hieronymus, Adranodorus, Zoippus Themistus, Hippocrates and Epicydes

(*Continued*)

Table A.1 Comparative sample of gendered AUC history in Livy (*Continued*)

Book	Female representation	Reference in Livy and other sources + uses of *femina* and *mulier*	Related male representations
	Roman widows	24.18.13-14	Censors of 218 BCE
	Wife of Hannibal (from Castulo in Spain)	24.41.7	Hannibal
26	Mistress of Campanian deserter	26.12.17	Fulvius Flaccus, Hannibal
	VESTIA OPPIA and PACULA CLUVIA	26.33.8	Capuan ambassadors
	Daughters of Indibilis and *virgines*; wife of Mandonius; female hostages	26.49.11-16	P. Cornelius Scipio Africanus, trusted male
	Fiancé of Alluccius	26.50.1-14	P. Cornelius Scipio Africanus, Alluccius
27	Young woman from Tarentum	27.15.9-11 *amore mulierculae* (27.15.9)	Q. Fabius Maximus Verrucosus (Cunctator), commander of Bruttian guard, brother of young woman
	POLYCRATIA	27.31.8	Philip V of Macedon, Aratus, Q. Sulpicius
29	CLAUDIA QUINTA and the *matronae primores civitatis*	29.14.12-14	P. Cornelius Scipio Nasica, the Senate, and the *populus frequens*
	Wife of Mezetulus (daughter of Hannibal's sister)	29.29.12 *nobilem feminam* (29.29.12)	Mezetulus, king of the Massylians, Masinissa
	SOPHONI(S)BA (daughter of Hasdrubal; wife of Syphax and Masinissa)	29.23.3-6; 30.3.4; 30.7.8-9; 30.11.3; 30.12-15	Hasdrubal Gisgo, Syphax, Masinissa and P. Cornelius Scipio
32	APEGA (wife of the tyrant Nabis of Sparta), *singulae illustres*, and *plures genere inter se*	32.40.10-11 *ad feminas spoliandas uxorem Argos [Nabis] remisit* (32.40.10)	Nubis
34	The *frequentia mulierum* (34.1.6; 34.8.1) or *agmen* (34.8.2) of *matronae* (34.1.5), supporting the repeal of the *lex Oppia*	34.1.5-7; 34.8.1-2 *frequentia mulierum* (34.1.6; 34.8.1)	M. Porcius Cato and L. Valerius (Tappo?)

(*Continued*)

Table A.1 Comparative sample of gendered AUC history in Livy (*Continued*)

Book	Female representation	Reference in Livy and other sources + uses of *femina* and *mulier*	Related male representations
	The *coniuratio muliebri*	34.2.3 *coniuratio muliebri* (34.2.3)	M. Porcius Cato, referring to the episode of HYPSIPYLE, her father Thoas, king, and the **Lemnian women** (Herod. 6.138; Hyg. *Fab.* 15)
	Roman women, characterised in Cato's speech as *secessio mulierum* (34.2.7; cf. 34.5.5 [Valerius]), *agmen mulierum* (34.2.8) and *seditio muliebrum* (34.3.8; cf. 34.5.5 [Valerius])	34.2-5 *secessio mulierum* (34.2.7); *agmen mulierum* (34.2.8); *seditio muliebrum* (34.3.8)	M. Porcius Cato, referring to the Roman women agitating for the repeal of the *lex Oppia*
	Roman women, characterised in Valerius' speech as *matronae* (34.5.3, 5. 7, 8, 9, 10, 34.6.8, 9, 15), *coetum muliebris* (34.5.5), *honestae feminae* (34.5.1) and *filiae, uxores,* and *sorores* (34.7.11)	34.6-7 *coetum muliebris* (34.5.5), *honestae feminae* (34.5.1)	L. Valerius (Tappo?), referring to the Roman women agitating for the repeal of the *lex Oppia*
	The *intercursus matronae*	34.5.8-9 *secessionem muliebrem* (34.5.5); *viros feminae* (34.5.12); *honestis feminis* (39.5.13)	M. Porcius Cato, referring to the episode of the SABINE WOMEN (Liv. 2.35.6-40.10)
	Latin women *(sociorum Latini uxoribus)*	34.7.5-6 *feminis* (34.7.4); *haec feminarum insignia sunt* (34.7.9)	L. Valerius (Tappo?), referring to the wives of the Latin allies
38	CHIOMARA	38.24 *mulieri* (38.24.4); *mulieris* (38.24.6, 7); *mulier lingua sua* (38.24.8)	Cn. Manlius and C. Helvius, Orgiagon (Tectosagi chieftain), female captives (*captivae*), personal slave (*servus*)
	CORNELIA MINOR, mother of the Gracchi. CORNELIA MAIOR,	38.57	P. Cornelius Nasica, L. Cornelius Scipio Asiaticus, P. Cornelius

(*Continued*)

Table A.1 Comparative sample of gendered AUC history in Livy (*Continued*)

Book	Female representation	Reference in Livy and other sources + uses of *femina* and *mulier*	Related male representations
	wife of P. Cornelius Scipio Nasica Corculum, and AEMILIA, wife of Scipio Africanus, mother of Cornelia the elder and Cornelia the younger.		Scipio Africanus, Tiberius Sempronius Gracchus
39	HISPALA FAECENIA et alii	39.9-18 *viros mulieresque* (39.8.5); *mixti feminis mares* (39.8.6); *ingenuorum feminarumque* (39.8.7); *ipse Sulpiciam gravem feminam* (39.11.4); *probam et antique moris feminam* (39.11.5); *lacrimae mulieri [Aebutiae]* (39.11.7); *nobilem et gravem feminam* (39.12.2); *Sulpicia, tali femina* (39.12.3); *mulier, mulieris* (39.13.1); *gravissimae feminae* (39.13.3); *permixti viri feminis* (39.13.10); *plura virorum inter sese quam feminarum* (39.13.10); *sacerdotes eorum sacrorum seu viri seu feminae* (39.14.7); *primum igitur mulierum ... feminis mares* (39.15.9); *mulierum ac virorum* (39.15.12)	
	Prostitute from Placentia	39.43.2-4	L. Quinctius Flamininus
40	ARCHO and THEOXENA	40.4 *Theoxena ... mulieribus* (40.4.3); *ferox interim femina* (40.4.13)	Philip V and Poris

(Continued)

Table A.1 Comparative sample of gendered AUC history in Livy (*Continued*)

Book	Female representation	Reference in Livy and other sources + uses of femina and mulier	Related male representations
	QUARTA HOSTILIA (wife of C. Calpurnius Piso; mother of Q. Fulvius Flaccus)	40.37.5-7 *Quarta Hostilia uxore* (40.37.5)	C. Calpurnius Piso, Q. Fulvius Flaccus
41	ORTHOBULA	41.25.6 *Orthobula uxore* (41.25.6)	Proxenus
45	Crowds of Roman women	45.2.7 *turba ... feminarum* (45.2.7)	Roman men

were almost invariably registered as the *privati* who had not chosen a senatorial career (e.g., scholars and lawyers), the lower magistrates (particularly tribunes), members of the lower classes, municipals, foreigners (including, with notable exceptions, their aristocracy), freedmen, slaves, and any male member of the upper classes whom the author wished to insult.[4]

If Livy applied a similar linguistic demarcation with respect to representations of individual women and female collectives, then he should be seen to inscribe this explicitly gendered differentiation in the range of statuses comported by the words *femina* and *mulier*. *Feminae* will, of course, refer to women of the upper class who appear synonymous with Roman ideals and standards of behaviour applicable to the idealised female of elite society; whereas, in keeping with the *uir/homo* binarism, *mulieres* should incorporate those individuals and/or groups who inhabit socio-political or geographical spaces regarded as exemplary of the subordinate (foreign or low-born) antithesis of representative femaleness.[5] Since *uir/homo* and *femina/mulier* are linguistically redundant terms,[6] they may be viewed as appositive epithets, used for various kinds of rhetorical emphasis: exaggeration, invective, exemplification, intensification, and so on.

Two data points suggest that Livy may have adopted the use of a gendered vocabulary to denote differences in the relative social standing and cultural (or national) tradition of women and men, but it is also clear that the historian complicated the technical simplicity of this stylistic pattern when composing episodes featuring female protagonists.[7] In Chapter 1, uses of the terms *femina* and *mulier* were identified in the surviving traces of *Ab Urbe Condita* (AUC) history: 66 items within the broader annalistic or narrative episodes treated explicitly in Tables 1.1–2 and A.1; 8 instances in relation to sacrificial notices and prodigy lists; and 53 associated references through the extant corpus.[8] However, as Table A.1 indicates, Livy did not always follow the rhetorical conventions of this socio-linguistic strategy. Indeed, while there are frequent correspondences between named women belonging to a particular stratum of Roman society or of non-Roman origins and either under Roman rule or in conflict with the Roman state, it is not always the case that Livy's narrative distinguishes his female representations according to such a rigorous, status- and ethnic-based paradigm. For example, the reader should expect that women closely associated with men belonging to the upper echelons of pre-Roman or Roman society, and whose actions are key to the resolution of social or political relations or historical crises of one kind or another would be identified as *feminae*. However, in episodes where Livy deploys this gendered terminology the expected concordance is not always evident. Named women like Lavinia and Tanaquil, as well as female collectives such as the Sabine women and the *matronae* supporting the repeal of the *lex Oppia*, are identified as *mulieres*. In these instances, it may be the case that the ethnic origins of women like the wives of Aeneas and L. Tarquinius Priscus or the brides, wives, and mothers of the founding fathers of the early city of Rome required Livy to differentiate them from idealised females of Roman society such as Sulpicia, the mother-in-law of Sp. Postumius Albinus, or the *honestae feminae* agitating for the repeal of the *lex Oppia*. However, it should also be clear that these women were instrumental to the foundation, progress, and, in certain instances, transformation of the Roman state. Similarly, the historian designated women like Cloelia, the daughter of Hannibal, and the wives of Rome's 2nd century BCE Latin allies as *feminae* in the same way as more complex female protagonists like Apega and Theoxena, wives of the Spartan tyrant Nabis and the first citizen of the Aenianes.

Consequently, the literary representations in Livy's history featuring individual women or female collectives that reflect this symbolic grammar of gendered identity display a complementary if variable linguistic field of sexual and social vocabulary. Women and men may be identified in AUC by a range of explicit, qualitative signifiers and the horizontal and vertical relationships of Roman society defined in literary contexts by insertive-receptive and status-specific designations. That said, although Livy represented women primarily in terms of filiation, marital condition, reproductive agency, and civic status, he did not always inscribe female and male identity solely with respect to relations of blood, marriage, birth, and citizenship. In certain instances where the character or actions of particular women demanded a more nuanced representation, Livy applied gendered rhetorical descriptors so as to highlight their moral, psychological, or behavioural distinctiveness as persons in situations whose resolution or complication held very particular implications for the historical trajectory of the *res Romana*.

The two-fold referential significance of gendered terminology – in helping to determine and evaluate the discursive standpoints of Livy's source material – should be evident. A second pre-supposition of this study relates to the currents of political, social, and economic power identified by the structural function of language. As Marilyn Skinner notes, any examination of late Republican and early Imperial social history will find it difficult to ignore the socio-political transformation of the Roman city-state, the radical demographic shift in the megalopolitan population, and the fundamental centrality of patronage to the reconstituted cultural experience.[9] While a late modern society like ours would more likely disseminate information regarding aspects of class, ethnicity, lifestyle, or politics in statistical or quantitative form, it has been argued that specifically sexualised or gendered discourses in the ancient Mediterranean provided "an ordered, semantic system for articulating social anxieties."[10] In this schema, problematic sociological modifications in the traditional environments of Graeco-Roman experience would have been codified in terms of a sexual *alia oratio* (allegory, or "other speech"), a species of metaphor which reflected the "proofs of status and badges of identity" most desired in times of anxiety or transition.[11] In Livy's history, this symbolic exchange of ideas is most often expressed in scenarios of normative confusion or violation, and frequently intersects with the depiction of anomalous gender roles and moral irregularities of behaviour.[12]

What this necessarily brief survey of analytical theory and interpretative method indicates is that Livy – and, if the exercise were to be extended, other historians of Classical antiquity – was deeply concerned with ancient codes of behaviour and modes of representing cultural conflicts and tensions. Similarly, a written composition like AUC was firmly embedded in highly specific sets of social relations, reinforced by small-group or collective cultural practices. No less than modern historiographical narratives, the rhetorical culture of the Graeco-Roman Mediterranean formed part of a concrete process of social exchange, class- and gender-based, and was therefore a product of historical hierarchies of value and power. From this perspective, studying Livy's representations of the social identity of women and men living under Roman rule must engage with the system of critical differences which structured the ideological framework of Roman culture, society, and state.

Distinctions of public and private

A second idea arising from study of episodes in Livy's narrative that include female representations is that Roman society blurred the distinction between domestic and public spheres. The indefinitude of *res publica* as a signifier of the state illumines the notion. For Livy (and, by implication, the weight of his audience), the dichotomy between female/domestic and male/public realms was discerned of special interest. While it is difficult to ascertain the extent to which the historian identified distinctions between the desired/idealised and behavioural/normative affective values ascribed to social and political activity, the usefulness of the intervening space as a device for explicating and reinterpreting problematic elements of the received historical and cultural tradition is beyond question. As an adjunct to this critical or reflexive quality of gendered AUC history, it is instructive to note the manner in which Livy questions or distorts specific personality types conventionally invoked as either portraying recognisable (female) traits – for instance, Tullia Minor, L. Tarquinius Superbus' high-spirited, greedy, ambitious, and violent wife; Vitellia, who exposes her sons to a conspiracy to restore the exiled Tarquins; Damarata, who urges her tyrant husband Adranodorus to retain sovereign power at whatever cost and by whatever means; Sophonisba, who prevailed on her husband Syphax to pursue the war with Rome; and Apega, who subjects Argive women to suffering and violence and steals nearly all their gold jewellery and valuable clothing – or as performing the subordinate part of illustrating (male) virtues – Hersilia, Romulus' wife and mediator between the Sabine women and their parents; Horatia, Lucretia, and Verginia, sacrificial victims whose deaths benefit the evolving Roman state; Cloelia, who liberates her fellow female hostages and is honoured with an equestrian statue on the highest part of the Summa Via; the unnamed Pandosian woman who stands between the mutilated body of Alexander, king of Epirus, and a crowd pelting it with javelins and stones and returns the bones to the king's wife; Busa, an Apulian woman who aids Roman soldiers escaping from Cannae; Claudia Quinta, singled out by Rome's most prominent *matronae* due to her chastity, assists in conveying the statue of Magna Mater into the Temple of Victory on the Palatine.

As a single instance of this element of the historian's representational strategy, episodes featuring female ritual activity offer a useful additional point of reference and illustration. For example, Livy and Obsequens speak about groups of *matronae* and *puellae* taking part in processions and singing and bringing gifts *Graecu ritu* for Ceres and Proserpina.[13] Livy also recounts a procession of 27 *uirgines* singing a hymn to the goddess.[14] So, too, in the process of representing the communal presence of men and women in what will come to be the ritual environment of Augustan Rome's festival-rich year, Livy describes the origin of the Apolline Games, ordered by the Senate on the advice of the *decemviri sacris faciundis* (board of 10 priests for over-seeing sacred matters) after the loss of Tarentum to Hannibal in 212 BCE. According to the historian, when the praetor had seen to it that the games were performed in the Circus Maximus for the sake of a victory over the Carthaginian enemy, the Roman people watched, adorned with garlands as the city's matrons held a *supplicatio* (*matronae supplicavere*), after which the whole crowd dined with open doors, outside, and the day was taken up with every sort of celebration.[15] While scholarship on Livy's reference to such a formally sanctioned religious observance conducted by elite married Roman women discounts its historical authenticity, it is clear that the histo-rian's use of technical terminology to describe a female-led public religious act conforms to his deployment of the verb *supplicare* elsewhere in AUC to describe the action taken after the *decemviri* recommend that precisely such a ritual take place.[16]

Arguing for or against women participating in the first phase of public, semi-public, or household sacrifice cannot omit[17] the handling and drinking of undiluted wine. Similar rhetorical asymmetries may be found in pertinent

Ciceronian fragments; for instance, the ideological equation between *pudicitia* and abstention.[18] Festus notes that women dedicated to religious matters also use the *simpulum*.[19] According to this item, a *simpulum* was a small utensil not unlike a *cyathus*, a ladle for dipping out wine from a mixing-bowl.[20] Apparently, it was used to make a drink offering; specifically, one in which pure wine was poured out during sacrifices.[21] The women who performed this offering were known as *simpulatrices*. These women may be compared with the category of *simulatrix* previously noted as officiating in some way over sacrificial space (Festus 232L). This definition indicates that wine and women, and by implication, women and sacrifice, were not as indissolubly separate as modern commentators argue.[22]

What Livy achieves here may be understood more broadly as indicative of the historian's rhetorical dislocation of structural symmetries (passive-active, private-public, female-male) throughout the AUC. The historian's vivid account of Tanaquil may owe much to legend but his portrait of the Etruscan queen's power and political activity can be argued to represent an historical reality – albeit one where Livy's representation is formulated in such a way that she will have been seen to exercise her social independence and civic visibility on behalf of her family.[23] Nonetheless, as Livy records, "like most Etruscans, Tanaquil was a woman skilled in interpreting celestial prodigies."[24] If Livy's implication is historically accurate and Etruscan women were as active in and talented at practices like divination as Etruscan men were reputed to be, then he may provide proof of official Etruscan female religious activity.[25] In a similar fashion, Livy's account of the Bacchanalian conspiracy reinforces the epigraphic evidence of the *Senatus consultum de Bacchanalibus* which demonstrates that the cult of Dionysus was a mixed-gender organisation and may have been the only such group in which both men and women occupied the same leadership positions.[26]

Returning to his formulation of Rome's history, Livy's description of Rome's ritual obligations incorporates the heterodox nature of Roman religious practice, the distinctive spaces where the city dedicated gifts to the gods, and the variable hierarchies of gender, class, and race participating legitimately in these cultural activities. In relation to these interdependent categories of representation, it is sufficient to note that Livy registers essentially elite (*dedicatio*), popular (*celebratio*), and mixed (*sacrificium*) sacral experiences, conducted in diverse though neighbouring urban localities. These comprise a less hierarchical complexity of citizen- and non-citizen-populations than is normally understood.

It is usually argued that status, space, and the *mos maiorum* define the limits of male and female participation in Roman civic rituals. According to Ariadne Staples, religious observances marked the *only* public space where women played a "significant formal role."[27] John Scheid is somewhat more prescriptive: "[Roman women] were, to be sure, excluded from the celebration of the most important rites ... in religion, which was always related to the expression of community power, men played the leading role in every situation."[28] Of course, if one defines a fixed action as paradigmatic to any understanding of shared physical or symbolic space, then the boundaries within which women could operate will be narrow indeed. However, a performative act does not of its nature require official sanction in the sense of "presiding over" or "supervising" a ritual occasion; nor is a participant necessarily a privileged member of the celebrating community. For instance, allocating discrete activities like "killing," "consecrating," or "presenting" to the concept of performing a religious ceremony (*sacrum facere*) immediately restricts the ownership of agency to a select core of male presiding figures: magistrates and priests. But as we have just seen, performing a ceremony like the Roman sacrifice comprises a four-fold series of interdependent ritual elements operating within a common civic context. Certainly, women could not generally sacrifice – that is, fell the victim, butcher it, and open the corpse for the purpose of *extispicium* – on behalf of the whole community. However, by definition, this understanding of sacrifice equally excludes from direct involvement the majority of the citizen-male population. It seems prescriptive to characterise a civic act of homage, thanks offering or contractual ritual obligation in terms which automatically excluded the wider community by which and for whom the deed was done. Such a standpoint equates legitimate male capacity to officiate liturgically in the context of *forum* or *atrium* with a general female incapacity to represent others customarily or otherwise in any context. Yet oftentimes this is exactly what happens by implication or intention to the category of female in the sources and description of many ancient cultic practices.[29]

Alternatively, conceptualising Roman ritual as a systemic process allows for the necessary complexity of involvements underpinning cults and practices in a diverse suburban community. In this context, a female presence may be discerned far more readily. For example, men and women are known to have participated in the lustral processions leading the victims to the altar. The "Salian virgins" participated in processions, witnessing to the seasonal limits of state military action.[30] Similarly, women of diverse statuses ritually displayed their cohesion and expressed spatial control in celebrating the cults of the Matronalia (March 1) and Fortuna Muliebris (July 6). The Matronalia's honoured deity Juno features relatively prominently within the narrative of Book 5 of the AUC history.[31] Livy records that Juno's statue (and hence the goddess) was brought into Rome from the neighbouring city of Veii and established on the Aventine; and it was her sacred geese which alerted the Roman sentinels to the Gallic invasion, leading to her epithet *Moneta*, the one who warns. Like the Salian priesthood, the cult of Fortuna Muliebris (July 6) associated women with civic life and the security of the city. Livy's relatively expansive etiological narrative offers a fascinating window into the construction and interpretation of women's priestly service during the republican period. As we have seen, Livian tradition locates the foundation of the cult of Fortuna Muliebris to the year 488 BCE, when Rome's *matronae* persuaded the wife and mother of the disgraced general Coriolanus, who led a Volscian army against Rome, to join in an embassy to the enemy camp outside the walls of the city.[32] This *ingens mulierum agmen* were determined, according to Livy, "that since the arms of men could not defend the city, the women should defend it with their prayers and tears."[33] Livy recounts how this female collective broke through Coriolanus' resolution – Veturia's inflamed speech, the embraces of his wife and children, and the tears of the entire company of women – resulting in the general's withdrawal of the Volscians and personal exile far from the limits of Rome's territory and the construction and dedication of a temple to Fortuna Muliebris.[34] What goes unstated in Livy's account is that the Senate permitted Valeria, the woman who Dionysius of Halicarnassus claims had instigated the embassy, to serve as the cult of Fortuna Muliebris' first priestess, and who commemorated the first anniversary of what came to be a renowned and celebrated event in the history of Rome with a sacrifice on behalf of the people.[35] Importantly, despite Livy's failure to mention Valeria's role in the subsequent history of the cult of Fortuna Muliebris, his representation of the *agmen* of wives, mothers, and female citizens demonstrated the fundamental interest that *matronae* possessed in the security and success of Rome and that they were capable of ritually and politically significant action.

Similarly, the Vestals are regularly associated with the preparation of sacrificial ingredients like *mola salsa*.[36] Apart from the Vestals' indirect ubiquity in every public *immolatio*, and their participation in the sacrifices honouring Tellus (April 15), Bona Dea (May 1 and December 3), Consus (August 21), and perhaps Ops Consiva (August 25), other women known to have participated directly or otherwise in the stages of ritual sacrifice include the *flaminica Dialis* and the *regina sacrorum*, the *Saliae uirgines*, and the *matronae* (especially *uniuirae*) belonging to the cults of Juno Regina, Fortuna Muliebris, Pudicitia Plebeia, Carmenta and Rumina, and Bona Dea.[37] In these contexts, one should also mention the extraordinarily vivid triple supplication of imperial, Vestal, and matronal *sellisternes* following the Severan Secular Games of 204 CE.[38] In this regard, Livy's citation of "crowds of women ... seen praying and offering sacrifice" in the forum and on the Capitol during the Hannibalic War (212 BCE) seems to associate such activity with a broader disruption of specifically Roman forms of worship.[39] However, the senatorial decree issued to deal with various manifestations of *superstitio* in the city, of which female sacrificial activity is one instance, prescribed that "nobody henceforward should offer sacrifice according to foreign or unfamiliar rites in any public or consecrated place."[40] It may be argued that Livy's concern is not so much with men and women taking part in offering public or, for that matter, private sacrifices; rather, that the acts occur in the context of unaccustomed rites. In other words, what the annalist sees as operating transformatively on traditional ideological constructs of divinity and humankind appears to be associated with the influx of foreign cult practices into public sacral space, not women's public or private role in prayer and sacrificial ritual.[41]

Reading Livy's accounts of women participating in roles traditionally performed by men in civic spaces shows how important it is to connect interpretations of the actions taken – in this case, ritual as repetitive activity expressing and reinforcing societal values – with the heterogeneous nature of Roman society. In regard to the representation of women acting with impunity in contexts involving public sacrifice – the Apolline Games, the Matronalia, the aftermath of the battle at Cannae during the Hannibalic War – not to mention with expertise and authority in private or sequestered locations – Tanaquil's skill in the interpretation of prodigies, the priestesses of the 2nd century BCE Dionysian cult – it is still possible to see Roman festival rituals as maintaining traditional divisions of citizen status, gender, age, and office, and thereby reasserting traditional social orders. Equally true, however, they incorporate non-hierarchical, status inclusive, mixed gender experiences, and consequently promote a sense of shared identity among Roman and non-Roman affiliations.[42] As Peter Dorcey argues, "to study only the public aspect of Roman religion is to misunderstand the entirety of the pagan experience."[43]

To recognise in AUC history a particular cultural activity in Roman society as interdependent and reciprocal in nature and practice – and, importantly, understood to apply restrictions in relation to the acquittal in public or private contexts of particular roles dependent on gender and status – addresses and confirms the socio-scientific distinction between informal power and legitimate authority. As MacDonald notes, it is important to understand the significance of women's activities with a view to "the substantial amount of informal influence and power exercised by women in a variety of social contexts."[44] In other words, authority is an official quantity or category, encompassing the capacity to sanction and ensure the performance of certain acts; whereas power may be conferred as an adjunct to the exercise of authority, or exist in its own right, in which case it represents the recognition and operation of informal influence over others. Dubisch goes further, suggesting that "not only may [power and authority] both be effective (and illegitimate power may be even more effective than legitimate power, since the way it is used is less circumscribed by social rules), but also they may be both culturally recognized."[45] Such an apparent theoretical dichotomy neatly juxtaposes the historical submission of men and women to authority structures exercising power, in this instance, over Rome's festival and cult institutions, against the radical possibilities of informal male and female involvement as represented by Livy in the working and experiences of these civic entities.[46] On the one hand, then, it is usual to find the fathers of families, male leaders of social groups, male officials of the city, and male sacerdotal functionaries, wielding authority in references to Republican and Augustan religious organisations. Less identifiable in secondary historical commentary is an appreciation of the variety of manifestations of non-standard male and female power, linked to the considerable weight of epigraphic evidence and literary citations. In addition to the evidence provided by votive offerings and dedicatory inscriptions, it is clear that textual references in Livy speak to the prominence of men and women in mediating the human and divine elements of public religious life as priestesses, quasi-sacerdotal officials, or prophetesses. Once- and remarried wives, unmarried and divorced women, widows, including the often idealised *univirae*, and prostitutes may be seen to participate widely in the exercise and assignation of agreed ceremonial roles. In addition, there is ample evidence of the interest many women took in the cosmopolitan diversity of Roman and non-Roman belief systems, whether or not they may have adhered to accepted and acceptable customary practice.

Conjunctions of literature and history

Livy's use of a variety of rhetorical instruments in his depiction of female engagement in the process of historical change helps the modern student to clarify the intent and value of Roman historiography. The degree to which Livy distorted, elaborated, and transformed the traditional record in episodes featuring mythological, legendary, and historical female protagonists – from Egeria's insertion as divine adviser of Numa to Hispala Faecenia's role in the suppression of the Bacchanalian conspiracy – is evident. Going beyond text and context in order to identify the conjunction between literature and history, it has become clear that emphasis on a defined link between turning points in *res Romana* and an exploitation of the category of "woman" as narrative device is deliberate, and represents an intentionally revisionist treatment of the annalistic imagination. While it was an historiographical convention to claim that one's work surpassed that of one's precursors, the incorporation of a gendered component to his composition may be viewed as radical, and acts to confirm Livy's design to supersede the annalists. The female in AUC history is a part of the author's project to extend, refine, and elaborate a received, invented, yet incomplete historical and socio-political tradition.[47]

In addition to the incidents in AUC that have been previously examined, a category of female representation reflecting Livy's gendered historiographical approach relates to his accounts of poisoning in Rome and the wider Mediterranean. The earliest known incidents of alleged mass poisoning in AUC history occurred at times when Rome suffered severe epidemics. According to Livy,[48] in 331 BCE the leading men of the Roman state were falling ill and in almost every case died as a result. As we have seen in relation to other episodes – where a woman, usually young and often from a non-elite stratum of Roman society, acts in a way that precipitates an official response from sanctioned state authority, and sometimes wider legislative or civic action resulting in longer-term social transformation – a female slave (*ancilla*, euphemistically translated into English in many editions of AUC history as "maid servant") reveals to one of Rome's curule aediles, Q. Fabius Maximus, and then to the senate that certain *matronae* were compounding poisonous drugs. Cornelia and Sergia, 2 of 20 elite Roman women discovered in possession of, or in the process of concocting, poisons, claimed that the drugs were medicinal preparations. When confronted, both women consult with their fellow *matronae*, all of whom had been brought into the Forum after their houses were seized; after taking counsel together, they all consented to drink their concoctions, whereupon they fell victim to the poison's effects. While we must assume that all 20 women died, as Livy leaves confirmation of their demise unstated, this did not mark the end of the episode. The slaves of the seized households were subsequently arrested and denounced a large number of other *matronae* as guilty of the same offence, out of whom 170 were found guilty. Livy's final observation is instructive: "The whole incident was regarded as a portent and thought to be an act of madness rather than deliberate wickedness."[49]

The historian's assessment of the motivation underlying the criminal practices of 170 (or 190 if we include the original 20 *matronae* implicated in the *ancilla*'s testimony) – insanity rather than felonious intent – reinforces his practice of including episodes to evoke the psychological climate in Rome. Barely half a century after the Gallic sack in 390 BCE, following which ensued decades of conflict with neighbouring states, periods of interregnum, and the intermittent impact of fire, flood, and disease, it is likely that many innocent citizens were wrongly condemned at this early stage in the 4th century BCE, when superstition was rife in Rome and scapegoats were sought. As we learn from the historical narrative immediately preceding the episode, the Aurunci, at war with the Sidicini, appealed to Rome, deserted their *oppidum* (then destroyed by the Aurunci), and fortified their most important settlement, Suessa Aurunca. Rome did not send an army to support the Aurunci, instead dispatching a military force to engage the Ausones of Cales, now allied with the Sidicini. Cales was besieged, captured, and colonised, but the Sidicini remained unsubjugated. Finally, while a census was conducted and Acerrae incorporated as a *civitas sine suffragio*, rumours of Samnite unrest and a Gallic War lead to the appointment of a Dictator and Master of Horse. While it has been argued that the *matronae* acted as they did in order to provoke a rupture in elite society, leading to a revision of the city's patriarchal order, it seems more likely that Livy sought to use the episode as a way of reinforcing the fragile nature of the Roman state, expressed through exemplary narrative contingent on a reported historical incident.[50] When the social, political, and moral perturbations stirred up in the wake of the incident achieve resolution and explanation, Livy follows the pattern of historical development adopted whenever the role of women has proven crucial to the rhetorical construction of *res Romana*. Thus, after accomplices of the *matronae* informed on those participating in the production of deadly potions, leading to the conviction of 170 (or 190) in total, Rome goes to war against the Volscian town of Privernum. Rome is victorious, Privernum capitulates, and the town is granted Roman citizenship. The creeping progress of the Roman state, momentarily under threat from within as well as without, continues its inexorable forward march.

It would appear that there was considerable anecdotal material in support of female participation in *veneficium* as applied to the crime of poisoning.[51] Livy notes in passing extensive investigations of poisoning by women and men consequent to the introduction of the worship of Bacchus in 186 BCE and again between 184 and 179 BCE.[52] In 184 BCE, the praetor Q. Naevius condemned 2000 people for poisoning; in 180 BCE, C. Maenius condemned a further 3000; and further *quaestiones*, for which no conviction totals are given, occurred in 180 and 179 BCE.[53] Finally, there is reference in one of the later summaries to an investigation of poisonings in 154 BCE, leading to accusations that two elite patrician women, Publilia and Licinia, murdered their husbands and were executed by a decision of their relatives.[54] As already noted, such incidents frequently coincided in Livy's narrative with crises such as wars and epidemics; and the historian's representation of these events will almost certainly have been coloured by the view prevalent from the late 1st century BCE on that certain persons (mostly women) dispensed poison. Cicero (*Clu.* 26–27) records the extraordinary case of Aulus Cluentius Habitus whose stepfather Statius Albius (or Abbius) Oppianicus was required to murder his three sons by Sassia before she would consent to marry him. In his account of the year 19 CE, Tacitus (*Ann.* 2.19) tells us of the death by suspected *ueneficium* of Germanicus, son of Nero Drusus, the emperor Tiberius' step-brother, accomplished (it would seem) by a certain Martina, a woman infamous for poisonings in the province of Syria (*infamem ueneficiis ea in provincia*).[55]

Aligned to the historiographical paradigm we have traced throughout this volume, then, whether or not supported by documentary or anecdotal testimony, Livy incorporated the association of women and poison into his account of incidents reflecting Roman society's politico-military and psychological insecurity in the face of authentic or perceived attack from unprecedented aggressive threats from neighbouring states or as a result of infectious disease. Such a rhetorical strategy, designed to portray the human face of momentous experiences which marked the oscillation of the Roman state as it negotiated the peaks and troughs of mid-republican historical circumstance, may also be discerned in Livy's accounts of Vestal Virgins accused and convicted of unchastity. When domestic conflict between patricians and plebeians distracted from the greater threat of war with Veii and the Volscians, for instance, Livy records that the Vestal Oppia was charged and found guilty of *incastitas*, in response we are told to the pronouncement of soothsayers that sacred functions had been profaned.[56] In similar fashion, as domestic strife ensued between plebeian tribunes and *interreges* and, again, drove patricians against plebeians, the Vestal Postumia was accused – wrongly, it transpired – of unchastity and acquitted.[57] During the final tense negotiations leading to the settlement after the Latin War (340–339 BCE) that provided Rome with a secure system of incorporated states and subject allies, Minucia was accused in 337 BCE of unchastity on the evidence of a slave, tried and found guilty by the college of *pontifices*, and buried alive in the Campus Sceleratus ("the accursed field").[58] In a more positive turn, over a period of 3 years (275–273 BCE), the consul Curius Dentatus defeated Pyrrhus, expelling him from Italy; the state was declared ritually cleansed after a *lustrum*; and a treaty of friendship concluded with Ptolemy II Philadelphus of Egypt. In the wake of these events, Sextilia was condemned for adultery and buried alive.[59] Likewise, in 237 BCE, while the *pontifex maximus* L. Caecilius Metellus may have saved the *sacra* from a fire in the Temple of Vesta, and Faliscan, Sardinian and Corsican revolts were suppressed, nonetheless Tuccia was condemned for adultery.[60]

It is hard not to recognise in this catalogue of inclemency towards allegations of Vestal intemperance marking the rejection of their sacred vow of chastity – an action considered to have a direct and pivotal bearing on the health of the Roman state – a representation qualitatively commensurate to that of female poisoners of the degree to which the continuance and security of Rome relied on the actions of women, in this instance, correct and unwavering observance of sexual abstinence by priestesses of the goddess Vesta. What is interesting, however, is that Livy's narrative subsequent to the deaths of these named Vestals fails occasionally to provide his readers with clarity in relation to the impact of state-sanctioned violence against the bodies of those convicted and put to death for the crime of unchastity or with respect to the sole priestess criminalised without legitimate grounds. According to the conventional historical ledger balancing just retribution against treasonous action, the readers of AUC history should expect favourable consequences arising from the condemnation and execution (or exoneration) of the named Vestal Virgins. Assuredly, certain episodes provide entirely expected results: Minucia's burial while living is recorded just prior to Rome establishing the first Latin colony after the Latin settlement of 338 BCE; Rome subdued Tarentum immediately after Sextilia was buried alive; and, in triumphant succession, following Tuccia's condemnation war was declared against the Illyrians, who were defeated and surrender, and the Roman people and Latin allies crossed the Po for the first time to defeat an invading Gallic army. However, not all incidents have the desired outcome: civic dissension escalated and the Veientine and Aequo-Volscian wars began after Oppia's death; and, while a slave plot to set fire to the city was foiled in the wake of Postumia's acquittal, the renewal of hostilities with Aequi was also mooted.

What these brief case studies of Livy's approach to his representation of female poisoners and Vestal Virgins accused of unchastity reflect does not only bear on the many and varied conjunctions between literature and history: they are crucial to our understanding of his wider rhetorical strategy regarding the inclusion of women in his historical narrative – and, indeed, his larger historiographical project. In many ways, we must return to Livy's personal historical context and what we may infer about his contemporary socio-cultural experiences. While modern historians of the Augustan Age have traditionally praised its political and cultural achievements, whenever one reads the account of the younger Octavianus in the history of Cassius Dio or the biography of Suetonius, it is difficult not to mark the extremes of violence and hostility directed towards Rome's established order. Moreover, whether one examines Appian's history of Rome's civil wars, the moralising tales of Valerius Maximus, or Cassius Dio's extensive coverage of events, it is impossible to avoid the conclusion that the triumviral period was remembered as a traumatic series of events.[61] Given Livy's knowledge and understanding of the final decades of the 1st century BCE – grounded in archival research, anecdotal reports, his family's experiences in northern Italy, and his own life journey, personal encounters, and eyewitness observations – his representation of historical events will almost certainly have been coloured to some extent by what can only be described as the deeply distressing or disturbing events of Roman history in the decades prior to and during the early years of Livy's composition of AUC. It is, I would argue, because of these profound personal experiences, shared as a nation that we may locate something of a rationale underlying Livy's deployment of women at certain moments of historical disturbance, disorder, or suffering. In regard to the present incidents under review, the historian's accounts of mass poisonings in the 3rd and 2nd centuries BCE reflect an underlying breakdown of peaceful and law-abiding public behaviour, and so may reasonably be explained by recourse to the conception of the female as cognitively and behaviourally different, subject to inconsistent, unpredictable, and emotional action. However, moments placing extraordinary strain on the very fabric of Roman society, like the shattering of the existential bond between the ongoing security of the state and the chastity of the priestesses of Vesta, could not always be accommodated by recourse to the rhetorical pattern of historical continuity adopted to memorialise Rome's teleology of progress and prosperity as it approached the golden age of Augustan rule.

Conclusion

The *res populi Romani* of T. Livius' AUC is a literary and social document remunerative of close study. In structural terms, evidence examined in this volume adduces a link between significant individual or collective female interventions and episodes involving crisis or revolution.[62] The historian locates these incidents throughout AUC history: from Helen of Sparta as the mythological link between Greek and Roman epic and the founding of Rome to Lucretia as the catalyst for the expulsion of the Etruscan kings; from Vitellia, Cloelia, and Veturia at the beginning of the Republic to the recognition of Juno Regina, Roman *matronae*, and the Vestal Virgins as central to the religious identity and customary tradition of the city after the sack of Rome by the Gauls and the rebuilding of the city; from the tale of the Fabiae Ambusti marking Rome's second foundation and the political evolution of the constitution to Verginia's creation of the cult of Pudicitia Plebeia as Roman power in Italy continued to expand; and, between the scant fragmentary references to accusations of Vestal unchastity in the lost books of Pentads III and IV and tantalising glimpses of women better known from other historical, documentary, and epigraphic sources in the epitomies of Books 46–142, we read about the exploits of a heterogeneous group of Roman, Latin, and other non-Roman women during the period of the Macedonian and Eastern Wars, not least the events depicting crowds of women agitating for the repeal of the *lex Oppia* and the suppression of the Bacchanalia. What is remarkable about Livy's narrative of the incidents featuring these women is the relational and mutable nature of his representations of female identity. While it is clear that Livy deploys women as partial elaboration of his declamation concerning the edifying use of *exempla*, the fact that he portrays individual or collective female action across a multitude of crucial historical contexts renders their identity fluid and subject to change. In much the same way as Livy seeks to chart the interdependent events that comprised a lasting record of the evolving *res Romana*, so his formulations of how women's actions, ideas, personalities, and roles impinge on, precipitate, complicate or resolve moments in AUC history emulate broader cultural discourse where identities are socially mediated and performed through embodiment and action.[63] Strategic and positional, the identities of Livy's women can by turns be hybrid or multiple and the intersection between different types of identities – female and male – enriches the literary and historical monument he seeks to create. In this regard, if Livy coopted his representations of female identity as constructs through which the protagonists (and readers) of his narrative perceived themselves, and others saw them, namely, as belonging to certain groups and not to others, then the Roman and non-Roman women Livy incorporated into the AUC must, of necessity, be seen to actively engage in the fabric of memorialised historical accounts – and, as such, their identity – fictive, historical, or a composite thereof – should not be understood as a static quantum, but rather, like history itself, a continual (and continuing) process.

It is in this sense that Livy depicts women as playing a role in the resolution to critical situations which threaten Roman society. Whether uniting private household and state or setting in motion significant re-orderings of the *res publica*, Livy's vignettes of individual women – like Hersilia, mediator between the Sabine women and their parents, or Vestia Oppia, who sacrifices every day during the siege of Capua for the safety and victory of the Roman people – and female collectives – from the *matronae* who contributed toward the necessities of the commonwealth to assist the government in discharging its responsibility in the fight against the Etruscans or when the ransom was being raised to buy off the Gauls to the crowds of prominent married women receiving the cult statue of the Magna Mater at the height of the Hannibalic War – are more frequently than recognised something other than passive caricatures of the ideal or non-normative female stereotype commonly associated with classical historical literature. Just as society should be viewed as something that cannot exist independently of the people of whom it is comprised, so too it is through the actions and practices of the women Livy represents at key points in the historical narrative of the city that Roman society is constituted and sustains its forward progress. In other words, through his depictions of female agency, and the engagement of women – like Rhea Silvia and Larentia, Lucretia and Verginia, and Hispala Faecenia and Sulpicia – with Rome's social and institutional structures, that aspects of the world of AUC history – such as the foundational acts leading to the creation of the city, the establishment of the *res publica* and the ratification of the Valerio-Horation legislation, and the suppression of the cult of Dionysus – were transformed.

Within this model of Roman history, and particularly with respect to those events where women's roles prove pivotal, Livy portrays the structuring principles of social institutions inextricably bound to the interactions of women and men – codes of personal behaviour and civic conduct; family and gender relations; legal regulations, religious practices – as both the medium and outcome of their reproduction through female action. Importantly, in these scenarios women should not be categorised either as entirely free agents or helpless, passive individuals, or groups. Although it is true that the actions of these women can be constrained by other individuals or larger institutional entities – on many occasions fathers, sons, brothers, husbands, and lovers; or the political, military, legal, or religious structures of patriarchal society – Livy demonstrates that they have varying degrees of knowledge about how their society functions and they may use that knowledge in order to achieve personal or communal goals. While it will have been impossible for any ancient writer to deconstruct or reformulate the constraints of gender, sexuality, ethnicity, religion, or class which permeated all social and cultural relations in the classical Mediterranean world, nonetheless Livy's representations of women afforded him opportunities to reinterpret, problematise, and negotiate the form and function of his monumental history of Rome from its foundation.

Notes

1 Robbins (1995: 76).
2 For a schematisation of the Roman insertive-receptive sexual vocabulary, see Williams (1999: 161–162, with 326n.4).
3 See especially l'Hoir (1992) and Viden (1993).
4 The late Republican category of the "new man" (*nouus homo*) is perhaps the most concrete instance of this phenomenon. On the one hand, individuals like M. Porcius Cato, C. Marius, or Cicero rose from outside the senate to the consulship; on the other, each measured the terms of his advancement as part of a self-fashioning regime *per se cognitus* ("known through himself"). In contrast to the *nobilitas* of the "known" men, *noui homines* were required to justify their origins and defend the pattern of their career. Demonstrable moral excellence (*uirtus*) and hard work (*industria*) were insufficient; patronage or circumstances determined the registration of a new man's achievement. In these respects, the socio-linguistic resonances of the *uir*(nobilis)/(novus)*homo*

dichotomy stand confirmed. For a particularly apt expression of the rhetorical slipperiness of these denominations, consider Cicero's attack on the lineage and achievements of the son (?) of one of Sulla's "new" senators, the infamous C. Verres, in 2 *Verr.* 5.180.

5   For references supporting the *feminal mulier* distinction, see L'Hoir (1992: Chapter 2). It should be noted that, while L'Hoir's (1992: 77) socio-linguistic approach to the analysis of female figures in Roman literature is a useful heuristic tool, her characterisation of Livy's representations of women – "[Livy's] female characters are shadowy impersonations of womanhood, subordinated to the males who are themselves ancillary to the virtues and vices that form the woof on the loom of Roman history" – does not accord with the evidence underlying the overarching thesis of the present volume.

6   Sexual distinctions can be expressed in Latin (and Greek, for that matter) by substantives (demonstrative and relative pronouns).

7   L'Hoir (1992: 77–78).

8   For a detailed list of references, see Section 1 of Chapter 1 (n.46).

9   Skinner (1998: 4–5).

10 Skinner (1998: 5).

11 For a discussion of sexualized allegory following these principles, see Warner (1985).

12 Cognate parallels to this formulation would seem to obtain in referential and sociological fields. For useful introductory remarks on the relationship between social anxieties in ancient Rome and the genres of political invective and erotic love elegy, see Skinner (2004: 19, 217–218, 221–226, 240–241).

13 Liv. 27.11.1-16; 27.37.4-15; Obsequens 34, 36, 43, 46, 53. On the public women's cult of Ceres at Rome and the post-midsummer festival called *sacrum Anniversarium Cereris* (cf. Cic. *Leg.* 2.21, 36), see Spaeth (1996: 12, 13, 105–107) and Fantham (1998: 393n.). In this regard, Fantham (ead., and 2002: 39–40) emphasises that "the only references to contemporary ritual acts [relating to the cult of Ceres] are to *Greek* practices" (italics included); cf. Ov. *Fast.* 4.493, 535–536, 547–548; Cic. *Verr.* 2.4.114-5, *Balb.* 55; Festus 86L. The presence of *sacerdotes publicae* from Magna Graecia and the performance of *sacra Graeca* do not preclude the participation of Roman women in cult and festival action.

14 Liv. 27.37 (207 BCE). Cf. Phlegon of Tralles, *On Wonders* 10.16-18 (133, 125, or 83 BCE). This procession moves from the temple of Apollo, through the *porta Carmenta*, to the *forum Romanum*; and then by way of the *uicus Tuscus* and the *Velabrum*, through the *forum Boarium*, to the temple of Juno Regina on the Aventine. Consider, too, Tibullus's evocation of the Ambarvalia ceremony (*El.* 2.1.1-26), Ovid's 'eyewitness' account of the Robigalia festival (*Fast.* 4.905-941), Lucretius's description of a procession in honour of Cybele (2.594-601, 606–614, 618–632) and Apuleius's account of asinine Lucius's initiation into the cult of Isis (*Met.* 11.7, 9–11, 16, 17, 22–24). Add to these instances the plethora of wedding, funeral, triumphal, and racing day processions in which women took part as bridesmaids, mourners, observers, or in some other capacity, and perceived structural limits to their participation in this aspect of community life diminish accordingly; contra Beard et al (1998: 296–300).

15 Liv. 25.12.14-15; cf. Macrob. *Sat.* 1.17.27-28.

16 Schultz (1995: 30–33).

17 As does de Casanove (1987: 159).

18 Cic. *Rep.* 4.6: *carent temeto mulieres.*

19 Festus 455L: *et mulieres rebus diuinis deditae.*

20 Festus 455L: *uas paruulum non dissimile cyatho.*

21 Festus 455L: *quo uinum in sacrificiis libabatur.*
22 de Casanove (1987); Scheid (1992: 380 with n.11), relying on de Casanove; Beard et al (1998: 297 with n.157), citing de Casanove and Scheid.
23 Glinister (1997). According to Plutarch (*Quaest. Rom.* 30) and Pliny (*HN* 8.194), Tanaquil was famed for her wool working, the traditional occupation of the virtuous and dedicated *matrona.*
24 Liv. 1.34.9: *Tanaquil perita ut vulgo Etrusci caelestium prodigiorum mulier.*
25 According to Lundeen (2006: 36), "Tanaquil ... is the only Etruscan woman recorded as performing such a religious act and she does so in private, not public settings." In this respect, if such a role as the Etruscan priestess existed, she is not to be found in the literary record. Cf. Rallo (1989); and, for the archaeological and epigraphic evidence, see Bonfante (1981), Nielsen (1998). See also Cornell (1995) and Haynes (2000: xvi–xviii, and *passim*) for discussion about the historical accuracy of ancient texts when compared with archaeological findings.
26 Liv. 39.8-19; *CIL* I².581 = *CIL Imagines* 392 = *ILLRP* 511 (Tirolo): *sacerdos nequis vir eset; magister neque vir neque mulier quisquam eset* (l. 10).
27 Staples (1998: 3). I would extend Staples' useful analytic view of Roman polytheism as a complex network of cults and rituals conferring meaning on each other to the related categories of gender- and status-hierarchies. In particular, Staples finds strategies mediating sexually defined ideological boundaries in such areas as the ostensibly female-only spaces of Bona Dea, the feminised practices and practitioners of Mater Magna, the counter-intuitive valuations of normatively polarised female categories of *matrona* and *meretrix* in the worship of Ceres and Flora, and the non-sexualised associations of the multitude of Venuses. I suggest that similar participatory strategies – blurring the extent of and coincidentally permitting status-inclusive, male and female ritual participations – may be identified across a broad spectrum of Roman cult practices.
28 Scheid (1992: 377, 379).
29 Scheid (1995) characterises "women's unfitness for sacrifice" as integral to any understanding of organized religious practice in public, private, or semi-public, and household Roman community life. Female performative incapacity, according to Scheid, hinges on a threefold prohibition excluding women from the most important elements of Roman ritual; that is, preparation of flour, the slaughter, skinning, and butchery of animals, and drinking undiluted wine. It is interesting to note that Scheid (1992: 405) concludes his detailed study with the codicil that "it is purely for reasons of convenience that I separate religious behaviour from other social practices." However, by classifying "different sources of community practice" in this way, Scheid's attempt to access "a global view of women's roles" not so much "bridge[s] the gap between theory and practice, between rule and custom,'" as conspires with "the general representation of the female sex" implicit in the ancient discourse on female religious roles. For Scheid (1992: 408), then, finding that "[e]ven for women the religious paradigm was male" is a foregone conclusion, participating in and corroborating "the totalising representations of the [ancient Roman] city and its component parts" formulated by the masculinist uses of cult.[29] Consider, in the same light, this assessment of gender as a factor in the organization of cult in Beard et al (1998: 297): "[A]lthough the attendance of women at most religious occasions (including *ludi*) was not prohibited, they had little opportunity to take any active religious role in state cults." To simply be present within the confines of cultic space was, it would seem, a self-evidently passive state; only by doing something specific could one overcome this marginal mode of existence. Once again, exclusion from the central defining ritual of civic religious activity is represented in neuter-male terms; in this case, from the standpoint of those included in officiating roles.

30 Festus 439L = Cinc. Alim. fr. xxx Peter; cf. Virg. *Aen.* 8.663-6: *hic exsultantis Salios nudosque Lupercos/lanigerosque apices et lapsa ancilia caelo/extuderat, castae ducebant sacra per urbem/pilentis matres in mollibus.* Here, Virgil inscribes on the shield bearing Italy's history the extraordinary collocation of leaping Salii, naked Luperci and chaste mothers participating in a procession of the *sacra* through the city of Rome.

31 Liv. 5.21-22; 47.1-6.

32 Liv. 2.40. See Section 3 of Chapter 2 for a discussion of this episode.

33 Liv. 2.40.2: *quoniam armis viri defencere urbem non possent mulieres precibus lacrimissique defenderent.*

34 Liv. 2.40.9-12.

35 Dion. Hall, *Ant. Rom.* 8.55.4.

36 Serv. *Ecl.* 8.82.

37 Flaminica Dialis and regina sacrorum: Macrob. *Sat.* 1.16.30, 1.15.18. Saliae virgines: Festus 439L. Juno Regina: Tac. *Ann.* 15.44. Fortuna Muliebris: Liv. 2.39; Dion. Hal. *Ant. Rom.* 8.22-62; Plut. *Coriol.* 37.4; Val. Max. 5.2.1. Pudicitia Plebeia: Liv. 10.23.3-10. Carmenta and Rumina: Plut. *Quaest. Rom.* 56, 57. Bona Dea: Juv. *Sat.* 2.86; Macrob. *Sat.* 1.12.23; Cic. *Leg.* 2.9.21. For an intriguing reference to public contestation over female participation in official ritual actions, see Cic. *Dom.* 136. Here, a certain Licinia – a Vestal, daughter of C. Licinius Crassus (trib. 145 BCE), granddaughter of C. Licinius Crassus (cos. 168 BCE; see RE 13. 497 {181}) – dedicates an *ara, aedicula* and *puluinar* – in the location (*sub Saxo*) corresponding to Ovid's reference to the temple of Bona Dea (*Fast.* 5.150), in a *loco publico* rejected as invalid both by *pontifices* and the Senate; see further, Herbert-Brown (1994: 138).

38 *CIL* 6.32329; *NSc* 1931, 313–345. Recorded in Pighi (1965: 155ff).

39 Liv. 25.1.7: *mulierum turba erat nec sacrificantium nect perecantium deos patrio more.*

40 Liv. 27.1.12: *neu quis in publico sacrove loco novo aut externo ritu sacrificaret.*

41 For a discussion of salient examples in the *inscriptiones sacrae* found in or near Rome (*CIL* 6.1-871) of male and female dedication to particular deities, abstract or otherwise, by free, freed, and slave men and women with or without explicit collegial or cult status, see Keegan (2014: Chapter 5).

42 Contra Beard and Crawford (1985: 35–36): "Although proof is impossible ... the vast majority of such (private and family) cults essentially represented the state cult on a smaller scale – practised within the smaller social unit of the family."

43 Dorcey (1992: 3).

44 MacDonald (1996: 41), in a section of the introduction to her study of the lives of early Christian women in the Graeco-Roman world entitled "A social-scientific concept of power" (1996: 1–46, esp. 41ff), referring to Michelle Zimbalist Rosaldo's ground-breaking article "Women, Culture, and Society: A Theoretical Overview," in Rosaldo and Lamphere (1974: esp. 21).

45 Dubisch (1986: 17–18).

46 For a survey of the rhetorical representations of female power and influence in Tacitus and Cassius Dio, see Keegan (2005).

47 While this view of Livy's historical writing may conform in certain respects to what Forsythe (1999: 7) refers to as "the literary school" of Livian historiography, it should be clear that much which has been examined in this volume rejects what he characterizes as the limitations of "mechanical and subjective source criticism" in favour of a more nuanced examination of Livy's historical method and judgement as they apply to his representation of women in AUC history.

48 Liv. 8.18.4-9; cf. Val. Max. 2.5.3; August. *De civitate Dei* 3.17.

49 Liv. 8.18.11: *prodigii ea res loco habita captisque magis mentibus quam cons-celeratis similis uisa.*

50 Hermann (1964); cf. Bauman (1974), (1992: 13–15).

51 Cilliers and Retief (2000: 96).

52 Liv. 39.8.2, 7 (under the jurisdiction of the consuls Sp. Postumius Albinus and Q. Marcius Philippus): "to both consuls the investigation of secret conspiracies were decreed. ... likewise, poisonings and secret murders" (*consulibus ambobus quaetio de clandestinis coniurationibus creta est ... venena indidem intestinaque caedes*); Liv. 39.38.3: "[Matho received jurisdiction of) Sardinia and the additional task of investigating cases of poisoning (*Sardiniam et ut idem quareret de veneficiis*), 41 (under the praetor C. Claudius, within ten miles of the city; beyond the tenth milestone by the praetor C. Maenius).

53 Liv. 39.41.5 (184 BCE); Liv. 40.43.3 (180 BCE); Liv. 40.37.4, 44.6 (180 and 179 BCE).

54 *Per.* 48.6-7: *de veneficiis quaesitum. Publilia et Licinia, nobiles feminae, quae viros suos consulares necasse insimilabantur, cognita causa, cum praetori praedes vades dedissent, cognatorum decreto necatae sunt.*

55 Following Livy's time, one of the most celebrated *ueneficae* of the Julio-Claudian period was a certain Locusta, who poisoned Claudius at the command of Agrippina (in 54 CE), and Britannicus at that of Nero (the year after), the latter of whom even placed persons under her to be instructed in the art. According to Tacitus (*Ann.* 12.66, 13.15), Locusta was a person skilled in *ueneficium*, a mistress of the art, a professional in the designation of such matters (*artifex talium uocabulo*). She is held to have possessed a vast reputation for crime (*multa scelerum fama*) and had been condemned for poisoning (*ueneficii damnata*). To these historical citations may be added Horace's extended and incidental references to the "poetic" (fictive construct) Canidia (= Gratidia?): *Ep.* 3.7-8, 5, 17; *Sat.* 1.8, 2.1.48, 8.94.5. In this regard, Currie (1998) convincingly uses Pliny the Elder's treatment (in Books 21–27 of his *Historia naturalis*) of *remedia* and *uenena* as a case study to "go beyond cataloguing venomous women and posit reasons for the association of women and poison and for poison's assumed feminizing power." The literary evidence is borne out by certain provisions of the *lex Cornelia de sicariis et veneficis*, passed in the time of the dictator Sulla (82/1 BCE). This law not only provided for cases of poisoning, but contained provisions against those who made, sold, bought, possessed, or gave poison for the purpose of poisoning (Cic. *Clu.* 54; cf. Marcian, *Dig.* 49.8.3; Gai. *Inst.* 4.18.5). Interestingly, by a *senatusconsultum* passed subsequently to the *lex Cornelia*, a female, who gave drugs or poison for the purpose of producing conception even without evil intent, was banished (*relegatus*), if the person to whom she administered them died in consequence (*Dig.* 49.8.3).

56 Liv. 2.42.11.

57 Liv. 4.9.4-6.

58 Liv. 8.15.7-8.

59 *Per.* 14.7.

60 *Per.* 20.5.

61 App. *BC* 4.8-45; Val. Max. 5.3.4; 5.7.3; 6.7.2; 6.7.5-7; 7.3.8; 9.11.6-8; Cass. Dio 47.3-14.

62 See Figs. 1.1–2 and A.1 for synthetic catalogues of key episodes and female actors, with accompanying references.

63 Useful discussions of identity in the Roman world include: Gruen (1992); Dench (2005); Berry and Laurence (2009).

BIBLIOGRAPHY

Ampolo, C. 1983. "La storiografia su Roma arcaica e i documenti." In *Tria Corda: Scritti in Onore Di Arnaldo Momigliano*, ed. Gabba, E., 9–26. Como: New Press.

Arieti, J.A. 1997. "Rape and Livy's View of Roman History." In *Rape in Antiquity: Sexual Violence in the Greek and Roman World*, ed. Deacy, S., K.F. Pierce, 209–29. London and Swansea: Duckworth/The Classical Press of Wales.

Arjava, A. 1996. *Women and Law in Late Antiquity*. Oxford: Oxford University Press.

Auerbach, E. 1953. *Mimesis: The Representation of Reality in Western Literature*. Princeton: Princeton University Press.

Badian, E. 1966. "The Early Historians." In *Latin Historians*, ed. Dorey, T.A., 1–38. London: Routledge and Kegan Paul.

Badian, E. 1993. "Livy and Augustus." In *Livius: Aspekte Seines Werkes*, ed. Schuller, W., 9–38. Constance: Universitätsverlag Konstanz.

Balsdon, J.P.V.D. 1962. *Roman Women: Their History and Habits*. London: Bodley Head.

Balsdon, J.P.V.D. 1979. *Romans and Aliens*. London: Duckworth.

Barrow, R.J. 2018. *Gender and the Body in Greek and Roman Sculpture*. Cambridge: Cambridge University Press.

Bartman, E. 1999. *Portraits of Livia: Imaging the Imperial Women in Augustan Rome*. Cambridge: Cambridge University Press.

Bauman, R. 1993. "The Rape of Lucretia, Quod Metus Causa and the Criminal Law." *Latomus* 52: 550–66.

Bayet, J. 1940. *Tite-Live. Histoire Romaine I*. Paris: Les Belles Lettres.

Beard., M., M. Crawford. 1985. *Rome in the Late Republic*. London: Duckworth.

Beard, M., J. North, S. Price. 1998. *Religions of Rome. Volume 1: A History*. Cambridge: Cambridge University Press.

Beard, M. 1999. "The Erotics of Rape: Livy, Ovid and the Sabine Women." In *Female Networks and the Public Sphere in Roman Society*, ed. Setälä, P., L. Savunen, 1–10. Rome: Institutum Romanum Finlandiae.

Beard, M. 2018. *Women & Power: A Manifesto*. New York and London: Liveright Publishing Company.

Begbie, C.M. 1967. "The Epitome of Livy." *CQ* 17: 332–38.

Beness, J.L., T.W. Hillard. 2016. "Wronging Sempronia." *Antichthon* 50: 80–106.

Bérard, F., D. Feissel, N. Laubry, P. Petitmengin. 2000. *Guide de l'épigraphiste: Bibliographie Choisie des épigraphies antiques et médiévales*. Paris: Éd. Rue d'Ulm.

Berg, R. 2002. "Wearing Wealth. *Mundus Muliebris* and *Ornatus* as Status Markers for Women in Imperial Rome." In *Women, Wealth and Power in the Roman Empire*, ed. Setälä, P. et al, 15–74. Rome: Institutum Romanum Finlandiae.

Berg, R. 2016. *The Material Sides of Marriage: Women and Domestic Economies in Antiquity*. Rome: Institutum Romanum Finlandiae.

Berg, R., R. Neudecker. 2018. *The Roman Courtesan: Archaeological Reflections of a Literary Topos*. Rome: Institutum Romanum Finlandiae.

Berger, V. 2011. "Orality in Livy's Representation of the Divine. The Construction of a Polyphonic Narrative." In *Sacred Words: Orality, Literacy, and Religion*, ed. Lardinois, A.P.M.H., J.H. Blok, M.G.M. van der Poel, 311–27. Leiden, Boston: Brill.

Berry, J., R. Laurence. 2003. *Cultural Identity in the Roman Empire*. London and New York: Routledge.

Bettini, M. 1991. *Anthropology and Roman Culture*. Translated by J. van Sickle. Baltimore: Johns Hopkins University Press.

Bloch, R. 1963. *Les prodigies dans l'antiquité classique*. Paris: Presses Universitaires de France.

Blondell, R. 2013. *Helen of Troy: Beauty, Myth, Devastation*. Oxford: Oxford University Press.

Blok, J., P. Mason (ed.). 1987. *Sexual Asymmetry: Studies in Ancient Society*. Amsterdam: J.C. Gieben.

Boatwright, M.T. 2011. "Women and Gender in the Forum Romanum." *TAPhA* 141: 105–41.

Bodel, J. 2001. *Epigraphic Evidence: Ancient History from Inscriptions*. London: Routledge.

Boëls-Janssen, N. 1993. *La vie religieuse des matrons dan la Rome archaïque*. Rome: Ecole française de Rome.

Bolchazy, L.J. 1977. *Hospitality in Early Rome. Livy's Concept of its Humanizing Force*. Chicago: Ares.

Bolton, C.M. 2009. "Gendered Spaces in Ovid's Heroides." *CW* 102: 273–90.

Bonet, V. 1998. "Les maladies des enfants et leur traitement d'après le témoignage de Pline l'Ancien." In *Maladie et maladies dans les textes latins antiques et médiévaux*, ed. Deroux, C., 184– 98. Brussels: Latomus.

Bonfante, L. 1981. "Etruscan Couples and Their Aristocratic Society." *Women in Antiquity: Women's Studies* 8: 157–87.

Bosch, M.J.B. 2011. "El iudicium domesticum." *Revista General de Derecho Romano* 17. https://dialnet.unirioja.es/servlet/articulo?codigo=3877561. Accessed May 12, 2020.

Boyd, B.W. 1987. "Virtus Effeminata and Sallust's Sempronia." *TAPhA* 117: 183–201.

Bowman, A.K., E. Champlin, A. Lintott (ed.). 1996. *Cambridge Ancient History Vol. 10. The Augustan Empire, 43 BC – AD 69*. 2nd ed. Cambridge: Cambridge University Press.

Bradley, K.R. 1994. *Slavery and Society at Rome*. Cambridge: Cambridge University Press.

Braund, S.M. 1992. *Roman Verse Satire*. Oxford: Oxford University Press.

Breglia Pugli Doria, L. 1983. *Oracoli sibillini tra rituali e propaganda. Studi su Flegonte di Tralles*. Naples: Liguori.

Brennan, T.C. 2012. "Perceptions of Women's Power in the Late Republic. Terentia, Fulvia, and the Generation of 63 BCE." In *A Companion to Women in the Ancient World*, ed. James, S.L., S. Dillon, 354–66. Malden WA: Wiley-Blackwell.

Briscoe, J. 1981. *A Commentary on Livy Books XXXIV-XXXVII*. Oxford: Clarendon.

Briscoe, J. 2008. *A Commentary on Livy Books 38-40*. Oxford: Oxford University Press.

Brouwer, H.H. 1989. *Bona Dea*. Leiden: Brill.

Brown, P. 1988. *The Body and Society: Men, Women, and Sexual Renunciation in Early Christianity*. New York: Columbia University Press.

Brown, R. 1995. "Livy's Sabine Women and the Ideal of Concordia." *TAPhA* 26: 291–319.

Brownmiller, S. 1975. *Against Our Will: Men, Women and Rape*. New York: Simon and Schuster.

Brunt, P.A. 1980. "On Historical Fragments and Epitomes." *CQ* 30: 477–94.

Bryson, N. 1986. "Two Narratives of Rape in the Visual Arts: Lucretia and the Sabine Women." In *Rape: An Historical and Cultural Enquiry*, ed. Tomaselli, S., R. Porter, 152–73. Oxford: Oxford University Press.

Burck, E. 1934. *Die Erzählungskunst des Titus Livius*. Berlin: Weidmann.

Burck, E. 1991. "Livius und Augustus." *ICS* 16: 269–81.

Burck, E. 1992. *Das Geschichtswerk des Titus Livius*. Heidelberg: Carl Winter.

Burden-Strevens, C., M. Lindholmer (ed.). 2018. *Cassius Dio's Forgotten History of Early Rome: The Roman History, Books 1-21*. Leiden: Brill.

Burgess, J.S. 2001, *The Tradition of the Trojan War in Homer and the Epic Cycle*. Baltimore: Johns Hopkins University Press.

Burton, P. 2000. "The Last Republican Historian: A New Date for the Composition of Livy's First Pentad." *Historia* 49.4: 429–46.

Cairns, F. 2011. "Tarpeia Pudicitia in Propertius 1.16.2 – and the Early Roman Historians." *Rheinisches Museum für Philologie* 154.2: 176–84.

Caldelli, M.L. 2015. "Women in the Roman World." In *The Oxford Handbook of Roman Epigraphy*, ed. Bruun, C., J.C. Edmundsen, 582–604. Oxford: Oxford University Press.

Caldwell, L. 2015. *Roman Girlhood and the Fashioning of Femininity*. Cambridge: Cambridge University Press.

Calhoun, C.G. 1997. "Lucretia, Savior, and Scapegoat: The Dynamics of Sacrifice in Livy 1, 57–59." *Helios* 24.2: 15–169.

Cameron, A., A. Kurht (ed.). 1993. *Images of Women in Antiquity*. London and New York: Routledge.

Canevaro, L.G. 2018. *Women of Substance in Homeric Epic: Objects, Gender, Agency*. New York: Oxford University Press.

Cantarella, E. 1987. *Pandora's Daughters: The Role and Status of Women in Greek and Roman Antiquity*. Baltimore: Johns Hopkins University Press.

Cappelli, R. (ed.). 1991. *Il Tesoro Ritrovato: Mulierum Ornamenta*. Roma: Ministero per i Beni Culturali e Ambientali, Soprintendenza Archeologica per il Lazio.

Carson, R.A.G. 1990. *Coins of the Roman Empire*. London and New York: Routledge.

Casevitz, M. 1985. "La femme dans l'oeuvre de Diodore de Sicile." In *La Femme Dans Le Monde Méditerranéen. I. Antiquité*, ed. Vérilhac, A.M., 113–35. Lyon: Maison de l'Orient.

Cavaggioni, F. 2004. *Mulier Rea: Dinamiche Politico-Sociali Nei Processi a Donne Nella Roma Repubblicana*. Venezia. Istituto Veneto di scienze, lettere ed arti.

Champeaux, J. 1982. *Fortuna. Recherche sur le culte de la Fortune à Rome et dans le monde romain, des origines à la mort de César. I. Fortuna dans la religion archaïque*. Rome: Ecole française de Rome.

Chaplin, J. 2000. *Livy's Exemplary History*. Oxford: Oxford University Press.

Chaplin, J.D., C.S. Kraus (ed.). 2009. *Livy. Oxford Readings in Classical Studies*. Oxford: Oxford University Press.

Cheesman, C. 2011. *Personal Names in the Roman World*. London: Duckworth.

Chiu, A. 2016. *Ovid's Women of the Year*. Ann Arbor University of Michigan Press.

Chrystal, P. 2017. *Roman Women. The Women Who Influenced the History of Rome*. London and New York: Fonthill.

Claassen, J.-M. 1998. "The Familiar Other." *AClass* XLI: 71–103.

Clark, G. 1993. *Women in Late Antiquity. Pagan and Christian Lifestyles*. Oxford: Oxford University Press.

Cleland, L., G. Davies, L. Llewellyn-Jones. 2007. *Greek and Roman Dress from A to Z*. London and New York: Routledge.

Coarelli, F. 1983. *Foro Romano, 1. Periodo Arcaico*. Rome: Edizioni Quasar.

Cohen, D. 1995. *Law, Violence, and Sexuality in Classical Athens*. Cambridge: Cambridge University Press.

Collingwood, R.G. 1946. *The Idea of History*. London: Oxford University Press.

Collins, P.A. 2015. "Intersectionality's Definitional Dilemma." *Annual Review of Sociology* 41: 1–20.

Connerton, P. 1989. *How Societies Remember*. Cambridge: Cambridge University Press.

Corbett, P.E. (1930). *The Roman Law of Marriage*. Oxford: Clarendon Press.

Cornell, T.J. 1995. *The Beginnings of Rome: Italy and Rome from the Bronze Age to the Punic Wars, 1000-264 BC*. London and New York: Routledge.

Cornell, T.J. (ed.). 2013. *The Fragments of the Roman Historians. Vol. 2. Texts and Translations*. Oxford: Oxford University Press.

Crawford, M.H. (ed.). 1996. *Roman Statutes*, Vol. 2. London: Institute of Classical Studies.

Crawford, O.C. 1941. "Laudatio funebris." *CJ* 37: 17–27.

Croom, A. 2002. *Roman Clothing and Fashion*. Stroud, Gloucestershire: Amberley.

Csillag, P. 1976. *The Augustan Laws on Family Relations*. Budapest: Akadémiai Kiadó.

Culham, P. 1987. "Ten Years after Pomeroy: Studies of the Image and Reality of Women in Antiquity." *Helios* 13: 9–30.

Culham, P. 1997. "Did Roman Women Have an Empire?" In *Inventing Ancient Culture: Historicism. Periodisation. and the Ancient World*, ed. Golden, M., P. Toohey, 192–205. London and New York: Routledge.

Cutolo, P. 1983. "Sugli Aspetti Letterari Poetici E Culturali Della Cossidetta Laudatio Turiae." *AFLN* 26: 33–65.

D'Ambra, E. 2007. *Roman Women*. Cambridge: Cambridge University Press.

Daube, D. 1972. *Civil Disobedience in Antiquity*. Edinburgh: Edinburgh University Press.

Davies, J.F. 1986. "The Circle and the Tragic Chorus." *G & R* 33: 38–46.

Deacy, S., K.F. Pierce (ed.). 2002. *Rape in Antiquity. Sexual Violence in the Greek and Roman Worlds*. London: Classical Press of Wales/Duckworth.

de Arena, D.H. Granados. 1986. "Actitud admirable de dos mujeres en eıpocas difi-
ciles. La uxor ignota de a Laudatio funebris y Hortensia, la hija del orador." *REC*
17: 93–107.

de Casanove, O. 1987. "Exesto. L'incapacité Sacrificielle Des Femmes à Rome."
Phoenix 41: 159–74.

Dean, C. 1994. "The Productive Hypothesis: Foucault, Gender, and the History of
Sexuality." *History and Theory* 33.3: 271–96.

Della, D. 1991. "Fulvia Reconsidered." In *Women's History and Ancient History*, ed.
Pomeroy, S., 197–217. Chapel Hill: University of North Carolina Press.

Demand, N. 1994. *Birth, Death, and Motherhood in Classical Greece*. Baltimore:
Jophns Hopkins University Press.

Dench, E. 2005. *Romulus' Asylum. Roman Identities from the Age of Alexander to
the Age of Hadrian*. Oxford: Oxford University Press.

Dench, E. 2009. "The Roman Historians and Twentieth-Century Approaches to
Roman History." In *The Cambridge Companion to the Roman Historians*, ed.
Feldherr, A., 394–406. Cambridge: Cambridge University Press.

Dench, E. 2018. *Empire and Political Cultures in the Roman World*. Cambridge:
Cambridge University Press.

Deninger, J. 1985. "Livius und der Prinzipat." *Klio* 67: 265–72.

Develin, R. 1983. "Tacitus and Techniques of Insidious Suggestion." *Antichthon* 17:
64–95.

Diels, H. 1890. *Sibyllinische Blätter*. Berlin: G. Reimer.

Di Fazio, M. 2018. "Figures of Memory. Aulus Vibenna, Valerius Publicola and
Mezentius between History and Legend." In *Omnium Annalium Monumenta:
Historical Writing and Historical Evidence in Republican Rome*, ed. Sandberg, K.,
C. Smith, 279–300. Leiden and Boston: Brill.

Dix, T.K., G.W. Houston. 2006. "Public Libraries in the City of Rome from the
Augustan Age to the Time of Diocletian." *MEFRA* 118.2: 671–717.

Dixon, S. 1985. "Polybius on Roman Women and Property." *AJP* 106.2: 147–70.

Dixon, S. 1988. *The Roman Mother*. London, Sydney: Routledge.

Dixon, S. 1992. *The Roman Family*. Baltimore and London: Johns Hopkins
University Press.

Dixon, S. 2001. *Reading Roman Women: Sources, Genres, and Real Life*. London:
Duckworth.

Dixon, S. 2007. *Cornelia, Mother of the Gracchi*. London: Routledge.

Doherty, L. 2001. *Gender and the Interpretation of Classical Myth*. London:
Duckworth.

Dolansky, F. 2012. "Playing with Gender: Girls, Dolls, and Adult Ideals in the Roman
World." *ClAnt* 31.2: 256–92.

Donaldson, I. 2002. *The Rapes of Lucretia: A Myth and Its Transformations*.
Cambridge: Cambridge University Press.

Dorcey, P.F. 1992. *The Cult of Silvanus. A Study in Roman Folk Religion*. Leiden,
New York, Köln: E. J. Brill.

Dover, K.J. 1978, *Greek Homosexuality*. Cambridge MA: Harvard University
Press.

Dubisch, J. (ed.). 1986. *Gender and Power in Rural Greece*. Princeton: Princeton
University Press.

Durry, M. 1950. *Eloge funébre d'une matrone romaine (éloge dit de Turia)*. Paris:
Collection des Universités de France.

Eder, W. 1990. "Augustus and the Power of Tradition: the Augustan Principate as Binding Link between Republic and Empire." In *Between Republic and Empire: Interpretations of Augustus and His Principate*, ed. Raaflaub, K.A., M. Toher, 71–122. Berkeley and London: University of California Press.

Edmundsen, J.C. 2015. "Roman Family History." In *The Oxford Handbook of Roman Epigraphy*, ed. Bruun, C., J.C. Edmundsen, 559–81. Oxford: Oxford University Press.

Edwards, C. 1993. *The Politics of Immorality in Ancient Rome*. Cambridge: Cambridge University Press.

Evans, J.K. 1991. *War, Women and Children in Ancient Rome*. London and New York: Routledge.

Fantham, E., H.P. Foley, N.B. Kampen, S.B. Pomeroy, H.A. Shapiro. 1994. *Women in the Classical World*. Oxford: Oxford University Press.

Fantham, E. 1994. *Women in the Classical World. Image and Text*, Oxford: Oxford University Press.

Fantham, E. (ed.). 1998. *Ovid. Fasti. Book IV*. Cambridge: Cambridge University Press.

Fantham, E. 2002. "The *Fasti* as a Source for Women's Participation in Roman Cult." In *Ovid's Fasti. Historical Readings at its Bimillennium*, ed. Herbert-Brown, G., 23–36. Oxford and New York: Oxford University Press.

Fantham, E. 2006. *Julia Augusta, the Emperor's Daughter*. Abingdon, Oxon., New York: Routledge.

Fayer, C. 1994. *La familia Roma. Aspetti giuridici ed antiquari*. Roma: L'Erma di Bretschneider.

Faustoferri, A. 2016. "Women in a Warrior's Society." In *Burial and Social Change in First-Millennium BC Italy: Approaching Social Agents*, ed. Perego, E., 97–110. Oxford, Philadelphia: Oxbow Books.

Feldherr, A. 1997. "Livy's Revolution: Civic Identity and the Creation of the *res publica*." In *The Roman Cultural Revolution*, ed. Habinek, T.N., A. Schiesaro, 136–57. Cambridge and New York: Cambridge University Press.

Feldherr, A. 1998. *Spectacle and Society in Livy's History*. Berkeley CA: University of California Press.

Flannery, H.W. 1920. "Roman Women and the Vote." *CJ* 16: 103–7.

Flemming, R. 2000. *Medicine and the Making of Roman Women. Gender, Nature, and Authority from Celsus to Galen*. Oxford: Oxford University Press.

Flory, M.B. 1996. "Dynastic Ideology, the Domus Augusta, and Imperial Women: A Lost Statuary Group in the Circus Flaminius." *TAPhA* 126: 287–306.

Flory, M.B. 1993. "Livia and the History of Public Honorific Statues for Women in Rome." *TAPhA* 12: 287–308.

Flory, M.B. 1988. "The Meaning of Augusta in the Julio-Claudian Period." *AJAH* 13.2: 113–38.

Flory, M.B. 1984. "Sic Exempla Parantur: Livia's Shrine to Concordia and the Porticus Liviae." *Historia* 33: 309–30.

Flower, H.I. 2011. *Roman Republics*. Princeton and Oxford: Princeton University Press.

Foley, H.P. (ed.). 1981. *Reflections of Women in Antiquity*, New York: Gordon and Breach Science Publishers.

Fornara, C.W. 1983. *The Nature of History in Ancient Greece and Rome*. Berkeley and Los Angeles: University of California Press.

Forsythe, G. 1999. *Livy and Early Rome: A Study in Historical Method and Judgment.* Stuttgart: F. Steiner.

Forsythe, G. 2006. *A Critical History of Early Rome: From Prehistory to the First Punic War.* Berkeley: University of California Press.

Foubert, L. 2011. "The Impact of women's Travels on Military Imagery in the Julio-Claudian Period." In: *Frontiers in the Roman World: Proceedings of the Ninth Workshop of the International Network 'Impact of Empire' (Durham, 16-19 April 2009),* ed. Hekster, O., T. Kaizer, 349–61. Leiden, Boston: Brill.

Foxhall, L. (ed.) 1998. *When Men Were Men: Masculinity, Power, and Identity in Classical Antiquity.* London and New York: Routledge.

Fraenkel, E. 1932. "Senatus Consultum de Bacchanalibus." *Hermes* 67: 369–96.

Fraschetti, A. 2001. *Roman Women.* Chicago: University of Chicago Press.

Freund, S. 2008. "Pudicitia saltem in tuto sit: Lucretia, Verginia und die Konstruktion eines Wertbegriffs bei Livius." *Hermes* 136.3: 308–25.

Frier, B.W. 1979. *Libri Annales Pontificum Maximorum: The Origins of the Annalistic Tradition.* Rome: American Academy in Rome.

Fronza, L. 1947. "De Bacanalibus." *Annali Triestini* 17: 205–27.

Gabba, E. 1991. *Dionysius and the History of Rome.* Berkeley: University of California Press.

Gagé, J. 1963. *Matronalia. Essai sur les devotions et les organisations cultuelles des femmes dans l'ancienne Rome.* Rome: Ecole française de Rome.

Gagé, J. 1976. "Coriolan entre les deux Fortunes." In *La chute des Tarquins et les débuts de la République romaine,* 167–93. Paris: Payot.

Galinsky, H. 1932. *der Lucretia-Stoff in der Weltliteratur.* Breslau: Priebatsch.

Galinsky, K. 1996. *Augustan Culture: An Interpretive Introduction.* Princeton: Princeton University Press.

Galsterer, L. 1990. "A Man, A Book, A Method: Syme's *Roman Revolution* after Fifty Years." In *Between Republic and Empire: Interpretations of Augustus and His Principate,* ed. Raaflaub, K.A., M. Toher, 1–20. Berkeley and London: University of California Press.

Garcia Barraco, M.E., I. Soda, G. Giannelli. 2017. *Virgines Vestales, Il Sacerdozio delle Vestali Romane: origine, costituzione e ordinamento.* Roma: Arbor Sapaientiae.

Gardner, J.F. 1986. *Women in Roman Law and Society.* Bloomington: Indiana University Press.

Gardner, H.H. 2013. *Gendering Time in Augustan Love Elegy.* Oxford: Oxford University Press.

Gelzer, M. 1936. "Die Unterdrückung der Bacchanalien bei Livius." *Hermes* 71: 276–87.

Girard, R. 1961. *Mensonge romantique et vérité Romanesque.* Paris: Grasset.

Glei, R.F. 2009. "The Show Must Go On: The Death of Marcellus and the Future of the Augustan Principate (*Aen.* 6.860-86)." In *Vergil's Aeneid. Augustan Epic and Political Context,* ed. Stahl, H.P., 119–34. Bristol: Classical Press of Wales.

Glinister, F. 1997. "Regal Myths." *CR* 47.1: 115–18.

Gourevitch, D. 1996. "La gynècologie et l'obstètrique." *ANRW* II 37.3: 2083–147.

Grillet, B. 1975. *Les Femmes et les fards dans l'antiquité grecque.* Lyon: Centre national de la recherche scientifique.

Grubbs, J.E. 2002. *Women and the Law in the Roman Empire. A Sourcebook on Marriage, Divorce, and Widowhood.* London and New York: Routledge.

Gruen, E.S. 1990. *Studies in Greek Culture and Roman Policy.* Leiden: E.J. Brill.

Gruen, E.S. 1992. *Culture and National Identity in Republican Rome*. Ithaca, NY: Cornell University Press.

Hallett, J.P. 1984. *Fathers and Daughters in Roman Society: Women and the Elite Family*. Princeton: Princeton University Press.

Hallett, J.P. 1989. "Woman as Same and Other in Classical Roman Elite." *Helios* 16.1: 59–78.

Hallett, J.P. 1992. "Heeding Our Native Informants: The Uses of Latin Literary Texts in Recovering Elite Roman Attitudes Toward Age, Gender and Social Status." *Echos du monde classique* 11.3: 333–55.

Hallett, J.P. 2009. "Absent Roman Fathers in the Writings of their Daughters." In *Growing Up Fatherless in Antiquity*, ed. Huebner, S., D.M. Ratzan, 175–91. Cambridge: Cambridge University Press.

Hallett, J.P. 2011. "Ballio's Brothel, Phoenicum's Letter, and the Literary Education of Graeco-Roman Prostitutes. The Evidence of Plautus' *Pseudolus*." In *Greek Prostitutes in the Ancient Mediterranean, 800BCE-200CE*, 172–96. Madison: University of Wisconsin Press.

Halperin, D.M. 1990. "Why Is Diotima a Woman?" In *One Hundred Years of Homosexuality and Other Essays on Greek Love*, 113–52. New York: Routledge.

Hammond, M. 1963. "Res olim dissociabiles: Principatus ac Libertas: Liberty under the Early Roman Empire." *HSPh* 67: 93–113.

Hänninen, M.-L. 1999. "Juno Regina and the Roman Matrons." In *Female Networks and the Public Sphere in Roman Society*, ed. Setälä, P., L. Savunen, 39–52. Rome: Institutum Romanum Finlandiae.

Hardie, P. 1993. *The Epic Successors of Vergil*. Cambridge: Cambridge University Press.

Harris, W.V. 1979. *War and Imperialism in Republican Rome*. Oxford: Clarendon Press.

Harris, W.V. 1989. *Ancient Literacy*. Cambridge and London: Harvard University Press.

Harrison, E.B. 1988. "Greek Sculptured Coiffures and Ritual Haircuts." In *Early Greek Cult Practice: Proceedings of the Fifth International Symposium at the Swedish Institute at Athens 26–29 June 1986*, ed. Hägg, R., N. Marinatos, and G.C. Nordquist, 247–54. Stockholm: Svenska Institutet i Athen.

Hartog, F. 1988. *The Mirror of Herodotus*. Translated by J. Lloyd. Berkeley: University of California Press.

Harvey, D. 1985. "Women in Thucydides." *Arethusa* 18.1: 67–90.

Harvey, T. 2020. *Julia Augusta. Images of Rome's First Empress on Coins of the Roman Empire*. London and New York: Routledge.

Haynes, S. 2000. *Etruscan Civilisation. A Cultural History*. Los Angeles, CA: Getty Publications.

Hays, S. 1987. "Lactea Ubertas: What's Milky About Livy?" *CJ* 82.2: 107–16.

Hawley, R., B. Levick. 1997. *Women in Antiquity: New Assessments*. London, New York: Routledge.

Heath, J. 2011. "Women's Work: Female Transmission of Mythical Narrative." *TAPhA of the American Philological Association* 141.1: 69–104.

Heiduk, J.D. 2008. *Clodia. A Sourcebook*. Norman OK: University of Oklahoma Press.

Hellegouarc'h, J. 1963. *Le vocabulaire latin des relations et des partis politiques sous la République*. Paris: Faculté des Lettres et Sciences humaines de l' Université de Lille.

234

Hemelrijk, E.A. 1987. "Women's Demonstrations in Republican Rome." In *Sexual Asymmetry: Studies in Ancient Society*, ed. Blok, J.A., P. Mason, 76–131. Amsterdam: Gieben.

Hemelrijk, E.A. 1999. *Matrona Docta. Educated Women in the Roman Elite from Cornelia to Julia Domna*. London and New York: Routledge.

Hemelrijk, E.A. 2013. *Women and the Roman City in the Latin West*. Leiden, Boston: Brill.

Hemelrijk, E.A. 2015. *Hidden Lives, Public Personae: Women and Civic Life in the Roman West*. Oxford: Oxford University Press.

Hemker, J. 1985. "Rape and the Founding of Rome." *Helios* 12.1: 41–7.

Herring, E., K. Lomas. 2009. *Gender Identities in Italy in the First Millennium BC*. Oxford: Archaeopress.

Herrman, C. 1964. *Le Rôle judiciaire et politique des femmes sous la République romaine*. Brussels: Latomus.

Hillard, T.W. 1989. "Republican Politics, Women, and the Evidence." *Helios* 16: 165–82.

Hillard, T.W. 1992. "On the Stage, Behind the Curtain. Images of Politically Active Women in the Late Roman Republic." In *Stereotypes of Women in Power. Historical Perspectives and Revisionist Views*, ed. Garlick, B., S. Dixon, P. Allen, 37–64. Westport CT: Praeger.

Hinard, F. 1985. *Les proscriptions de la Rome republicaine*. Rome: Ecole francaise de Rome.

Holbrook, A.L. 2009. *Constructions of the Family in Livy's AUC*. Unpublished thesis, McMaster University.

Hölscher, T. 2018. *Visual Power in Ancient Greece and Rome: Between Art and Social Reality*. Oakland, California: University of California Press.

Horsfall, N. 1983. "Some Problems in the 'Laudatio *Turiae*." *BICS* 30: 85–98.

Houston, G.W. 2014. *Inside Roman Libraries: Book Collections and Their Management in Antiquity*. Chapel Hill: University of North Carolina Press.

Humphrey, J.H. 1991. *Literacy in the Roman World*. Ann Arbor: Journal of Roman Archaeology (supplementary series 3).

Irigaray, L. 1977. *Ce sexe qui n'en pest pas un*. Paris: Éditions de Minuit.

Jaeger, M. 1997. *Livy's Written Rome*. An Arbor: University of Michigan Press,

Jensen, E. 2018. *Barbarians in the Greek and Roman World*. Indianapolis and Cambridge: Hackett Publishing Company.

Joplin, P.K. 1990. "Ritual Work on Human Flesh: Livy's Lucretia and the Rape of the Body Politic." *Helios* 17.1: 51–70.

Joshel, S.R. 1992a. *Work, Identity and Legal Status at Rome: A Study of the Occupational Inscriptions*. Norman and London: University of Oklahoma Press.

Joshel, S.R. 1992b. "The Body Female and the Body Politic: Livy's Lucretia and Virginia." In *Pornography and Representation in Greece and Rome*, ed. Richlin, A. New York and Oxford: Oxford University Press.

Joshel, S.R., S. Murnaghan. 1998. *Women and Slaves in Greco-Roman Culture: Differential Equations*. London and New York: Routledge.

Kajanto, I. 1965. *The Latin Cognomina*. Helsinki: Keskuskirjapaino.

Kampen, N. 1981. *Image and Status: Roman Working Women in Ostia*. Berlin: Gebr. Mann Verlag.

Kampen, N. 1992. "Between Public and Private: Women as Historical Subjects in Roman Art." In *Women's History and Ancient History*, ed. Pomeroy, S., 218–48. Chapel Hill: University of North Carolina Press.

Keegan, P. 2005. "Boudica, Cartimandua, Messalina and Agrippina the Younger. Independent Women of Power and the Gendered Rhetoric of Roman History" *Ancient History: Resources for Teachers* 34.2: 99–148.

Keegan, P. 2014. *Roles for Men and Women in Roman Epigraphic Culture and Beyond. Gender, Social Identity and Cultural Practice in Private Latin Inscriptions and the Literary Record.* Oxford: Archaeopress.

Keith, A.M. 1997. "*Tandem venit amor:* A Roman Woman Speaks of Love." In *Roman Sexualities*, ed. Hallett, J.P., M.B. Skinner, 295–310. Princeton: Princeton University Press.

Keith, A.M. 2000. *Engendering Rome: Women in Latin Epic.* Cambridge: Cambridge University Press.

Keith, A.M. 2006. "Women's Networks in Vergil's Aeneid." *Dictynna* 3: 211–33.

Keith, A.M. 2011. "Lycoris Galli/Volumnia Cytheris. A Greek Courtesan in Rome." *Eugesta* 1: 23–53.

Keith, A.M. 2018. "Historical Roman Courtesans." In *The Roman Courtesan: Archaeological Reflections of a Literary Topos*, ed. Berg, R., R. Neudecker, 73–86. Rome: Institutum Romanum Finlandiae.

Kellum, B.A. 1994. "What We See and What We don't See. Narrative Structure and the Ara Pacis Augustae. *Art History* 17: 26–45.

Keltanen, M. "The Public Image of the Four Empresses – Ideal Wives, Mothers and Regents?" In *Women, Wealth and Power in the Roman Empire*, ed. Setälä, P. et al, 105–46. Rome: Institutum Romanum Finlandiae

Kennedy, D.F. 1992. "'Augustan' and 'anti-Augustan': Reflections on Terms of Reference." In *Roman Poetry and Propaganda in the Age of Augustus*, ed. Powell, A., 26–58. Bristol: Bristol Classical Press.

Keuls, E.C. 1985. *The Reign of the Phallus: Sexual Politics in Ancient Athens.* Berkeley: University of California Press.

Kierdorf, W. 1980. *Laudatio Funebris. Interpretationen und Untersuchungen zur Entwicklung der romischen Leichenrede.* Meisenheim am Glan: Haim.

King, H. 1997. "Reading the Female Body." *Gender and History* 9.3: 620–24.

Kleiner, D.E.E. 1977. *Roman Group Portraiture: The Funerary Reliefs of the Late Republic and Early Empire.* New York and London: Garland Publishing.

Kleiner, D.E.E. 1978. "The Great Friezes of the Ara Pacis Augustae: Greek Sources, Roman Derivations, and Augustan Social Policy." *MEFRA* 90: 753–85.

Kleiner, D.E.E. 1996. "Imperial Women as Patrons of the Arts in the Early Empire." In *I, Claudia*, ed. Kleiner, D.E.E., S.B. Matheson, 28–41. New Haven: University of Texas Press.

Kloppenborg, J.S., S.G. Wilson (ed.). 1996. *Voluntary Associations in the Graeco-Roman World.* London and New York: Routledge.

Knapp, R.C. 2013. *Invisible Romans.* London: Profile Books.

Koenen, L. 1970. "Die Laudatio Funebris des Augustus für Agrippa auf einem neuen Papyrus." *ZPE5*: 217–83.

Kokkinos, N. 1992. *Antonia Augusta: Portrait of a Great Roman Lady.* London and New York: Routledge.

Konstan, D. 1986. "Narrative and Ideology in Livy: Book I." *ClAnt* 5: 198–215.

Konstan, D. 1992. "Introduction: Documenting Gender: Women and Men in Non-Literary Classical Texts." *Helios* 19: 92–103.

Koptev, A. 2003. "Lucretia's Story in Literature and the Rites of Regifugium and Equirrii." *Studies in Latin Literature and Roman History* 11: 5–33.

Kraemer, R.S. 1988. *Maenads, Martyrs, Matrons, Monastics. A Sourcebook on Women's Religion in the Greco-Roman World*. Philadelphia: Fortress Press.

Kramer, S.N. 1969. *The Sacred Marriage Rite: Aspects of Faith, Myth, and Ritual in Ancient Sumer*. Bloomington: Indiana University Press.

Kraus, C.S. 1991. "Initium turbandi omnia a femina ortum est: Fabia minor and the election of 367 BC." *Phoenix* 45: 314–25.

Kraus, C.S. (ed.). 1994. *Livy. Ab Urbe Condita: Book VI*. London: Cambridge University Press.

Kraus, C.S., A.J. Woodman. 1997. *Latin Historians*. Cambridge: Cambridge University Press.

Kuhrt, A., A. Cameron. 1983. *Images of Women in Antiquity*. London: Croom Helm.

Labate, M. 2003. "Tra Grecia e Roma: l'identità culturale augustea nei Fasti di Ovidio." In *Fecunda Licentia*, ed. Gazich, A.C., 77–118. Milano: Vita e Pensiero.

Langlands, R. 2006. *Sexual Morality in Ancient Rome*. Cambridge: Cambridge University Press.

Larmour, D.H.J., P.A. Miller, C. Platter. 1997. *Rethinking Sexuality: Foucault and Classical Antiquity*, Princeton: Princeton University Press.

Latte, K. 1960. *Römische Religionsgerschichte*. Munich: C.H. Beck.

Leeman, A.D. 1963. *Orationis Ratio: The Stylistic Theories and Practice of the Roman Orators, Historians and Philosophers*. Amsterdam: A.M. Hakkert.

Lefkowitz, M.R., M.B. Fant. 2005. *Women's Life in Greece and Rome. A Source Book in Translation. 3rd* ed. Baltimore: Johns Hopkins University Press.

Le Glay, M. 1978. "L'evolution des mentalités collectives sous le second triumviral." In *Le dernier Siécle de la République romaine et l'epoque augustéenne*. Strasbourg: Association pour l'êtude de la Civilisation Romaine. 63–73.

Lennox, J. 2001. *Aristotle's Philosophy of Biology: Studies in the Origins of Life Science*. Cambridge: Cambridge University Press.

Lerner, G. 1986. *The Creation of Patriarchy. The Origins of Women's Subordination*. Oxford: Oxford University Press.

Levene, D.S. 2010. *Livy on the Hannibalic War*. Oxford and New York: Oxford University Press.

Levene, D.S. 1993. *Religion in Livy*. Leiden: E.J. Brill.

Lewis, C.T. 1953. *A Latin Dictionary for Schools*. Oxford: Clarendon Press.

Lind, G. 1979. "Roman Social Conservatism." In *Studies in Latin Literature and Roman Social History I*, ed. Deroux, C., 7–58. Bruxelles: Latomus.

Lindner, M.M. 2015. *Portraits of the Vestal Virgins: Priestesses of Ancient Rome*. Ann Arbor: University of Michigan Press.

Lindsay, H. 2009. *Adoption in the Roman World*. Cambridge: Cambridge University Press.

Lintott, A.W. 1968. *Violence in Republican Rome*. Oxford: Clarendon Press.

Lipovsky, J. 1984. *A Historiographical Study of Livy VI-X*. Salem, New Hampshire: Ayers Company.

Luce, T.J. 1965. "The Dating of Livy's First Pentad." *TAPhA* 96: 209–40.

Luce, T.J. 1977. *Livy: The Composition of His History*. New Jersey: Princeton University Press.

Luce, T.J. 1993. "Livy, Augustus and the Forum Augustum." In *Between Republic and Empire: Interpretations of Augustus and His Principate*, ed. Raaflaub, K.A., M. Toher, 123–38. Berkeley and London: University of California Press.

Lundeen, L.E. 2006. "In Search of the Etruscan Priestess: A Re-Examination of the *Hatrencu*." In *Religion in Republican Italy*, ed. Schultz, C.E., P.B. Harvey Jr., 34–61. Cambridge: Cambridge University Press.

MacDonald, M.Y. 1996. *Early Christian Women and Pagan Opinion. The Power of the Hysterial Woman*. Cambridge: Cambridge University Press.

Macmullen, R. 1980. "Roman Elite Motivation: Three Questions." *P & P* 88: 3–16.

Manassa, C. 2009. "A Depiction of Paris in Luxor Temple and the 'eidolon' of Helen." *ZPE* 136: 141–49.

Mantzilas, D. 2018. "Female Domestic Financial Managers: Turia, Murdia, and Hortensia." In *The Material Sides of Marriage: Women and Domestic Economies in Antiquity*, ed. Berg, R., 169–74. Rome: Institutum Romanum Finlandiae.

Marincola, J. 2009. "Ancient Audiences and Expectations." In *The Cambridge Companion to the Roman Historians*, ed. Feldherr, A., 11–23. Cambridge: Cambridge University Press.

Marshall, A.J. 1984. "Symbols and Showmanship in Roman Public Life: The Fasces." *Phoenix* 38: 120–41.

Martin, D.B. 1996. "The Construction of the Ancient Family: Methodological Considerations." *JRS* 86: 40–60.

Martin, R.H., A.J. Woodman. 1989. *Tacitus: Annals Book IV*. Cambridge: Cambridge University Press.

Mastrocinque, A. 2014. *Bona Dea and the Cults of Roman Women*. Stuttgart: Steiner.

Mastrorosa, I. 2006. "Speeches Pro and contra Women in Livy 34.1-7." *Latomus* 65.3: 590–611.

Matthes, M.M. 2000. *The Rape of Lucretia and the Founding of Republics: Readings in Livy, Machiavelli and Rousseau*. University Park PA: Pennsylvania University Press.

Mauersberger, A. 1968. *Polybius-Lexikon I: 1 (α – γ)*. Berlin: Akademie-Verlag.

McDonald, A.H.1957. "The Style of Livy." *JRS* 47: 155–72.

McGinn, T.A.J. 1998. *Prostitution, Sexuality and the Law in Ancient Rome*. Oxford: Oxford University Press.

McHardy, F., E. Marshall (ed.). 2004. *Women's Influence on Classical Civilisation*. London and New York: Routledge.

McManus, B.F. 1997. *Classics and Feminism: Gendering the Classics*. New York: Twayne Publishers.

Meautis, G. 1940. "Les aspecs religieux de l'affaire des Bacchanales." *REA* 42: 476–85.

Mellor, R. 1999. *The Roman Historians*. London and New York: Routledge.

Mette, H.J. 1961. "Livius und Augustus." *Gymnasium* 68: 269–85.

Miles, G.B. 1986. "The Cycle of Roman History in Livy's First Pentad." *AJPh* 107.1: 1–33.

Miles, G.B. 1993. "The First Roman Marriage and the Theft of the Sabine Women." In *Innovations of Antiquity*, ed. Hexter, R., D. Selden, 161–96. London and New York: Routledge.

Miles, G.B. 1995. *Livy: Reconstructing Early Rome*. Ithaca and London: Cornell University Press.

Milnor, K. 2005. *Gender, Domesticity and the Age of Augustus. Inventing Private Life*. Oxford: Oxford University Press.

Milnor, K. 2012. "Women in Roman Society." In *The Oxford Handbook of Social Relations in the Roman World*, ed. Peachin, M, 609–22. Oxford: Oxford University Press.

Moles, J. 1993. "Livy's Preface." *PCPhS* 39: 141–68.

Momigliano, A. 1991. *The Classical Foundations of Modern Historiography.* Berkeley: University of California Press.

Moore, T.J. 1989. *Artistry and Ideology: Livy's Vocabulary of Virtue.* Frankfurt am Main: Athenäum.

Moore, T.J. 1993. "Morality, History, and Livy's Wronged Women." *Eranos* 91: 38–46.

Moses, D.C. 1993. "Livy's Lucretia and the Validity of Coerced Consent." In *Consent and Coercion in Sex and Marriage in Ancient and Medieval Societies*, ed. Laiou, A.E., 39–81. Washington: Dumbarton Oaks.

Murray, O. 1990. "Sympotic History." In *Sympotica: A Symposium on the Symposion*, 3–13. Oxford: Clarendon Press.

Mustakallio, K. 1990. "Some Aspects of the Story of Coriolanus and the Women Behind the Cult of Fortuna Muliebris." In *Roman Eastern Policy and Other Studies in Roman History*, ed. Solin, H., M. Kajava, 125–31. Helsinki: The Finnish Society of Science and Letters.

Mustakillio, K. 1999. "Legendary Women and Female Groups in Livy." In *Female Networks and the Public Sphere in Roman Society*, ed. Setälä, P., L. Savunen, 53–64. Rome: Institutum Romanum Finlandiae.

Newlands, Carole. 1995. *Playing with Time: Ovid and the Fasti.* Ithaca: Cornell University Press.

Nielsen, M. 1989. "la donna e la famiglia nella tarda società etrusca." In *Le donne in Etruria*, ed. Rallo, A., 121–45. Rome: L'Erma di Bretschneider.

Nissen, H. 1863. *Kritische Untersuchungen über die Quellen der vierten und fünften Dekade des Livius.* Berlin: Weidmann.

North, J.A. 1979. "Religious Tolerance in Republican Rome." *PCPhS* 25: 85–103.

Nussbaum, M., C.J. Sihvola. 2002. *The Sleep of Reason: Erotic Experience and Sexual Ethics in Ancient Greece and Rome*, Chicago: University of Chicago Press.

Oakley, S.P. 1997. *A Commentary of Livy, Books VI-X*, Vol. *i*: Book VI. Oxford: Clarendon Press.

Oakley, S.P. 1998. *A Commentary of Livy, Books VI-X*, Vol. *ii*: Books VII-VIII. Oxford: Clarendon Press.

Oakley, S.P. 2005. *A Commentary of Livy, Books VI-X*, Vol. *iii*: Book IX. Oxford: Clarendon Press.

Oakley, S.P. 2005. *A Commentary of Livy, Books VI-X*, Vol. *iv*: Book X. Oxford: Clarendon Press.

Ogilvie, R.M. 1963. *A Commentary on Livy: Books 1-5.* London: Oxford University Press.

Olson, K. 2008. *Dress and the Roman Woman. Self-Presentation and Society.* New York: Routledge.

Olson, K. 2009. "Cosmetics in Roman Antiquity: Substance, Remedy, Poison." *Classical World* 102. 3: 291–310.

Ortner, S. 1974. "Is Female to Male as Nature Is to Culture?" In *Women, Culture, and Society* ed. Rosaldo M., L. Lamphere, 67–88. Stanford: Stanford University Press.

Osgood, J. 2014. *Turia. A Roman Woman's Civil War.* Oxford: Oxford University Press.

Packard, D.W. 1968. *A Concordance to Livy.* Cambridge, Mass.: Harvard University Press.

Pailler, J.-M. 1988. *Bacchanalia. La repression de 186 avant J.-C. à Rome et en Italie.* Rome: École française de Rome.

Pailler, J.-M. 1995. *Bacchus, figures et pouvoirs.* Paris: Belles lettres.

Pais, E. 1915. *Storia critica di Roma durante i primi cinque secoli. Volume II.* Rome: Ermanno Loescher and Company.

Päivi, S., L. Savunen. 1999. *Female Networks and the Public Sphere in Roman Society,* Rome: Institutum Romanum Finlandiae.

Papi, E. 1995. "Domus: Livia." In *Lexicon Topographicum Urbis Romae,* ed. Steinby, E.M., 116–17. Roma: Edizioni Quasar.

Parenti, M. 2003. *The Assassination of Julius Caesar. A People's History of Ancient Rome.* New York: New Press.

Patterson, C.B. 1998. *The Family in Greek History.* Cambridge: Harvard University Press.

Pearce, T.E.V. 1974. "The Role of the Wife as Custos in Ancient Rome." *Eranos* 72: 16–33.

Pédech, P. 1964, *La méthode historique de Polybe.* Paris: Les Belles Lettres.

Peppe, L. 2017. "Women and Civic Identity in Roman Antiquity." *Austrian Law Journal* 1: 23–38.

Peradotto, J., J.P. Sullivan (ed.). 1984. Women in the Ancient World. *The Arethusa Papers,* Albany: State University of New York.

Petersen, H. 1961. "Livy and Augustus." *TAPhA* 92: 440–52.

Petersen, L.H. 2006. *The Freedman in Roman Art and Art History.* Cambridge: Cambridge University Press.

Pittenger, M.R.P. 2008. *Contested Triumphs. Politics, Pageantry, and Performance in Livy's Republican Rome.* Berkeley and London: University of California Press.

Pfohl, G., C. Pietri. 1983. "Grabinschrift I (Griechisch)" *[Pfohl] and "Grabinschrift II (Lateinisch)" [Pietri], Reallexicon für Antike und Christendum* 12. Stuttgart: Anton Hiersemann. 467–514, 514-90.

Phillips, J.E. 1982. "Current Research in Livy's First Decade" *ANRW* 2.30 2: 998–1057.

Philo, J.-M. 2016. "Tudor Humanists, London Printers, and the Status of Women: The Struggle Over Livy in the Querelle des Femmes." *RenQ* 69: 40–79.

Plant, I.M. 2004. *Women Writers of Ancient Greece and Rome.* Norman OK: University of Oklahoma Press.

Pomeroy, S.B. 1975. *Goddesses. Whores. Wives and Slaves: Women in Classical Antiquity.* London: Pimlico.

Pomeroy, S.B. 1991a. *Women's History and Ancient History.* Chapel Hill: University of North Carolina Press.

Pomeroy, S.B. 1991b. "The Study of Women in Antiquity: Past, Present, and Future." *AJPh* 112.2: 263–68.

Porciani, L. 2017. "Thucydides' Predecessors and Contemporaries in Historical Poetry and Prose." In *The Oxford Handbook of Thucydides,* ed. Forsdyke, S., E. Foster, and R. Balot, 551–66. Oxford and New York: Oxford University Press.

Proietti, G. 2012. "Memoria Collettiva E Identita Etnica. Nuovi Paradigm Teoritico-Metodologici Nella Ricerca Storica." In *Forme Della memoria E Dinamiche Identitarie Nell-Antichità Greco-romana,* ed. Franchi, E., G. Proietti, 13–40. Trento: Università degli studi di Trento.

Purcell, N. 1986. "Livia and the Womanhood of Rome." *PCPhS* 32: 78–105.

Raaflaub, K.A., M. Toher (ed.). 1990. *Between Republic and Empire: Interpretations of Augustus and His Principate*. Berkeley and London: University of California Press.

Rabinowitz, N.S., A. Richlin. 1993. *Feminist Theory and the Classics*. New York and London: Routledge.

Rabinowitz, N.S., L. Auanger (ed.). 2002. *Among Women: From the Homosocial to the Homoerotic in the Ancient World*. Austin, TX: University of Texas Press.

Raditsa, L.F. 1980. "Augustus' Legislation Concerning Marriage, Procreation, Love Affairs and Adultery." *ANRW II* 13: 278–339.

Rallo, A. 1989. *Le Donne in Etruria*. Rome: L'Erma di Bretschneider.

Ramsby, T.R., B. Severy-Hoven. 2007. "Reshaping Rome: Space, Time, and Memory in the Augustan Transformation." *Arethusa* 40.1: 43–71.

Rawson, E. 1971. "Prodigy Lists and the Use of the Annales Maximi." *CQ* 21: 158–69.

Rawson, B. 2011. *A Companion to Families in the Greek and Roman Worlds*. Malden, MA and Oxford: Wiley-Blackwell.

Reynolds, J. 1982. *Aphrodisias and Rome: Documents from the Excavation of the Theatre at Aphrodisias Conducted by Professor Kenan T. Erim, Together with Some Related Texts*. London: Society for the Promotion of Roman Studies.

Richardson, J.H. 2015. "The Complications of *Quellenforschung*: The Case of Livy and Fabius Pictor." In *A Companion to Livy*, ed. Mineo, B., 178–89. Chichester, West Sussex: Wiley-Blackwell.

Richlin, A. 1981. "Approaches to the Sources on Adultery at Rome." In *Reflections of Women in Antiquity*, ed. Foley, Helene P., 225–50. New York: Gordon and Breach.

Riggsby, A.M. 2010. *Roman Law and the Legal World of the Romans*. Cambridge: Cambridge University Press.

Rives, J.B. (ed.). 1999. *Tacitus: Germania*. Oxford: Clarendon Press.

Rives, J.B. 2012. "Interpretatio Romana." In *Oxford Classical Dictionary*[4], ed. Hornblower, S., A. Spawford, E. Eidonow, p. 739. Oxford: Oxford University Press.

Rizzelli, G. 2000. *Le Donne Nell-Esperienza Giuridica Di Roma Antica Il Controllo Dei Comportamenti Sessuali: Una Raccolta Di Testi*. Lecce: Edizioni del grifo.

Robbins, V.K. 1995. "Oral, Rhetorical, and Literary Cultures: A Response." In *Semeia 65: Orality and Textuality in Early Christian Literature*, ed. Dewey, J., 75–91. Atlanta: Scholars Press.

Rosaldo, M.Z., L. Lamphere. 1974. *Women, Culture and Society*. Stanford: Stanford University Press.

Rosenthal, M. 1992. *The Honest Courtesan. Veronica Franco, Citizen and Writer in Sixteenth-Century Venice*. Chicago: University of Chicago Press.

Rousselle, R. 1989. "Persons in Livy's Account of the Bacchic Persecution." In *Studies in Latin Literature and Roman History V*, ed. Deroux, C., 55–65. Bruxelles: Latomus.

Ruggini, L.C. 1989. "Juridical Status and Historical Role of Women in Roman Patriarchal Society." *Klio* 71: 604–19.

Rüpke, J. 2007. *Religion of the Romans*, Translated by R. Gordon. Malden, MA: Blackwell.

Russell, A. 2015. *The Politics of Public Space in Republican Rome*. Cambridge: Cambridge University Press.

Rutherford, R.B. 2010. "Tragedy and History." In *A Companion to Greek and Roman Historiography*, ed. Marincola, J., 504–14. Oxford: Blackwell.

Rutherford, R.B. 2012. "Structure and Meaning in Epic and Historiography." In *Thucydides and Herodotus*, ed. Foster, E., D. Lateiner, 13–38. Oxford and New York: Oxford University Press.

Sacks, K.S. 1990. *Diodorus Siculus and the First Century*. Princeton: Princeton University Press.

Sande, S., T.K. Seim. 2009. *Woman as Subject and Object*. In: *AAAH* 22 (n.s. 8).

Sailor, D. 2006. "Dirty Linen, Fabrication, and the Authorities of Livy and Augustus." *TAPhA of the American Philological Association* 136.2: 329–88.

Salway, B. 1994. "What's in a Name? A Survey of Roman Onomastic Practice from C. 700 BC to AD700." *JRS* 84: 124–45.

Sandberg, K. 2018. "*Monumenta, Documenta, Memoria*: Remembered and Imagining the Past in Late Republican Rome." In *Omnium Annalium Monumenta: Historical Writing and Historical Evidence in Republican Rome*, ed. Sandberg, K., C. Smith, 351–89. Leiden and Boston: Brill.

Santoro L'Hoir, F. 1992. *The Rhetoric of Gender Terms: Man. Woman, and the Portrayal of Character in Latin Prose*. Leiden: E.J. Brill.

Scafuro, A. 1989. "Livy's Comic Narrative of the Bacchanalia." *Helios* 16.2: 119–42.

Scheid, J. 1991. "Indispensibili 'straniere'. I Ruoli Religiosi Delle Donne a Roma." In *Storia Delle Donne in Occidente: L'Antichità*, ed. Duby, G. et al, 424–64. Rome: Bari.

Scheid, J. 1992. "The Religious Role of Roman Women." In *A History of Women: from Ancient Goddesses to Christian Saints*, ed. Schmitt Pantel, P. 377–408. Cambridge MA: Harvard University Press.

Scheid, J. 2012. "Sacrifice." In *Oxford Classical Dictionary 4th* ed., ed. Hornblower, S., A. Spawforth, E. Eidinow, 1345–46. Oxford: Oxford University Press.

Scheidel, W. 1995. "The Most Silent Women of Greece and Rome: Rural Labour and Women's Life in the Ancient World." *G & R* 42.2: 202–21.

Scheidel, W. 1996. "The Most Silent Women of Greece and Rome: Rural Labour and Women's Life in the Ancient World (2)." *G & R* 43.1: 1–10.

Schubert, W. 1991. "Herodot, Livius und die Gestalt des Collatinus in der Lucretia-Geschichte." *RM* 134: 80–96.

Schultz, C.E. 2006. *Women's Religious Activity in the Roman Republic*. Chapel Hill: University of North Carolina Press.

Schultz, C.E., P.B. Harvey Jr. (ed.). 2006. *Religion in Republican Italy*. Cambridge: Cambridge University Press.

Scott, J.W. 1988. "Gender: A Useful Category of Historical Analysis." In *Gender and the Politics of History*, 28–50. New York: Columbia University Press.

Sebesta, J.L. 1997. "Women's Costume and Feminine Civic Morality in Augustan Rome." *Gender and History* 9.3: 529–41.

Sedgwick, E.K. 1992. *Between Men. English Literature and Male Homosocial Desire*. New York: Columbia University Press.

Sertima, I.V. 1985. *Black Women in Antiquity*. New Brunswick, NY: Transaction Books.

Setälä, P., L. Savunen (ed.). 1999. *Female Networks and the Public Sphere in Roman Society*. Rome: Institutum Romanum Finlandiae.

Setälä, P. et al (ed.). 2002. *Women, Wealth and Power in the Roman Empire*. Rome: Institutum Romanum Finlandiae.

Severy, B. 2003. *Augustus and the Family at the Birth of the Roman Empire*. London and New York: Routledge.

Shackleton-Bailey, D.R. 1977. *Cicero: Epistulae ad Familiares 1, 62–47 B.C.* Cambridge: Cambridge University Press.

Sharrock, A.R. 1997. "Re(ge)ndering Gender(ed) Studies." *Gender and History* 9.3: 603–14.

Sharrock, A.R. 2002. "Gender and Sexuality." In *The Cambridge Companion to Ovid*, ed. Hardie, P., 95–107. Cambridge: Cambridge University Press.

Sherwin-White, A.N. 1967. *Racial Prejudice in Imperial Rome*. London: Cambridge University Press.

Sherwin-White, A.N. 1978. *The Roman Citizenship*, 2nd ed. Oxford: Oxford University Press.

Sirago, V.A. 1983. *Femminismo a Roma nel primo impero*. Rome: Soveria Mannelli.

Skinner, M.B. 1987a. *Rescuing Creusa. New Methodological Approaches to Women in Antiquity*. Lubbock: Texas Tech University Press.

Skinner, M. 1987b. "Classical Studies, Patriarchy and Feminism: The View from 1986." *Women's Studies International Forum* 10: 181–86.

Skinner, M.B. 2005. *Sexuality in Greek and Roman Culture*. Malden, MA: Blackwell.

Skinner, M.B. 2011. *Clodia Metelli. The Tribune's Sister*. Oxford: Oxford University Press.

Slater, P.E. 1968. *The Glory of Hera: Greek Mythology and the Greek Family*. Princeton: Princeton University Press.

Smethurst, S.E. 1959. "Women in Livy's History." *G & R* 19: 80–87.

Smith, C.J. 2015. "Urbanization and Memory." In *A Companion to the Archaeology of Religion in the Ancient World*, ed. Raja, R., J. Rüpke, 362–75. Malden, MA; Oxford: Oxford University Press.

Solin, H. 1996. *Die Stadrömischen Sklavennamen. Ein Namenbuch*. Stuttgart: Steiner.

Solodow, J.B. 1979. "Livy and the Story of Horatius, 1.24-26." *TAPhA* 109: 251–68.

Spaeth, T. 1994. *Männlichkeit und Weiblichkeit bei Tacitus. Zur Konstruktion der Geschlechter in der römischen Kaiserzeit*. Frankfurt & New York: Campus.

Spawforth, A. 2012. *Greece and the Augustan Cultural Revolution*. Cambridge: Cambridge University Press.

Stadter, P.A. 1972. "The Structure of Livy's History." *Historia* 21: 287–307.

Staples, A. 1998. *From Good Goddess to Vestal Virgins. Sex and Category in Roman Religion*, London and New York: Routledge.

Stehle, E. 1989. "Venus, Cybele, and the Sabine Women: The Roman Construction of Female Sexuality." *Helios* 16: 143–64.

Steinby, E.M. 2000. *Lexicon Topographicum Urbis Romae. Vol. VI. Addenda et Corrigenda. Indici*. Rome: Edizioni Quasar.

Stevenson, T. 2011. "Women of Early Rome as Exempla in Livy AUC Book 1." *CW* 104.2: 175–89.

Strocka, V.M. 1981. "Römische Bibliotheken." *Gymnasium* 88: 298–32.

Sumi, G.S. 2004. "Civil War, Women and Spectacle in the Triumviral Period." *AncW* 35: 196–206.

Syme, R. 1939. *The Roman Revolution*. Oxford: Clarendon Press.

Syme, R. 1959. "Livy and Augustus." *HSPh* 64: 27–87.

Syme, R. 1968. *Ammianus and the Historia Augusta*. London: Oxford University Press.

Syme, R. 1991. "Fictional History Old and New. Hadrian." In *Roman Papers VI*, ed. Birley, A.R., 157–81. Oxford: Clarendon Press.

Syme, R. 2016. "The Gay Sempronia." In *Approaching the Roman Revolution: Papers on Republican History*, ed. Santangelo, F., 173–81. Oxford: Oxford University Press.

Takács, S.A. 2000. "Politics and Religion in the Bacchanalian Affair of 186 B.C.E." *HSPh* 100: 301–10.

Tarditi, G. 1954. "La Questione dei Baccanali a Roma nel 186 a.c." *La Parola del-passato* 9: 265–87.

Thomas, R. 1992. *Literacy and Orality in Ancient Greece*. Cambridge: Cambridge University Press.

Thomson, R. 1980. *King Servius Tullius: A Historical Synthesis*. Copenhagen: Kibenhavn Glydendal.

Toher, M. 1990. "Augustus and the Evolution of Roman Historiography." In *Between Republic and Empire: Interpretations of Augustus and His Principate*, ed. Raaflaub, K.A., M. Toher, 139–54. Berkeley and London: University of California Press.

Traina, G. 2001. "Lycoris the Mime." In *Roman Women*, ed. Fraschetti, A, 82–99. Chicago: University of Chicago Press.

Treggiari, S. 1991. *Roman Marriage. Iusti Coniuges from the Time of Cicero to the Time of Ulpian*. Oxford: Oxford University Press.

Treggiari, S. 2007. *Terentia, Tullia and Publilia. The Women of Cicero's Family*. London: Routledge.

Ullmann, R. 1927. *La Technique des discours dans Salluste, Tite-Live et Tacite*. Oslo: Dybwad.

Valentini, A. 2012. *Matronae Tra Novitas E Mos Maiorum: Spazi E Modalità dell'azione Pubblica Femminile Nella Roma Medio Repubblicana*. Venezia: Istituto Veneto di Scienze, Lettere ed Arti.

Vandiver, E. 1999. "The Founding Mothers of Livy's Rome: The Sabine Women and Lucretia." In *The Eye Expanded: Life and the Arts in Greco-Roman Antiquity*. ed. Titchener, F.B., R.F. Moorton, 206–32. Berkeley: University of California Press.

Vasaly, A. 1987. "Personality and Power: Livy's Depiction of the Appii Claudii in the First Pentad." *TAPhA* 117: 203–26.

Vasaly, A. 2018. *Livy's Political Philosophy: Power and Personality in Early Rome*. New York: Cambridge University Press.

Vidén, G. 1993. *Women in Roman Literature. Attitudes of Authors under the Early Empire*. Göteborg, Sweden: Acta Universitatis Gothoburgensis.

Virlouvet, C. 2001. "Fulvia the Woman of Passion." In *Roman Women*, ed. Fraschetti, A., 66–81. Chicago and London: University of Chicago Press.

Vivante, B. 2007. *Daughters of Gaia. Women in the Ancient Mediterranean World*. Westport, CT: Praeger Press.

Vuolanto, V. 2002. "Women and the Property of Fatherless Children in the Roman Empire." In *Women, Wealth and Power in the Roman Empire*, ed. Setälä, P. et al, 203–24. Rome: Institutum Romanum Finlandiae.

Walbank, F.W. 1957. *A Historical Commentary on Polybius I: Books I-VI*. Oxford: Clarendon.

Walbank, F.W. 1972. *Polybius*. Berkeley and Los Angeles: University of California Press.

Walcot, P., I. Mcauslan. 1995. *Women in Antiquity*. Oxford: Oxford University Press.

Wallace-Hadrill, A. 1983. "The Social Structure of the Roman House." *PBSR* 56: 43–97.

Wallace-Hadrill, A. 2009. "Family and Inheritance in the Augustan Marriage Laws." In *Augustus*, ed. Edmundson, J., 250–74. Edinburgh: Edinburgh University Press.

Walsh, P.G. 1955. "Livy's Preface and the Distortion of History." *AJPh* 79: 355–75.

Walsh, P.G. 1961. "Livy and Augustus." *Proceedings of the African Classical Association* 4: 26–37.

Walsh, P.G. 1970. *Livy: His Historical Aims and Methods*. London: Cambridge University Press.

Walsh, P.G. 1978. Review of T.J. Luce, *Livy: The Composition of His History*. *Phoenix* 32: 271.

Walsh, P.G. 1994. *Livy: Book*, Vol. *39*. Warminster: Aris and Phillips.

Walsh, P.G. 1996. *Livy: Book*, Vol. *40*. Warminster: Aris and Phillips.

Watson, A. 1976. *Rome of the XII Tables: Persons and Property*. Princeton: Princeton University Press.

Watson, A. 1979. "The Death of Horatia." *CQ* 29: 436–47.

Watson, P.A. 1995. *Ancient Stepmothers. Myth, Misogyny, and Reality*. Leyde: Brill.

Welch, T. 2012. "Perspectives on and of Livy's Tarpeia." *EuGeSTa* 2: 169–200.

Wheeldon, M.J. 1989. "'True Stories': The Reception of Historiography in Antiquity." In *History as Text: The Writing of Ancient History*, ed. Cameron, A., 33–63. London: Duckworth.

Wheeler, E.L. 1988. *Stratagem and the Vocabulary of Military Trickery*. Leiden: E.J. Brill.

White, H. 1973. *Metahistory: The Historical Imagination in Nineteenth-Century Europe*. Baltimore: Johns Hopkins University Press.

White, H. 1978. *The Tropics of Discourse*. Baltimore: Johns Hopkins University Press.

White, H. 1987. *The Content of the Form*. Baltimore: Johns Hopkins University Press.

Wiedermann, T.E.J. 1983. "ἐλάχιστον … ἐν τοῖς ἄρσεσι κλέος: Thucydides, Women, and the Limits of Rational Analysis." *G & R* 30.2: 163–70.

Wiedemann, T. 1981. *Greek and Roman Slavery*. Baltimore and London: Johns Hopkins University Press.

Wild, J.P. 2003a. "The Romans in the West, 600 BC–AD 400." In *The Cambridge History of Western Textiles*, Vol. *1*, ed. Jenkins, I., 77–92. Cambridge: Cambridge University Press.

Wild, J.P. 2003a. "The Eastern Mediterranean, 323-31 BC." In *The Cambridge History of Western Textiles*, Vol. *1*, ed. Jenkins, I., 102–17. Cambridge: Cambridge University Press.

Wildfang, R.L. 2006. *Rome's Vestal Virgins: A Study of Rome's Vestal Priestesses in the Late Republic and Early Empire*. London: Routledge.

Wille, G. 1973. *Der Aufbau des Livianischen Geschichtswerkes*. Amsterdam: B.R. Grüner.

Williams, C.A. 2010. *Roman Homosexuality*, 2nd ed. Oxford: Oxford University Press.

Williams, G.W. 1968. *Tradition and Originality in Roman Poetry*. Oxford: Oxford University Press.

Winkel, L. 2015. "Roman Law and Its Intellectual Context." In *The Cambridge Companion to Roman Law*, ed. Johnston, D., 9–22. Cambridge: Cambridge University Press.

Wiseman, T.P. 1979. *Clio's Cosmetics: Three Studies in Graeco-Roman Literature.* Leicester: Leicester University Press.

Wiseman, T.P. 1983. "The Wife and Children of Romulus." *CO 33*.2: 445–52.

Wiseman, T.P. 1985. *Roman Political Life 90 BC – AD*, Vol. 69. Exeter: University of Exeter Press.

Wiseman, T.P. 1994. *Historiography and Imagination.* Exeter: University of Exeter Press.

Witke, C. 1983. *Horace's Roman Odes: A Critical Examination.* Leiden: E.J. Brill.

Witte, K. 1910. "Über die Form der Darstellung in Livius' Geschichtswerk." *Rheinisches Museum für Philologie* 65: 270–305.

Wood, S.E. 2001. *Imperial Women. A Study in Public Images, 40 BC – AD*, Vol. 68. Leiden: Brill.

Woodman, A.J. 1988. *Rhetoric in Classical Historiography.* London: Croom Helm.

Wyke, M. 1994. "Women in the Mirror: The Rhetoric of Adornment in the Roman World." In *Women in Ancient Societies: An Illusion of the Night*, ed. Archer, L.J., S. Fischler and M. Wyke, 134–51. London: Macmillan.

Wyke, M. 2002. *The Roman Mistress: Ancient and Modern Representations.* Oxford: Oxford University Press.

Yavetz, Z. "The Personality of Augustus: Reflections on Syme's Roman Revolution." In *Between Republic and Empire: Interpretations of Augustus and His Principate*, ed. Raaflaub, K.A., M. Toher, 21–41. Berkeley and London: University of California Press.

Zanker, P. 1988. *The Power of Images in the Age of Augustus.* Translated by A. Shapiro. New York: Ann Arbor.

Zanker, P. 2000. "Die Frauen und Kinder der Barbaren auf der Markussaule." In *Autour de la Colonne Aurélienne*, ed. Scheid, J., V. Huet, 163–74. Turnhout: Brepols.

Zanker, P. 2016. *Roman Portraits: Sculptures in Stone and Bronze in the Collection of the Metropolitan Museum of Art.* New York: Metropolitan Museum of Art.

Ziegler, D. 2000. *Frauenfrisuren der römischen Antike. Abbild und Realitat.* Berlin: Weißensee-Verlag.

Zorzetti, N. "The Carmina Convivialia." In *Sympotica: A Symposium on the Symposion*, ed. Murray, O., 289–307. Oxford: Clarendon Press.

INDEX

Names and categories of persons found in gendered episodes of Livy's AUC history
Female individuals are listed under their family name (*nomen*), followed by their
first name (*praenomen*), if known, their role and/or other status in parentheses
and/or their relationship to a named male individual by marriage or betrothal,
as mother, sister, or daughter if unmarried, or by name only if no role, status,
and/or relationship is identified; female collectives are listed under the generic
category, "women," followed by their social, cultural, or ethnic designation
(e.g. wife or *virgo*; women, Vestal Virgins; or women, Sabine or Latin). The
names and categories of female individuals and collectives are emboldened.
Male individuals are listed under their family names (*nomen*) and additional
or third names (*cognomen*), followed by their first names (*praenomen*) and
offices, or according to their role; or according to their relationship to named
individuals by kinship. Generally, only the first office held by a particular
individual is listed.
Abbreviations: cos. = consul; cos. suff. = suffect consul; mil. trib. c.p. = military
tribune with consular power; dict. = dictator; tr. pl. = tribune of the plebs.
Unless otherwise indicated, all dates are BCE.

INDEX

For Product Safety Concerns and Information please contact our EU
representative GPSR@taylorandfrancis.com
Taylor & Francis Verlag GmbH, Kaufingerstraße 24, 80331 München, Germany